# DREAMS AND REALITIES

# DREAMS AND REALITIES

*selected fiction of*
*Juana Manuela Gorriti*

Juana Manuela Gorriti

*Translated from the Spanish by*
Sergio Waisman

*Edited with an Introduction and Notes by*
Francine Masiello

OXFORD
UNIVERSITY PRESS

2003

# OXFORD
### UNIVERSITY PRESS

Oxford New York

Auckland Bangkok Buenos Aires Cape Town Chennai
Dar es Salaam Delhi Hong Kong Istanbul Karachi Kolkata
Kuala Lumpur Madrid Melbourne Mexico City Mumbai Nairobi
São Paulo Shanghai Taipei Tokyo Toronto

Published by Oxford University Press, Inc.
198 Madison Avenue, New York, New York 10016

www.oup.com

Oxford is a registered trademark of Oxford University Press

Library of Congress Cataloging-in-Publication Data
Gorriti, Juana Manuela, 1816–1892.
Prose works. English. Selections
Dreams and realities : selected fiction
of Juana Manuela Gorriti / Juana Manuela Gorriti;
translated from the Spanish by Sergio Waisman;
edited, with an introduction and notes, by Francine Masiello.
p. cm. — (Library of Latin America)
0195117379 (cl)    0195117387 (pbk)
1. Short stories, Argentine—Translations into English.
2. Gorriti, Juana Manuela, 1816–1892.
I. Waisman, Sergio Gabriel. II. Masiello, Francine. III. Title. IV. Series.
PQ7797.G6A27 2003 863/.5 21

2 4 6 8 9 7 5 3 1

Printed in the United States of America
on acid-free paper

# Contents

# Series Editors'
# General Introduction

The Library of Latin America series makes available in translation major nineteenth-century authors whose work has been
neglected in the English-speaking world. The titles for the translations from the Spanish and Portuguese were suggested by an editorial
committee that included Jean Franco (general editor responsible for
works in Spanish), Richard Graham (series editor responsible for
works in Portuguese), Tulio Halperín Donghi (at the University of
California, Berkeley), Iván Jaksić (at the University of Notre Dame),
Naomi Lindstrom (at the University of Texas at Austin), Eduardo
Lozano of the Library at the University of Pittsburgh, and Francine
Masiello (at the University of California, Berkeley). The late Antonio
Cornejo Polar of the University of California, Berkeley, was also one
of the founding members of the committee. The translations have
been funded thanks to the generosity of the Lampadia Foundation
and the Andrew W. Mellon Foundation.

During the period of national formation between 1810 and into
the early years of the twentieth century, the new nations of Latin
America fashioned their identities, drew up constitutions, engaged in
bitter struggles over territory, and debated questions of education,

government, ethnicity, and culture. This was a unique period unlike the process of nation formation in Europe and one that should be more familiar than it is to students of comparative politics, history, and literature.

The image of the nation was envisioned by the lettered classes—a minority in countries in which indigenous, mestizo, black, or mulatto peasants and slaves predominated—although there were also alternative nationalisms at the grassroots level. The cultural elite were well educated in European thought and letters, but as statesmen, journalists, poets, and academics, they confronted the problem of the racial and linguistic heterogeneity of the continent and the difficulties of integrating the population into a modern nation-state. Some of the writers whose works will be translated in the Library of Latin America series played leading roles in politics. Fray Servando Teresa de Mier, a friar who translated Rousseau's *The Social Contract* and was one of the most colorful characters of the independence period, was faced with imprisonment and expulsion from Mexico for his heterodox beliefs; on his return, after independence, he was elected to the congress. Domingo Faustino Sarmiento, exiled from his native Argentina under the dictatorship of Rosas, wrote *Facundo: Civilización y barbarie,* a stinging denunciation of that government. He returned after Rosas' overthrow and was elected president in 1868. Andrés Bello was born in Venezuela, lived in London, where he published poetry during the independence period, settled in Chile, where he founded the University, wrote his grammar of the Spanish language, and drew up the country's legal code.

These post-independence intellectuals were not simply dreaming castles in the air, but vitally contributed to the founding of nations and the shaping of culture. The advantage of hindsight may make us aware of problems they themselves did not foresee, but this should not affect our assessment of their truly astonishing energies and achievements. Although there is a recent translation of Sarmiento's celebrated *Facundo,* there is no translation of his memoirs, *Recuerdos de provincia (Provincial Recollections).* The predominance of memoirs in the

Library of Latin America series is no accident—many of these offer entertaining insights into a vast and complex continent.

Nor have we neglected the novel. The series includes new translations of the outstanding Brazilian writer Joaquim Maria Machado de Assis' work, including *Dom Casmurro* and *The Posthumous Memoirs of Brás Cubas*. There is no reason why other novels and writers who are not so well known outside Latin America—the Peruvian novelist Clorinda Matto de Turner's *Aves sin nido*, Nataniel Aguirre's *Juan de la Rosa*, José de Alencar's *Iracema*, Juana Manuela Gorriti's short stories—should not be read with as much interest as the political novels of Anthony Trollope.

A series on nineteenth-century Latin America cannot, however, be limited to literary genres such as the novel, the poem, and the short story. The literature of independent Latin America was eclectic and strongly influenced by the periodical press newly liberated from scrutiny by colonial authorities and the Inquisition. Newspapers were miscellanies of fiction, essays, poems, and translations from all manner of European writing. The novels written on the eve of Mexican Independence by José Joaquín Fernández de Lizardi included disquisitions on secular education and law and denunciations of the evils of gaming and idleness. Other works, such as a well-known poem by Andrés Bello, "Ode to Tropical Agriculture," and novels such as *Amalia* by José Mármol and the Bolivian Nataniel Aguirre's *Juan de la Rosa*, were openly partisan. By the end of the century, sophisticated scholars were beginning to address the history of their countries, as did João Capistrano de Abreu in his *Capítulos de história colonial.*

It is often in memoirs such as those by Fray Servando Teresa de Mier or Sarmiento that we find the descriptions of everyday life that in Europe were incorporated into the realist novel. Latin American literature at this time was seen largely as a pedagogical tool, a "light" alternative to speeches, sermons, and philosophical tracts—though, in fact, especially in the early part of the century, even the readership for novels was quite small because of the high rate of illiteracy. Nevertheless, the vigorous orally transmitted culture of the gaucho and the urban underclasses became the linguistic repertoire of some of the most interesting nineteenth-century writers—most notably José Hernández, author of the "gauchesque" poem "Martín Fierro," which enjoyed an unparalleled popularity. But for many writers the task was not to appropriate popular language but to civilize, and their literary works were strongly influenced by the high style of political oratory.

The editorial committee has not attempted to limit its selection to the better-known writers such as Machado de Assis; it has also selected many works that have never appeared in translation or writers whose work has not been translated recently. The series now makes these works available to the English-speaking public.

Because of the preferences of funding organizations, the series initially focuses on writing from Brazil, the Southern Cone, the Andean region, and Mexico. Each of our editions will have an introduction that places the work in its appropriate context and includes explanatory notes.

We owe special thanks to the late Robert Glynn of the Lampadia Foundation, whose initiative gave the project a jump start, and to Richard Ekman of the Andrew W. Mellon Foundation, which also generously supported the project. We also thank the Rockefeller Foundation for funding the 1996 symposium "Culture and Nation in Iberoamerica," organized by the editorial board of the Library of Latin America. We received substantial institutional support and personal encouragement from the Institute of Latin American Studies of the University of Texas at Austin. The support of Edward Barry of Oxford University Press has been crucial, as has the advice and help of Ellen Chodosh of Oxford University Press. The first volumes of the series were published after the untimely death, on July 3, 1997, of Maria C. Bulle, who, as an associate of the Lampadia Foundation, supported the idea from its beginning.

—*Jean Franco*
—*Richard Graham*

# Chronology of Juana Manuela Gorriti

| | |
|---|---|
| 1818 | June 15. Juana Manuela Gorriti is born in Horcones, in the province of Salta, bordering Tucumán. |
| 1823 | The Gorriti family moves to the city of Salta. |
| 1831 | November 13. The Gorriti family flees Argentina, escaping the forces of Facundo Quiroga. They settle in Tarija, Bolivia. |
| 1833 | April 20. Juana Manuela marries Manuel Isidoro Belzú. |
| 1841–42 | She secretly returns to Salta, disguised as a man. |
| 1847 | June 4. Belzú stages an uprising against his superiors and fails. He leaves with his family for Arequipa, Peru. Juana Manuela travels alone to Lima. |
| 1848 | Belzú stages a successful coup d'état in Bolivia and assumes power. |
| 1850 | Juana Manuela remains in Lima and opens a school for girls. |
| 1851 | Gorriti's first work of fiction, "The *Quena,*" is published first in La Paz and then in Lima. Gorriti's daughters leave |

Peru to live with Belzú, who is inaugurated as legitimately elected president of Bolivia.

1852    Gorriti writes "The Black Glove."

1861    Gorriti publishes "If You Do Wrong, Expect No Good" in *Revista de Lima.*

1863    Gorriti publishes "The *Mazorquero*'s Daughter" in *Revista de Lima.*

1864    Gorriti travels to La Paz and opens a school for girls.

1865    *Sueños y realidades* is published in Buenos Aires. Belzú is murdered on March 27, and Juana Manuela speaks at his funeral. She then returns to Lima.

1866    During a Spanish naval attack on Peru, Juana Manuela volunteers in nursing brigades of field hospitals in Lima. She continues to work as a volunteer nurse during yellow fever outbreaks in Lima.

1868    *Biografía del General Don Dionisio de Puch* is published in Paris.

1871    Gorriti publishes the first article in newly inaugurated Argentine newspaper, *La nación.*

1874    She founds and directs *La alborada* with Numa Pompillo Llona.

1875    Gorriti is named member of the "Literary Club" of Lima. She travels to Argentina in order to secure a monthly pension for descendants of patriots of the independence wars against Spain. The First Lady of Argentina, wife of President Nicolás de Avellaneda, assists Gorriti in this project. Once relocated in Buenos Aires, Gorriti collaborates in *La ondina del Plata.* Argentine intellectuals award her a *Palma literaria,* or festschrift, in her honor. After eight months in Buenos Aires, she returns to Lima and reopens her primary school.

1876      The Peruvian government honors Gorriti for her volunteer work on the war front in 1866. She inaugurates her literary salon. In Buenos Aires, her *Panoramas de la vida* appears.

1877      Gorriti makes her second journey to Buenos Aires. She travels this time with her son, Julio Sandoval. In Buenos Aires, she prepares the cultural journal, *La alborada del Plata*. She is awarded an honorary membership by the Scientific and Literary Circle of Buenos Aires. Later that year, she initiates a literary salon in Buenos Aires.

1878      After nine issues, *La alborada del Plata* closes. She travels to the north of Argentina and later returns to the Argentine capital. After her *Misceláneas* is published in Buenos Aires, she petitions for permission to leave Argentina for two years and returns to Lima.

1879      Her daughter Mercedes dies. With the outbreak of the War of the Pacific, Gorriti is unable to return to Buenos Aires and asks that Lola Larrosa de Ansaldo direct the second run of *La alborada del Plata,* which she had planned from Lima.

1881      She embarks for Buenos Aires.

1883      She attempts to open a dialogue with Eduarda Mansilla de García, apparently without a warm response from the senior Argentine author whose family's political allegiances to Rosas were in marked opposition to the Gorriti's Unitarian projects.

1885      She returns to stay definitively in Buenos Aires.

1886      She travels to Salta where she publishes *El mundo de los recuerdos.*

1888      She publishes *Oasis en la vida.*

1889      *La tierra natal* appears.

1890      *Cocina ecléctica* appears.

1892    She publishes *Perfiles,* and completes her autobiographi-
        cal account, *Lo íntimo,* twelve days before her death. She
        dies on November 6, 1892. Soon after her death, her son,
        Julio Sandoval, sees to the publication of her *Veladas liter-
        arias de Lima.*

# Introduction

The most important woman writer in nineteenth-century
Argentina, Juana Manuela Gorriti (1818–1892) draws her fiction
from themes of time and remembrance, fortune and political crisis. In
the process, she helps us understand Spanish America's emergence
from the shadow of the Spanish Crown and its debut on the stage of
modernity. Her fiction covers more than half a century of rapid social
change and registers both a nostalgia for the narrative heroics of the
wars for independence and an ongoing desire to accelerate progress
toward a cosmopolitan, urban future. A towering presence who
dramatized the dilemmas of the displaced intellectual and nomad,
Gorriti straddles two worlds: She longs for the solace of home while
insisting on travel to points unknown. This dual desire runs through
the landscape of the Americas as Gorriti draws upon legends from
the preconquest Incas to the forty-niners of California's gold rush.
The narrative movement of this writing allows today's reader a
glimpse into cultures on the verge of monumental change.

In *Lo íntimo,* a memoir completed shortly before her death, Gorriti reflects on the negative aspects of this exciting time. She describes
her condition as a person in exile, an existence marked by constant

displacement and economic distress, a life seized by the violent transformations of Spanish America as it moved from colony to independent state. Her text begins this way:

> Horcones! Paternal home, now a mound of ruins inhabited
> only by jackals and snakes. What remains of your former splen-
> dor? Your walls have decayed, the pillars of your arches have
> crumbled as if once erected upon an abyss. The sinuous roots of
> the fig tree and the golden trunk of the citrus barely signal the
> site of your gardens. Silence and loneliness have settled upon
> your once festive days. Now your paths are abandoned and the
> herb of oblivion grows over your forsaken thresholds.[1]

True to the romantic spirit of her times, Gorriti begs us to notice
the construction of memory as it rises from ruins. A common trope
of her generation, the ruins allow her to reminisce about a past inhab-
ited by illustrious men; the present moment, by contrast, is devoid of
people and voices. Only nature offers a point of contact between the
past and the present. Though the roots of the fig and citrus extend
back in history to touch a once splendid garden, the herbs of forgetfulness reverse that flow; moving toward the future, they proliferate
beyond control. Memory advances through time—it is contained in
branches and fallen stone; in the final instance, we might even claim
that memory acquires a body.

For its scenes of decay, this text also recalls the first page of
Domingo F. Sarmiento's *Facundo* (1845), perhaps the most canonized
text of nineteenth-century Latin America. Writing in the abandoned
baths, etching graffiti on the walls of those spaces once reserved for
cleansing, Sarmiento contrasts the fragility of the body with the per-
severance of abstract thought: "You can murder men, but not their
ideas," he tells us, recalling the words of Enlightenment thinkers in
order to explain the savagery of the present. This gesture claims the
continuity of intellectual work in the face of tyranny and oppression.
Gorriti, however, stages a reversal of this position. If Sarmiento
strives to create a legend in which ideas prevail over bodies, Gorriti
instead sustains corporeality as the basis of legend itself. In fact, she

tells us time and again that ideas persist because edifice and body prevail, because the materiality of the vessel survives. Gorriti will constantly ride the disorder between body and ideas, experience and representation. Her work is a recitation of this central conflict. Not only does she return in her writing to these same references and quotations, but she also carries an obsession with origins as if, with each visit to her lost home, a new turn on the truths of history and the human body might be revealed to both herself and the reader. In fact, the passage cited above appears many times in Gorriti's earlier works. It introduces several stories and novellas and makes a final textual appearance in *Lo íntimo* to convey the illusion of autobiographical truth. The reference indicates, more importantly, the persistence of a problem—the author's obsession with bringing the relationship between past and present into alignment, the disordered flow of memory, and the seemingly linear advance of history. In the process, Gorriti reveals herself as a subject in need of reinvention, a restless yet weary traveler wanting repose but driven to take her inquiries across a vast, transnational landscape.

To progress, Sarmiento sought to rehabilitate his enemies and then to destroy them once and for all with words, but Gorriti needs to leave her phantoms indefinitely alive, rushing their images circuitously through past and present. In her fiction, she insists on these dual markers. Her writing is also complicated by mismatched fates, ambiguous crossings of voices and names, and the elision of significant moments in history. In her historically based narratives, for example, legendary men still alive in Gorriti's time are represented as fallen soldiers: Living heroes are portrayed as ghosts. Other historical figures are positioned in cities that, in real life, they had long since abandoned. This intentional anachronism is used to lament the reversals of national destiny, to show how the once glorious plans for progress were later thwarted by civil strife. At the same time, people travel under pseudonyms, women are disguised as men, and characters roam in a masked adventure through which they balance mystery and revelation. This prolonged play with contradictory forms of representation, the stock of melodrama, is in Gorriti's case utterly serious insofar as it articulates a concern for memory and history and for the individual's role as citizen in a modern Spanish-American state.

Gorriti's fiction is organized around multiple sites of focus: Some directly evoke scenes of the past—the home, the garden, the lost grandeur of the colonial period, the battlefields of the independence wars, and others trace the course of characters in a slowly emerging modern world. Here, the path of return itself becomes the object of Gorriti's interest, allowing her to track the networks of composition that move memories through space and time. Perhaps this dualism is required of all second beginnings (and here I'm borrowing from Edward Said), a disposition that emerges from conflicts between the familiar and the new, between faith in the historical past and doubt in its founding precepts. If it is true that each society reinvents itself after crucial historical moments, it does so by drawing upon a double system of representations, taking the reader in two directions at once. José Joaquín de Olmedo's "Victory of Junín" (1825) and Andrés Bello's "Ode to Agriculture in the Torrid Zone" (1826) give evidence of the way in which literature, following Spanish America's independence from Spain, works through these horizons, simultaneously mapping a historical past for the new republics and signaling a course for the future. These texts sustain their energy from contradictory forces of accumulation and uncertainty, order and transgression, stasis and dispersal, all taken from a given body of American landscape and from the complex liberal fantasies for its elaboration and change. For later readers, these fundamental texts have come to serve as cues to evoke *la patria*, a recitation of the conflicts between visible reality and national desire.

It was perhaps the overarching challenge of thinkers at an early moment of postcolonial freedom to narrate what had not been told before, to find a venue for previously untellable tales, to advance a claim for originality despite a proclaimed necessity for philosophical quotation that would take Latin American intellectuals back to a masterly European source. More than an effort to insert their autobiographies as part of the founding fictions of the nation (and this, of course, was always the passion of romantic writers), their challenge was to draw upon the elements of a refractory, disassembled past to sketch a plan for the future. The materiality of space—the pristine countryside, the decayed architectural structures that defined the once great estates—often upheld this fabric of narration, as we saw in the inaugural citation from Gorriti's memoir. But the images to explain this transition were also found in economic models, in a transformation of systems of exchange that signaled a move from colonial agrarianism to urban modernization.

In *La tierra natal,* Gorriti wrote, "I contemplated the village, which showed me the steps toward progress where earlier I had sought only a trail of remembrance." [2] Gorriti invites us to rethink the operations of memory that dominated nineteenth-century texts, especially the inverse relationship between nostalgia and progress. This process is sustained by images of a once verdant forest now in decline, joined with descriptions of a metallic glow that awakens a desire for money. Memory is thus pulled between an ongoing longing for the family estate at Horcones and a fear of thieves and swindlers who threaten the New World. These visions fill the gap between nature and culture, but they also allow her to track past experience as she faces an uncertain future. Finally, it is impossible to read Gorriti without thinking about where autobiography intersects fiction.

### *The Intolerable "I"*

In *Lo íntimo,* Gorriti writes of her determination to "flee the intolerable 'I'," [3] suppressing the emphasis on personal events and affections, erasing the texture of any intimate encounter with others. This claim not withstanding, her writing reveals an autobiography rich in the details of privilege accorded one of Latin America's exceptional families. She constantly returns to this source, to the life that that notable lineage often supplied to its progeny. Juana Manuela Gorriti was born in Horcones, in northern Argentina, to an illustrious family of landowners, military officers, and clerics whose wealth and prestige had been assured by the advantages of the late colonial order. Their power was rooted in the countryside and the control that they exercised over the rural economy and commerce with adjacent regions. Her father, José Ignacio Gorriti, was trained in the law and later earned distinction in the Spanish-American War, fighting alongside military leader Manuel Belgrano and acting in the decisive Congress of Tucumán (1816), in which River Plate independence was proclaimed. He subsequently became an officer under General Martín Güemes in Salta and then served as governor of that province from 1822 to 1824 and again from 1827 to 1829. His appointment prompted one of many shifts in domicile for the family, obliging the Gorritis to move from the tranquil Horcones estate to the budding city of Salta. More disruption was to follow for the young girl. After independence, when political disarray resulted in years of civil strife, roughly defining an ideological competition between Federalists and Unitarians, the Gorriti family challenged Federalist strongman Juan Manuel de Rosas (1829–1832 and 1835–1852).[4] Since part of the Federalist program was to rein in the powerful northern provinces, such as Salta, an inevitable conflict arose, leading to Gorriti's loss of prestige, financial ruin, and exile. In defense of his threatened estate, Gorriti joined the forces of Rudecindo Alvarado, fighting against the *montonera* troops led by Facundo Quiroga, who stood at that time for the powers of Rosas. Quiroga's triumph at La Ciudadela in November of 1831 inflicted heavy losses on the *salteños,* an event recorded by Gorriti in her story "The Deadman's Fiancée" (included in this volume). Acknowledging the power of the Federalists over local elites, the family decided to leave Argentina for the duration of the Rosas regime.

The Gorritis abandoned their notable estate in Salta and headed for Bolivia, first traveling to Tarija and then settling in Chuquisaca (later renamed Sucre), an intellectual center and destination for many émigrés from Argentina. Although her father was to live out his remaining years in poverty and exile there, Juana Manuela met the man who would become her spouse and bring her into the theater of politics once more. In La Paz, she married Manuel Isidoro Belzú in 1833. Of humble Arabic origin, Belzú (1808–1865) rose from the rank of military captain, at the time of his first encounter with Juana

Manuela, to become president of Bolivia (from 1848 to 1851). His rapid ascent, his successful coup d'état, and his later election as president have left behind an image of Belzú as both populist hero and dictatorial strongman. Some regard him as the "Bolivian Mohammed" or the "Apostle of the Indians," while others claim his public service career was notable for scandal and outlandish ideas.[5] An authoritarian figure who, for a while, had secured an extremely enthusiastic backing from the Bolivian people, Belzú left a conflicted legacy and was considered by some a demagogue and by others a revolutionary socialist *avant la lettre*.[6] His tumultuous career included leading repeated uprisings and making an attempt at sedition. After a failed uprising within military ranks, Belzú was driven from Bolivia in 1847 only to return the following year to seize presidential power through a coup. He was elected president in 1851 and enjoyed a vast popular following. Years of political strife followed, culminating in his betrayal and assassination in 1865 by the forces of General Melgarejo. Juana Manuela spoke at his funeral, announcing a commitment to adopting her husband's popular causes, although she soon departed for Lima where she reopened a school for girls that she had established during her first extended visit there.

Gorriti's biography of Belzú, published in *Panoramas de la vida* (1876), overlooks the sordid details of his regime and instead focuses on his compassionate intelligence; she also omits the details of the troubled marriage they endured, although this aspect has intrigued recent biographers and creative writers.[7] For example, in a fictionalized biography, Analía Efrón records the extramarital betrayals of both husband and wife: President Belzú with his paramours, and Gorriti in trysts with Belzú's acknowledged political rival, General José Ballivián. Efrón writes, "Belzú failed to make her happy, but their cloudy marriage allowed Gorriti to become the person she was."[8] She goes on to say that the affair between Ballivián and Gorriti was simply the product of gossip, although the scandal circulating among high society drove Gorriti to leave Bolivia for Peru. By contrast, Bolivian biographers and defenders of Belzú explain the couple's marital conflict as having resulted from Juana Manuela's envy of her brilliant spouse, and voracious Ballivián's grand seduction of her. "The fact is that Gorriti always felt like a satellite of that giant star," Fausto Reinaga writes.[9] Taking revenge against Ballivián and as a challenge to his privileged position, Belzú staged a coup d'état in 1848 with the support of the indigenous masses. Other versions of the couple's marriage exist. For example, in *Juanamanuela mucha mujer* (1980), a resoundingly successful novel that reintroduced the figure of Gorriti to the modern reading public, Marta Mercader represented the couple as deeply loyal to one another despite their separations.[10] The truth about the dynamics of the pair may never be known, but it is certain that the couple brought two children into the world—Edelmira and Mercedes. The couple took exile in Arequipa, Peru, when Bolivian politics forced them to leave; when Belzú subsequently returned to Bolivia, Gorriti remained in Lima, though she visited Bolivia often. In 1847 Gorriti once again went to Arequipa, traveling with her two daughters and leaving Belzú behind. She journeyed to Lima in 1848, initiating a series of separations and tenuous reconciliations with her husband that continued until his death.

Their rocky marriage acquired characteristics of what might be called a modern relationship, with each partner pursuing separate lives, but remaining intellectually loyal to the other in a camaraderie unusual even today. After Belzú called for his daughters to return to Bolivia, Juana Manuela struck forth on her own, establishing a primary school for girls in Peru. To be closer to her children, she returned to Bolivia for a while, teaching in Bolivian schools until 1855 and then traveling to Lima. During her years in Peru, Gorriti also bore two children, Clorinda and Julio, presumably through a relationship in the 1850s with local merchant Julián Sandoval.[11] She returned again to Bolivia in 1864, following the election in Peru of Juan Antonio Pezet, a declared enemy of Belzú.

From the time that she became directly involved in the transformative events of the nineteenth century, Gorriti expressed a clear disdain for political life. In *Perfiles,* a text published the year she died, Gorriti reflected on the tedium of politics:

Destiny, for its capriciousness, determined, from the cradle and during the best years of my youth, that an absorbing, bitter, destructive force would surround me—politics. . . . And when I could, at last, leave that dark world, I felt the sweetness of light, peace, and well-being to which Dante aspired when he left the dwelling of the reprobates.[12]

This double helix of desire for both politics and repose character-ized Gorriti's life, supplied the fundamental nutrients for her fiction, and set her on a course through South America. Despite her pro-claimed disdain for the political arena, Gorriti found herself attracted to public issues and recorded this in her writing. Her literature is steeped in legends of the Rosas regime, in which known political figures frequently make an entrance. Even in her final work of fiction, *Oasis en la vida* (1888), Sarmiento and Bartolomé Mitre briefly appear as characters to applaud the happy nuptials of the young protagonists of the novel![13] As a journalist and one engaged in cultural debate, Gorriti never strayed from politics, despite her abhorrence of civil strife and the toll it took on her family; similarly, politics was never far removed from her literary creations.

Juana Manuela did not begin to publish, to assume a public iden-tity as an author, until she moved to Peru. However, her preparation for the world of writing dates to her childhood years in Salta, where she benefited from her family's extensive library, considered the most significant in northern Argentina during the early years of independ-ence.[14] As prominent intellectuals in the postcolonial order (her uncle, Juan Ignacio Gorriti, authored significant treatises on colonial law and stood along with Mariano Moreno as one of the principal intellectuals in the so-called Revolution of May that began the inde-pendence wars against Spain; a maternal uncle, Facundo Zuviría, was devoted to journalism and jurisprudence), the Gorritis offered the female children of the clan the kind of private instruction and reli-gious education typical of elites. Fables told by indigenous members of the household retinue complemented Juana Manuela's readings in

European literature and the classics and undoubtedly provided her with material regarding the many local traditions that weave their way through her work. Among these traditional tales, the quest for lost Inca treasures, a motif that filled the imagination of the Gorriti children from their days at the Horcones estate, left a forceful impression on the aspiring writer. Although her autobiography records her father's attempt to distract his workers from the ongoing excavations for gold that were taking place on his land, Gorriti embraces this fantasy of riches as the basis of numerous stories. Her earliest works of fiction thus follow tales about the lost Incan wealth that lay hidden in the Andean highlands and trace legends told by native women who took a stand against Spanish greed. "The *Quena*" and "The Treasure of the Incas" capture this spirit of adventure and mystery by delving into the white man's search for indigenous fortune and the Incas' resistance to invasion. The early phase of her writing also recuperates a family anxiety about the tyranny of Rosas and the power that this leader wielded over the population. "The Black Glove" and "The *Mazorquero*'s Daughter," for example, are remarkable fictional treatments of the injustices that Rosas and his henchmen delivered upon Argentine citizens. Along with "The Deadman's Fiancée," they emphasize the damage wreaked by politics on family ties. "Gubi Amaya," meanwhile, records Gorriti's real-life journey in 1841 when, dressed as a man, she returned incognito to visit her native Salta. Under the pretext of narrating the adventures of highway robber Gubi Amaya, Gorriti defended her father's interests and protested the assaults by Federalist raiders who besieged the family estate. With few exceptions, these stories, written during Gorriti's exile, appeared in print following Rosas's defeat at Caseros. The dates of Gorriti's earliest publications continue to be debated: Some suggest that "The *Quena*" was written between 1841 and 1842, although it was first published in 1851 in *El comercio* of Lima; others cite 1850 as the year in which the first chapter of "Gubi Amaya" was written; "The Black Glove" followed in 1852 and "Una apuesta" ("A Bet") in 1855.[15] These early stories were to be gathered in her first collection of fiction, *Sueños y realidades* (1865), published in Buenos Aires with the assistance of her friend, Vicente Quesada.

Her experience in cultural journals and reviews dates from the 1850s, when she established herself in literary circles in Lima. In the city where she was to spend nearly 40 years of her life, Gorriti began to publish in newspapers, periodicals, and journals such as *El liberal*, *El nacional*, and the *Revista de Lima*. Her writings later appeared in Chile, in the *Revista de Sud-América* (Valparaíso), and in Argentina, in the *Revista del Paraná*; she also published a biography of Belzú (1865) and another of Dionsio Puch (1869), the latter published in Paris.[16] Her having published in such a variety of places suggests that a transnational dialogue was important to Gorriti and fulfilled her need to exchange style and ideas with writers throughout the Americas and Europe. This cosmopolitan outlook is also evidenced through other aspects of her literary career, notably through her literary salon—reputed to have been the most dynamic site of intellectual exchange in South America in the nineteenth century, the numerous editorial projects that she sustained in Peru and Argentina, and her extensive network of interlocutors and admirers in literary culture.

When Gorriti settled in Lima at mid-century, she entered a major intellectual center recovering from colonial rule and moving toward modernization. The city bubbled with exciting possibilities in the areas of theater and literary culture, expressing the conflicts of a world undergoing rapid change. Mid-century in Lima also witnessed an explosion of literary journals, cultural circles, and salons. Gorriti quickly engaged the attention of cultural elites and usually was among the few women to participate in Peruvian literary publications. Her famed *veladas literarias*—by any name, a cultural salon— received the most prominent figures in Peruvian literary life, among them Ricardo Palma. A topic of newspaper commentary, the salon drew intellectuals, writers, musicians, and painters whose reputation had spread throughout the Andean region. Through agendas set by the hostess, salon members heard musical compositions and readings of poetry, prose fiction, and critical commentary. The interest in folk-

lore, so important to Gorriti in her earliest stories, was here represented to the public through demonstrations of indigenous music.
The cultural circle also brought recognition of patriotic festivities
along with Indian culture. Inca traditions and drama in Quechua
were often presented at the meetings and gave evidence of Gorriti's
long-standing commitment to native expression, a theme in her earliest stories and a topic in her literary journals.

Gorriti delivered the inaugural lecture of each meeting of the literary salon, reminding her audience of significant issues of the day
and calling upon intellectuals to defend the cause of progress and the
advancement of nations. From the start, she introduced a debate
about the role and status of the intellectual in postindependence
America and also inquired about the participation of women in shaping the agenda of national culture. Although prominent men such as
Pastor Obligado and Ricardo Palma formed part of her literary salon,
she reached out for a conversation with the accomplished women of
her generation regardless of their national origin. Mercedes Cabello
de Carbonera, Carolina Freyre de Jaimes, Teresa González de Fanning, Clorinda Matto de Turner, María Nieves y Bustamante, and
Manuela Villarán de Plascencia, the principal women writing in Peru
in the nineteenth century, were her constant interlocutors. In Lima,
Gorriti also contributed to a number of journals and cultural reviews
for women. With Carolina Freyre de Jaimes, she directed *El álbum*
(1875); with Numa Pompillo Llona, she inaugurated *La alborada*
(1875).

Peruvian women devoted themselves to a variety of genres from
romantic novels to manuals of etiquette. Straddling a double field,
between the constraints of a colonial and Catholic legacy that
restricted women's role to the household, on the one hand, and train-
ing children for future roles as citizens of the republic, on the other,
these women were not of a single political disposition nor were their
successes uniformly made apparent. Though some took on the anti-
clerical cause, following the initiatives of Clorinda Matto de Turner,[17]
others, such as Mercedes Cabello de Carbonera, addressed the

impact of positivism in Peru and its consequences for the lives of women (a point she made repeatedly in her novel *Blanca Sol*); still others, such as Teresa González de Fanning, took up questions of curricular reform in order to advance the interests of Peruvian girls among the nation's students. In effect, women's limited access to formal education became a topic of constant concern.

Flora Tristán agreed with Gorriti and the women of the Peruvian elite when she observed that Lima had few public resources for the education of women: "Women in Lima have no access to learning; they don't read and [they] remain distant from everything that happens in the world."[18] In Gorriti's day, this was a matter of preoccupation for privileged women, who inevitably entwined their struggle for female emancipation with a critique of religious control over women's right to learn. The *Veladas* also captures some of Lima's newly found feminism. Some participants claimed that women needed a social education to alert them to the dangers of excessive consumerism and extravagant dress, and to warn them of the perils of reading provocative materials that might not be considered "respectable" knowledge.[19] Meanwhile, republican values were said to enable the expansion of a woman's mind and protect her soul. Finally, as Mercedes Cabello de Carbonera suggested, literature offers a moral solution for women's social woes.[20] Through these various strategies, Gorriti's collaborators made the image of women synonymous with republican virtue, inextricably linking the two to a concept of moral citizenship emerging in the Americas at that time.

Their persistence in these matters notwithstanding, these nineteenth-century thinkers often regarded with suspicion the more radical aspects of female emancipation. Female labor, civil rights, and the role of women in politics were topics that failed to make their way into Gorriti's forum. Instead, a domestic and bookish feminism gained favor in her salon, holding women's rights to the library and the pen as worthy of discussion. A poem by Manuela Villarán de Plascencia, a member of Gorriti's circle, observes the restrictions on the woman writer who is tethered to household obligations:

Bring pen and paper
And a bottle of ink;
It's time to write
A mosaic, I think.
But a knock on the door. Who can it be?
I drop my sheaf of papers to see...
It's a birdbrain who asks
If Don Fulano lives here.
I fly to my desk. And then a cry I hear
It's my youngest child who demands my care.
I run to calm her, a pen in my hand;
I return to my desk with a quartet in mind
I write two words and hear something unwind . . .
These are the good times used to distract;
I haven't yet told you of times that are black.[21]

Peruvian literature authored by women often inspired a negative reaction in avid Catholics and in those who saw a perilous challenge to prevailing social mores and traditional Christian values. Thus it is reported that when Clorinda Matto de Turner, as editor of the Peruvian weekly *El Perú ilustrado* (*Modern Peru*), published a story about a possible romance between Jesus and Mary Magdalene, so vehement was public protest against her that Matto was forced to resign her post.[22] For her continued anticlericalism and her support of liberal politicians, her figure was later burned in effigy and she was driven from Peru. The fate of women in the literary world is a concern apparent in Gorriti's publications; it also surfaced in the family of literary networks that she cultivated during her years in Lima and following her return to Argentina. For that reason, Mercedes Cabello de Carbonera and Clorinda Matto de Turner, among others, were usually present in the pages of her journals, memoirs, and notations. Even when she traveled to Buenos Aires, she continued to include these women in her literary publications and to cite them in her essays.

Gorriti's time in Peru bore witness to many contradictions about the recognition and advancement of women in nineteenth-century public life. Those years also represented a time of constant travel and upheaval as she regularly moved between Lima and Buenos Aires. In 1875, in pursuit of a pension owed to descendants of patriots of the independence wars, Gorriti returned to live in Buenos Aires. Her reputation preceded her. By the time she arrived in Buenos Aires, she had published in *La nación*, the important Buenos Aires newspaper founded by Bartolomé Mitre in 1871, and in the *Revista del Río de la Plata* (1873). The first lady of Argentina, wife of President Nicolás Avellaneda, facilitated Gorriti's arrival and guaranteed her a lifetime allowance of 200 pesos per month.[23] But recognition in the world of Argentine letters also awaited the author in the form of a *Palma literaria* (1875), a festschrift consisting of occasional texts written by friends, and a medal honoring her achievements. In 1876 the Peruvian government also bestowed an important prize upon Gorriti in recognition of her work as a volunteer in the medical brigades of the national army a decade earlier. She then returned to Argentina to welcome the publication of her second major collection of fiction and biography, *Panoramas de la vida* (1876), and to announce her plans to start a new cultural review, which saw the light in Buenos Aires in 1877 as *La alborada del Plata*. Through her many moves, and despite her economic misfortunes, Gorriti always managed to maintain an intense dialogue with elites, aware of the social and cultural transformations sweeping through the Americas. She stayed in touch with colleagues in both Argentina and Peru until 1885, when she established permanent residency in Buenos Aires and remained there until her death.

## *The Argentine Sisterhood*

When Gorriti returned to Argentina in 1875, she immediately cultivated a relationship with female writers in her native country. Almost upon her arrival, she rushed to visit Juana Manso de Noronja (1819–1875), who lay upon her deathbed. Closely allied with a range of interests similar to Gorriti's anti-federalism and known for her extensive commitments to the world of fiction and literary journalism,

Juana Manso had earned a reputation that reached Juana Manuela in Peru and awakened her admiration. Manso's most important fiction, *Los misterios del Plata: episodios históricos de la época de Rosas* (1846), a novel written from exile and not published until years after her death, shared an aesthetic and political vision with the fictions penned by Gorriti. A melodrama about the difficulties of Argentine life under tyranny, Manso's novel worked from the conceits of masking and revelation that she claimed all citizens must master in order to survive. Though focused on urban life—unlike the rural adventures of Gorriti—Manso's novel pursued the double entendre to explain the doubleness required of individuals resisting oppression. Living the drama of exile principally in Brazil, Manso also took up the abolitionist cause, translated Beecher Stowe, and wrote antislavery fiction such as *La familia del comendador,* which linked the plight of African slaves with the oppression of white women. In Brazil, she also initiated an important feminist journal, *O jornal das senhoras* (1852), a project that she would continue, upon her return to Buenos Aires, in her *Album de señoritas* (1854), a publication that protested domestic abuse and women's lack of access to formal education while it also observed the expansion of technology and modernization and their effects on women. A teacher and defender of Unitarian values, she assumed an important post in the Ministry of Education under Sarmiento's direction and wrote history textbooks while continuing to write works of fiction that exposed the horrors of the past. Her enterprises in the post-Rosas years included a basic school text on Argentina as well as important cultural and pedagogical reviews such as the *Anales de la educación común* (1873). This towering figure was surely a model for Juana Manuela Gorriti, as she shared with Manso the experience of exile and a strong anti-Rosas sentiment.

Upon her return, Gorriti also sought to establish a relationship with the other prominent woman writer who found her place in Argentine letters. She thus initiated contact with Eduarda Mansilla de García (1838–1892). This writer's cosmopolitan elegance, by contrast with Juana Manuela's simplicity, reflected the privilege she enjoyed because of her family's connection to Rosas and her long history of participation in diplomatic circles outside of Argentina. Long after Rosas's defeat at Caseros, she integrally defended his political world and the programs that benefited her family. Perhaps because of the politically dissonant camps that separated Gorriti from Mansilla de García, the budding exchange that Gorriti had hoped to pursue quickly wilted.[24] Nevertheless, Mansilla de García's literary legacy left its mark on Gorriti's imagination. Author of three important novels and the first travel book by an Argentine woman that covered the United States, Mansilla de García lived in Paris and Buenos Aires; she wrote elegantly in French in answer to the Unitarian Sarmiento, questioning his policies and projects for reform. Like Gorriti, Mansilla de García was also an avid traveler. Nevertheless, a curious contradiction emerges when we compare these two women: While Gorriti insisted on itinerancy as a theme in her fiction, Mansilla de García preferred country retreats and domestic repose. From her first novel, *El médico de San Luis* (*The Doctor from San Luis*) in 1860, she began exploring the idyllic country as she spoke of the value of a rural lifestyle to temper behavior and coordinate reason. But Federalist politics always assumed a place in Mansilla de García's fiction. In *Pablo ou la vie dans les pampas* (1868), she issued a rejoinder to Sarmiento in French to challenge the legitimacy of his presidential Unitarian projects. In that work, she explained the consequences of civil strife in the rural areas of the nation, the effective decimation of the countryside, the violent collapse of families, and the murder of women. The campaign against savagery, it would appear, held more complex ramifications than Sarmiento had suspected, for it took its toll on human life and disrupted domestic order. In a later work, *Lucía Miranda* (1884), Mansilla de García once again showed how war disrupted family life, but this time, she used the genre of the captivity novel—the white person held by the natives—to show that women's bodies were mediators between civilization and barbarism. Here, Mansilla de García returned to the period of the Conquest, the arrival of the Spaniards on the shores of the River Plate, to insist that the presence of women was essential to the first colonial encounter. Toward the end of her career, she also published a travelogue of her voyage to the United States, *Recuerdos de viaje* (1882), a handsome notebook of sharp observations about a rapidly changing society with mores and cultural habits strangely different from those of Argentina and France. Mansilla de García observed that, as progress continued in the United States, women would have an opportunity for advancement unequaled in the Americas.

Gorriti entered the world of Argentine letters fully aware of these female writers and their works. With her return to her native country in the 1880s, she quickly moved to promote her own ideas about literature and culture through periodical literature of her own. In Argentina, following the publication of *Panoramas de la vida* (1876), she also issued *Misceláneas* (1878) and other books of fiction. In these works, she left behind the intrigues of the Rosas regime as a focus of her narrative art to explore other themes, ranging from gothic adventure set in the Andes to literary treatments of melancholia, inspired by her own displacement and loss. At the same time, she actively entered the world of Argentine journalism and the excitement of periodical publications that spread cultural news throughout Spanish America. She quickly linked up with the staff of *La ondina del Plata,* a cultural periodical directed by Luis Santos Telmo (1876–1879), which had a wide circulation in Argentina and Peru. After she founded *La alborada del Plata* (1877–1878), she set to work on its sequel, *La alborada literaria del Plata* (1880). These journals offered a valuable glimpse into the cultural debates of the late nineteenth century, revealing both a preoccupation with transnational cultural alliance as well as a program of literary education tied to the objectives of modernization. In *La alborada del Plata,* her desire to reach an international audience was made clear from the start: *"La alborada del Plata* will be an international publication destined to link our literature with that of other American republics and to propagate its rapid progress."[25] Progress, modernity, and cosmopolitanism informed Gorriti's thinking as Argentina swept into the final decades of the century, fresh with hope for liberal reform and progress. These ideals accompanied enthusiastic discussion of fashion, theater, and the arts, while literary culture occupied writers and readers. Argentine literature introduced Argentine readers to texts and authors from the Americas; in particular, it placed Gorriti's Peruvian colleagues in wider circulation and fostered an inter-American awareness unique for the times. One could say that Gorriti's years outside of Argentina helped her cultivate a network of contacts that she would later use to assist her in the composite work of a cultural review. But the project is wider still for, here, Gorriti insists on expanding the breadth of a national literature. Trying to define the parameters of good taste and aesthetic value, Gorriti proposed to link modernization with the advantages of a literary education as if to follow in the footsteps of many Enlightenment thinkers before her. Nevertheless, the innovation of her project lies in a commitment to American yearnings, awakening a consciousness of transnational linkage among writers throughout the Americas.

This scope is remarkably original for the time of publication. It anticipates by a decade the cosmopolitan impulses of the *modernista* literary movement; it accelerates the cross-exchange of ideas that was to characterize modernization in Latin America in the 1880s. In particular, the publication manages to *feminize* the move toward modernity, showing that women were an integral part of the intellectual progress of Latin America. Perhaps this is the great revelation of Gorriti's review, uncovering the gendered components of a transnational modernization as it emerged in the south. In *La alborada del Plata*, Gorriti published essays on the value of American literary and cultural independence from Spain, the need to establish an intellectual autonomy free of foreign ties, the advantages of bilingual study, and the merits of female participation in public life; along with the value of travel, she celebrated the dawn of an urban style. Moreover, she provided a strong reminder of the role of women in public action.

Her feminism, as has already been noted, is often contradictory. By contrast to Juana Manso de Noronja, who urged an ironic reversal of the rules that held women captive in the home, Gorriti sought to provoke a gendered revolution consistent with domestic reserve, a recognition of woman in the public arena, but consonant with the law. This domesticated version of feminist militancy was aimed at achieving self-sufficiency for women while keeping them in less contentious public spaces. Other female writers were to follow Gorriti's editorial initiatives: In 1878, with the departure of Gorriti for Lima, Josefina Pelliza de Sagasta (1848–1888) assumed the stewardship of *La alborada del Plata*. And in its second run, commencing in 1880, while Gorriti was detained in Peru owing to the ongoing War of the Pacific, Lola Larrosa de Ansaldo (1859–1895)—an Argentine novelist of some achievement—took editorial charge of the journal and changed its name to *La alborada literaria del Plata*. By then *La alborada* had changed its voice and complexion, losing much of its earlier cosmopolitan thrust. Its defense of women's role in public space had been considerably diminished. In effect, when Gorriti returned in 1881, her impulse to continue the cultural review had been lost.

Periodicals in general, including newspapers, reflected a significant female contribution to lettered culture. Through these outlets, women not only found a way into national debate, but these media also produced a network of interlocutors, a *language* for recording the rise of liberalism from the "unofficial" side of political life. Writing also served to connect a network of nineteenth-century intellectuals from the distaff perspective. In this respect, Gorriti's *La cocina ecléctica* (1889) deserves our brief attention. Evoking the participation of the most accomplished female writers in Argentina and Spanish America, this cookbook brought together a wide variety of talent, drawing the 108 collaborators from countries as far apart as Colombia and Chile. The global cartography indicated in the book reflects Gorriti's ongoing concern for dialogue through the art of writing, as well as for threading her concepts of Americanism as it might flow through the regional recipes of her community of acquaintances. Equally important, it shows the power of women in the domestic space to intervene in a transnational arena. In this respect, Gorriti's work—far beyond the cookbook itself—promotes unequivocal respect for those women, regardless of their reputation, who traversed the American landscape. Her project is to merge different circles of social prestige, to unite local and international concerns, to speak of public politics from the space of domesticity. She also defended an ethic of contact that grew on the obverse side of nationalist rhetoric and, by its very practice of dialogue and exchange, surpassed provincial boundaries. In this project of blending lies a major epochal shift in which a new consciousness about mixture and *mestizaje* would erupt in the minds of liberal thinkers. Gorriti's writing shows a concern for integration as part of what Mary Louise Pratt has recently termed the "art of the contact zone."[26] Indians, Africans, and Californians all take a role in her fiction, announcing an awareness of movement between nations and the need for cross-cultural exchange. Like other elites in South America, Gorriti spoke Aymara and Quechua and was intensely aware of the plight of indigenous groups resulting from the urban rush toward modernization. Race often became a placeholder for a wider set of issues in a newly independent America, allowing a reflection on identity and citizenship as well as a claim for women of European descent to link their fate to that of subalterns. The economic plight of indigenous groups, in this instance, allowed Gorriti to reflect on her own impoverished condition in the post-Belzú years. Central to the foundational projects of the nineteenth century, the race question was to become a major focus of interest in Gorriti's work and was usually linked to matters of money.

The final years of Gorriti's life were dominated by a concern for funding. She was worried not only about securing a state pension offered to descendants of the independence wars (an obsession that brought her to return and eventually remain in Argentina), but also about acquiring the subventions that might make her life as a writer possible. Like with other female writers in Argentina who earned their living by the pen—Juana Manso de Noronja most notable among them—writing was not considered a luxury, but a source of income.[27] From the time of publication of her *Sueños y realidades,* Gorriti publicly discussed her economic problems and called upon Vicente Quesada to back her writing.[28] Among her final works, *El mundo de los recuerdos* (1886) was published with support of the municipality of Salta; *Cocina ecléctica* (1889) was written under a patron's support; and her last novel, *Oasis en la vida* (1888), refers to goods and products promoted by sponsors, principal among them a financial institution located in Buenos Aires. In the plot of this novel, characters were thus guaranteed happiness and allowed to marry when they located an insurance policy underwritten by the sponsoring Sud-Americana Bank! Finally, the Ministry of War assumed expenses for her funeral.

Emphasis on earning a living through writing is not, as some have proposed, a sign originating in *modernismo,* the Spanish-American literary movement emerging in the 1880s and promoted by Rubén Darío. Angel Rama, for example, claimed that the defining characteristic of this literary movement was seen in the separation of the writer from a system of patronage that had dominated the nineteenth century. Only in the 1880s could writers enter the market in effect to "sell" their works. The secret desire of each author was to reach "professional" status, to leave behind the patronage system.[29] The activity of Gorriti and her female colleagues complicates Rama's observation, for it shows that women shared an anxiety for the market that surfaced many years before Darío achieved celebrity for his radical innovations in the field of poetry. In effect, the professionalization of the writer, which Rama ascribes to the generation of *modernistas,* is in evidence from the time of Gorriti's first publication, when she expressed a desire for salaried compensation for her literary art; similarly, the *fin de siglo,* which promised autonomy for the writer, failed to relieve the financial distress that plagued Gorriti. Her emphasis on the manifestations of greed and the fight for survival in evidence from her earliest stories to her tale of the California gold rush, remind us that themes of acquired wealth were never far from her mind. Indeed, solvency was always a problem in Gorriti's life; it directed her literary plots and resurfaced as a form of nostalgia, a longing for an idealized past in which economic matters were not in disarray and self-sufficiency was guaranteed.

## The Routes of Memory

Remembrance in Gorriti's works always grows from conflict. Conflicting Creole and indigenous worlds and rural and urban experience allow Gorriti to find varying explanations for history and privilege. Her texts are never monolingual, but include indigenous and Spanish languages, drawing also upon the tempo of musical composition that serves as the backdrop of many of her works. Memory is never pure in lineage, but instead always depends on the blending of colonizing and colonized voices, on liberals and conservatives meeting in distant lands, on the measures of song and opera that set a secondary temporal pace for movement. Memory is also shaped by the forceful disposition of the romantic imagination, by the opulence of a narrative self that imposes its presence in the text and then serves as a crossing point for the integration of a modern political world with one's longing for a lost place of origin.

Let me thwart a possible objection: How can we speak today of the construction of memory in nineteenth-century texts with a clear mind, without suffering from our present-day biases, without being overtaken by the dominant economic and social concerns that drive Latin America today? When individuals made way for democracy, after the dictatorships of the 1970s and 1980s, they sought to rectify the violations of human rights enacted under authoritarian rule, to create a public memory, a shared knowledge of history that would overcome the legacy of an unresolved past. By contrast, in the mid-nineteenth century, following the reign of caudillos, intellectuals structured remembrance with a different goal in mind: to make way for the liberal state and build plans for a republic. Their goal was not simply to bring to account the abuses cast by political oppression, to reconcile private recall of horrors with public restitution of justice, to restore the realm of feelings over the increasing gloss of indifference. Instead, the exercise of public and private memory in the nineteenth century served plans of modernization. The representations of bodies and landscape were tools of that implementation.

The nineteenth century begs us to reflect upon the transition from colony to nation, to account for a transformation in politics and social life, to abandon an attachment to folklore, and to move instead into a horizon of multiple and conflicting ideals about narrating history. How to be *original* in America was set on a plane of competing interests, narrated through stories about one's place in an as-yet unstructured civil society caught in the throes of progress and unstoppable, rapid change. Latin American literature of the nineteenth century draws attention to this constellation of differences; it reveals a compulsive production of narrative that eludes our complete control.

In the nineteenth century, Gorriti was not alone in seeking original material by combining rural and urban resources and confusing temporal chartings. Many thinkers, in fact, had invested themselves in a similar concern, lamenting—after the independence wars—the effects of colonial ideology. Against a singular identity, they pointed to multiple chartings. Their literature often confused binary logic, not for lack of clarity in thinking, but in response to the mixed realities dominating local culture. In this way, as they sought a useful past that would assist them in planning a future, they crossed the networks of cause and effect—they upset chronological progression.

Vicente Fidel López wrote of the urgency of studying a philosophy of history. This meditation would be crucial for a new nation, he wrote, "since it explains the connection between what is and what will be." Nineteenth-century intellectuals well understood the importance of establishing a functional past from which to organize a theory about identity and nation; it was also an invitation to an aesthetic project and a theory of narrative form. Articulated as national literature, fiction postulated a past and future that maintained a moralizing principle. But literature also expressed a contradictory and disordered desire that worked against singular readings. Far from convincing us of the essential truths underlying the concept of "nation," literary texts represented the homeland as a denaturalized construct, often fragmented and without a fixed center. Indians, Africans, and migrant Creole subjects thus entered the panoply of literary texts to destabilize any fixed ideal of home. Central to these projects is the dispute for memory and justice. Here, Gorriti emphasizes the contracts established among characters to retain a common understanding of the past and also shape the future. Multiple voices emerge to echo shared beliefs or to dispute the truths held by others. Ghosts, giants, monsters, and phantoms (the stock of gothic fiction) remind us of a past that still haunts us and lacks clear resolution. These figures also remind us that national memory is often constructed upon troubled ground.

Gorriti's texts guide us through the course of this project. In her early stories, she attacks the moral failures of the government of Rosas, but also writes against the ethical shortcomings of Spanish colonialism. Her first novella, "The *Quena*," illuminates the dual routes available for this condemnation. A story of wide resonance in Peruvian literary traditions, "The *Quena*" was published in Peru at a time when statesmen were beginning to organize national projects under the presidency of General Ramón Castilla (1845–1851 and 1855–1864). The debates sustained by men of letters at that time raised serious questions about the modes of citizenry that would accompany the liberal state and the role of indigenous groups in shaping the nation. In particular the liberal landowning classes, eager to maintain Indian labor, were careful to protect Indian rights in order to control social unrest.[30] In this vein, "The *Quena*" registers both a general anxiety for the plight of Indians in Peru as well as a strong objection to the faults of colonial rule. The story thus operates on multiple levels although, on the surface, it supplies a simple melodrama of impossible love: Ramírez, a ruthless Spaniard elected governor of the Philippines, and Hernán, a mestizo of Incan and Spanish descent, both compete for the love of Rosa. The triangle is common enough in any romance, but Gorriti develops the wide political significance of this trope when she positions the innocent Rosa between two conflicting spheres of influence marked by the power of the colonizer and the weakness of the vanquished. Torn between the savagery of the Spaniard's unrelenting greed and the noble enlightenment of indigenous subjects, Rosa's plight leads us to speculate on an endangered world that can no longer offer protection to its people. Rosa is thus portrayed as a woman lacking freedom: She cannot marry the man she loves due to her father's interventions. At the same time, as a mestizo subject, Hernán is also shown to have no rights: He cannot claim a history or exercise choice in matters of love. Removed from his Indian mother at an early age and raised in Spain, he is marked as a half-breed who lacks control over his racial destiny. The two are thus condemned to separate lives. With this narrative strategy in place, Gorriti requires us to recognize that the plight of the Indian is somehow analogous to the fate of Creole women insofar as both are exiled from the sphere of citizenry and are denied basic rights. The triad formed by Church, state, and individual greed prohibit the kind of love that might overstep the boundaries between races. In a style that surely recalls the journeys of exile suffered in life by Juana Manuela Gorriti, Hernán and the luckless Rosa are banished from protection by law. Greed, dating from colonial times, continues to drive their misfortune.

This impasse is often resolved as a conflict of tongues. Rosa is swayed by the deceptive language of the colonial elite and so rejects Hernán; in turn, Hernán is persuaded by rumors of an African slave (called Francisca or Zifa) to believe that Rosa no longer loves him. There is no basis for alliance among members of the same social class, nor is there a claim of integrity among individuals who assume the roles of "outsiders" in a new world order. Instead, havoc reigns; one marginal race betrays another and, finally, linguistic confusion (evident in the multiple lies and bilingual misfires that orchestrate the style of the story) leads to madness and death. In the end, Hernán survives to express his "pains of love" (a literal translation of the word "quena," which gives the story its title) by carving a musical instrument from the dead Rosa's bones and thus giving birth to the "quena."

With so much violence wreaked upon bodies and souls, Gorriti's stories assault the integrity of nation. A time of menacing greed and relentless usurpation of indigenous treasures, the years between conquest and independence were fraught with contradictions, as Gorriti handily points out. In this respect, her fiction reveals a personal and ideological dam about to burst, with a reconciliation between Indians and Creole elites seen as impossible. Reciprocal betrayals abound and, even among subaltern figures, deception is the word of the day. Not only does one group deceive another, but even the representation of characters is guided by Gorriti's aesthetic and racial confusion. Her

noble Indian figures, for example, assume the countenance and gestures of courtiers—their desire, language, and self-expression are
manifestly European—yet Indian culture is shown to be the reposi-
tory of ethical value, in contrast to the sordid habits of the colonizer
in America. Can this bring us to an early conclusion about Gorriti's
misreading of the cultures around her? Is Gorriti willing to overlook
the specificities of the Andean zone in order to whiten indigenous
culture, to make it appealing to her readers? Or have we simply met a
convention common to nineteenth-century Latin American writers
from Jorge Isaacs to José de Alencar, in whose works indigenous customs are transformed in order to defend the concept of the "noble
savage"? The answers lead us to other inquiries in the fertile American terrain.

Unlike those stories that elevate the status of Indian and slave,
Gorriti's fiction erects cultural barriers that one can examine only
through negotiations within language. This is seen not only in the
bilingual condition of characters and their agility in moving through
cultures, but also through the roadblocks that are erected as a result of
this process. If, on the one hand, the Spanish invasion demanded that
native American or African figures alter their given names in order to
enter the colonial orbit; on the other, it produced a literature in which
the collision of multiple cultures oddly confused any concept of an
emerging Peruvian nation. Gorriti's work thus situates us within this
spectrum of contradictions and shows us the logical limits of all
searches for authentication. Far from drawing tales of complicity
within colonial regimes, she convinces us that the half-breed condition produces irrational desire. Neither colonial law nor the projects
sustained by liberal elites can eliminate that confusion; indeed, their
intervention exacerbates all conflict.

In "The *Quena*," Hernán is the child of a racial mixing who
assumes his condition as orphan; his mother, an Inca princess unable
to protect the rights of her son, loses the boy to his Spanish father;
similarly, an African slave in the story tells of the voyage from Africa
in which she lost her children. All experience the displacements of
exile and acknowledge their unhappiness as an effect of colonial rule.

And, of course, with the Philippines in the background of "The *Quena*," we see yet a second set of displacements in which colonial subjects from one part of the Spanish empire are poised to exploit colonial subjects residing in another. The union of different worlds, Gorriti appears to tell us, can only take place after death, when hybrid passions can at last find reconciliation and peace. These triple exiles show us that Peru is but a backdrop for a larger movement of bodies; lacking its own constitutive identity as nation, it only serves as a stage for grander colonial theater. Finally, underlying all of this, Gorriti obliges her readers to look at temporal flow—time as counted by the heartbeats of love that link the living and dead, time that separates the pristine past from the moment of colonial invasion. The unstable present brackets these extremes.

The paradigm established in Gorriti's first work of fiction is reiterated in subsequent texts. "Treasure of the Incas" tells the story of the leader Yupanqui, who has been dispossessed of his lands in Cuzco. His children are his only wealth. However, his daughter Rosalía falls in love with Diego de Maldonado, a Spaniard who is driven by greed and seeks to learn the secret location of the treasure of the Incas that only Yupanqui's family holds. Love and gold are thus intimately tied, generating Diego's adventurism in America as well as his cruelty and acts of deception. As in "The *Quena*," interracial attraction constitutes the basis of melodramatic romance. Hidden truths and false identities also drive the story, while thieves and gamblers and shifty characters serve to remind us of corruption under colonial law. Gorriti structures this reading through tropes of blindness and revelation. Rosalía is blind to the lies of Diego; Diego, meanwhile, extracts secrets from a blind woman in the countryside who confuses Diego with her son; blindfolded, Diego is permitted to reach the location of the Inca treasure where he sees the desired gold. But the real blindness is ultimately conveyed through Diego's ignorance of ethics and virtue. He is blind to the tenacity of Inca honor and all rules of justice.

The early stories link love and avarice in a melodramatic structure that often evokes interracial conflicts. At the same time, Gorriti's despair over the plight of Argentina finds expression in a cycle of fictions devoted to the horrors of the Rosas regime. Here, hallucinatory madness becomes a literary expression of Argentine social unrest. In "The Deadman's Fiancée," the conflict between Federalists and Unitarians refuses a quick resolution. Set in Tucumán, in northern Argentina in the 1820s, the fiction recalls significant people and events in Argentine civil war history, leading us to the battle of La Ciudadela in 1831, in which Facundo Quiroga's forces issued a colossal blow to Unitarian soldiers. These events form the backdrop for scenes of family conflict, as Gorriti places the bulk of the weight of political strife upon women. Vital, daughter of Federalists, falls in love with Horacio Ravelo, a Unitarian soldier of high achievement. This doomed love is explained through literary allusions. Vital, as a reader, is chastised for her excessive devotion to literary fiction. Too much reading, her interlocutor advises, encourages unbridled fantasy. Nevertheless, Gorriti counsels us to read this national conflict and tale of warring families in terms of the tragic romance of Romeo and Juliet. Also imposed upon this critique of reading is a gothic narration featuring apparitions, phantoms, and premonitions of danger that haunt the female characters. The triumph of Federalists at La Ciudadela thus inspires strange hallucinations and disturbs the stability of realist narration, the building block of historical fiction. At the story's end, Vital wanders aimlessly, reminding readers of the close ties between Federalist triumph and madness, between the power of the female gaze and the instruments that give it meaning in history. Gorriti appears to tell us that 30 years of Federalist tyranny might produce eternal happiness for some; for others, it yields a grotesque experience driven by hopeless dementia.

"The *Mazorquero's* Daughter" once again dramatizes Federalist and Unitarian conflict through the medium of the family. This time, however, Gorriti focuses specifically on the figure of Roque Black-Soul, head of the Mazorca, the secret police force that protected Rosas and drove out dissident forces. To emphasize the heinous crimes of this terrible figure, Gorriti places Roque in opposition to his lovely daughter Clemencia, a girl who seeks to correct the atrocities of Federalist rule. Modeled on Rosas's real daughter Manuelita—a celebrated figure in Unitarian literature and folklore, in which she was seen as opposing her father's tyranny, Clemencia—as her name indicates—represents mercy and hope, a symbol of unblemished virtue. Gorriti uses the structural opposition of father and daughter to contrast good and evil. If Clemencia's gift of generosity is made evident by her melodious voice, Roque Black-Soul generates a vocabulary of "cruelty and irreverence"; if the sweet name Clemencia soothes the spirit, Roque's criminality provokes fear. These ironies are reinforced by many errors in perception. Roque hopes that his spies will reveal the identity of traitors and ensure the safety of the state, but Clemencia uses different tactics, cloaking the identity of Unitarian figures behind the veil and the mask, and intervening to dupe Federalist agents. The opposition of good and evil is thus registered in the energetic pairings of deception and revelation, error and recognition, that the father-daughter dyad supplies. The contrast of speech and silence also supports this opposition. As the story advances, Roque's garrulous discourse overcomes Clemencia's silence. Roque holds the power of naming and purports to account for all truths that circulate in Argentina. His voice determines the fate of the innocent, condemning individuals to death. Nevertheless, he fails to control ironic reversals of fate and to note the meaning behind Clemencia's muted gestures. In this respect, the power of the gaze and one's faith in surveillance reveal their limited functions. The state, in an attempt to control its inventories of citizen-subjects, exposes its tragic flaw: It cannot hear the warnings of silence.

Gorriti's fiction operates from scenes of misrecognition in which darkness enshrouds identity and the veil covers the oppositional body. At the same time, abundant syntactic crossovers occlude the origins of meaning and set the pace for errors of interpretation and ongoing ironic confusion. Buenos Aires is the setting for these early stories, serving as the backdrop for this rhetorical crisscross, represented by its threatening darkness and the hovering presence of Rosas. (The city was unknown to Gorriti until the later years of her life; like Sarmiento, she described Buenos Aires long before she ever set foot

in the growing city). "The Black Glove" brings us close to the horrors
of this ominous city and depends upon the Federalist and Unitarian
wars for its dual narrative structure. In this instance, however, the
switch from one world to another depends upon the presence of a
single object, the black glove of a lover whose symbolic force radiates
among different characters, driving narrative action and condensing
signs of devotion and betrayal. In this way, the keepsake negotiates
extremes of political allegiance and introduces secrecy and deception
as principal tropes of the story. The glove represents the romantic
inconstancy of Wenceslao, who hurts the two women who love him.
Wenceslao receives the devotion of Manuela Rosas and Isabel, one
the representative of Federalist politics, the other a Unitarian supporter. To cultivate the love of these women, Wenceslao alters his
political allegiance, endangers his standing with his Federalist father,
and eventually pays with his life. The story is told, however, from the
perspective of Isabel, thus allowing Gorriti to emphasize a feminine
world of intuitive (and Unitarian) wisdom that drives an alternative
version of history.

These conflicting visions motivate a number of secrets that move
the story forward. Trick doors, concealed identities, and letters of
confession gone astray lead to the unfolding of plot and guide the
story toward its inevitable conclusion. Gorriti also makes apparent an
ongoing attention to the human body as a source and flow of meaning. The bleeding wound of Wenceslao, for example, floods the
minds of characters and reminds us of the Federalist preference for
crimson as a sign of allegiance to Rosas. The gushing blood also generates a call for action and awakens the passions of the women who
rush to Wenceslao's aid. But the returning trope of bloodshed
reminds us of the drained national body, devastated by civil war,
despoiled on the landscapes of an emerging nation in which individuals can no longer heal. All conflict leads to a final scene on the battlefield of Quebracho Herrado, site of a notorious Unitarian defeat in
November 1840, in which General Lavalle's 1,300 troops were lost to
the Federalists. Just as the wound of Wenceslao will not heal, this
civil war will not see a tranquil end in Gorriti's tale. Instead, she

leaves her characters in a realm of hallucination and madness in which they wander in search of meaning. Only the voice remains to haunt future generations.

Opera is significant in Gorriti's fiction. Setting the pace of the stories, operatic arias warn of danger and anticipate the tragic unfolding of love amidst civil war. Singing voices not only contrast with the silence enforced by the state, but also serve as a reminder of an ongoing ethical loss. They structure the rhythms of prose in order to link text to musical composition, but the voices also allow Gorriti to link her American landscape to the cloak-and-dagger dimensions of European romantic opera, with its cast of political intrigues and double entendres. In "If You Do Wrong, Expect No Good," the story opens with conflicting voices that offer differing versions of history. The voice of indigenous conscience is challenged by European aggression and might. In this story, a military officer, representing the Spanish Crown, rapes an indigenous woman. The woman gives birth to a girl who is later abducted and raised in Europe where she meets and marries a young man who turns out to be her half brother, the son of the same official who violated her mother. When the couple returns to Peru, the young girl discovers her hidden past. Unable to bear it, the military officer responsible for fathering the luckless siblings dies from despair, his body abandoned to vultures. Using this scenario, Gorriti attacks the colonial regime that fails to protect the rights of indigenous women, while also blaming the Peruvian nation for its ongoing confusion of values. Sexual licentiousness carries the dangers of eventual incest; in an unruly state, dysfunction marks the family. Unable to restrain its military personnel or protect its wards, the regime is held responsible for the dissolution of society. Efraín Kristal has explained this story in terms of the pacts between the export oligarchy and the landowning elites to stimulate immigration and improve the racial composition of Peru.[31] The crossing of races, which lies at the center of Gorriti's story, needs the powers of the liberal republic to set things straight. Nevertheless, Gorriti also points to elites' ongoing malice toward rural women and family morals. In this regard, it is no surprise that violation and madness are tropes that give meaning to the fiction, just as the old colonel's lasciviousness is uncorrected until the moment of final revelation. The incest between siblings anticipates Clorinda Matto de Turner's *Aves sin nido* (*Torn from the Nest*) in 1889, a landmark Peruvian novel that exposed the corruption of the Church and the wanton desires of its clerics. Uprooting families and disregarding the rights of women and Indians, the traditional church, in Matto de Turner's eyes, had little to offer the nation. Gorriti, however, goes one step further by insisting upon the interchangeability of subjects, representing the Indians as surrogates in a complex play of European desires. The indigenous groups and rural poor thus come to function as placeholders in fiction, redistributing allegiances and substituting for the loved ones lost by Creole elites; they temporarily fill in for whiteness. In this capacity, they are tokens of shifting meaning and remind us that patterns of racial resemblance and difference are the sustaining tropes of a national project. Indigenous figures in this literature are a clue to the systems of differentiation that separate America from Europe, just as doubling and mirroring are the bases of the gothic fiction that Gorriti sets before us. But the indigenous groups in Gorriti's work also create a double time that is incomprehensible to colonial elites. Indeed, they introduce the possibility of parallel worlds that lie beyond European grasp.

To orchestrate this double time, Gorriti insists on movement and massive upheaval, always evoking the nomadic aspects of characters to advance her plot. While this fiction wanders between Europe and America, between the chasms of the Andean highlands and the Parisian cemetery of Père Lachaise, in other stories Gorriti points to characters' movement between country and city and to subjects' migration around America. It is no wonder that travelers and highway bandits are the constant stock of her literary world.

Gorriti's work is pure movement: Her itinerant characters are depicted in exile, on the run, in defiance of the law. She weaves the adventures of postcolonial elites with those of popular figures. Robbers and bandits, highwaymen and servants, the principal figures represented in her early stories, are integrated in the adventures of Creole would-be aristocrats and rising military officers who seek to gain instant wealth from stealing inheritances or Inca treasures. The dreams of overnight profit contrast with an ongoing nostalgia for the primitive wealth of the land.

These conflicting interests produced a contentious style of writing, but they also signaled a rupture of paradigms, a hybrid approach toward assessing the ground rules of a new nation. On the one hand, a revision of the past, seriously steeped in nostalgia, may be read as a strategy to preserve local history while also amassing an inventory of local histories upon which to build a future. On the other hand, the frenzied dual course of narration, incited by repetitions and doubling, by masquerade and disguise, puts the alignment of any national narrative in question. Each time a story was retold and familiar facts were reintroduced in fiction, the history of the nation changed slightly to show the inconsistencies of progress and the futility of defining national subjects. The conflicts lay bare the tensions between elites and emerging popular figures excluded from the province of the law.

Hayden White observed that in order for an event to be historical, it must have two possible interpretations.[32] These necessary conflicts were always present in the writings of Latin America's founding fathers, sustaining a double movement in narrative style as a way to depict the problems of nations. Often this became the equivalent of locating one's culture in a geopolitical elsewhere, on the borders, in hybrid articulations, in spatial representations outside of one's homeland. It signaled one's estrangement from *patria* and opened an area that Homi Bhabha once described as the "realm of the beyond."[33]

In Chile, for example, Sarmiento debated the merits of public voice, but also set the terms for a mid-century style, inaugurating a restless movement that blended complex, popular forms with a singular categorization of citizenship. In debate with Bello, Sarmiento also theorized possible roles for the *letrado,* different ways to articulate public authority in the postcolonial administration of knowledge. Distance from his country allowed him to tell of the plight of Argentines, to generalize about tyranny and freedom, but it also allowed him to set terms for budding intellectual projects in Chile, showing not only that national discourse was shaped by ideas from abroad, but also that intellectuals in exile affected the debates of their host countries. Like Sarmiento, Gorriti also placed before the public the conflicts between rules of state and elements of dissidence and protest, shaping from beyond Argentina the crisis emerging in her homeland.

In this respect, her fiction offers a trail of multiple possibilities, inserting contradiction in inherited philosophical systems and challenging univocal implications of theory with the power of interstitial logic. Her example allows us to understand a nation through discordant readings, through a gesture against totalizing thought. Here, in the space that Silviano Santiago named as the advantage of the "in between," Gorriti allows us to reflect on the conflicting materials that sustain projects of representation.[34] In this respect, it comes as no surprise that marginal figures—Indians and blacks among them—sustain so much of her fiction, challenging the limitations of administrative projects belonging to the emerging state. Taking us beyond standard novels in defense of nationhood, wayward subjects become a guiding incentive for Gorriti's philosophy about the need for community ethics. They also offer the components for a local style that, after independence, initiated the possibility for theoretical reflection to grow in Latin America. As a material site to register change, the popular or marginal subject works as a placeholder to register the flows of history and to point to the inadequacy of any singular vision in planning for new beginnings.

In "Gubi Amaya," Gorriti tells of returning, disguised as a man, to her native Horcones. Masked identity is a constant in her stories, as if to say that disguise is a sine qua non for the emerging personality in America. The motif is repeated in nineteenth-century texts: Think only of the tale of Catalina de Erauso, the ensign nun—a woman disguised as a man—whose legacy circulated in fiction and historical texts by Chileans José Victorino Lastarria and Diego Barros Arana; the heroine of Juana Manso's novel, *Los misterios del Plata* (1846), who purposefully eluded state surveillance when she dressed in men's clothing; and the veiled women of Mercedes Cabello de Carbonera's novels who tried to escape control by the state. These dramas of confused identity are the stock of the literary landscape, and Juana Manuela Gorriti's fiction is no exception. What is interesting, however, is her fascination with the topic as a way to subvert the Rosas regime and introduce the possibility of women moving beyond the traditional domestic sphere assigned to them. Domesticity appears to offer no cure for her luckless protagonists; rather, moving through the Americas bespeaks the female desire for independence and freedom. For nomads, false identities abound; no authority is absolute; no experience is fixed in time. Disguise enables movement.

The Spanish-American travelers who emerge in Gorriti's fiction suggest that identity is all about the tricks of eye and tongue, staged upon a national platform in which memories of the past and rules of the present remain uncertain. More than any final destination, it is the voyage that counts, provoking new subjectivities and different ways of feeling. "I was two persons," Gorriti's narrator advises her readers in the early pages of "Gubi Amaya." Beyond the recourse to disguise, the urgency to travel awakens a dual self, a crossed vision that confuses past and present moments, sentimental and political life. This doubleness is everywhere: in the dual identities of strangers who cross the narrator's path, in the interpolated stories that conflict with the major narration, in the dual memories of home and exile that divide the loyalties of all nomadic subjects, in the ironies posed by the law and its multiple transgressions.

Gorriti's narrator, Emma, attempts to return to her native land, but a series of digressions raises other concerns and interests. "How can I ever describe it?" she asks. This split between experience and narration now becomes the fundamental division governing all reflection in "Gubi Amaya." The protagonist, who bears two names—Gubi Amaya and Miguel—personifies this split. A highway robber who nonetheless maintains an ethical stance, Gubi Amaya is both cruel and delicate, aware of his heinous crimes but critical of those who disregard human interest. His is the story of a delinquent whose identity lies beyond the limits of the law. Other conflicts follow: One person's nostalgia is cut short by the narrated adventures of another; one's exercise of memory is countered by another's narration of current experience; one's good fortune is challenged by the poverty sustained by his double. Duality reigns in a topsy-turvy world that refuses absolute answers. The only authority, as characters remind us, is found in the art of telling.

It is not surprising that Gorriti and her contemporaries consistently tell tales of travel. As might be expected, travel moves not simply the eye and mind, but the physical self as well. When Gorriti's traveler returns to the past to revisit the homeland, the voyage is marked by a clash of identities and geographic displacements. Travel produces a material response to landscape, exaggerating the contact between individuals and the land through sensation and feelings. As a result, we are directed to the physical basis of experience; we train our eyes to the body. Travel also creates a space for the naming of new subjectivities, mediated through variants of speech and often through translation. In this respect, linguistic shifts—from French, English, Portuguese, Aymara, and Quechua into Spanish—become a graphic, material way to expand possible fields of knowledge. Through their bilingualism, the foreigners expand the range of debates about the other nation named. As a result of their bilingual skills, these traveling subjects begin to doubt the authority of their native tongues. The exercise creates both a minor genre and breaks up the singularity with which one equates nation, language, and home.

With so much discussion of movement and stasis, perhaps it is time to address the question of narrative structure. I am referring to the apparent swing in Gorriti's works between a desire for a comprehensive explanation of history and an ongoing representation of the components of past and future. This tension leads us to focus on artifice in the text. Images of ruins, remnants of a monumental past, traces of precious metal or buried treasure litter Gorriti's stories; in this respect, they reveal Gorriti's desire for collection. The ruins are certainly like souvenirs, but, in a literal sense, they are stones in the ongoing project of building a house for literature. Mined from nature's quarries, they sustain a partial memory of the past, but they also create sites for future longings. More important, they remind us of a transformation of sensibility from romantic melancholia about the experience of loss to the *modernista* habits of the urban consumer; they move us from the rural past to a modern consumerist fetish for the catalogue of goods that marked a new cosmopolitan culture emerging in the late nineteenth century. It is an interesting case, in which the fragment, usually the basis of allegory, here overturns allegory itself and comes to stand for an aesthetic process belonging to modernization.

Gorriti places the edifice of allegorical narration (the ruins that stimulate remembrance, the accumulation of objects that allow the narrator to assemble a "typical" past, the romantic desire to show the waning of time through remnants, the artifice of melancholic longing) against the wanderings of characters who collect remote and partial experiences en route to some future project. Permanence against futurity; duration against uncertain choice. These are different ways of making use of the fragment in terms of a textual economy: If the first reminds one of the colonial regime, the second moves inevitably to the experience of consumerism that will be dominant under the liberal state and the aegis of *modernismo* in the *fin de siglo*. The fragment now leads to a contemplation of the relationship between experience and naming; it registers a split between feeling and object, between personal and public experience.

Gorriti took to chronicling the progress of nineteenth-century America—the advent of trains and electric lights, the buzz of industry and machines, the availability of more consumer goods. She began to publish this kind of fiction and history after the death of Belzú, an event that left her virtually impoverished. From that time, she abandoned entitlement and wealth and began to redesign her stories around earning a living. Her rural scenes of the independence wars were contrasted with an almost obsessive meditation on consumerism in the city. This is a crisis between tradition and modernity, between the founding moment of a nation and a cosmopolitan assertion of personal need. This crisis disturbed any supposed unity in her cultural texts, fragmenting her work into multiple realms of experience. One might claim that Gorriti's fiction announces a division between the state's explanation of history and the individual's private drama concerning the effects of modernization.

This emerged as the principal narrative in her later career: tales of survival juxtaposed against memories of distant wealth, stories of travelers in search of fortune on the trade routes of modern America. While her autobiography suggests a constant preoccupation with financial solvency and the economic well-being of her colleagues and friends, in her fiction the topic of finance is articulated through chaotic movements, differing styles of managing the anxiety of lost prestige and current economic distress, conflicting interests in negotiating one's legal rights and adequate venues of representation.

In one of a long line of tales about the gold rush, "A Year in California," a novella she first published in serialized form in 1869,[35] Gorriti follows characters who travel north from Chile to join the forty-niners' search for gold and adventure. She thus indulges a genre that has always been popular with Spanish speakers and that ranges from Vicente Pérez Rosales's saga of the Chilean journey north in 1849 to Isabel Allende's novel, *Daughter of Fortune,* which retraces the same ocean course leading to California. Gorriti, however, uses the gold rush background to try her hand at representing avarice and unrelenting sexual desire. She focuses on her characters' longing for a safe and cozy past that they know is beyond their reach, but she also dwells on a general fear of predatory sexual urges and irrepressible greed. The novel features an impoverished orphan forced to join an adventurer traveling by ship from Chile to California. When their boat stops in Peru, the orphan meets an innocent young woman who will become the object of his affection. Here all tranquility ends for, in the voyage from Chile to the gold mines, a reckless copper-skinned man emerges to disrupt social life; Gorriti describes him as a nameless "hombre de cobre," a possible allusion to indigenous races that was commonly used in the nineteenth century, but that also refers to the copper coins that adventurers so passionately sought.[36] By his constantly shifting identities, the "hombre de cobre" threatens the couple and dismantles the rules of law. His sinister presence reminds us of the dangers that the Creole elites associate with modernization; equally important, he embodies concupiscence, guilt, and shame.

Similarly, the gold rush fever that is the underlying theme of this story produces uncontrollable excess. The text thus presents a crisis in the values of an emerging liberal society, a materialism that distorts ethical principles and separates children from their families. The chaos of the new society takes shape through fragmented narration and uneven stories; useless objects litter the text without clear direction or function. Foreign populations appear, introducing new languages and crossing borders. Newspapers, gossip, and hearsay inform the tale. Against the linear authority of traditional narration, which serves to detail the colonial past, unknown voices intrude in the text; origins are suspect, racial purity is placed in doubt. No certain proof exists of one's identity or name. These are the byproducts of a society undergoing rapid change.

Among the figures driven by greed, the copper-skinned man awakens fears in other characters. His race is uncertain: He passes as hunter and miner and is alternately described as Navajo and English (and even as a Central American muckraker); in San Francisco, he performs in vaudeville. A quick reading of this figure will lead us to speak of the Creole elites' racial fears in a time of transition, but his corporeal form also generates a secondary reading. Only observed in transit, the copper-skinned man inspires a haunting fear, a blurred but ongoing reminder of an unnamable danger that never quite solidifies or dissolves. He stands for an elusive presence that the state cannot hope to control. Awakening undefined sexual desire in the female protagonist, his lurking figure motivates fear, but it is also clear to the reader that he is described by the color of money. The multiple positions maintained by characters like the copper-skinned man thus confuse the boundaries of nations and threaten the integrity of family. In this environment of economic advancement, danger lurks in all corners; it threatens the possibility of love and menaces the safety of all.

In *The Confidence Man* (1857), Herman Melville also introduced a character with multiple disguises, a trickster who represented the dangers of a new ethos in North American culture. From South America, as well, Gorriti's example makes clear the anxieties of a generation that vacillates between the goals of law and order and serious plans for resistance. The objective of the tale is to denounce the ethos of the modern age through ceaseless narrative movement, tracing not simply a destination, but the path of discovery that leads to it. It is not coincidental then this inquiry takes place on the new frontier, in the United States.

Gorriti was always suspicious of the ethos of North American business, the ethos of profit and gain. In *Lo íntimo,* she wrote:

> I admire as few do the grandeur of [the United States], today the first in everything, but endowed with a superlative national ego. Everything is for them, everything is for them. The Monroe doctrine has two faces.
>
> I greatly fear at the present moment that the issue is reduced to a few questions: "How much will you pay me to stop them from hanging you?" "How much will you pay me so that you can hang another?"[37]

Money facilitates identity, establishes the terms of the contract, and sets the guidelines for polity and exchange that govern the nineteenth century. Gorriti's stories are densely packed with concerns about financial gain; theft, robbery, and deception form the substance of her melodramatic adventure. In her last works, she was disturbed by the growing materialism of the 1890s: the greed, the desire for material goods, the betrayals of friends.[38]

In the nineteenth century, intellectuals actively debated the meaning of emerging republicanism, testing it as a matter of rights and representation. It offers a record of conflicting political languages and incessant discord, tremendous disagreements about how to identify citizens and construct an image of the common good. The heated arguments, of course, reflect an asynchrony between civil society and the state and express the *letrados'* uneasiness before the multiple, uncharted subjects who cannot be brought to order. In this respect, think only of the confusion in Chile in the 1840s when Bello and Sarmiento debated the future of language in Spanish America. Their lively exchanges focused on the state's grip over deviant expressions and the possibility of a normative speech that would run the length of the *cordillera*. These debates were also about questions of individual conformity, wayward desire, and the ways in which we should exercise control over the free flow of identities and voices. Their exchanges led to what is perhaps the dominant, overarching question of nineteenth-century philosophy, that concerning the formation of the "liberal republic."[39] What, after all, is the "liberal republic"? For its liberal side, it suggested the autonomy of civil society, the flow of particular interests and the exercise of free will; for its republican aspect, it suggested a common and collective project, faith in consensus, and the negotiation of a standard, universal ideal. As such, the liberal republic redirected the power of popular beliefs and set patterns for national memory; paradoxically, it controlled the multiplication of difference as it sought to construct a semiotic field based on principles of exclusion. Nevertheless, the project locked Latin American nations in ambiguity and confusion. Instead of a cohesive, regulated language, Babel flourished in its multiple practices and defied a singular logic. Moreover, the question of association (as confederacy or federal state) was never resolved in terms that could lead to a general understanding of "we." The collective was set against particular interests, locked in unrelieved tension; normative exercises of the state stood against any protection of individual free will.

Political philosophers have covered these issues; however, they rarely take into account the literary and gendered contribution to the republican project. My question here, of course, is about the ways in which Juana Manuela Gorriti's writing falls within this debate. Gorriti tracks a host of characters who readily bridge two worlds, always speaking in two tongues, always wearing masks, one determined by the state's demands and another marked by private desires. But the mask presumes a confidence in some original identity, a fixed, symbolic ordering that will later be cloaked or disguised. The liberal republic repeatedly insists on this paradox and Gorriti, in particular, exploits this, showing how her characters come to exemplify the tensions between conformity and fluid free will, between one language in conflict with another. Her characters carry this doubleness in language and dress, and in staged public performances, they often defy the rules of state. The mask they wear negotiates Latin America's past and future. In this respect, Gorriti's stories cannot be read as examples of simple nostalgia; rather, her career spans nearly a century of literary modernization and sustains the possibilities of transit and change to overcome inertia and longing. Her work pivots on the ambiguities of a decisive nation-building movement that will usher Latin America from colony to modern state. Most synthetically, then, her texts investigate ways of entering a modern historical movement while recognizing that memory and progress do not stand still.

## Notes

1. Juana Manuela Gorriti, *Lo íntimo* (Buenos Aires: Ramón Espasa, 1892), 3.

2. Juana Manuela Gorriti, *La tierra natal* (Buenos Aires: Felix Lajouane, 1889), 171.

3. Gorriti, *Lo intimo*, 2.

4. On the history of Unitarian and Federalist conflicts, see David Rock, *Argentina, 1516–1987. From Spanish Colony to the Falklands* (Berkeley and Los Angeles: University of California Press, 1987), 96–117.

5. On Belzú, see Fausto Reinaga, *Belzú, Precursor de la revolución nacional* (La Paz: Editorial Rumbo Sindical, 1953), and Fernando Diez de Medina, *Literatura boliviana: introducción al estudio de las letras nacionales* (Madrid: Aguilar, 1953).

6. Alfredo Sanjinés even refers to Belzú as a "mestizo Quijote" (cited in Reinaga, *Belzú*, 34).

7. Juana Manuela Gorriti, "Belzú," in *Panoramas de la vida* 2 (Buenos Aires: Imprenta y Librería de Mayo, 1876).

8. Analía Efrón, *Juana Gorriti, una biografía íntima* (Buenos Aires: Sudamericana, 1998), 66.

9. Reinaga, *Belzú*, 26.

10. Marta Mercader, *Juanamanuela mucha mujer* (Buenos Aires: Sudamericana, 1980).

11. Hebe Beatriz Molina debates the paternity of these children in *La narrativa dialógica de Juana Manuela Gorriti* (Cuyo: Editorial de la Universidad Nacional de Cuyo, 1999), 304–5. Analía Efrón notes the birth of a fifth child, after 1860, born after Gorriti's separation from Sandoval (Efrón, *Juana Gorriti*, 136).

12. Juana Manuela Gorriti, *Perfiles* (Buenos Aires: Felix Lajouane, 1892), 27–28.

13. Juana Manuela Gorriti, *Oasis en la vida* (Buenos Aires: Felix Lajouane, 1888), 110.

14. Molina, *narrativa dialógica*, 298; Efrón, *Juana Gorriti*, 11.

15. On the dates of composition of Gorriti's early work, see José María Torres Caicedo's prologue to Juana Manuela Gorriti's *Sueños y realidades* (Buenos Aires: Casavalle, 1865), i–xv. On dates of subsequent material, see the chronologies supplied by Rocío Ferreira, "Cocina ecléctica: Mujeres, cocina y nación en el Perú decimonónico" (Ph.D. diss., University of California at Berkeley, 2001).

16. Dionisio Puch was a member of the family through marriage and a hero in the wars of independence.

17. On Clorinda Matto de Turner's anticlericalism in Peru, see the introduction by Antonio Cornejo Polar to Clorinda Matto de Turner's *Torn from the Nest* (New York: Oxford University Press, 1998).

18. Cited in Graciela Batticuore, ed., *El taller de la escritora. Veladas literarias de Juana Manuela Gorriti* (Rosario: Beatriz Viterbo, 1999), 29.

19. See, for example, the contributions of Abel de la E. Delgado, "La educación social de la muger," Batticuore, *Veladas literarias de Lima*, 27–39; and Mercedes Eléspuru y Lazo, "La instrucción de la muger," 145–49. Cited in Juana Manuela Gorriti, *Veladas literarias de Lima, 1876–1877*, vol. 1 (Buenos Aires: Imprenta Europea, 1892).

20. Mercedes Cabello de Carbonera, "Importancia de la literatura," in *Veladas literarias de Lima, 1876–1877*, ed. Gorriti, 6–12.

21. Manuela Villarán de Plascencia, "Inconvenientes para la emancipación de la mujer," *La alborada del Plata*, vol. 1, no. 12 (February 3, 1878): 94. Cited and translated by Francine Masiello in *Between Civilization and Barbarism: Women, Nation, and Literary Culture in Modern Argentina* (Lincoln: University of Nebraska Press, 1992), 67.

22. Cornejo Polar in *Torn from the Nest*, ed. Matto de Turner, xviii.

23. See Lily Sosa de Newton, *Las argentinas de ayer a hoy* (Buenos Aires: Ediciones Zanetti, 1967), 115.

24. Gorriti, *Lo íntimo*, 73.

25. Juana Manuela Gorriti, Untitled editorial, *La alborada del Plata*, vol. 1 (1877): 1.

26. See Mary Louise Pratt, *Imperial Eyes. Travel Writing and Transculturation* (New York: Routledge, 1992), 7.

27. Juana Manso notes in the final issue of her journal, *Album de señoritas* (1854), that, for lack of funds, she cannot continue publication. Like Gorriti, Manso made financial support a constant topic of her publications. On this, see Francine Masiello, *La mujer y el espacio público: el periodismo femenino en la Argentina del siglo XIX* (Buenos Aires: Feminaria, 1994).

28. Vicente G. Quesada wrote in defense of Gorriti and lamented the sorry economic state that befalls all writers: "Although literary works do not enjoy financial compensation in America, the literary scene nevertheless attracts the presence of notable and capacious minds. Poverty is almost the only laurel that can be harvested by the tranquil work of the mind yet has not discouraged those novices who often have to abandon their writing and secure other work in order to survive. Knowing the history of many writers, living in poverty, but working with faith, inspires our true pity. . . . Before the indifference of the public regarding this literary work, we also have to take into account the guilty neglect of governments: the person of letters thus enjoys neither stimulation nor financial benefits. Why write then? Because it responds to a higher law than mere physical need, because it satisfies the needs of the spirit." Cited in his review, "Sueños y realidades," *La revista de Buenos Aires*, vol. 2 (1864): 407–8.

29. See Angel Rama, *Rubén Darío y el modernismo* (Caracas: Alfadil Editores, 1985), 13.

30. Efraín Kristal makes this argument, linking the emergence of a Peruvian literature dedicated to the representation of indigenous groups to debates and conflicts among landowning oligarchy in *The Andes Viewed from the City: Literary and Political Discourse on the Indian in Peru, 1848–1930* (New York: Peter Lang, 1987).

31. Kristal, *The Andes Viewed from the City*, 61–71.

32. See Hayden White, *The Content of the Form: Narrative Discourse and Historical Representation* (Baltimore: John Hopkins University Press, 1987), 57–58.

33. See Homi Bhabha, *The Location of Culture* (New York: Routledge, 1994), 66–67.

34. See Silviano Santiago, "O Entre-Lugar do discurso latino-americano," *Uma literatura nos trópicos* (Rio de Janeiro: Editora Perspectiva, 1975), 11–28.

35. The translation presented here is based on the 1869 story serialized as "Un año en California," in *La Revista de Buenos Aires,* nos. 18–19 (1869). A revised version also appeared as "Un viaje al país de oro" in Juana Manuela Gorriti, *Panoramas de la vida* (Buenos Aires: Imprenta y Librería de Mayo, 1876).

36. The relationship between coinage and identity demands further investigation. In the nineteenth century, the obsession with copper is everywhere to be seen, as Benjamín Vicuña Mackenna makes clear in his classic book, *El libro del cobre i del carbón de piedra en Chile* (Santiago de Chile: Imprenta Cervantes, 1883). For a recent fruitful study on the significance of metal from the perspective of economic history, see Jeremy Adelman, *Republic of Capital. Buenos Aires and the Legal Transformation of the Atlantic World* (Stanford: Stanford University Press, 1999).

37. Gorriti, *Lo íntimo,* 59–60.

38. Gorriti, *Lo íntimo,* 90, 101–2.

39. On the debates within the liberal republic, see Luis Castro Leiva, *El liberalismo como problema* (Caracas: Monteavila, 1992).

# Bibliography

## A. Works by Juana Manuela Gorriti

*Sueños y realidades.* 2 vols. Buenos Aires: Carlos Casavalle, 1865.

*Biografía del General Don Dionisio de Puch.* Paris: Imprenta Hispano-Americana, 1868.

*Panoramas de la vida.* 2 vols. Buenos Aires: Imprenta y Librería de Mayo, 1876.

*Misceláneas: colección de leyendas, juicios, pensamientos, discursos, impresiones de viaje y descripciones americanas.* Buenos Aires: Biedma, 1878.

*El mundo de los recuerdos.* Buenos Aires: Felix Lajouane, 1886.

*Oasis en la vida.* Buenos Aires: Felix Lajouane, 1888.

*La tierra natal.* Buenos Aires: Felix Lajouane, 1889.

*Cocina ecléctica.* Buenos Aires: Felix Lajouane, 1889.

*Perfiles.* Buenos Aires: Felix Lajouane, 1892.

*Lo íntimo.* Buenos Aires: Ramón Espasa, 1892.

*Veladas literarias de Lima: 1876–1877.* Buenos Aires: Imprenta Europea, 1892.

## B. Further Readings

Adelman, Jeremy. *Republic of Capital. Buenos Aires and the Legal Transformation of the Atlantic World.* Stanford: Stanford University Press, 1999.

Batticuore, Graciela, ed. *El taller de la escritora. Veladas literarias de Juana Manuela Gorriti.* Rosario: Beatriz Viterbo, 1999.

————, ed. *Juana Manuela Gorriti. Ficciones patrias.* Buenos Aires: Editorial Sol, 2001.

Berg, Mary. "Juana Manuela Gorriti (1818–1892). Argentina." In *Escritoras hispanoamericanas: una guía bio-bibliográfica,* edited by Diane Marting. Mexico: Siglo XXI, 1990.

Castro Leiva, Luis. *El liberalismo como problema.* Caracas: Monteavila, 1992.

Chaca, Dionisio. *Historia de Juana Manuela Gorriti.* Buenos Aires: El Centenario, 1940.

Conde, Alfredo O. *Juana Manuela Gorriti: dolor, belleza, trabajo, patriotismo.* Buenos Aires: Biblioteca Popular de C.E. XX, 1939.

Denegri, Francesca. *El abanico y la cigarrera. La primera generación de mujeres ilustradas en el Perú.* Lima: Flora Tristán and Institute of Peruvian Studies, 1996.

Diez de Medina, Fernando. *Literatura boliviana: introducción al estudio de las letras nacionales.* Madrid: Aguilar, 1953.

Efrón, Analía. *Juana Gorriti, una biografía íntima.* Buenos Aires: Sudamericana, 1998.

Ferreira, Rocío. "Cocina ecléctica: Mujeres, cocina y nación en el Perú decimonónico." Ph.D. diss., University of California at Berkeley, 2001.

Fletcher, Lea, ed. *Mujeres y cultura en el siglo XIX.* Buenos Aires: Feminaria, 1994.

Guerra Cunningham, Lucía. "Visión marginal de la historia en la narrativa de Juana Manuela Gorriti." *Ideologies and Literatures* 2, no. 2 (1987): 59–76.

Iglesia, Cristina, ed. *El ajuar de la patria. Ensayos críticos sobre Juana Manuela Gorriti.* Buenos Aires: Feminaria, 1993.

————. *Letras y divisas. Ensayos sobre literatura y rosismo.* Buenos Aires: Eudeba, 1997.

Kristal, Efraín. *The Andes Viewed from the City: Literary and Political Discourse on the Indian in Peru, 1848–1930.* New York: Peter Lang, 1987.

Martorell, Alicia. *Juana Manuela Gorriti y "Lo íntimo."* Salta: Fundación del Banco del Noroeste, 1991.

Masiello, Francine. *Between Civilization and Barbarism. Women, Nation, and Literary Culture in Modern Argentina.* Lincoln: University of Nebraska Press, 1992.

————. *La mujer y el espacio público. El periodismo femenino en la Argentina del siglo XIX.* Buenos Aires: Feminaria, 1994.

Matto de Turner, Clorinda. *Torn from the Nest.* Translated by John H. R. Polt, and edited by Antonio Cornejo Polar. New York: Oxford University Press, 1998.

Meehan, Thomas C. "Una olvidada precursora de la literatura fantástica argentina: Juana Manuela Gorriti." *Chasqui* 10, nos. 2–3 (1981): 3–19.

Mercader, Marta. *Juanamanuela mucha mujer*. Buenos Aires: Sudamericana, 1980.

Molina, Hebe Beatriz. *La narrativa dialógica de Juana Manuela Gorriti*. Cuyo: Editorial de la Universidad Nacional de Cuyo, 1999.

Pratt, Mary Louise. *Imperial Eyes. Travel Writing and Transculturation*. New York: Routledge, 1992.

Quesada, Vicente G. "Sueños y realidades." *La revista de Buenos Aires* 2 (1864): 407–16.

Rama, Angel. *Rubén Darío y el modernismo*. Caracas: Alfadil Editores, 1985.

Reinaga, Fausto. *Belzú, Precursor de la revolución nacional*. La Paz: Editorial Rumbo Sindical, 1953.

Rock, David. *Argentina, 1516–1987. From Spanish Colony to the Falklands*. Berkeley and Los Angeles: University of California Press, 1987.

Rojas, Ricardo. *Historia de la literatura argentina*. Vol. 8. Buenos Aires: Librería La Facultad, 1922.

Royo, Amelia, ed. *Juanamanuela, mucho papel*. Salta: Robledal, 1999.

Scott, Nina M. "Juana Manuela Gorriti's *Cocina ecléctica*: Recipes as Feminine Discourse." *Hispania* 75 (May 1992): 310–14.

Sosa de Newton, Lily. *Las argentinas de ayer a hoy*. Buenos Aires: Ediciones Zanetti, 1967.

Vicuña Mackenna, Benjamín. *El libro del cobre i del carbón de piedra en Chile*. Santiago de Chile: Imprenta Cervantes, 1883.

Villavicencio, Maritza. *Del silencio a la palabra. Mujeres peruanas en los siglos XIX y XX*. Lima: Flora Tristán, 1992.

# DREAMS AND REALITIES

# 1

# The *Quena*[1]

## I. THE MEETING

Midnight had just sounded on the cathedral clock in Lima. The streets were dark and deserted, like the rows of a cemetery. The houses, so full of life and light earlier in the evening had, by then, a somber and sinister aspect to them. The beautiful city was asleep, buried in a deep silence interrupted only occasionally by the melancholic sounds of some lover playing the vihuela,[2] or by the distant murmuring of the sea, which the night breeze brought along with the fragrance of the orange trees that form aromatic forests outside the city's walls.

A man appeared in the darkness, his face covered by his long cloak. He moved forward quickly, looking around him very carefully, and stopped before the golden railings of a palace window, where he ran his fingers softly over the latticework.

The latticed window opened.

........

[1] In Andean traditions, a *quena* is a reed flute played by indigenous groups. —Trans.
[2] An early Spanish stringed musical instrument; an ancient type of guitar. —Trans.

"Hernán?" a voice asked, sweet and harmonious as the notes of a lyre. At the same time, the very beautiful face of a young woman came forward, framed by long, black curls scented with jasmine and fragrances.

"Rosa! Do not fear, my love, it is I," the man with the covered face answered passionately, pressing against his chest the white, delicate hand that the young woman stretched out to him.

"Oh! It took you so long to come tonight!" she said, sighing. "I counted the seconds by my beating heart; but it beat so quickly that I feel I have lived centuries since eleven o'clock."

And opening the latticed window completely, she kneeled against the sill to lean closer to her lover. Then she crossed her arms—lathed and white as alabaster—outside the railing. It was a gesture that combined childish confidence and voluptuous grace—a combination found only in our American virgins, to whom the influence of our hot sun gives the full seductive beauties of a woman, with all its refinements, without taking anything from their adorable childhood innocence.

The man whom she called Hernán contemplated her enchanting face almost touching his own in an anguished rapture.

"Rosa! My love!" he said. "I have never seen you as beautiful as you are right now; never have your eyes shone with such divine fire, nor has your voice ever sounded more magical to my heart."

"And yet you are about to leave me. You say all this, but are ready to abandon me to the unbearable persecutions of the hateful Ramírez—who, armed with the approval of my father, of whom he is a friend and colleague, insolently considers me his future property, completely ignoring my wishes. But I shall make them learn the strength of my will, which they ignore. For even if you abandon me, I shall fight this terrible battle on my own; my courage shall not fail me. Go on then, keep to yourself that fateful secret that you refuse to confide to your beloved, and which—since it impedes you from asking my father for the hand of his daughter, who has already given you her heart—might, for all I know, be some tie that binds you to another. . . ."

The voice of the beautiful young woman, which had begun in a firm, adolescent tone, dropped to a very sweet diapason as she said these last words, then faded into a long sigh.

"Rosa! My angel! Do not increase the horrible grief that fills my heart with your tears. Oh! I have been postponing the moment when I must destroy your heart with the weight of my secret, but the hour has arrived. . . . So be it!

"Do you wish to know who this Hernán is, the man whom you met at that bullfight as you sat next to the viceroy? This Hernán de Camporeal, educated with the sons of the great men of Spain, is a descendent of the exiled race, which all of you, especially your father, look upon with so much scorn, having dethroned it and enriched yourselves with its wealth. The man who loves you—the proud daughter of Judge Osorio, the man whom you prefer over the powerful and magnificent Judge Ramírez, is the son of an Indian woman. The man who loves you is an unfortunate soul who does not possess anything in this world, though his feet tread upon the treasures that his forefathers confided to the depths of the earth to keep them from the sanguinary greed of their tyrants."

Hernán interrupted himself and stared deeply into his beloved's eyes as if he wanted to read what was in her soul. But she had crossed her hands over her chest and was looking at him in ecstasy.

"What is this I hear?" she exclaimed. "Hernán, my heart's choice, is a son of the Incas! Oh! I had a premonition of this! Or else why did I get such an intense feeling, even before I knew you, at the mere sound of the name Manco-Capac or Atahualpa?[3] One might say that there was a vibrant link connecting my heart and those heroes' forgotten graves, through which the heat of my young blood communicated with their cold ashes. I used to attribute this strange feeling to

........

[3] Atahualpa entered into a vicious and cruel war against Huascar in order to claim his rights as son and heir of Huayna Capac. Although he won the battles, Atahualpa never assumed power because of Spanish intervention; he fell prisoner to Pizarro and was executed in 1533. Manco-Capac, named for the first Inca, was then selected by Pizarro to assume the throne of the Incas and to rule in accordance with the dictates of Spain. He then incited rebellion against Pizarro and was killed in battle in 1545. —Ed.

the vehement sympathies that youth feel even for beings who have been gone for centuries—when, in fact, it was a premonition of my love for you. But tell me, Hernán, even if my father looks upon your mother's lineage with scorn, how does this impair our love, since the noble Count de Camporeal made your mother a Spaniard when he gave her his name?"

Hernán's proud face turned pale when he heard these words.

"Oh! My blessed mother!" he exclaimed, turning his eyes toward heaven with a look of infinite love. "That name that was refused to you, as noble as it may be, was still not worthy of you. It could not have augmented the glow of your honor and heroism. . . . No! Rosa, my mother never carried that name; a horrendous injustice deprived her of it. Oh! If that had been the only thing he had stolen from her. . . . Just listen to her story, my love. Your heart is the only one worthy of understanding it—you whom she has sent to me from heaven to replace her here on earth.

## II. THE MOTHER

"My first memory is of a day in which I was very little, sitting at my mother's feet. She was a tall young woman, marvelously beautiful, with large, almond-shaped eyes. . . ."

"Like yours!" Rosa whispered in a voice that revealed immense passion, as she ran her slender fingers over Hernán's long eyelashes.

"She had a small mouth," he continued, "with pink lips that always formed a sweet, melancholy smile, revealing two equal rows of teeth white as mountain snow. Four long braids descended from her beautiful head all the way to the ground, and her forehead was adorned with a purple sash, the only emblem with which her people, in their fanatical veneration, distinguish the daughters of the old kings of Perú.

"We lived in Cuzco, in a small house whose walls were raised before the Conquest. The sun was shining in a cloudless sky, and a stream of sunlight poured through a window and died at our feet.

"My mother was spinning in a sad and pensive mood, stopping only occasionally to reach down and caress my hair. I was leaning against her legs, playing—either trying to stop her moving distaff, or playing with the atoms of sunlight, trying to catch them in my hands.

"'María! My daughter, are you there?' a broken voice asked from the doorway.

"'Come in, Cacique,' my mother answered, and stood up to welcome an old Indian with white hair and a venerable countenance. 'Come in, my good adoptive father. My heart is very sad today.' The old cacique looked at my mother with anguished tenderness.

"'Yes, very sad,' she repeated, answering his look. 'I have seen evil omens of an impending misfortune. But I do not know what it is! Just last night a strange and distressing dream filled me with terror. Will you listen to me, you to whom God reveals his mysterious meanings, and tell me what I have to fear?

"'My son was sitting on my lap, and we were in a delightful garden so beautiful that, by comparison, our fertile canyons seem like arid deserts. I was surrounded by all kinds of trees, bearing rich fruits, and countless, varied, gorgeous flowers intoxicated me with their penetrating aromas. And yet, even though everything there inspired happiness, I was sad, and a sense of anguish and restlessness made me hold my son tightly against my chest.

"'All of a sudden, I saw a man of colossal size, a giant with green branches for limbs, whose features—oh, it was so strange!—shifted about like an image reflected on moving water.'

"'The sea!' the old Indian mumbled.

"'The sight of the apparition was so frightening that it caused an extraordinary effect in me. My limbs became numb; my tongue, as if glued to the roof of my mouth, was unable to utter a single cry; and of my entire physical being, only my eyes remained alive. And I saw with my eyes how the giant took advantage of my helplessness and grabbed my son by the neck, tearing him from my arms despite his screams, and took him away to an endless plain, where he disappeared.'

"'The sea!' the cacique said again.

"'The pain that shattered my heart woke me up. My body, shaken by horrible convulsions, was covered in cold sweat, and my temples throbbed as if they were about to burst. But once I opened my eyes and saw my son sleeping in my arms, I hugged him tightly, and all my fears dissipated. They were replaced by an immense pleasure, impossible for anyone other than a mother who has lost her child to understand.'

"And lifting me up in her arms, she covered me with kisses and tears.

"The old Indian, after a long, pensive spell, asked my mother anxiously:

"'Where is he now?'

"'He went,' she replied, 'to Buenos Aires to carry out one of the missions for which he came to America. I have not heard from him in two years. Oh! My father, tell me: Do my ominous dreams and those thousands of evil omens around me refer to my beloved Fernando, my handsome Count de Camporeal?'

"'So you love that Spaniard very much?' the Indian asked bitterly.

"'Yes, I love him!' my mother answered in a passionate voice. 'My heart, my soul, my entire being belong to him. To increase his happiness I would have God double each of his gifts and abilities.'

"The Indian stared at my mother with a look of tender and anguished compassion and murmured sadly, 'She, too, like her forefathers, had to fall into the traps that that impious race lays for our simple, affectionate hearts!

"'It would be in vain, unfortunate daughter of Cuzco, for me to reveal the dark future that I read right now on your countenance and on that of your son—for no one, in any case, can escape their own destiny. Besides, the voice of love, sweet and harmonious, would drown out the quivering, even if inspired, voice of an old man. But it is necessary to put your conscience between our secret and the impassioned weakness of a woman's heart.'

"The cacique stood up and addressed my mother with a majestic gesture and a solemn voice: 'Granddaughter of Atahualpa,' he exclaimed, 'do you swear upon your son's head, and upon your grandfather's blood, that neither love, nor hate, nor caresses, nor tortures can force your lips to reveal to the tyrants the secret that your father left to you on his deathbed?'

'I swear!' she answered in a firm voice, resting one of her hands upon my head and extending the other toward the sun. 'But, oh, my father, I, who have sat upon our forefather's immense treasures and shivered from cold and languished with hunger and fatigue so that the tiny piece of gold that could have strengthened her would not fall into the hands of those who have deprived us of our lands and our inheritance, do not need an oath in order to hold my tongue.'

"The cacique's severe majesty disappeared from his eyes, and paternal tears fell from them.

"'I know, my daughter!' he said. 'But the voice of love is more powerful than that of hunger, or cold, or fatigue. I have fulfilled my duty!' And staring into space with a deep gaze that seemed to penetrate the immensity of the future, he exclaimed:

"'A day shall come in which man's science will discover those treasures; but by then men will be free and equal, and they shall use the wealth to serve humanity! The reign of worries and despotism will have ended, and only man's genius will rule the world, whether it reside upon the head of a European, or upon that of an Indian. Meanwhile, my daughter, may God fulfill his will with you.' Then he wiped a tear from his venerable cheek with his dry, wrinkled hand, turned around, and walked slowly away.

"My mother remained a long time without moving, her head resting on mine.

"The sound of someone quickly approaching shook her out of the deep pensiveness in which the old Indian's words had left her. A tall, elegant gentleman with a handsome, imposing countenance entered, his spurs clanking against our doorstep as he walked in.

"'Camporeal!' my mother exclaimed, running with me in her arms into the arms of the stranger.

"'María!' he answered, pressing both of us against his chest, which was adorned with crosses. 'Is this my son?'

"'Our son,' she replied timidly.

"'Oh! My son is so beautiful!' he continued, apparently without noticing my poor mother's attempt to correct him. Then, taking me in his arms, despite my curt resistance, he said to me with great volubility:

"'My dear Hernán, one day you will be an arrogant gentleman of the court. The queens will fight over you for their ladies! Until then, however, you must come with me to Lima.'

"'To Lima!' exclaimed my mother. With the count's first words, she began to feel all sense of joy freeze in her heart; now she pulled back, her eyes downcast and her head bowed. 'Oh, Fernando! That is not what you promised me! Does a Spanish gentleman so easily break his word?'

"'María,' the Count answered, 'the promises a man makes to a woman, especially to the mother of his son, are not like those that bind him to other men. They are rather like those we make to ourselves: subject to change with unexpected circumstances. If you love me, and if you love your son, you must understand that neither he nor I can confine our future to the small circle of a country lost among deserts just because I made a stupid promise to you one day. In any case,' he added in a resolved tone, 'my son—and you, if you wish—is leaving with me tomorrow. Good-bye!'

"My mother did not express her anguish in complaints and exclamations; instead, like all tender souls, she kept it hidden in her heart. She closed up her house and made the sign of the cross at the door as a farewell. Then she went with me in her arms to spend the entire day on the heights above the city, where she repeated, through silent tears, the words the cacique had said to her that morning: 'Love is stronger than anything else!' And Jephthah's daughter looked down from the summit of the mountains at the homeland she was about to leave, and cried for it.

"We left the next morning."

### III. THE ABDUCTION

"When we arrived in Lima, her sorrow, her fatigue, and perhaps the sad presentiments that had arisen in my mother's heart led to her becoming violently ill. She was overcome by a high fever; her reason went astray and was replaced by a terrible delirium, reaching a frantic state whenever I was taken from her side even for a moment. The dream she had had in Cuzco recurred constantly, causing her fits of terror. At these times she would press me against her chest, choking me and screaming wildly; this would be followed by an overwhelming exhaustion.

"One night, when she had fallen into this lethargic state, in which only her eyes were not susceptible—they looked out, wide open and attentive like two sentinels—I was lying down next to her, resting my cool hands on her burning forehead. As I lay there in the reigning silence around us, I began to fall asleep. But then I saw the door open, and a tall man wrapped in a long, black cape, his face covered by his hat, came in.

"When she saw him, my mother's large eyes dilated even further; her inert limbs shook in a violent convulsion; her lips trembled in supreme anguish; and her tongue, breaking the steel force that held it, articulated in a voice that I shall never forget:

"'The giant!!!'

"I let out a sharp scream and held on to my mother's neck tightly. The man, his face covered, approached, put one hand over my mouth and used the other to separate my mother's stiff, inanimate arms from my body, and he tore me away as if I were a poor chick stolen from its nest. Then he wrapped me up in the long folds of his cape and took me away.

"After I struggled in vain to free myself from the arms that tightly held me, my anger, my pain, and my fear led me to lose consciousness.

"When I came to, I found myself all alone in a low, narrow room, lying down in a strangely shaped bed. A slow, steady motion made all the objects around me oscillate; a muted sound, like a torrent heard from a distance, was the only thing that interrupted the deep silence that reigned in that kind of grave, that vault with a lamp fading before the light of the approaching day.

"My first thought was one of fear; my second was for my mother. Calling out to her in a pitiful voice, I jumped out of the bed with difficulty. I ran everywhere looking for a door, but there was not one in the room. Then I saw some stairs at the other end, and climbed them in a hurry.

"What a scene I beheld before me—I, a poor child, whose feet had never gone beyond the radius drawn by his mother's eyes!

"The land of the living had disappeared, along with its mountains and its prairies, its trees and its people. An immense blue plain stretched out before my astonished eyes as far as the thick clouds along the horizon.

"Oh! I shall never forget the horrible sorrow that broke my heart at that point. A child's soul feels pain more deeply than a man's, because a child does not have the faculty of reason—that crude consolidating force, which, unable to tear the pain away, freezes it in our heart.

"I turned my gaze from the horizon to the objects around me.

"The Count de Camporeal, my father, was standing before me. He answered my desperate cries with caresses, and sought to tell me of the happiness I would enjoy in Spain, to which we were sailing. But, oh! If the count's soul was susceptible to remorse, then even as large as his crime was, in tearing a son from his dying mother's arms, his punishment was even worse! In response to every tender thing he named, I answered by calling for my mother, and broke out crying. After the crying came a somber and silent sorrow, accompanied by a sentiment of repulsion toward my father, which neither reason nor the passing of the years has enabled me to overcome.

"We disembarked in Cádiz; when we reached Madrid, my father placed me in a school. There I spent three years so sad, so pale, that I never wish to recall them; they were like a nightmare. My external life was not made up of games and joys like those of the other children; I devoted all of my time to my studies, in which I made astounding progress. But this did not elicit the envy of my schoolmates, as it usually does. For seeing me experience neither pleasure nor pride in my triumphs, they forgave me for them. I was as indifferent to their benevolence, in any case, as I would have been to their hostility. Only one thing lived in my heart, in the shape of sorrow: my mother's memory! Every time I closed my eyes and fell asleep, I saw once again the horrible scene in which we were torn apart, and I felt, despite myself, that sentiment of rancorous fear that my father had bred in me. So when he came to see me, or when I would go to his palace, the best moment for me was when we said farewell. And he knew it, too. Oh, I saw so many clouds of sorrow and despair pass across his brow! And yet, thinking about my mother's pain, picturing her alone, abandoned, calling out in vain to her son, I felt a sharp and bitter satisfaction at the grief I caused him.

"One day, sitting in the garden, trying to smile at my schoolmates' games as they ran around me, I saw a woman with a svelte figure, her face covered by a long veil, walking under the trees toward us. She appeared agitated, deeply moved; she walked quickly, and, like a shadow, seemed not to touch the ground. When she reached us, she looked around quickly. Then she threw back her veil, ran to kneel before me, hugged me tightly, and exclaimed in my mother's sweet and tender voice:

"'My son! My son! I have found my son!'

"It was she! It was my mother! Abandoned, alone, and dying in Lima, a mother's love had found enough strength to triumph over being abandoned, over being isolated, and over dying, and had crossed an immeasurable distance and braved infinite dangers to come to see her son! She cried and laughed at the same time, hugged me convulsively, and then held me out to look at me, repeating the whole time in a voice filled with tears:

"'My son! My son! I have found my son!'

"When my first overwhelming emotions had partially receded, I was able to take a good look at my mother and was surprised at the havoc that grief had wreaked on her. Of that marvelous beauty that everyone who had looked at her had always loved, and which had earned her the name *Mama Oello*,[4] only her long, black hair and her large eyes remained. The latter had sunk into their orbits; grown larger, they were made more beautiful by that somber hue that sorrow leaves forever behind.

"But I was too young to guess at anything fateful in my mother's altered countenance. Entirely immersed in the joy of seeing her, in the caresses and the sound of her voice, and in the pleasure of hearing each one of her words, I did not notice that her face became more pale and her eyes more languid each day; that her voice was becoming softer, as if it were leaving for another world; and that her words, sadder all the time, had acquired the solemnity of the last farewell of someone who is dying.

"One day, she came to the school, and after talking for a long while with the rector, took me aside.

"'Hernán, my beloved son,' she said to me, 'today is your tenth birthday, and when one has suffered as we have, reason already begins to mature by this age. Besides,' she continued in an emotional voice, 'I do not have time to wait for you to grow stronger; I must hurry and deposit in your chest the secret that my father left in mine, just as my grandfather had left it in his. Listen carefully to what I am about to tell you, my dear son, and commit each of these words to memory.'"

### IV. THE UNDERGROUND CITY

"'I was keeping vigil over my dying father in our house in Cuzco. It was nighttime. A deep silence reigned in our humble abode; no priest had wanted to abandon his pleasant sleep to bring a word of comfort to this man who was about to depart from our world. I alone was there, praying, crying on my knees at the head of the deathbed;

........

[4] Mama Oello: Wife and sister of Tupac Inca Yupanqui, hence the great mother of the Incas. Oello thus refers to a beautiful girl, usually of noble lineage, revered for her grace and chastity. —Ed.

my moans were answered only by the whistling of the wind in the night, moaning also through our straw roof.

"'All of a sudden, my father's face, already pale and immobile, seemed to come back to life, as if through a supreme effort of his will. His eyes glowed with that last light of a fading life; then, after giving me a long, deep look, he exclaimed, "My daughter, I feel the cold of death invading my body; before it reaches my heart, I must reveal to you a secret known only to the descendants of the Incas, and passed on from father to son in this last hour of life. I would have wanted to deposit it in a strong chest, one able to hold its immense weight. But God, who has given me you as my only heir, shall also lend you, my daughter, the strength necessary to keep it. Listen.

"When the oppressors invaded our hapless homeland, setting loose their iron and fire upon it, the simple sons of our homeland thought that they could placate the fury of the tyrants by putting mounds of the fateful metal they so desired at their feet. But very early on they learned that those men's fierce greed grew with every treasure they conquered, as a tiger's hunger grows with the number of prey it devours. Therefore, those living in the interior, not having been surprised like those along the coast, decided to hide all the gold they possessed. To this end, they made use of the immense subterranean cities that our forefathers had wisely built under each of our cities. Do you see, my daughter, how big our city is? Well, below it there is an underground city just as big. And do you see all the thousands of people who live here, walking along our city's streets and filling its plazas? Well, even larger is the number of gold statues that reside in the other's dark galleries. The treasures gathered there are so immense that, if the sun were to shine upon them, merely the glow from their reflection would suffice to illuminate the entire world. This vast shelter of riches had one hundred doors, the keys and secret to which were held by a hundred of our kings' closest descendants. Each one, at his death, was to bequeath it to his first-born son; if a holder of a key did not have a successor, the key was to be thrown into the lake in the center of the underground, and its door locked. Oh! Of the hundred keys, 98 lie at the bottom of those waters. And in a few moments, of the two remaining, one shall lie in an old man's trembling hands, and the other in the weak ones of a girl.

"My daughter," he continued in a quickly fading voice, "you have seen me live in misery, depriving myself of basic needs, entrusting our survival to the labor of my hands, to the sweat of my brow, without ever letting either your suffering or that of your poor mother lead me to entertain the thought of taking even a single carat of the gold that is destined to reestablish our forefather's throne and the old glory of our homeland. Do as I have done, then, my dear María. In the name of our homeland, I ask you to work as well, to be sober and strong in all things. And when you become a mother, teach your children these two virtues, so important, and so necessary, for us."

"'Then he untied a cord from around his neck with his faint hand, from which a strangely shaped key hung.

"My daughter," he said, "keep this key upon your bosom, and its secret in the bottom of your heart. Trust only he who shows you the other one. . . . And now, my poor orphan, come closer, so that I may kiss and bless you."

"'Crying, I threw myself on my father's already cold hand, while he stretched his other one over my head to bless me.

"'When I looked up, frightened by the long silence, my father's face was motionless; his eyes, staring out into space, had glazed over and become glassy. He had died while I kissed his hand.

"'On the other side of the bed, a friend of my father's was praying on his knees. He was an old cacique, worshipped among the Indians as a prophet with infallible predictions.

"Come here, my daughter," he said to me. "Do you recognize this object?" He uncovered his chest and showed me a key that was in every way similar to the one my father had given me. I showed him mine in silence. "That is fine, my daughter," he said. "Now we must give your father his last rites, and place his remains beside your mother."

"Oh!" I answered, crying. "I have no idea where my poor mother is buried. My father never wanted to tell me, no matter how much I wished to go and pray at her grave."

"You will find out soon enough," he replied. And piously closing his friend's eyes, he sat next to me to keep vigil over my father's corpse.

"The following evening, once the last bells of midnight had rung, the cacique got up with a solemn gesture and closed all the doors in the house. He went up to the corpse lying on the bed, lifted it in his arms—along with all the sheets on which it was resting, and exposed the bed, which was a layer of hardened soil right on the ground. He had me dig a short distance there until I uncovered a small door, which he ordered me to open with my key. I followed his instructions; as soon as I turned the key in the keyhole, the door opened outward, revealing a long set of stone stairs that led deep underground and disappeared into shadows.

"The old man extinguished all the candles burning around the corpse, except for one, which he had me carry as I descended underground, while he followed with his gloomy load.

"My shaky feet had taken me down fifty steps, when my eyes saw a strange spectacle. The light from my large, heavy candle, instead of becoming lost in the subterranean darkness, seemed to reflect off of objects that multiplied its strength a hundredfold. Full of fright, I turned to look back at my companion, but he indicated that I should continue. The further down I went, however, the brighter the glow from the reflections from the underground area.

"I finally reached the hundredth stone step. At that point, the scene that opened before my eyes astonished me, forcing me to lean against the cacique's shoulder.

"My feet stood on enormous masses of gold, which covered the ground and the walls of an immense gallery extending out in endless circles. There was gold worked in the form of statues, altars, idols, vases, fruits, and flowers, as well as gold in its primitive form, in wide stones and huge, loose pieces.

"I had stopped, and was completely absorbed, contemplating the magical scene before my eyes. But the old man, not moved by these wonders, continued walking, forcing me to go on ahead of him. We walked for some time along the marvelous path; then we turned to the left and entered a vast cave. There terror joined my admiration. All along the length of the cave, there were two rows with gold niches, extending all the way to the end, and ending at the foot of a large throne made of the same metal. The throne and almost all the niches were occupied by corpses that seemed to have been alive just the day before, some decorated in wonderful clothes, others covered with the rags of our current misery. The cacique went to one of the empty niches and placed my father in it; then, without allowing me to kneel down and kiss my father's feet, he took me by the hand to the last tier by the throne.

"Descendant of Manco-Capac,"[5] he said to me, "greet your grand-father."

"The subterranean echoes repeated the old man's words a thousand times, as if everyone there were giving me the same order. I knelt, trembling, and brought my lips to touch the foot of the illustrious dead king. Then the cacique introduced me to all of our other ancient kings, all sleeping their eternal sleep there, from the son of the sun, to the hapless Atahualpa, whose sacred remains, recovered secretly by the Indians to be deposited in the burial place of his fore-fathers, ended that long, majestic line, now annihilated. After the monarchs, came their descendants, their miserable tatters in sad contrast with the magnificent sarcophagi in which they lay.

"As we retraced our steps, I recognized my mother's corpse in the niche next to the one occupied by my father. It was so little disfigured by the long years in its grave that it looked just as it had the day in which I saw her die in my arms, when I was still a girl. Seeing her renewed my sense of my double loss; but the old man dried my tears with his severe gaze. "My daughter," he said, "you and I are now the only guardians of our kings' relics and of their immense treasures. To fulfill our mission, we must be brave; yet you begin by showing your weakness at the feet of their majestic shadows. Those who have an exceptional destiny, like you and I, are not allowed tears. The last words of him over whom you are crying entreated you to be strong.

........

[5] Manco-Capac: First ruler of the Incas, revered as a foundational figure. —Ed.

Obey his order now, and be strong against your pain and your sorrow, so that you may have the strength necessary to face misery and persecution later."

"Then he quickly grabbed me by the arm, led me out of the subterranean city, and covered the door behind us with the same layer of soil that was there before.'"

## V. THE CURSE AND THE PROMISE

"'Eight years later, when I saw you taken from my arms on that fateful night, my extreme anguish led to a crisis that, in turn, saved me.

"'At first I feared I would give in to my feelings of desperation. These would have led to my death and deprived you of a mother's love—that guardian angel, with wings of fire, so powerful that it could fly from one pole to the other to save a child, or to give him a kiss, and which neither oceans nor deserts could stop. I wanted to live so that I might see you again; and, I thought, trembling with pleasure and terror, that I knew a way that was certain, although terrible, to achieve my goal: I could disobey my father's dying wish!

"'I returned on foot up the same road that only a few days before had seen me heading in the other direction with you in my arms. Oh, I suffered so! Each stone, each detail in the landscape, awoke heartbreaking memories. Under the shade of this boulder, I had stopped so that you might have a rest; on this stone, I had sat to let you sleep; from that fountain, I had taken water to quench your thirst. Oh! So many times, overwhelmed by such painful memories, I thought about death, which brings everything to a close! Oh! So many times, walking along the edge of a cliff, I allowed my body to lean over, and my foot dangled over the abyss! But each and every time, your image appeared before me to save me, like a guardian angel. Your image filled my heart, occupied my soul, absorbed my thoughts, made me indifferent to anything that was not you. A mother's love is a magical torch whose flame, for the mother, eclipses all the other lights of Creation and shines alone in her horizon.

"'When I arrived in Cuzco, I went and locked myself up in my abandoned house. Then, fighting off my panic and my terror, I removed the heavy layer of soil covering the door to the underground city and opened it. A gust of wind, cold and humid, blew against my face, making me step back, frightened. It seemed to me that the frozen hand of he whose will I was about to break was trying to keep me out, threatening to curse me. I felt that the strength that had driven me there was weakening; then, as always, I called my memory of you, my son, to help me. I recalled you as you were on that horrible night, your arms stretched out toward me, crying, calling out to me in vain, and my fears and remorse dissipated. I descended the wet staircase with determination and ran to the funereal gallery, where I knelt before my parents' remains. "Oh! You who have bequeathed the key to these treasures to me," I exclaimed, "you know how religiously I have obeyed your last wishes. You know that I have lived in poverty and darkness, when love asked me to use these golden riches to lift myself to the stature of the object that gave birth to this love in my heart. The orphan suffered her isolation and misery with patience; the lover carried her humiliation in silence; but—oh, dear Father!—the mother cannot resign herself to lose her son, and I wish to recover mine! Have pity on a poor mother! Allow me to take just a little bit of gold, which helps overcome the impossible, which can return my son to me, and which would be to these immense treasures but what a drop of water is to the ocean. And if you do not take pity on my sorrow, if you remain unyielding—oh, father—then let your curse fall upon me, for I cannot obey you!"

"'The echoes repeated from everywhere in the subterranean city: "Curse! Curse!" But I heard those sinister voices impassively. Determined, I got up and took the gold I needed for my plans. Then I left the underground city, as well as the city of Cuzco. Without ever stopping, I began the long pilgrimage that has brought me to you. But my father's curse has followed me; it weighs upon my head and consumes my life like a fire from the other world.

"'Hernán, my beloved son, promise me that my crime will not have been fruitless; promise me that you will redeem it with the good that you will do for our nation!'

"'Tell me, Mother, tell me! What should I do?' I exclaimed, letting my tears fall at my mother's feet.

"'Listen, my son,' she said, lifting me up on her lap. 'Our prophecies speak of a liberator who will live a long time among our enemies, learn the conqueror's science, and return to break the chains enslaving our homeland, leading it to a greater glory and happiness.

"'Promise me that you shall be that liberator, but that to liberate our brothers you will not use the hatred that demands the blood of our masters, but rather the enlightenment that shall make us their equals—enlightenment, the most sublime and certain means of liberation.

"'Look around you, my son, for nothing binds you to this land any longer. Your father, no doubt fearing that the poor Indian woman who once had faith in him will claim her son's rights, has hurried and given his hand to another. It is her children who will own your name and your title.'

"I barely even heard these last words, for the first had awoken in my heart a chord that had never sounded before. I was overcome by a strange excitement, and a glorious vision flashed across my mind. I thought I saw the man from the prophecies, surrounded by a glowing light, swinging a fiery sword in one hand and discarding the chains of slavery with the other. And with my heart full of a burning faith, I swore to my mother that I would do as she asked.

"She hugged me many times, crying. Then, after untying from around her neck the cord that held the inherited key, she placed it around mine, and said: 'Thank you, my son, thank you! When you go back to our homeland, do not return alone; do not leave your mother in a foreign land, take her remains with you. If the sun of exile has no heat for the living, how can it possibly warm those in the grave. . . ?'

"Someone came to interrupt her. It was nighttime already, and they were about to close the doors.

"My mother heard this announcement with grief. She held me tightly in her arms for a long time, murmuring strange words under her breath. These were perhaps her last prayers. Then, raising her hands over my head, she exclaimed in a muted voice: 'Father! Oh Father, up in heaven, I leave him to you!'

"And she disappeared.

"I never saw her again! She had come in the middle of her final anguish to say her last farewell to me. . . !

"I devoted the next ten years to studying science so that I might fulfill her last wish. When I was twenty years old, I returned to my homeland, my heart empty of all sentiments other than the memory of my mother, to fulfill the double mission that she had entrusted to me: to bury her remains under our skies and to liberate my brothers by taking them out of the abyss of ignorance into which their tyrants, in their hateful calculations, bury them deeper and deeper every day. But my mother loved me too much to make me wait very long to reward my obedience. She has sent you to me, oh, my heavenly angel, to smile upon her son's life, so that when he has fulfilled her plans and covered himself with glory before his own country and before Spain, you shall be his reward."

A long whistle interrupted Hernán's story.

"My God!" Rosa exclaimed. "That is Francisca, my favorite slave, the one who knows our secret, letting me know that my father has already awoken. The time for us to separate has come! But before you leave, my dear Hernán, say you will forgive the injustice with which I judged your noble heart! Oh! If God's will allows us to meet again, and for me to be yours, as you anticipate, then you will find infinite treasures of love in my heart to compensate for your past isolation! I shall be your friend, your sister, your mother, your lover, your slave. But, oh! A dark foreboding veils the future from me with a shroud, and through it I see only the shadows of death. A sinister voice, which I cannot identify, seems to arise in my soul, and yell, 'One of you must fall! You must choose!' Oh! If one of us must die, let it be me, let it be me! My existence on this earth is worthless; let me be a poor flower who lives only a day, while you live to carry out your sublime plans. . . and also to cry over me. Oh! All I ask is that I am allowed to sleep my last sleep next to you, like your mother! Hernán! Tell me that if my premonitions are not wrong, you shall carry the mortal remains of she whom you loved wherever you live. Promise that you shall identify your life with mine, even if death has carried my soul away, and that you will not bury me in the ground, where it is wet and cold, and your gaze cannot reach me!'

Hernán put his arms through the railing and brought his beloved closer to himself.

"My dear Rosa!" he said. "Your grief leads your mind astray. Stop tormenting your heart and breaking mine with such gloomy thoughts. Look at your countenance, glowing with youth and beauty; look at your eyes, so full of charm and life; feel how your chest beats with vitality and love; and tell me if it is possible for death to be near you! Oh! Allow me, instead, to make myself drunk during the short time that I have left tonight and contemplate you with the delightful thought of seeing you again when I am illustrious, powerful, and finally worthy of you; allow my heart to feel the pride that your love has given me. Man's will is all-powerful, and while you love me, mine shall allow me to fulfill everything that I ask of it. And now, my love, would you not concede to your fiancé a wife's first favor, so that I may savor this gift in the bitterness of your absence?"

Leaning forward through the railing, the virgin's red, voluptuous lips came to rest on the young man's ardent, yearning mouth, and a long, burning kiss filled the air around the two lovers with its fire.

The whistle was heard again, louder than before.

A moment later, the street was completely empty, and the only sound that could be heard around the closed window was the warbling of the Santa Rosa doves greeting the first light of dawn.

### VI. THE SLAVE

Six months after the scene we have just described, on a very similar night, another man whose face was also covered by his cloak, stopped before the railings of the same palace window. Like the other man, he ran his fingers along the lattice. But when the window opened in response, instead of Rosa's white, soft, and adorable face, instead of the fortunate Hernán de Camporeal's lover and very beautiful fiancée, a pair of shining eyes and the white teeth of a Negress appeared, surrounded by darkness.

Like the white apparition from the other time, this one also leaned forward on the windowsill and spoke in a soft voice:

"Señor Ramírez, are you there?"

"Yes, Francisca. I have come to carry out my end of our deal, for your plan has gone better than even I could have hoped."

"How do you mean, sir?"

"My spy has written that not having the letters that you intercepted had Rosa's lover full of grief and anxiety. But the letter you wrote, in which you tell him of the infidelity that you forged so astutely, transformed that restlessness into a sense of desperation as terrible for him as it is wonderful for me."

"Did he kill himself?"

"He has taken the vows to be a priest."

"A priest? I expected it to turn out differently," the Negress thought, "but so be it. In any case, I will not be here by the time it all unfolds. Still, that young Camporeal did not inspire the same hatred in me as other white men do. Like me, he had some great sorrow brewing in his heart." Then, addressing the man whose face was covered: "In any case, sir, I have not only done everything that you wished me to do, but also everything that my devotion to you has inspired in me. You may judge how great my devotion was by how great my sacrifices have been. Only out of an unyielding loyalty to you was I able to deliver to my good and beautiful mistress's heart the most terrible sorrow that the human soul is capable of experiencing: the death of the object one loves. Oh! If you had only seen her, as I did, sir, when I told her that dark lie. . . ."

"Stop! Francisca! Stop! Do not speak to me about her love for that man, for you do me—and her, too—a horrible wrong. Thanks to your shrewdness, as you know, she has finally given in to her father's will and is going to be my wife. But I would not wish to recall too frequently that she decided to give me her hand because of a trick, and that her heart might belong to another forever! Oh! I do not wish to think about that, as it would mean so much suffering for her. Let us speak about you, instead, Francisca. Here is a token of my appreciation," he continued, uncovering his face and handing the Negress a large pouch. "With this gold you will be able to recover your freedom and be happy wherever you wish. Good-bye!" he added, and left quickly.

The Negress closed the latticed window. Then, holding the bag of gold tightly against her chest, she rushed through the large halls, crossed the patio, and ran up the spiral staircase of the palace's watchtower, where she had a room at the very top. With her eyes dilated and her heart beating wildly, she fell to her knees in front of a small lamp lit in a corner, and untied the cord that held her treasure with a trembling hand. "Ten! . . . Twenty! . . . Fifty! . . . One hundred! . . . Two hundred! Two hundred ounces of gold!"

She closed her eyes, as if they were blinded by the brightness of the gold, or by some burning vision of happiness.

She stretched her hand over the pile of gold, and counted again: "Ten! . . . Twenty! . . . Thirty! . . . There lies your freedom, Zifa—or Francisca, as the white people have called you ever since they made you kneel down among two hundred of your fellow compatriots in chains, and their priest gave you that strange name that does not mean anything to you, and took away your name, Zifa, which was the first word your children murmured in your arms!"

Then she got up quickly, rushed to the window, forced it open, and, stretching her arms out toward some distant point on the wide horizon, exclaimed: "Africa! My beautiful land, you who keep in your bosom of fire the only two beings I love in the whole wide world! I shall soon be free and able to kiss your blessed shores again! Aibar! Leila! My beloved children! My beautiful little twins! Who could have known when I went to that ill-fated fountain where I was captured, and I laid you down to sleep in your wicker crib in our cabin under the shade of the palm trees—who could have known that five years would go by without my seeing you? But our good idol has finally taken pity on my sorrow. He will soon return your mother to you; and before too long, I will take each of you under each of my arms, as I did before, and sing of our joy to the echoes of the desert. And it shall be repeated in the caverns, where it will delight the lions, who are less fierce than the white people, who replied to a mother's desperate moans with insults and blows, and gagged her so that she would not even have the comfort of saying your names!"

The Negress's eyes, filled with a mother's inexpressible love, flickered with a somber fire as she said these words. Gritting her alabaster teeth together, the muscles of her neck bulging out, she stretched her hand out like a magical spirit sifting over the palace, and exclaimed, "Oh, you white people! You did not take any pity on me then; I shall not take any on you now! You stole my happiness from me; I have rescued it by selling yours. In exchange for a mother's being returned to her children, two lovers have been thrown into immense despair, a father, a wife, and a husband will be dishonored . . . and . . . who knows what else may happen? . . . I am saving myself, and taking my vengeance! To save myself and take my vengeance at once! What fortune! Freedom! Vengeance! I salute you. My land! My children! I shall see you soon!"

A kiss of fire resounded in the air, and the window was closed abruptly, leaving the palace buried in deep darkness.

## VII. THE RETURN

It was a hot morning in January. The sun reigned alone in a parched, empty sky, shining its piercing rays down on the beautiful Lima; she, gracefully standing in the middle of a delightful oasis, seemed to look back at her bright father contentedly and smile as if she were making eyes at him.

On one of the last mountains of the semicircle around her, a traveler had stopped to contemplate her.

It was a young, handsome priest; but stamped on his countenance was the mark of a deep and gloomy sorrow. He gazed at the magical city with his arms crossed, and with a look that expressed both sadness and resignation.

"Dear God!" he said, looking up with his large, black eyes. "I thank you for allowing my heart to remain strong, despite the bitterness of my memories, now that I return to the place that witnessed my former happiness! The lover who was deceived by his fiancée, his heart betrayed by a heart he had thought so pure and so loving, remembered your sublime call—'Come to me, oh sufferers, and I shall be your comfort'—and ran to your bosom, and you welcomed him, and comforted and strengthened him. And now, oh merciful God, I ask you to finish your work! Close off my soul to everything that is not you, and . . . forgive, dear God, this request, in memory of a life full of sorrow, but I ask you to shorten the length of my path in this world, which, although so brief, is so full of pain. I ask you to call me quickly to your side, where my poor mother has awaited me for so long at the feet of your mother!"

And bowing his head as a sign of submission to God's will, he walked slowly down the steep mountainside.

## VIII. SACRILEGE

One Sunday, in the early hours of the morning, the solicitous faithful were gathered as the bells rang announcing the commencement of mass. A large crowd filled the Church of Santo Domingo. The most noble and beautiful women of Lima were there, dressed in those skirts that are the envy of women everywhere else in the world; their faces were partially covered by the mysterious and seductive shawl, through the folds of which, like stars among the clouds, shone eyes, unrivaled in the entire world, which must move God's heart with delight when they are raised to him in prayer. Near the first step of the altar, a young woman whose beauty was so extraordinary that none of the other beautiful women in the church could compare themselves with her knelt. But her coloring, opal white, was as pallid as a corpse's; her wide, gorgeous, black eyes were raised upward with an expression of deep and hopeless sorrow; her mouth, adorable and small, still seemed to retain the mark of the cries that had distorted it; and even her clothes, in strict mourning, announced that she suffered one of those immense and incurable sorrows that take over our existence, tearing it apart in its iron grip, not only destroying our present, but also breathing its poisonous breath over the most distant memories of our past, into the eternity of our future.

The woman seemed lost in silent prayer. Seeing her with her hands crossed upon her chest, her eyes looking up and surrounded by bluish circles, one might have thought her the statue of Mary at the foot of the cross.

All of a sudden, her lips quivered, and she murmured a name under her breath.

"Hernán!" she said, sighing. "If you find heaven so beautiful that you will not leave it even for a moment to come and see the woman you once loved, at least reveal yourself to me in my dreams; allow me to see you smile at me in that fantastic and impalpable world, the only one in which I can see you now. Meanwhile, my beloved, join your prayer with mine, and ask God to shorten my exile here on this world, so sad and dark since you ceased to inhabit it. Oh! If I could at least devote myself entirely to my sorrow, and sob, and scream, and let out the heart-rending cries that fill my soul! But no! After being destroyed by the horrible blow of the news of your death, I was forced to return to life and give my hand to another, whose vigilant eye watches my tears and measures my sighs. For after making himself the owner of my physical being, he pretends to intrude on the sanctuary of my memory, where my soul has taken refuge alongside your image and remains completely yours!"

While she prayed and cried, while her eyes searched among the clouds of rising incense for the shadow of the one who inhabits the other world and whose memory filled her heart—a young priest, tall and pale, dressed in the sacred vestments, took his place behind the altar.

His countenance revealed a deep, religious absorption that contrasted with the distracted and loose air with which some of the other priests of the Church celebrated the holy sacraments around that time.

After reciting the words of Jesus Christ in a pious tone, he turned toward the crowd to give the brotherly greeting of the apostle.

But, instead, two screams were heard simultaneously under the church's dome, and were then drowned out by the sounds of the organ and the sacred canticles.

"He is alive!!!" the woman in mourning exclaimed, and fainted into the arms of the slave women surrounding her.

"She loves me!!!" the priest said, leaning against the altar, pale and shaking.

And when the moment of divine mystery came to an end, he who had begun to say it with a pure heart, full of piety, knew he had been guilty of being idolized by the people—for the priest had forgotten the sacrosanct words of the consecration!!!

### IX. THE VIAL

That night, in an old house lost among the orchards of the Cercado, two mysterious-looking men were speaking in an underground laboratory. One was old and had a repugnant appearance; his vulture-like eyes, curved nose, and thin lips revealed that he belonged to the degenerate race of Jacob. The other was covered by a long cloak, his face hidden among its folds.

The red flame of a small kerosene burner illuminated the scene, and surrounded the two men with a sinister glow. Anyone who had seen them at that hour, at the bottom of that black cave, in the somber glow of the light, would have thought them two demons scheming over a soul's damnation.

"So you mean to say that this liquid will render the coldness, the rigidity, and the immobility of death?" the man shrouded in the cloak said as he looked at a small vial filled with a ruby-colored liquid, holding it to the light.

"Yes, my noble sir," the old man replied. "It is a powerful narcotic extracted from magical plants found in Yemen; no more than three drops of it are needed to produce the effect you have just described."

"Without any of the conditions necessary for the preservation of life?"

"This fabulous liquid already contains them all."

"Weigh your words carefully, evil Jew, for, with God as my witness, I swear that if you are lying to me, the blade of my dagger will find you, even through your vile spells."

"I swear by the God of Abraham, my noble sir, that what I am telling you is the pure truth. This divine elixir is designed to preserve life in all its vigor, under the cold appearance of death, in any place that the one under its influence is put. . . . Whether it be used," the old man added, staring into the shrouded man's face with a deeply evil look, "whether it be used by a jealous husband, for example, who obtained a lady's hand through treachery, and who wanted to put his wife in a tomb and have her die before her homeland and her old love, and return her to life under the hot sun of the Philippines, or—"

As soon as he had uttered these words, the old man felt himself grabbed around the throat, and he saw a dagger's blade shine against his chest.

"You miserable wretch!" the shrouded man yelled. "How do you know? Tell me, or else you will die."

"Eh! Noble sir, would you stain your hands with a Jew's blood? If I know who you are, what difference does it make if you do or do not learn how I found out? Besides, am I not an astrologer? Very well, then. I have drawn your horoscope, and I can tell you that instead of being my murderer, you will thank me three times. In the first place, for the work it took me to consult the stars to determine your fate; then for that fragment of God's power held in this vial; and finally, for Solomon's seal," the Israelite concluded, placing his finger on his lips.

The shrouded man shoved the old man back brutally, threw him a bag of gold, put away the vial, and wrapped himself even more tightly inside his cloak. Then he climbed a spiral staircase, crossed an orchard, and, jumping over an adobe wall, left down the street, taking long, quick steps.

Half an hour later, he stopped in front of a secret door that led, through the back, into a large, magnificent house. He opened the door with a small key, closed it behind him, and lighted a candle. He was in a room lined with silk wall hangings and filled with expensive decorations.

The man threw off his cloak. He was an agreeable and handsome gentleman; but his hard features, and the angry scowl clouding his brow, revealed a man of impetuous character and violent sentiments. He went to a writing desk, left the candle he had lit, removed from a breast pocket the vial he had gotten from the old man, and studied it for a long time with a somber expression. Then he went to a door, raised the tapestry in front of it, and entered a sumptuous alcove softly illuminated by an alabaster lamp. In the center of the alcove stood a golden bed with scarlet velvet curtains; inside, beautiful and pale as a fantastic dream, a woman was sleeping in darkness, her head resting on one of her arms, her chest veiled by her long, black hair. Sad images no doubt bothered her sleeping mind, for, every so often, a convulsion would shake her body, her half-open lips would mumble a moan, and a tear could be seen to shine at the end of her long eyelashes.

At the foot of the bed, sitting on a chair, a black slave girl was keeping vigil—or, more accurately, was sleeping soundly. Near her, within arm's reach, was a night table with several medicinal liquids and a gold goblet containing a drink.

The nocturnal visitor quietly approached the bed, looked at the sleeping woman's beautiful face for a moment, and, going to the night table, poured three drops of the red liquid from the vial into the gold goblet. Then, after making sure that the lady and the slave were asleep, he quickly left, as silently as he had come, and disappeared behind the tapestry.

The next morning, the city of Lima was in distress over a very sad incident. One of the most beautiful and distinguished ladies of the viceroy's court, the wife of Judge Ramírez, the governor-elect of the Philippine Islands, had died at the height of her youth and beauty. Her husband was inconsolable in his loss; dressed in strict mourning attire, he brought up the rear of the mourning party at the funeral and carried his love where all loves come to an end: He himself carried his wife's corpse into the burial vaults beneath the cathedral and laid her to rest in a sumptuous tomb, the key to which he kept by his heart.

## X. THE TWO SHROUDED MEN

Once the evening prayers had ended and the thousand candles around the tabernacle were extinguished, the cathedral's sacristan, alone amidst the shadows of the vast church, went about closing all of the doors. His sluggish steps had already covered the tripartite nave when he stopped before the door that opens out to the plaza's atrium. He was sliding the lock on the last postern when a cold hand fell upon his, paralyzing his every muscle and leaving him frozen with fright.

"Jesus! Dear Lord! What do you want with me?" exclaimed the terrified sacristan. For, with the oscillating light from a lamp behind him, he had seen a ghost arise before him, shrouded in a long, black cloak.

"Silence!" said an imperious and curt voice from inside the dark shroud. And the same freezing hand dragged the terrified guardian of the church toward the sepulchral vaults. There the ghost stopped, and, turning to the sacristan, pointed at the door. From his fit of fear, the poor warden heard the shrouded shadow say with an other-worldly voice: "Open it!" So he opened the funereal door, and the ghost descended into the house of the dead. "A vampire!" the sacristan exclaimed, and ran away, stricken by a deep horror. But as soon as he stepped outside the church, the little strength that he had left abandoned him all together. He fell on his knees and stayed there, motionless, dumbfounded, feeling only an immense fear, which continued to work on his mind and disturb him, presenting him with a long succession of specters passing before his eyes time and again, all giving him fierce looks. Among these unreal visions, one suddenly appeared that was more distinct, and more horrible, than the others. The sacristan, his hair standing on end, saw it advance toward him under the somber arches and pass by him, disappearing behind the columns of the postern. It was the vampire. He was covered, as before, in his large, black cloak, and he was carrying a white shape in his arms, wrapped in long veils that floated like a nocturnal haze around the ghost. When he saw this vampire, the sacristan fell face first to the ground; a cold sweat covered his body, and he did not see or hear anything else until, a long time later, the bells above his head struck midnight. At that very moment, a hand, and this time a very human and strong hand, grabbed him by the arm, shook him roughly, and made him stand up. A shrouded man, who, despite the sanctity of the place, wore his hat drawn down over his eyes, placed a bag of gold in his hand and a dagger against his chest, and said with a voice more sinister than the ghost's had been: "Choose."

"What do you wish me to do, sir?" the poor man answered, taking hold of the heavier of his two options.

"Silence and obedience," the shrouded man replied, pushing the sacristan forward. And he, too, headed toward the underground pantheon. When they reached the doorway to the lugubrious area, the unidentified man said, "Listen. Every night, at this hour, you will wait for me here. If you are on time, and discrete, you will receive each time a bag of gold like the one I have given you tonight. But if you do not come, or if a single word escapes your lips . . . Do you understand me? Now, open the door."

The shrouded man took out a muffled lantern from under his cloak, and, like the other, also descended into the dark asylum of death.

The sacristan, for whom the mundane words of the unidentified man had dissipated all superstitious apprehension, was starting to recover, when he heard the man curse horribly from below. A short while later, the shrouded man appeared again; leaping toward him, he exclaimed, stammering with fury, "You miserable wretch! Speak up! Who has entered here before me?"

"Have mercy, sir!" the sacristan yelled, terrified by the dagger that the man held against his chest.

"Silence! Who has entered here?"

"Oh! It is not my fault, sir. There is nothing we can do against spirits. A shadow visited the tombs, and then disappeared among a multitude of specters from the church."

"I recognize your hand in this, you vile Jew!" the shrouded man mumbled, smashing a vial filled with a red liquid against the ground. "But I will find you, I promise. And you, his accomplice, who let someone steal the dead from their tombs, here is the price for your crime," he said, and drove his dagger three times into the chest of the hapless sacristan.

The next day, the unfortunate man was found dead, in a pool of his own blood, at the foot of the altar.

Shortly after this tragic event, the future governor of the Philippines, followed by an ostentatious retinue, embarked in a Spanish galley for India, setting off on the express voyage under royal orders.

The ship sailed off, and disappeared with the fading light of day. But a few fishermen sailing around Chorrillo Bay with their nets out saw the galley skirt behind the rocks of San Lorenzo and drop a boat with a man aboard who then rowed toward land.

## XI. THE BALLAD

In the waning hours of a spring day, a man wandered along one of the rugged paths that wind through the snowy heights of Illahuaman, seemingly uncertain of his destination. His pace, now slow and hesitating, now quick and self-assured, revealed a battle between a vigorous soul and a fatigued body. He wore a pilgrim's dark robe; his head was covered inside his hood, and his face was hidden by a black mask.

When he reached the summit, he stopped and looked down, gazing deeply and avidly at the pleasant valley of Urubamba that stretched out below him.

"There it is," he exclaimed with a focused fury, as he stretched his hand toward a point somewhere in the striking landscape before him. "There it is, as the stars predicted: a palace built upon heathen ruins .... Your diabolic science will serve for something after all, infernal Jew. It promised me fortune, and it will, in the end, deliver it to me.... But it shall be the fortune of a desperate soul, for it will come in the form of vengeance! Yes, vengeance! Executed, terrible, and merciless."

The traveler continued with determination on the march he had briefly interrupted, and soon disappeared down the mountain's steep cliffs.

The last frosts of winter had recently melted with the warm breezes of spring. Already, in their place, irises and fragrant lilies whitened the sandy shores of the creeks; rushes and violets smiled in the grass under the shadow of the willow trees; and in the hollows between the boulders, the bromeliads and gillyflowers opened their wild petals to the evening wind. The blooming orchards exhaled the acrid fragrance of their blossoms; and the soft murmuring of the wind through the foliage combined with the songs of the thrushes, nightingales, and the *tuyas,*[6] to add even more charm to the mysterious magic of the late hours of the day.

In an unexpected turn in the valley, at the end of a row of willows, and in the middle of a forest of ceiba trees—whose scarlet flowers contrasted sharply with the dark green of their leaves—stood a palace of Arabian architecture, elevated on a platform of ancient ruins, which gave off an air of shadow and mystery. It was surrounded by delightful gardens, and the fragrance of orange blossoms and jasmines, roses and cherimoya trees perfumed its many halls. Cool fountains pleased the ear with the sweet whispering of their spouting water, saturating the evening breeze with a moist and fragrant aura. Under the green dome of a pavilion of myrtle and honeysuckle, her

........

[6] The *tuya* is a Peruvian bird. —Trans.

hands on the cords of an ivory harp, a woman—beautiful as the moonlight draped over her—reclined against brocade pillows.

There also was a man sitting in the shadows close to her. It was the pilgrim with the black mask. Beside him was a table full of fruits and wine.

"Rest, blessed pilgrim," the lady said with a heavenly smile, "rest, and enjoy the fruits of our gardens. . . . But please, do me the favor of uncovering your face, so I may see your venerable countenance."

"I deeply regret not being able to fulfill your request, oh beautiful lady," the pilgrim answered in a shy and humble voice; "for I carry a stain marked upon my forehead that is like a cursed stamp, and I have sworn to keep it hidden until it has been erased. Until then, my food is bitter; I cannot accept your hospitable banquet."

"Keep your sacred oath, then. But at least listen to my singing while you rest."

Her white fingers played the prelude to a soft and tender melody. Then she raised her angelic voice through the silence of the night in the sweet language of the Incas, and sang:

"Between the shores of the rough waters of the Rimac and the blue waves of the ocean, there is a vast enchanted valley, where spring sleeps perpetually upon a bed of flowers.

"Above this valley the sky is always blue; orange trees and grapevines, bananas and palm trees provide it with shade; and below the ground there is a powerful magnet that attracts the gazes and the hearts of people from every corner of the world.

"Everything there smiles, and life is a delightful dream, from which one would never wish to awake, even to enter heaven. Yes! For there, as in heaven, beauty and love make their home.

"The angels that travel through the skies descend there to rest and replenish their wreaths. But there, too, the cursed cherub comes to relieve the immensity of his supreme sorrow for a moment.

"Thus the daughters of this blessed valley have the divine eyes of the angels, and Lucifer's irresistible powers of seduction.

"Do not look at them, if you do not wish to lose your heart to them. For all alone it will flee from your chest and jump into the fire of their eyes.

"Women reign there, with absolute power. For there they possess the kingdom of the elements and are the queens of creation.

"And yet, in this place where everything bows down before them, where women rule with all sovereignty, and happiness is found in the very air they breathe, there was a woman who moaned and called out for death to come to her.

"Young and beautiful, the blood of the conquerors ran through her veins, and power and opulence had rocked her golden crib.

"Why did she turn away from such bright horizons?

"She lived in an atmosphere of adoration and was the wife of a man who idolized her.

"So why did she wish to die?

"Because she hated this man; and her heart, closed off to him, belonged to another. For this daughter of Spain loved a son of the sun; and by the time the proud Iberian had taken possession of her body, her soul already belonged to Chaska-Naui Inca,[7] and had done so for a long time.

"And that is why she was withering and perishing like a flower plucked from its stem. Then, while she slept in her sorrow, the angel of death appeared with a goblet in his hand and said to her, 'Do you wish to die?'

"And the white lips of the dying woman trembled, and mumbled an anxious, desperate 'yes.'

"The Angel put three drops from his goblet on that supreme word. And all life fled from the woman's body, and fled into her heart, which, although it had stopped beating, burned like a raging fire, while her limbs lay cold and motionless, and her eyes glassed over, and could see no more.

"Strange echoes resounded in her breast, repeating sobs, cries of

........

[7] Chaska-Naui: Proper name; literally, "Eyes of the Morning Star." —Ed.

sorrow, funereal songs, and blows like those of a hammer on the lid of a coffin.

"Then, silence—a long, sepulchral silence. Where was she? Was she crossing the nether regions of eternity? Or rather—oh, horror! That cold and silent darkness, was it the abyss? The abyss of nothingness in which her soul was to vanish!

"But the echo inside the frozen chest woke up and made out a grave, sad, and melodious voice. It was a familiar voice, which she had loved in another time, in another world, perhaps in heaven.

"The dear voice sounded sweeter and nearer.

"In the depth of that dark space, she began to make out the outlines of an ethereal and illuminated figure. It was not the scowling countenance of the angel of death, no. It was the beautiful, soft, and melancholy face of one of those spirits of love who roam about gathering the sorrowful of the world to their bosoms.

"The heavenly apparition came nearer. And his hand moved the white shroud of death aside, and his lips came to rest on the corpse's cold forehead, and her body trembled at the divine touch.

"The fire of life, hidden at the bottom of her heart, spread and ran through her veins in burning waves; her pallid lips regained their red; her chest shuddered with deep sighs; her eyelids opened; and her eyes looked around with a fervent gaze.

"Where was she? In heaven? No! Heaven does not contain among its treasures the delightful intoxication that she felt in her enraptured soul.

"For under the golden domes of an enchanted palace lost among the foliage of dense gardens, Chaska-Naui held her in his arms. . . ."

"Yes," the pilgrim yelled, getting up suddenly; and he no longer spoke in a humble tone, but rather in the angry one of the terrible traveler from Illahuaman. "Yes! Under those mysterious domes, in the shadow of those quiet gardens, she gave herself to the pleasures of a guilty love, not aware that the man who had taken possession of her body before—and had hidden her in a tomb—was also there. With a dagger in his hand, and vengeance as his guide, this man slid, silent as a snake, among the walls of the garden, and stood up suddenly before her. 'Behold me here,' he said to her. 'You may have given your soul to another, but your life belongs to me, and I am here to claim it.'"

The pilgrim had thrown off his mask, and stood there, implacable and terrible. The lady turned pale before the evil apparition; but then, turning her beautiful eyes toward heaven, she tore her veils from her chest, and, with the sublime expression of those who yield before destiny, said:

"Here is my heart. Strike!"

The dagger's blade flickered in the shadows, and then sank three times into the woman's naked chest. And the white moonlight that before illuminated the beautiful resident of the enchanted palace shone now only upon a bloody corpse.

## XII. THE *Quena*

The winds of the tempest had descended upon the land. Its destructive force had blown through the narrow ravines of the mountain range, swept the dry grasses it found along the way, formed whirlwinds between the granite walls, and crashed, roaring furiously, against a small Indian town at the foot of the mountains. Torrents of water and snow had flooded the town's narrow streets, and the tumultuous thunder, repeated an infinite number of times by the echoes of the cliffs, had filled all the houses with fright. But the tempest had now passed. A gloomy night reigned over the mountains, the town, and the plains; the deep darkness that makes all objects equal was interrupted only occasionally by the yellowish, flashing light of the distant lightning. Nature itself seemed to be asleep after the terrible crisis that had upset her; everything that lived in the land had suffered through the fear, and now rested quietly.

There were no signs of life among the houses; and yet, at the top of one of them, a light could be seen, shining like a lighthouse in that ocean of darkness.

All of a sudden, a strange and sweet melody, at once heartbreaking and frightening, arose from there, and filled the air and the vast valley, and awoke the echoes of the mountains.

It was sublime music. Its magical tones, now tender and passionate like a departing lover's farewell, now melancholy and sorrowful as the sighs of loneliness, now somber and gloomy as the voice of the *De profundis*[8] imitated perfectly every kind of wailing that love or sorrow can tear from the human heart. Was it someone's voice? Was it an instrument? And who was the author of this melody, an angel or a demon?

It was a man. He was sitting at the feet of a woman in a small room where everything was in mourning, illuminated by a large, silver lamp, playing a strangely shaped instrument.

This man, dressed in black, was, like all the objects around him, tall and distinguished, with handsome features, although deathly pale. Even though he had deep, precocious wrinkles, his large, black eyes, with their long eyelashes, still had a very youthful brightness to them.

The woman, at whose feet he sat, was covered in a white tunic, and was lying down on a long divan, her face half-covered by her long, wavy, black hair, which fell along the folds of her clothes to the ground. One of her hands lay on her knee; the other held her head up as she reclined on the pillows of the divan.

Nothing could be more peaceful and beautiful than this scene, formed by the woman, dressed in white like a virgin lying on her nuptial bed, and the man who, sitting at her feet, looks at her with his deeply handsome, passionate eyes, and plays every note of that heavenly melody just for her. But if any living being had entered there and observed the scene up close, his hair would have stood on end, and he would have fled at once, terrified. For the woman's long hair had a metallic crispness to it; her beautiful, shapely hands were completely dry; her white tunic was actually a funeral shroud; the face that the young man was looking at had long ago received death's horrible stamp; and the instrument itself, which produced such a divine

........

[8] *De profundis* ("Out of the depths"—Lat.): The opening words of Psalm 130, one of the penitential psalms in Jerome's Latin version, which inspired a number of important musical pieces in the eighteenth and nineteenth centuries, as well as Oscar Wilde's letter to Alfred Douglas (published as an essay in 1905. —Trans.)

melody, was stolen from the grave—it was the femur of the woman's skeleton.

### XIII. CONCLUSION

Time—which ceaselessly extends its scythe over all creation to destroy and renew it—and even more, superstition and fear, turned this town into a desert. The traveler can barely distinguish the place it once occupied on the arid plains by a few ruins blackened by the rains and the freezing winds that blow down from the mountains. But neither the years, nor the omnipotent gaze of the Vatican, have been able to erase the memory of the unfortunate love or the strange mourning of Camporeal, the priest. For, in the depth of our valleys, and in the plazas of our cities, in the middle of the silent nights, he wails eternally through the voice of that instrument that he consecrated to his sorrow, and which the children of Peru have named the *Quena*, which, in the ancient Quechua language, means: "Love become sorrow."

If you hear the sound of that instrument when you are happy, you will hear the sweet melancholy that is so necessary to temper those aspects of happiness that are too overwhelming and exhausting for the soul. But, oh, to you who carry a great sorrow in your hearts: Beware of listening to it! Because for you it will have a terrible power. Like a magical mirror, it will show you everything that is gloomy about your past; it will reveal before your eyes the pale image of your sinister future; and the sorrow will grow inside your chest, causing it to burst.

# 2

# The Treasure of the Incas

*A Historic Legend*

I

The treasure of the Incas! These words take our minds immediately to the metropolis of the children of the Sun, to the center of their past grandeur—to Cuzco!

Cuzco is a city of fantastic legends, of wondrous myths and traditions. Its streets resound as if there were immense subterranean passageways beneath them; under the floors of its churches can be heard the roaring of unknown underground streams; the stones of its foundations lie atop mines of gold; and on dark nights when there is a conjunction in the vast skies, the common people look up at the pale celestial objects with as much longing as fear.

Combining the beauty of the ballad and the grace of the pastoral, they spill forth like a handful of jewels into the green hollows of a ravine. Enshrouded in its mantle of flowers, surrounded by eternal snows, the magical city feigns sleep and idleness, with no memory of its magnificent past. Her warriors have become shepherds; her virgins, the sacred fire now extinguished, have abandoned the temple; and her elders, crouching like beggars by the side of the roads, their gray hair covered with dirt, extend to the traveler a desiccated and famished hand.

But look closely at those elderly people, look at those virgins, and look at those shepherds, and you will see a somber, mysterious light shining in their eyes. Learn their beautiful language, listen to the conversations they have at home in the evenings, and you might just think that you are hearing the symbolic dirges of the exiles of Zion being sung under the willows of Babylon.

What thoughts burn behind the patient resignation with which they carry their misfortune? What hope is revealed by that festive dress that they have always saved, even in their eternal mourning? And what is the secret that they have passed from generation to generation, and guarded sacredly amid the rags of their misery?

The answer to all of these questions is, for them, found in one word:

*Hallpa-mama.* Motherland.

"*Hallpa-mama!*" they exclaim right after they say God's name in their prayers. "*Hallpa-mama,*" they repeat as they spill the first cup on the ground during their festivities. "*Hallpa-mama,*" they murmur during times of sorrow, when the burden of their everlasting servitude is too much to bear—and that mystic word gives their souls peace and courage, and seems to hold the secret of their very destiny.

## II

One day, early on a beautiful morning, while the city still slept and the bluish haze of dawn rose in the sky with the first songs of birds, like a hymn to the creator, a man wrapped in a dark hood, with a scowl on his face, his hair disheveled, and a long-feathered hat worn sideways over his brow, came out of a house, the door of which had opened repeatedly during the night, letting in numerous visitors.

He greeted the light of the new day with a curse, and, after hesitating for a moment, as if trying to decide in which direction he should go, he began to walk up the street, sticking close to the walls. He followed the slope of the streets to the first thickets beyond the city, and walked out into the countryside.

His pace, now slow, now fast; the somber expression on his face; and the abrupt motion with which he wrapped the upper part of his cloak around his head and shoulders from time to time all indicated that within that man's soul there was a tempest, the kind of storm that drives good men to heroics—and evil ones to crime.

He left the last houses of the city behind him without stopping and followed the path lined with weeds that leads to the Rodadero.

When he reached the first rocks of the steep slope, he turned right, without thinking, onto a narrow and difficult path that led around a large boulder; a short distance behind it was a group of elderberry trees whose yellowish-green branches filled with white tufts half covered the roof of a cabin.

When he saw the house among the branches of the trees, the man in the dark hood stopped in his tracks as if he were suddenly waking from a dream.

"Where am I going?" he said with a rough exclamation. "The devil take that damned Indian woman! Am I ready to hear cries and complaints and wooing now! To have to deal with her and her entire race for a mere twenty doubloons. Good-bye to all my dreams and aspirations! Goddamned four of spades!"

He turned back, retraced his steps, climbed back up the side of the Rodadero, and wandered through the rugged terrain of its rustic summit.

That night, the goatherds who gathered their flocks in the area saw him go down a winding path; shortly thereafter they spotted him again at the door of the cabin, his ear against the keyhole, like a prowler.

What was that man with fine scarlet breeches and gold spurs looking for in that poor cabin? What did he see? What did he hear?

Inside the home, three people sat around a small fire of dry elderberry branches—an old man, a youth, and a young woman. The old man's cupreous skin contrasted with his white hair, which fell in long locks over his shoulders. His countenance inspired meekness; the sweet look of his wrinkled eyes moved lovingly from the youth to the girl.

The old man was Yupanqui, the deposed cacique of the *Horcos;*[1] the boy and the girl were his children.

Stripped of his possessions after the appointment of the intendant of Cuzco,[2] the cacique had suffered his ill fortune with the resignation of an Indian: with patience and in silence. But he had one treasure left that that man's injustice could not take from him—the love of his work. And he had another that consoled him in the face of all his losses—a daughter as beautiful as the iris and as good as an angel.

Like the mystic dove in the "hollows of a rock," Rosalía had grown up within the walls of a cloister. Educated by the pious Abbess of the Nazarenes, her existence moved joyfully between the smoke of the incense and the glories of the Lord. Until one man's look came to stand between her and God.

One day, the insolent eyes of Diego de Maldonado stared into hers through the bars of the choir. From that moment on, all peace fled from Rosalía's heart; she became sad, pensive, and distracted.

No more quiet evenings around the lamp in the cell of the abbess, telling stories and decorating sugary pastilles; no more jumping about merrily during recess under the myrtles of the garden. Her days were now spent inside the church, kneeling on the cold tiles, her heart shaken with strange tremors; and while her lips uttered prayers, her eyes and thoughts turned to the spot that a man had come to occupy every day at Mass. When night fell, while her companions played, running under the arches of the cloisters, she, standing at the top of the tower of the convent, looked out with yearning eyes over the vast view of the city, her chest full of longing, her ears listening attentively in the dark as if she might hear among the many sounds below the echo of a beloved voice.

One day, soon thereafter, the abbess called Yupanqui in. She showed him his daughter, how she had grown pale and thin, and rec-

........

[1] Horcos: Indigenous group from the high regions of the Andes, near Cuzco. From *urku*, meaning hill (Quechua). —Ed.

[2] The intendancies were territorial subdivisions in the Spanish viceroyalties. The intendants, or governors of those lands, exercised great power over taxation, economic development, land grant distribution, and the administration of justice. —Ed.

ommended that he take her for a time to breathe the air of the country and the mountains.

If the old cacique had studied his daughter's countenance with a look other than a paternal one, he would have seen developing on it all the changes of fortune found in a drama: impatience, happiness, doubt, fear, anger. But the good Yupanqui only saw an illness caused by lack of fresh air and open space, and he took his daughter out into the neighboring valleys where there were orchards and large houses; he had her breathe the invigorating wind of the heights; he gave her sweet goat's milk to drink; he took her to his cabin, protected like a lark's nest in the dense foliage of the willows; and he made a bed for her on a swing hanging from the branches of the trees in a breeze perfumed by the breath of the cows.

The freshness of youth returned, after all this, to Rosalía's face. But it did not come from the flowers of the valleys, nor from the invigorating air of the heights, nor from the nectar of the goats, nor from the healing breath of the cows—it came from the love of Maldonado.

Who knows by what chance of fortune they were united! In any case, the fact remained that the cacique once again saw his daughter radiant in all her splendor and beauty, and he was content, and he never tired of looking at her, and he asked himself why he had not brought this inexhaustible source of happiness back to his side sooner. But woe to him who trusts his good luck! Just when the old man was raising his shining eyes filled with joy to thank God, he heard Andrés whisper in his ear:

"Father, Rosacha is crying!"

He saw a tear sliding furtively from Rosalía's eyes to fall on the herbs she was cleaning to season the next day's meals.

She dried the trace the tear had left on her cheek with one of her black braids and turned to the cacique.

"Father," she said to him, "is it possible for someone who loves another to make that person suffer?"

"What are you saying, my daughter!" Yupanqui exclaimed, putting the girl's head against his chest. "Do you not know that I would give my life to prevent any unhappiness from falling upon you? Speak up!

What do you need? . . . Ah! . . . I know. You cannot get used to the poverty of our simple cabin? You miss the sweet home of the convent and wish to go back there?"

"No, Father! Never! I will never leave your side! Oh! Where would I find more love than here? These smoky walls are filled with so many memories. My mother lived and died here. Her soul looks over our abode; I see her frequently in my dreams, bending over me, smiling with her sweet and melancholy smile. All the things around me have been touched by her hands. Here is the stool on which she usually sat next to the fire; there is her distaff and her loom. In the convent, my mother seemed more dead to me than she does here. Here, doing what she used to do, devoting myself as she did to serving you and taking care of my brother, I feel like I am continuing to live her life. . . . And then, the threshold of our door leads out to freedom; I can go as far as my eye can see. It is so good to let the winds carry away all the worries of life! . . . So you see, Father, what can I possibly miss when I am at your side?"

"But you were crying just now."

"You saw me cry? Now see me laugh."

And kissing the old man on his white head, she smiled enchantingly.

"Oh! And yet you were crying. Tears from your eyes are screams from the soul. Perhaps the daughter of the kings feels humbled, dragging about the livery of misery among the grandeurs of the world?"

"And what are those grandeurs to me after my eyes have beheld our own? Can all the riches of all the cities that rise up throughout the world put together compare with those that our underground city holds? Are you not the owner of one of its hundred doors? Have I not entered through it, treading with my princess feet the tiles of gold that covered the palaces of the Incas? Contemplating them, I have gotten to know those treasures that are greater than anyone could ever dream of, surpassing even what the greed of the Europeans has imagined. I carry the misery that exists above them with pride."

A strange sense of anxiety came over the cacique and drove him to the door. He stopped there and listened. But everything was quiet outside, and the only sound that could be heard was the wind rustling the leaves of the willow trees.

If the old man's eyes could have penetrated the door, he would have seen a man crouching down, his ear to the keyhole, his heart in his throat, pale, shaking, terrible; and if Rosalía had seen him, she would have fled to the furthest corners of the convent, to the deepest corners of the grave.

The old man, his doubts quieted by the deep tranquillity that reigned outside, returned to his daughter's side, gave her a kiss, blessed her, and retired to bed, calling Andrés to join him so that they might get the rest necessary to recover from the extreme weariness of a day's work.

Andrés pretended not to hear him. Instead, he stayed behind, sitting before his sister, looking at her fixedly.

"Brother," she said to him, "our father is waiting for you to turn in. You sleep by his side. Go on."

"Our father has left reassured; but I am not. He is old and has forgotten what goes on in the hearts of the young; but I have read yours, and I know that you are suffering, and that you are crying, and that you are wretched. I am but a boy, only sixteen years of age, and cannot offer you any advice; but the day you need a devoted heart and a strong arm, remember me."

Rosalía did not answer; she rested her head on her brother's chest and cried in silence.

Andrés dried her tears, gave her a hug, and left to go lie down next to his father.

Rosalía remained alone by the fire, her hand on her cheek, looking distractedly at the dying fire in their home. Her fingers were moving of their own accord, and her lips murmured:

"Ten. . . twelve. . . fourteen. . . today, Friday, makes fifteen days! Fifteen days since Diego has forgotten me! . . . Today is Friday! . . . I hear the rooster crowing; it must be midnight! I will check my fortune with the *Guarmi del Peñascal.*[3] Oh! The abbess does not allow

........

[3] *Guarmi*: Woman (Quechua). —Ed.

me to have such beliefs! . . . But what does the abbess know, what does anyone know who, like her, lives in peace and happiness? . . . What do they know about the mysteries of God?"

She got up and went to get the hard, dry, green leaves of an herb from a small, black cloth bag hanging on the wall.

She piled them carefully one by one on the palm of her hand and blew. The leaves spun in the air and came to rest on her knees. The young Indian woman looked at them anxiously, concentrating; as she examined their precarious position on her dark lap, she said:

"He is coming! . . . Then he leaves. . . he climbs up some boulders . . . he climbs down a ravine. . . then he comes closer again. . . he arrives. . . he stops. Oh! What is that dark shadow spreading about him. . . !"

At that moment, the door of the cabin, opened by a cautious hand, gave way to a man.

When she saw him, the daughter of the cacique let out a hushed cry and threw herself into his arms.

### III

The man was he who had been pacing furiously at dawn, and who had been lurking about suspiciously that night. But now the expression on his face was sad and somber. The young Indian woman noticed it at once and took a step back in fright.

"Diego," she exclaimed, "what ill-fated news have you brought with you? Tell me! I have suffered so much that it would not take much for your words to kill me."

"You should not utter your lover's name anymore, Rosalía. That name now has a death sentence attached to it; and before long you will hear it pronounced by voices in the street who want to send me to the gallows."

"You, my Diego! My noble and handsome gentleman. . . !"

"Yes. I am proscribed, and every moment I spend here I risk my death. . . ."

"Oh, God! What has happened?"

"I work as a collector of the tribute,[4] and I recently received large sums. But I was greedily tempted by the devil and gave into his seduction. I lost my own money first, but ended up throwing the gold that belonged to the royal coffers on a miserable card table, which did not take long to devour it all.

"The revenue is set to leave tomorrow, and I should have turned in those sums today. But I have lost them, and I am guilty of lèse-majesté; to avoid the humiliating death that awaits me from the king's justice, I must flee his large empire. In other words, I must put as much ground as possible between you and me.

Rosalía fell to her knees at her lover's feet.

"No! My Diego!" she exclaimed. "Do not leave me alone to suffer the horror of your absence. I will work; I will plow the ground with my hands and earn, *real* by *real*,[5] the amount you have lost. I will go ask my brothers, the errant Indians of the mountains, and they will not deny me."

"My poor beloved," Diego said with a sad smile, "your anguish leads you astray, and you forget that time is my greatest enemy. Two days is the longest time I might survive. After that, even if I had on the third the moneys that belong to the authorities, they would be worthless to me, for they could not save my honor."

A terrible idea crossed Rosalía's mind like a flash of lightning and made her murmur:

"*Hallpa-mama!* Take that thought and keep it far away from me."

"Good-bye, Rosalía," Diego said, removing the young woman's arms from around his neck. "Let us keep this sad moment as short as possible; the bitter cup must be drunk in one swift swallow."

The young Indian woman grabbed him around the knees.

........

[4] The "tribute" comes from an old Spanish tradition. In the Americas, the obligation of the tribute or tax fell on the new, non-Spanish lower classes. In the Spanish juridical conception, the Indians were to pay a tribute as part of their obligations as subjects of the Crown. A large number of sixteenth-century documents refer to the excesses of the collectors of the tributes. —Trans.

[5] A *real* is a small silver coin and monetary unit formerly used in Spain and the colonies. —Trans.

"No! Do not leave me!" she exclaimed, pale as death.

"Diego! . . . I would rather lose my own soul than lose you!

"Tomorrow. . . at midnight, wait for me at the corner of San Blas, and I will take the gold that you need to you."

Diego's eyes shone with an evil glow.

"Rosalía," he answered, holding the young woman in his arms, "I love you very much, but I could not accept that gold from you without knowing where it came from."

"Oh! Do not ask me, Maldonado; it is a secret that even death cannot make me reveal."

"Oh!" he replied, with feigned anger. "This is what my mistakes have led to: The woman I love, to save my life, is going to throw herself into the arms of one of those rich men that long after her, so that in exchange for her caresses they will throw back in her face the gold she needs to save me. No, Rosalía! I would rather die in the desert or on the scaffold before I accept the life you offer me. Good-bye."

"Majestic shadows of the dark city!" the Indian woman exclaimed. "I will have to break our terrible oath; but never will profane eyes see your sacred hallways or the secret corridors that lead to them.

"Diego," she continued, "have you heard of the treasure of the Incas? Well, we have it, and my father, the legitimate cacique of the Horcos and a descendant of Huascar,[6] holds one of its keys. A sacred oath holds us to keep its existence secret and to abstain from taking even a single carat from it. God knows that not even the most ardent pleas would have made me break our oath, but you need gold, and when I offer it to you, you doubt me. Forgive me, oh Father; forgive me, oh souls of the Incas."

"I still doubt, Rosalía. What would you want? I am jealous, and jealousy is the ruin of man. Make me ashamed of my weakness, show me how ugly my lack of trust is, take me with you."

........

[6] Huascar: An Incan prince, son of Huayna Capac. According to legend, when the prince was born, his father ordered a gold chain, measuring seven hundred feet in length, to be wrought for him. The child was called "Huascar," meaning "boy of the chain." —Ed.

"Take you with me! The vaults of the imperial palace would collapse; tradition has it that if a European lays his eyes upon the treasure, it will vanish."

"I will not look at it. Take me blindfolded."

"Blindfolded?"

"Yes, cover my eyes with a blindfold and guide my steps. Forgive me; but that is the only way that I will believe your words."

"So be it! And now, Diego, tell me that you love me, so that your words will drown out the voice of remorse in my heart."

Maldonado allowed himself to express raptures of affection that would have alarmed the young Indian woman if her soul had not been blinded by the love she felt for that man. But once she was alone again, with her own thoughts, the Indian woman dropped to her knees and prayed, full of fright.

The light of sunrise found Rosalía in the same position.

"My daughter," the old cacique said to her, when he went with his farming tools to give her a hug before heading out to the fields, "you are as pale today as you were in the convent. Do not spend so much time working; leave the distaff and go out to breathe the morning air. Today is a beautiful day; go for a walk among the rows of sown land; sit under the shade of the wheat. Look at how beautiful the red carnations are, and how fragrant the white flowers of the broad beans!"

"Rosacha," Andrés whispered in his sister's ear, while he placed his shepherd's purse diagonally across his back and grabbed his staff, "you no longer ask me to bring you the nests of woodpigeons or flowers from the hills. So do you know what I carry with me in my bag instead of food for the day? This!"

And he showed his sister the shining blade of a dagger.

"I know," he continued, "that someone is bringing sorrow into your soul. If last night I said to you, 'when you need a devoted heart and a strong arm, remember me,' I now say to you, Rosacha—whenever you should need such a heart, and such an arm, I will be there for you!"

The young Indian woman watched them walk away, the one with the fast pace and impetuous gestures of youth, the other curved over under the double weight of his many years and his long labors. She looked at them for a long time, without moving; when she saw them finally turn at a bend in the road and disappear, her heart tightened up in her chest, and a burning tear fell down her pale cheek. But the image of Maldonado, the memory of his caresses and the fear of losing him, drowned out the moans of remorse in her soul.

Who was the man for whom the daughter of the cacique was about to break her oath, and for whom she was about to betray her father and her homeland?

## IV

Toward the last years of the reign of Don Carlos III,[7] a nobleman named Alonso de Maldonado lived in a town in the region of Aragón. He was one of those nobles with a wealthy name, but an emaciated estate; one of those who is decorated with royal orders, but whose pouch is as empty as the escutcheon of his coat of arms; like one of the knights of Calatraba or of Alcántara, whose gowns, riddled with holes, have to be mended with gold from the Americas by their sons, and often through infamy and crime. The ancestral home of the Maldonados, blackened and pitted like all of its owner's fortunes, was right next to the opulent Palace of Valdeneira, which belonged to the marquis of the same name, an old courtier who returned every summer to live on his lands for a few days. On one occasion, he brought with him the beautiful Eleonora de Aranda as his brilliant ward; she was an apparition who spread light and joy on the sad town, and Maldonado's two sons, Diego and Sancho, were unable to lay their eyes upon her without falling in love with her.

And that is how discord entered into the relationship between the two brothers, splitting them apart; from that moment onward, they looked at each other with a deadly hatred and thoroughly despised each other.

........

[7] Carlos II (1716–1788), king of Spain from 1759–1788. —Trans.

Although they were noblemen, neither one of them could aspire to the hand of the marquis of Valdeneira's beautiful ward. For Eleonora, a descendent of one of the most illustrious houses of Spain, did not have any wealth whatsoever; it was thus necessary for her to enter into a very rich matrimony, one that would provide her the means of occupying the position in court to which her noble birthright entitled her.

One day, Diego heard his brother say to Alonso de Maldonado:

"Father, I need money; and to acquire it, I am going to the court to solicit employment in Mexico."

Those words were like a ray of light for Sancho's rival. He wondered, in a word, why he had not had that very idea himself. Why had he not thought of that *domus aurea* called America, whence he could get plenty of gold to buy Eleonora's love? Yes! He would go there, and with greater chances of success than his brother, for he would make no stops in between. The only problem was that he knew his father would not allow him to leave the kingdom, for, as the second-born son, he was destined to serve in the army; he would therefore leave secretly. That would be a desertion; but Diego longed for Eleonora too much to allow any scruples to stop him. Sancho had asked his father for a term of two years to have enough time to accumulate the necessary wealth; he would have to hurry to beat him to it.

And so Diego left Spain and came to the Americas.

When he arrived on the new continent he met with all the deceptions that greet those who go searching for the wonders of the world. He had imagined that the mines of Perú were thick veins of silver and gold open to whoever wanted to chisel them. He found, instead, the long, arduous work necessary to tear from the earth its stone entrails, pulverize it, and finally extract carat by carat the precious metal that he had thought he would find piled up on its rich surface.

It is true that he saw many men who had gotten rich from these labors; but they had spent many years working there, whereas he had no time to lose: He had to beat his rival and return to Spain before him.

Diego changed his plan of attack, and dedicated himself to trying to learn about secret, hidden treasures. He learned Quechua, Aymara, and the strange tongue of the Chiriguanos,[8] and he visited cities and places of historical importance in Upper and Lower Peru. But his efforts were in vain; the only thing he found were fantastic stories, unbelievable myths that only inflamed his Tantalean thirst to maddening levels in that land filled with so many rich veins.

In the middle of the second year of his ill-fated term, Diego, running out of resources, finally arrived in Cuzco.

This mysterious land held his last hope. He brought with him a precious itinerary that he had obtained in a strange fashion, thanks to his knowledge of various American languages; he expected it to lead him to possess immense wealth.

One night Diego got lost in the intricate labyrinth of a mountain range while looking for a hill where, according to tradition, there were hidden eleven gold flames that the Indians had taken there to help rescue their king, and which they had buried, still lit, in the same spot where they were when they heard the news of Atahualpa's death.

It was snowing, and the thick snow accumulated on the ground and covered all the paths.

Wandering randomly from ravine to ravine, Diego saw a light shining in the distance, and headed toward it.

It was a fire burning in a hut. Inside the hut, Diego found a dying, old, blind woman; when she heard his steps, she turned her unseeing eyes toward him, and exclaimed in a hushed voice:

"Sebastián! You have been gone so long!" And without waiting for a reply, she went on, doubtlessly under the influence of her delirium:

"You did not bring the priest with you? So much the better! After you left, I thought that if I disclosed to him where I hid that treasure that my father took from the lake of Horcos, he would not even take the time to say a prayer for me before I died. Instead, he would hurry away from here, gallop straight to Cuzco, dismount at the door of the

........

[8] These are the languages of the Incan and Guarani Indians. The Chiriguano Indians are an offshoot of the Guarani who migrated from Bolivia to Argentina. —Ed.

Convent of the Nazarenes, and go into the church, which he can do at any time. Then he would raise the dais of the main altar, dig two meters down, and spend eight days removing all the gold, gold, and more gold that it took me eight days to hide there after I had given the abbess ten blows, and then poisoned her that night in case it might occur to her to speak about or act on what I had done. . . . What is that noise?"

The blind woman's sharp ear had detected, in effect, what Diego soon heard: the approaching footsteps of a horse.

The greedy Aragonese, who had been leaning over the dying woman's leathery face, anxiously drinking in each of her words, now looked out through the slightly ajar door. Outside, in the white reflection of the snow, he saw a man approaching on horseback, and another man guiding him, trotting in front of the horse. The rider was wrapped in a black cloak.

Maldonado recognized the priest that the dying blind woman had just referred to. The priest whom she had had called to disclose to him where her secret treasure was, and who was now arriving, and would soon come in, speak with her, and with the pressure of his priestly influence, get from her the secret Diego himself had just uncovered. That secret was his only hope, his only means of possessing Eleonora. . . .

A red cloud passed before Diego's eyes, and his temples beat as if they were being hit by a hammer. The dying woman moved in her bed, agonizing.

"*Whlano* just spoke outside?" she murmured. "It is Sebastián's voice!

"Then who is the person next to me? Sebastián. . .!" but those were her last words. A pair of strong hands seized her throat and strangled her to death.

When the priest and his guide entered the hut, they found the blind woman already dead, and a sad, somber man sitting next to the fire.

V

The blind woman had predicted that the priest would head straight to Cuzco if he had come to know of her treasure; instead, it was Maldonado who did so as soon as he learned her secret.

His first concern, naturally, was to go directly to examine the place that contained the riches, which he already thought of as his own. Had he not, in essence, purchased them at the highest of prices, at the cost of a deadly crime?

He kneeled in the Church of the Nazarenes as if he were praying; his eyes were fixed on the dais that hid his treasure. The priest, the hall, the ceremony, the presence of God himself—everything had disappeared for him. Instead, it was his spirit that he saw, which, after covering great distances, hovered now with the image of Eleonora above the magnificent regions that the treasure would open for them.

But how could he take possession of it? By himself, there was nothing he could do; he needed somebody's help, and that somebody had to live inside the convent. Who would he be able to trust with the dangerous secret that had already taken the life of a previous abbess and cut short the sufferings of the old, blind woman?

Maldonado directed his gaze toward the choir. It was full of somber figures, on their knees, motionless, whose grave aspect ruled out any thoughts of a possible seduction. The Aragonese man looked at those austere countenances for some sign of a worldly emotion that might encourage his hopes; but he did not see anything in them other than the deep absorption of prayer.

All of a sudden, under one of the novices' white veils, Maldonado saw two beautiful black eyes meet his with a certain look. . . .

Maldonado left the church telling himself that he had found the accomplice he needed.

Oh! Sacrilegious mockery of love! That look that the daughter of the cacique had believed to be the mysterious meeting of two souls in search of each other was only the gaze of a thief looking longingly at the locks on a treasure chest!

Maldonado was short on resources and needed to procure them immediately.

But it was easy enough for him to get a hold of them. At that time the word "nobleman" was still a form of currency and could stand in the place of all other manners of recommendation. The Aragonese received a warm welcome from the intendant of Cuzco, who proposed naming him the collector of the Tribute. Maldonado accepted the job, a form of employment that would put him in contact with Indian women out in the country, from whom he expected to receive important information.

Meanwhile, he went every day to the Church of the Nazarenes, and, on his knees, looked adoringly at the treasure within those walls, the key to which, for him, was Rosalía.

One day, when he did not see her on the other side of the bars of the choir, Maldonado became furious, enraged; but when he learned that she had left the convent, the news he had thought would ruin his chances instead calmed him at once. He went looking for the cacique's daughter; he realized she had fallen in love with him, and when he found her, he seduced her, making her his.

From that moment on, he had been waiting for the right occasion to let her in on his secret intentions, and to convince her to return to the convent to carry them out.

He started pretending to be madly jealous, frightening the poor girl. Then, all of a sudden, he stopped going to visit her.

He wanted to tame her soul into obedience by drowning her in grief.

It was around that time that, one night, Maldonado found himself in the tempting confines of a gambling house. It was a magical place, continually dazzling to behold. The gold flowed in torrents, and the harmonious sound of the coins plucked the deepest chords of one's soul. All of the faces inside the house were pale, some with pleasure, others with desperation; and everyone's eyes glowed with the sinister flash of greed.

After losing his last *blanca*,[9] Maldonado sat motionless and thoughtful, leaning his elbow against a corner of the fateful card table. Every once in a while he would wipe his hand across his brow,

........

[9] A *blanca* is an ancient Spanish coin. —Trans.

as if he were trying to turn away an evil thought. But it kept returning, and for moments it could be seen to settle in his dark, fixed stare.

Meanwhile, the stakes of the game had grown to immense proportions. The green felt of the tabletop was all but completely covered by mounds of shining doubloons; the bets were in, and the card
was about to be turned over. Maldonado saw on the table, with a pile
of gold next to it, the card that had made him lose the previous couple of rounds. At the same time, in an ill-fated coincidence, another
player beside him said:

"I bet against this one, for no card is lucky enough to win three
times in a row!"

Maldonado did not need to hear anything else; he undid the clasp
of his sword, with the escutcheon of his coat of arms on it, and threw
it on the table, saying:

"I lay the escutcheon of a noble house as a bet of one thousand
doubloons."

And away it went, to be replaced by a bag of gold for the bet. But
the gambler's rule of thumb did not hold up, and Maldonado, in
order to recover his escutcheon, found himself forced to exchange the
extra gold he had with him. And this was the gold that came from
the blood and sweat of the poor Indians—for it was the gold of the
tribute, which the owners of this land were forced to pay to a sover-
eign foreigner, and which Maldonado was now stealing from the
royal coffers.

Terrified by the thought of the tremendous punishment to which
his crime condemned him, Maldonado thought about fleeing. But he
realized that running away from that country that was in the center
of everything was impossible—requisitions were certain to go out for
him and soon land him in the hands of justice.

So Maldonado decided to hurry the execution of his plan at all
costs, and went to find Rosalía to convince her to return to the convent.

But how surprised he was when she told him about that secret of
the descendants of the Americas, of which he had previously caught

whispers among the rustling of the winds, in the rushing of the streams and the echoes of the Andes!

After he had hooked the daughter of the cacique with his vile shrewdness and had gotten her to promise to take him to the mysterious place that contained the treasures of the kings of Peru, Maldonado began to think that he might be living a dream; he would have given his soul to hasten the moment that separated him from reality.

## VI

It has been a few hours since Yupanqui's cabin, the fire extinguished, went dark and silent. The rooster, perched on top of the willows, has crowed his first song.

It is midnight.

The sky is veiled with black clouds, and every once in a while distant flashes of lightning illuminate the inside of the cabin with a violet light.

The old cacique is asleep with the heavy sleep of the tired worker. Andrés is next to him, lying in the same bed.

Through the door that separates the two rooms of the cabin, a pale, trembling, and quivering woman comes, hidden in the darkness of the night.

The woman is Rosalía.

She extends her neck into the room, listens, and, encouraged by the silence, approaches the cacique. She leans over him, reaches out with her hand, opens a small bag lying on the old man's chest, takes out a key, and turns around to leave the room and the cabin. Outside, she takes the narrow path that leads down to the city.

Behind her, nimble and silent as a shadow, a black figure exits the cabin and follows her at a distance.

At the same time, a man standing on the corner of San Blas, wrapped in his cloak, waits anxiously, his eyes staring fixedly at the road that leads up to the Rodadero.

"Finally!" he exclaims.

Shortly thereafter, a woman, covered from head to foot in a large black shawl, stops in front of him and whispers in a somber tone:

"Here I am, Diego! I bring God's anger and the curse of my ancestors upon my head; but this is how you wanted it to be. Your foot will soon step into the sacred place where only the sons of the kings have stepped. I pray that the great Pachacamac[10] will only punish me for this offense and not extend his anger to you!

"Now let me tie your hands, blindfold your eyes, and cover you in my father's blanket, so that the souls of the Incas will not recognize you as you enter the sacred city."

VII

When the exquisite moment finally arrived, the greedy Aragonese man could barely contain his tremendous raptures of happiness, which seemed almost like raptures of horror.

"Here are my hands, Rosalía," he said, stretching them out to her, "tie them up; and blindfold me. . . . But tell me, why are you dressed like that?"

"In the place that we are about to enter, Diego, my name is not Rosalía; there, I am Mama Tica Suma.[11] I therefore leave my poor clothes behind, and under this long shawl I have the outfit that accords my social position, which I only reveal within the quiet shadows of the underground city."

The Indian woman wore a *topo*[12] fastening the shawl that covered her body. From under it, she took out and unfolded a long wool sash and covered Maldonado's eyes. Then she tied his hands behind his back, wrapped him up in a blanket like hers, and started walking, guiding him by the arm.

........

[10] Pachacamac: In the Incan tradition, "ruler of the world," one of the original deities. —Ed.
[11] Mama Tica Suma: Literally, "beautiful mother." —Ed.
[12] A *topo* is a large brooch used by Indian women to fasten their shawls. —Trans.

The Aragonese man felt himself being led for a long time on rugged roads, through intricate twists and turns, always climbing steeply toward some high summit. A cold, harsh wind howled in his face, blowing an occasional dry leaf against him. Every once in a while the hand guiding him would shake and tremble; and among the distant clash of the thunder, Maldonado thought he heard the Indian woman's voice whispering strange words under her breath, as if she were praying.

The shrewd Aragonese tried many times to free one of his hands with a furtive motion, thinking that he would then slide it under the blanket and up to his eyes. But he found that the knot that bound them was too tight; he was finally forced to give up.

Meanwhile, the nighttime sounds of the city, the barking of the dogs, the crowing of the roosters, reached him less and less frequently and at a greater distance as they went along; the strong wind was blowing harder, and Maldonado could breathe the thin air of the higher lands.

Suddenly, the terrain evened out under his feet, and he felt the wind blow even stronger and colder.

The Indian woman finally stopped, and Maldonado heard her kneel in prayer three times. Then he thought he heard a sound similar to that which a large boulder being moved might make. Immediately after that, he heard the crisp sound of flint being struck, and Maldonado felt himself taken quickly down a seemingly endless, winding staircase. He felt his foot slide against the wet surface of stone steps; the foul underground air of subterranean regions made it difficult to breathe; his temples throbbed strongly; and his footsteps, repeated infinitely by the echo, filled the unknown areas they were traversing with an immense sound.

The Aragonese felt all of this without stopping to think about it. His heart was absorbed by a single thought: the treasure! An unbelievable treasure—and guarded by a mere girl, a fragile reed so easy to break.

As he thought this, a vertiginous sensation grew inside of him; the names of Spain, of Sancho and Eleonora resounded in his ears, and a whirlwind of burning images raced through his mind.

"We have arrived. We are now in the sacred city!" the Indian woman whispered suddenly in Maldonado's ear. "Diego, your foot has passed through the entrance way of the imperial palace. We are now in the gallery of the statues. Touch them, Diego, and you will see that the Indians knew how to work gold much better than the artisans from your country."

"How can I touch them if my hands are tied?"

The trusting Indian woman untied the knot that had kept his hands tied behind his back. Once they were free, trembling with emotion, the Aragonese used them to touch and feel a long line of statues; the metallic contact made him quiver with pleasure.

"Over here," the daughter of the cacique said, "over here are the flowers of the gardens of the Inca. Touch these beautiful irises."

"Made out of gold!" the Aragonese murmured, his voice trembling.

"And here is the maize from their fields, and their blond ears."

"Made out of gold!"

"And the racemes of these shrubs with their wide leaves."

"Pearls! Thick pearls, and gold, gold everywhere!"

"Yes! Everything, from the tiles that both your steel spurs resound against, to the sand on which our warriors practiced their skills; from the Inca's canopied throne, to the small pebbles that the children played with, one of which you just kicked—everything here is made out of gold. But it is sacred gold, gold that no one has ever taken from here, not even a single carat of it; it is a precious deposit sealed with a holy oath that I am about to break for you. . . .

"But let us hurry. The shadows are asleep; let us not wake them by spending any more time here than is necessary. Over here there are mounds of the most beautiful pearls that our oceans produce; over there you have hills of the richest stones from our washeries. Take as much as you want, Diego, and let us leave quickly."

"Leave!" Maldonado exclaimed, in a delirious state. "Leave this huge treasure that could change the face of the world, but which you keep buried down here, you stupid Indian! No! I want all of this to be mine, and it shall be mine!"

And Maldonado, crazed out of his mind, tore off the sash that had been covering his eyes. . . .

What he saw then, in the space of an instant, was a tremendously large field of marvelous things that dazzled his eyes, an expanse containing all the wonders that his fantasy could ever have conjured for him. There were temples illuminated by an infinite number of lamps; halls and galleries filled with gold in all manner of forms: here in the shape of statues, vases, and altars; there in gardens with flowers that were constellations of precious stones. And standing next to him, adorned with pearl bracelets and necklaces, was the humble Indian woman who had led him there, dressed in an outfit of the highest rank, donning the purple sash of a Peruvian princess.

But, as was just said, the magical vision lasted but a moment. The moment the band fell from Maldonado's eyes, an iron hand seized him by the throat, threw him to the ground, blindfolded him again, and tied his hands behind his back with a double knot. Then he was lifted up by two strong arms, and the Aragonese felt himself being carried over a solid shoulder, away from that place filled with so many things he had not had time to see, and up the long staircase down which he had come but a few moments before.

Despite the suddenness of the attack, Maldonado did not lose his quick thinking. When he felt himself thrown to the ground, Maldonado anticipated the designs of his unknown enemy, and reached up to his chest to tear off his rosary, which all Spaniards had with them at all times back then, and clutched its beads in his closed fist as his attacker tied his hands behind his back.

The mysterious guide climbed the immense staircase very quickly, without stopping even once. Then Maldonado heard him open a door and push a boulder; shortly thereafter he felt the wind of the night blow against his face again.

From that moment on, the Aragonese, carrying out his spontaneous plan, began to drop the beads of his rosary one by one from the entrance to the secret city. Each one of those beads represented a letter to Maldonado, an integral part of the precious itinerary that would later give him possession of the immense treasure of which he had had time to catch but a glimpse.

After about half an hour, the arms that had been holding the Aragonese set him down on the ground. A hand untied his blindfold, and Maldonado found himself again on the same street corner of San Blas from where, a short while before, he had left with the daughter of the cacique. Standing before him was Andrés. The warrior who had attacked him and brought him under control was the sixteen-year-old boy!

But any possible vexation that might have wounded his pride was negligible compared to the tremendous happiness that filled his heart with the following idea: He had left the road to the treasure marked behind him!

Just imagine, then, the magnitude of his anger when, upon taking a step backward, Andrés, who had not said a single word before, stretched his hand out to the Aragonese to hand him something in the middle of the dark night, and said:

"Sir, here are the beads of your rosary, which you apparently dropped as we were coming back."

"Wicked Indian!" Maldonado yelled at him as he left. "You will pay for this!"

And he headed straight to find the intendant, with whom he had a very long meeting.

## VIII

Before he went back to his home, Andrés walked over to a nearby group of houses and knocked on the door of a cabin.

The door opened and a youth, of about the same age, stood at the entrance.

"Andrés! What are you doing here at this time of night? Something must be wrong. My father said today that the coca leaves were bitter, and you know that is a bad sign."

"Yes. And you know, too, Santiago, that when the *Saxsahuaman*[13] turns black, some misfortune threatens us. And look at it now!"

A large, dense group of clouds was blowing toward their hill, rumbling with thunder, covering the sky and the land below it with dark shadows. And everything, as the Indian youth had said, was turning black, black as the heart of night.

"*Hallpa-mama* is angry! Speak, Andrés!"

"I will; but let us talk so softly that not even the spirits that roam in the thin air will be able to hear us."

The two young men spoke for a long time, one into the ear of the other.

Later, the youth from the cabin embraced Andrés, and the latter handed him an object that shone brightly in the light of a sudden flash of lightning.

## IX

That same night the cacique and his children were attacked in their cabin. They were apprehended, gagged, and, with their hands and feet chained up, were taken to an isolated country house that the intendant of Cuzco had on the outskirts of the city, high in the mountains.

When they arrived there they were separated, and the intendant questioned each one of them about the existence of the treasure. But the cacique and his children shrouded themselves in a deep silence, and neither promises nor threats could get a word out of them.

Exasperated with that cold and silent obstinacy, the intendant decided to break the father by presenting him with the horrendous spectacle of seeing his children tortured in front of him.

To this end, they brought the three of them to a room that had the

........

[13] *Saxsahuaman*: Literally, "royal eagle of the Andes." In Incan history, the name of an important fortress built on a mountaintop in the vicinity of Cuzco. Here, Gorriti refers to the mountain itself. —Ed.

necessary evil implements prepared: a blindfold, a tourniquet, and a bonfire.

When the cacique was brought in, a masked man waiting near the door took him to the intendant who sat in an armchair at the other end of the room.

"Yupanqui," he said, "have you thought this through? Do you know to what point the hard silence that you keep can lead?"

"May God's will be done!" the old man answered with humble resignation.

"We will soon see if you say the same when you see your children given into the hands of the torturer."

The cacique shook all over, and the venerable white hairs that crowned his head stood on end.

At that moment Andrés and Rosalía were brought into the room.

The masked man went to meet them and brought them before the intendant.

The young woman stared straight into his eyes, and a livid indignation came over her countenance.

"Traitor!" she exclaimed. "Hurry and take me to my death. But here, in the presence of God who will judge you and me, I call you before his holy tribunal to account for today's actions."

A vague, sinister smile appeared on Andrés's lips as he heard his sister's words; she, in turn, threw herself into the arms of the cacique. The old man held her tightly in his arms and cried on his daughter's chained hands.

"Father!" she whispered in the old man's ear. "Dry your tears; I deserve death, for I gave away our secret. . . ."

The cacique turned pale and, holding his daughter away from him, said to her severely:

"If what you say is true, may God have mercy on you. Meanwhile, at least carry out your last duty: Remain silent and die."

The intendant made a sign, and the masked man grabbed Andrés, who was standing next to his father, his hands chained behind him. He made him sit on a bench solidly nailed down to a beam on the ground. He turned a lever and a rope sprung out from a hole in the center of the beam. The masked man put the rope around the young man's head, turned the lever again, this time in the opposite direction, and the rope became more and more taut, marking a blue circle around Andrés's temples.

The intendant turned to Yupanqui.

"Look at your son," he said to him; "he is going to die. Have pity on his youth! Do you value that gold of yours more than you value his life?"

"Do not worry, father," Andrés said, with the smile of a martyr, "look at me die and praise God for the strength he bestows upon his creatures."

The torturer turned the lever again, and the young Indian, looking straight at his father, kept on smiling even in the horror of his agony, the rope tightening more and more upon his head.

When the cacique heard his son's head implode, his son expiring without uttering a single moan, he tore at his chest with his nails, and turned his eyes with a last, supreme look at his daughter.

The young Indian woman had fainted.

It was now the wretched girl's turn.

The torturer seized her, stripped her naked, and put her on the wheel.

When she felt the impious touch of those dirty hands, the young woman opened her eyes and found herself naked and in front of the torturer. But her heroism overcame her modesty and her fear.

"Father!" she exclaimed, leaning back with a sublime gesture on the horrid implement. "Forgive me!"

"Keep quiet and die," the old cacique repeated.

The young Indian woman suffered her martyrdom with the firm stoicism of her ancestors. At each turn of the wheel, she turned to the cacique and said to him, smiling:

"Father! Are you proud of me?" And when she let out her last breath, her body torn asunder, she repeated: "Father, are you proud of me?"

"Oh, great *Pachacamac!*" the cacique exclaimed when he saw the corpses of his dead children. "God of my fathers, glory be to you, for you have given these children the strength necessary to face their torture and to take to their graves the secret kept through the centuries!"

And pushing the torturer aside, he ran of his own accord and jumped into the bonfire waiting for him.

"*Hallpa-mama!*" he yelled through the flames. "Save the treasure of the Incas in the deepest parts of your entrails! Be its guard, *Cora puna sara sara;*[14] and release your eternal snows upon he who dares try to find it!"

His mystical prayer rose from the fire in a whirlwind of sparks. . . .

X

His victims' obstinate silence led the intendant to believe that the story of the treasure had been a dreamed-up delirium of greed. He thought so little about the lives of the wretched Indians, however, that he did not even consider turning the execution of the cacique and his children into a punishable offense.

As far as Maldonado went, the pointlessness of his crime did not discourage him. Doubly pressed by his ambition and by his need to reinstate the sums he had lost, he left the intendant, went right back to the spot where he had lost his guide the night before, and started his search from there. He followed the same steps and made the same turns that he remembered; he began to distance himself from the city without realizing it, his mind blinded with the wondrous vision that his eyes had briefly beheld.

After that day, no one ever heard from Diego Maldonado again; he disappeared as if he had been swallowed up by an abyss.

But from the next day on, the residents of Cuzco saw an immense *apacheta*[15] on the summit of *Saxsahuaman*. Santiago the goatherd raised the *apacheta* above the bloody limbs of an Aragonese corpse. And every Indian that walks by the mound of stones spits on it, then immediately throws rocks on it and curses.

........

[14] *Cora puna sara sara*: Literally, great high land of corn. —Ed.
[15] *Apacheta*: Ceremonial mound of stones erected by the Incas. —Ed.

# 3

# The Dead Man's Fiancée

*For my dear friend Vicente G. Quesada*[1]

## I

In the delightful region that extends from the border with Bolivia to the Patagonian line, in the center of a region that contains all of heaven's beautiful creations, on a plain furrowed with crystal-clear fountains and lost like a bird's nest among roses and jasmines, stands a city that has an oriental appearance. Her white domes rise exquisitely above the dark greens of the forests of orange trees that surround her, drawing in the traveler who contemplates her from afar. Her roads are lined with flowers; her air is warm and fragrant; her days glow gold and blue; her starry nights are serene, filled with music and love songs. To visit her once is to remember her forever; and if one day that same person were to return, and even if God had rendered them blind, upon breathing her perfumed air they would immediately exclaim—Tucumán!

Destined to be the site of great events, she has been the stage of our glories and of our misfortunes. It was there that the first American congress declared our independence, and that we first claimed

........

[1] Vicente G. Quesada (1830–1913) was a diplomat, legislator, journalist, and patron of Juana Manuela Gorriti. —Ed.

our freedom.[2] It was there that we tore the covers of tyranny off for the first time, and for the first time the courage of America humbled the Spanish lions. It was there that the hydra of the civil war produced the most horrible monsters and the noblest heroes. It was there that the caudillo of vandalism, the bloodthirsty "Tiger of the Plains,"[3] followed by his savage hordes, descended one day from the wild heights of the Andes, and fell suddenly upon the National Army that had been lulled to sleep in the delights of that new Capua, turning it into an immense hecatomb.[4]

It is the very image of the Garden of Eden: Good and Evil engage in a perpetual battle to possess her. But which one shall triumph?

## II

For some time now the political horizon of the Río de la Plata area had been darkening by the day. The heroes of the Battle of Ituzaingó,[5] united around the sky-blue banner of the country, have raised their bold efforts in vain against the barbaric phalanxes who, invoking a principle of chaos, scandalized the world with the atrocities of a fratricidal war. The days of the Battles of Tablada and Oncativo[6] were followed by cruel setbacks, and General Paz, the victim of an ill-fated coincidence for the cause of order, had fallen into the hands of the enemy and was being held captive in the jails of Santa Fe.[7]

........

[2] At the Congress of Tucumán, Argentina declared its independence from Spain on July 9, 1816. —Ed.

[3] Common epithet for Facundo Quiroga (1788–1835), a caudillo who figured in the civil wars and was the subject of Sarmiento's masterpiece, *Facundo, civilización o barbarie* (1845). —Ed.

[4] Reference to Quiroga's battle staged at Ciudadela (November 4, 1831), a bloodbath for Unitarians, which prompted the Gorriti family to abandon Salta and seek exile in Bolivia. —Ed.

[5] Battle of Ituzaingó: Decisive action staged by the Argentine army, under the leadership of Alvear, against Brazil (February 20, 1827). —Ed.

[6] Battles of Tablada and Oncativo: Sites where Facundo Quiroga was defeated. At the Battle of La Tablada (June 23, 1829), Quiroga launched a solid attack against General Paz and was firmly beaten; Paz again triumphed over Quiroga at Oncativo (February 25, 1830). —Ed.

[7] General Gregorio Paz (1797–1857), hero of the independence wars against Spain and the ensuing civil wars against the caudillos. He was taken prisoner by the Federalists on May 10, 1831. —Ed.

Deprived of its leader, the National Army that he led, and of which he was the heart and soul, undertook a great retreat, like that of the *Berezina*;[8] but it turned out to be just as disastrous. The marvelous courage of the hero in charge of it[9] was not enough to prevent its becoming a defeat.

When they arrived in Tucumán, the army selected its new leader—the noble and courageous Alvarado.[10] Noble and courageous, yes; but unlucky and a bad omen for the armies who fought under his command.

In any case, he was skillful, a good strategist, and very well-versed in the art of war, and upon assuming his tremendous responsibility, he was able to assess the situation with just one look; he discovered what his weak points were, and he calculated his advantages. He, who had the ill-fated experience of past retreats, weighed the results of this one, and decided to stop right there, fortify his troops, and wait for the enemy in the same place that, at another time, under the same circumstances, had been the site of victory for the immortal Belgrano.[11]

He built quarters; he reviewed his troops; he reinforced his numbers; he gathered extra weapons and asked for additional assistance from the neighboring provinces—all with the quick, instant determination that characterizes great captains. In that formidable battle

........

[8] The heroic retreat of Napoleon's army across the Berezina, November 26–29, 1812. —Trans.

[9] Gregorio Aráoz de LaMadrid (1795–1857) distinguished himself in the independence struggles and the later civil wars. After the Battles of La Tablada and Oncativo, he was chosen to replace Paz when the latter was taken prisoner. Pursued by Quiroga, LaMadrid was defeated at the Battle of Ciudadela and then immigrated to Bolivia where he lived for seven years. —Ed.

[10] Rudecindo Alvarado (1792–1872), from Salta, officer in the independence wars who rose through the ranks and achieved the title of Grand Marshall of Peru in 1826 and, later, Brigadier General of Argentina. His military career was marked by many serious defeats, first during the struggles against the Spanish Crown, when he served under Belgrano, and later as leader of the United Army. For his liberal ideals, Alvarado was driven into exile from 1831 until 1838. When he returned, he served as governor of Salta (1854–1856). —Ed.

[11] Manuel Belgrano (1770–1820), founding father and military leader of the independence movement. —Ed.

with destiny, Alvarado did not forget anything. His genius did not fail him; as it always occurs, it was his fortune that failed him.

## III

Spring bestowed its green wreaths upon the city that had become a military camp. The acrid perfume of the new shoots scented the breeze; the songs of the lark and the nightingale mixed with the notes of bugles, and the clamor of the weapons was insufficient to drown out the sweet sounds of that beautiful time of the year.

The spring of Tucumán!—rushes of light and fragrances, blue skies streaked with mother-of-pearl clouds, orchards filled with flowers, gorgeous women whose eyes shone like bright stars—in a word, everything delightful and peaceful that nature has to offer. Thus, at the peak of the day, the soldiers of the Unitarian army gave their souls over to all the illusions of eternal love.

No one came to disturb the army during that delightful period, as October left its last rays of sun on the golden petals of the Spanish brooms. Those who were superstitious, however, looked to the distant horizon of the red sunsets, and, shaking their heads like prophets, exclaimed, "There is blood ahead! Blood!"

But the army bands answered those evil omens with festive quadrilles to which the daughters of Tucumán danced under bowers of jasmine with that strange joy that precedes catastrophes.

## IV

Toward nightfall on the third of November, two pretty young women were reclining and laughing in the embrasure of a window.

"Emilia!" one of them suddenly yelled, "come quickly. Here comes the handsome Ravelo!

'Riding his quick horse to-day
The one that leaves the wind behind.'"

"I have promised not to see him," answered a voice, with a heavy sigh.

"And who could have demanded such a high promise from you?"

"My tutor."

"Bah, what does that old dodderer care if you see Ravelo? Is he jealous, perhaps?"

"He says that he is guilty of having a certain complacent look in his eyes implying he will never love me."

"What does he know! I would like to see someone forbid me from doing something that I really wanted to do! No, sir! And I would especially not let anyone take from me the pleasure of contemplating someone as graceful, and above all having those dark eyes with that deep look. . . . Ah! Emilia, he is so beautiful! Listen at least to the footsteps of his horse," the mischievous girl added, smiling maliciously and lowering her voice as the one to whom she was referring passed right in front of them.

The man who so attracted the attention of those girls was, as a matter of fact, a beautiful young man in every sense of the word.

He wore a uniform and a cuirass, and a commander's epaulette hung from his right shoulder.

Like all the officers in the Unitarian army, following an oath that had heroic significance to them, he allowed his black, wavy beard to grow fully and fall in dark curls down to his bright breastplate. He rode a spirited colt from the pampas; and if there was anything that matched his horse's equestrian gracefulness, it was the dexterity with which the youth handled him.

Horacio Ravelo was the boldest of the bold whom Alvear[12] had taught to fight. He was barely twenty years of age; and yet, from Ituzaingó to that day, his life had been a series of glorious events.

His companions, unable to surpass him, had grown accustomed to admiring him, and applauded his triumphs with sincere enthusiasm.

........

[12] Carlos María de Alvear (1789–1852), military leader during the independence wars and leader of the Constituents' Assembly of 1813, which set in place the symbolic codes of the future Argentine nation. As leader of state for a brief period of time, he was both authoritarian and reckless. He regained his prestige with his stunning defeat of Brazilian troops at the Battle of Ituzaingó in 1827. —Ed.

All the young women of Tucumán were in love with him. When they saw him pass by, whether at the head of his regiment, with the soldiers wearing their helmets and their polished armor for the magnificent maneuvers of a review, or alone at the end of the day, wearing a blue hood, holding the croup of his great horse from the pampas, it made them dream of all the heroes from the past, from Orlando to Murat, and they would have given their souls for just one look from him.

But he, who was the lover in the dream of so many beautiful girls, did not favor any of them. He greeted them with exquisite gallantry when a march came to a stop, he rode next to them in outings to the country, and he danced with them in the dance halls. But always, just when they thought they had caught him, he would slip out of their arms, flee from the festive evening parties, and, jumping on his fast horse, would gallop off and disappear. Where did he go? What unknown star called out to him and dazzled his soul?

v

A stone's throw from the last houses of the city, at the end of a path lined with hawthorn hedges, and on the edge of the ceibo tree grove that extends to the town of Monteros can be seen the white facade of a country house surrounded by the dark foliage of a group of mulberry trees. Before it is a garden with lemon trees and dense vines, under the shade of which an old woman and a young lady stroll arm in arm.

The one, bent over and moving with difficulty, was gathering herbs in a fold of her shawl; the other, dressed in white crêpes, with her black hair up in braids, supported the old woman's slow steps with visible impatience. Every once in a while she looked up, listened, and searched the darkness of the night anxiously with her gaze.

That young woman was the daughter of Avendaño, the guerrilla soldier. And that country house was the hideout from which, each night, the daring caudillo left with his band of guerrillas, whom he dispersed at dawn, and with whom he sought to antagonize the army by stealing its supplies and intercepting its communications from the Unitarian army in the north.

"Even if you laugh at me," the old woman said, continuing an ongoing conversation, "even if you laugh at me, I insist that there is something in you as of late that has been making your beauty glow. Something. . . How can I say it? . . . Something like the splendor of a restless hope that makes your eyes shine and makes it look like you are wearing a halo."

"It is just spring, Aunt," the young woman answered. "Spring, whose carnations are reflected on the faces of all twenty-year-olds."

"No, on my word! For last year at this time your face looked the same in every one of God's days—white and pink, pretty and smiling. But now it is different; within just one minute, your countenance changes its color, its complexion, and its expression ten times. The rustling of the wind affects you, you turn pale when you hear the sound of a bugle. . . and the distant footsteps of a horse make you tremble; what is wrong with this girl, my Lord? One would say that she was in love, as if there were some man in Tucumán with whom a young lady could fall in love; but there is no one. . . no one except those evil Unitarians with those frightful beards."

"Horacio!" the young woman sighed passionately.

"Horacio? Ah! Ah! Go on! Some novel, one of those inflammatory gossipy books that keeps girls awake and sends their minds floating into the clouds. Yes, well, that is where those waves of restlessness and happiness, of sadness and anxiety, must be coming from; and that must be why you lock yourself up in your room from eight in the evening onward, leaving me alone, lost like a needle in this huge haystack of a house. And all that comes from reading novels. Such foolishness! And having the twelve volumes of the *Año cristiano*[13] within arm's reach. . . . In any case, Vital, tell me at least what this Horacio of yours is all about; it is not a forbidden book, is it. . . ?"

........

[13] In the tradition of the spiritual exercises of St. Ignatius, the *Año cristiano o ejercicios devotos para todos los días del año*, authored by P. J. Croisset, Society of Jesus (1656–1738), circulated widely, reaching Spanish America through a translation prepared by the Spaniard, Padre Isla. —Ed.

"My Horacio! He is a sublime poem, a beautiful mystery that the heart savors with pleasure—yes! Sadness and happiness, bliss and pain, everything comes from him!"

Vital's voice was so impregnated with emotion as she answered her aunt that she galvanized a number of dead memories in the frozen soul of the old woman.

"Jesus! What a girl!" she exclaimed. "She speaks with a rapture that makes the heart quiver; one would think that we were back in the times of Belgrano, when there were men worthy of a woman's love."

"Oh! The hero of my story is a soldier handsome as a dream and brave beyond all fear. Men admire and envy him; women love him passionately, but of them all only one has captured his soul, and his heart and love belong to her. Like Romeo and Juliet, they belong to two races that are mortal enemies of each other—he is a Colonna—she, an Orsini."

"In other words, as if some Unitarian were to fall in love with you, the daughter of Federals."

"Yes, but like Romeo and Juliet's love, theirs has bridged the chasm of hatred that separated them. . . ."

"Ah! Ah! As if you, taking advantage of your father's absences, mocking my guardianship. . ."

"Yes. While their desire searched the distant horizons of the future for a day of reconciliation that might join their fortunes in the same manner in which their souls had already been joined; while the two rival families sent each other deadly challenges from atop their walls, the shepherds of the surrounding lands witnessed two fantastic beings coming out each night. One covered in a black helmet, the other in a white veil, the two meet, intertwine their hands and stroll under the shady, wooded paths until the first rays of the sunrise separate them and they are forced to retreat into the darkness of their respective castles."

"That is more or less the same thing that Sebastian the farmer came to tell me yesterday."

"Ah! . . . And what did Sebastian say?"

"It was one of his silly stories. The other night, while he was watching over the skittish cattle at the watering place in the ceibo tree grove between midnight and one in the morning, he imagined that he saw a strange vision suddenly pass by his hiding place: a man, wearing armor and carrying a sword, walking arm in arm with a woman dressed in a white gown whose long folds blended with the silvery rays of the moon. . . . They were visions created by drink, girl, do not try to make anything of them. That youth has given himself to visiting the local store more than the average man, and those apparitions are nothing but children of the bottle. Bah! And how is it that your father never saw such figures, and he spends the entire night out with his mounted rebels in the neighboring forests?"

"My father!" the young lady said, shaking. "But. . . doesn't he spend the night at home?"

"Goodness gracious! Wouldn't you know it; how right is Avendaño for saying that you should not trust anything to an old woman? And here I am, telling you what he told me not to talk about. And I have his daughter right in front of me, frightened and shaking! Calm down, girl. What is so strange about it? Is your father not a Federal? What is wrong with it, if he sleeps like the dead during the day and opens his eyes at night like a bat? So much the better for our cause. Without Avendaño's watchfulness, the Unitarians would already have received countless reinforcements; whereas, thanks to him, they are not aware that Quiroga is approaching with a forced march and is going to attack them violently in the middle of their little parties. . . ."

"My God," Vital murmured, "have mercy on my love! If I do not speak, I lose him; if I do speak, I betray my father. . . ."

"What are you saying, girl?"

"I said that it is late already and that the dew is starting to fall."

"And it is so bad for me. Come, girl, I am ready for bed. Tomorrow we shall go to the Church of Santo Domingo to hear Mass at six in the morning. Good night. . . . Oh! Do not let your father know what I just told you, for he is rough as a devil; I would not want to take any chances with him."

Vital locked herself in her room. She prayed on her knees before a statue of the Virgin that was right next to her bed; then, getting up at once, after kissing the Divine Lady on the face as if she were a terrestrial mother, she went to the window and looked out, searching everywhere.

The moon was already shining its rays upon the deserted countryside, and the fireflies flickered like bright stars under the thick foliage of the orchards.

At that moment a man dismounted under the branches of a mulberry tree and tied his horse's reins to its trunk. "Quiet, old boy," he said, caressing the neck of the beautiful animal, "be quiet and silent, for your own good. Ah! When will the day come when I will be able to take her in my arms, hold her tightly against my heart, and gallop with you in the delightful fields of the pampas?" He stopped talking, for he thought he heard a sound among the branches. But it was only a frightened owl that had flown off, carrying away in the evil wind of its flapping wings the young man's exclamation of hope for the future.

Rider and horse remained hidden among the trees; but eyes that look for love know how to find it even in the dark.

"There he is!" Vital exclaimed. And turning back toward the Virgin, she exclaimed, "Mother! The hour of my fate has arrived; events have rushed in and now they grab and throw me into the arms of my beloved. Tomorrow I must be his and follow him. But meanwhile, and for the last time, lend me your sacred veil, that saintly talisman that has protected me to this day and blessed my love."

She covered herself with the Virgin's white humeral veil and walked to the window, where she removed a bar that had been stealthily filed off and reset with wax. Passing through the extra space now available, she slipped through the window and disappeared into the shadows.

It was six in the morning and the dawn was quite beautiful. A splendorous aurora of mother-of-pearl and gold streaked with brilliant rays arose in the east, and the clear, pure blue of the sky, the perfumed aromas of the breeze, the songs of the birds, and the joyful ringing of the bells gave every indication that the day was to be filled with good fortune—that day, the fourth of November, which was to fill Tucumán with such dismal memories.

The bugles played the reveille; from the heights of the towers the large bells called everyone to the early morning Mass, and the doors opened one after the other, letting out a multitude of beautiful early risers who—with their countenances softly colored by the warmth of their beds, their eyes still heavy with the rich languor of sleep, and their unplaited hair half-hidden by that fantastic haze of veils that the women from Tucumán so gracefully wore—ran to the Church of Santo Domingo to receive the indulgence that would be bestowed at that Mass by a Capuchin who was a monastic notable recently arrived from Rome with ample concessions from the Pontiff, of whom he was an honorary steward.

To those of you who stop to look at women at the doors of churches, you—who after praying to God inside the sanctuary adore him by contemplating the beauty of his creation outside: Do not search for those beauties when they cover themselves with those gaudy ornaments and disguise themselves with rouge and other cosmetics, when they follow the extravagant forms of fashion and thus lose their own. Look for them, instead, during those first hours of the day, and then the mysteries of their beauty, like those of nature, shall be revealed to you.

The Mass had begun amid the silent absorption that is inspired by the darkness of the old naves of churches, but the pink light that precedes the first rays of the sunrise reflected off the top of the dome, making the candles burning at the alter pale in their brightness, distracting the youth, as they looked around with that restless curiosity of 20-year-olds that is fed by all manner of frivolous things.

"There," one of them said into the ear of another, "we are all here now, all the dancers from last night. I missed you tremendously; I have had no one to joke with."

"And the love of your loves?"

"Ravelo? He was there for one hour, and then left. I swear! His heart is made of stone!"

"Hmph! Not as much as you would have me believe. I saw him just recently; perhaps he was coming to find you."

"Him! Oh! You do not know what I would give if that were true!"

"Well, really! Say, who is that young lady who just got up from beside that ugly old woman and who is right this moment disappearing behind that column?"

"Do you not know her? It does not surprise me. She is the daughter of a Federal and does not come to our dances. Have you not heard of the beauty of Vital, the daughter of the guerrilla Avendaño? Well, that is she."

And so it was that when the last Epistle of the Mass was sung, Vital left her aunt and went to meet a man who was waiting for her behind a column. It was Horacio Ravelo.

"Vital!" he said, taking her hand, "I ask you, who I have chosen as my partner, do you love me?"

"More than my own soul!" the young woman answered with vigorous emotion in her voice. And both kneeled down.

At that moment the priest turned toward the people in the church; calling on the Lord Almighty, he gave them his blessing.

"You are mine!" exclaimed the husband, pressing the hand of his beloved to his lips.

"You are mine!" she answered, staring into his eyes with a look of love.

"Damn!" grunted a voice in a hoarse murmur above the sacred book of the Tabernacle, "it is that fateful beauty that my eyes see in spite of me; the image that has set forth an impure fire in my blessed dreams; it is Eve, the temptress, who, without knowing it, has come to place herself between my soul and God...!"

All of a sudden, a loud noise, mixed with moans and wails, was heard from afar. Shortly thereafter a large crowd of people rushed into the church screaming in fear, "It is the Federals! The Federals!"

Vital started crying and threw herself into the arms of her husband, but he held her back; her lover now became a soldier. He kissed his wife on the forehead and whispered in her ear:

"I will see you tonight!"

"Ah!" she said passionately, "where will I be tonight?"

"Here!" he answered, crossing his arms over his chest. "For, dead or alive, I will be here!" Drawing his sword, he turned away from his wife and stormed out of the church.

A purple line streaked with lightning bolts wound its way toward Tucumán over the plains dotted with trees that extend toward the town of Monteros—they were the spears and the red shirts of Quiroga's army. The Tiger of the Plains, covering great distances with the speed of a hurricane, had reached the prey that fate was to deliver to him.

The National Army formed its troops in the field of the Ciudadela and awaited its enemy courageously.

History has recorded in its bloody pages that ill-fated day that cut short the life of half a generation and threw the other half out to face the horrors of exile. The guilty insubordination of one of the main leaders of the army, who later paid with his life for the consequences of his disobedience, changed the fortune of that day, transforming a sure victory into defeat. General López! May God's judgment have been merciful, and may the earth that covered his mutilated remains be light![14]

The battle was fought and lasted nearly the whole day. The entire infantry perished, fighting to the death without backing down. The cavalry fled the battlefield; but its leaders and officers jumped to the ground and, joining their troops, fought to the end with them. Two hundred of them, the cream of the army, were injured and captured in the field of battle, and were dragged to the central plaza of the city to be executed. At the last moment, one of them raised a weak arm with much difficulty and called for one of the priests who had come to attend to them. He whispered something to him and placed an object in his hand. There was a flash of recognition in the monk's eyes; but he lowered his hood, stretched his hand over the dying man's head, and gave him absolution.

........

[14] Felipe López (1795–1858), military officer in the independence wars and subordinate to LaMadrid at the battle of Ciudadela. —Ed.

A moment later the weapons fired; it was over. The bodies were to be left there unburied by order of the victor as a lesson to the people. The Tiger of the Plains, having gained possession of the city, grabbed her mercilessly with his terrible claws.

The unfortunate women whose dear ones were in the defeated army did not know of their fate; those mothers, sisters, and wives had to spend the entire night in their houses tormented by the unbearable uncertainty of not knowing whether they lived or not.

## VI

In the country house next to the ceibo tree grove, locked up in her white virginal alcove, on her knees, pale and shaking, Avendaño's daughter begged the Mother of God for her husband, while her father celebrated with his men the triumph of their cause with an endless feast.

Holding back the anguish in her soul, quieting her sobs so as to listen in the silence of the night, she was waiting for some sound—anything—from outside to provide some ray of hope in her heart.

But the suffering of that eternal night drained all her strength; her body was growing faint, and strange hallucinations began to invade her mind.

All of a sudden she felt her whole body shudder. She could not deny it; someone was approaching. She was completely in the dark, for she had extinguished her light to keep her watch secretly; but she saw quite distinctly now a shadow that came and stopped between the window and the weak light of the stars.

Shortly thereafter she heard the bar that had been filed down being removed, and a man entered her room.

"Horacio!" she wanted to shout, struggling to get up from where she was kneeling to welcome her husband; but her lips were met by a pair of passionate lips, two strong arms surrounded her body with an impetuous embrace, and the silence once again mixed with the darkness in that mysterious alcove. . . .

The cool breeze of dawn blowing her unbraided hair across her forehead woke Vital. She was alone; there was no indication anywhere of Ravelo's presence. Of that passionate night she had only a cold, terrifying memory. Had it really taken place? Had she dreamt it? What a strange mystery!

When she touched her forehead with her hand, Vital screamed, and an immense happiness filled her soul. She found on her finger a ring that she had given Ravelo on one of the first days of their love. She had not imagined it, she had not dreamt it; he in whose arms she had spent those long precious hours had not been a specter of death—it had been her husband.

The old aunt came to tear the youth from the ecstasy that absorbed her.

"Vital! Vital!" the good lady shouted as she came in. "Come with me, my daughter; your father has given permission for you to carry out an act of charity. Do you know what it is? It is to bury the unfortunate Unitarians who were executed by firing squad yesterday afternoon in the plaza. Quiroga has said that they may be buried, but under the condition that it be their mothers and their wives who escort them to their graves. Mother of God! Poor children! All of my hatred has turned to pity. Let us go, my daughter, let us go help carry out this painful duty."

Vital sighed, thinking of the poor souls she was going to see; she followed her aunt, thanking God for having spared her husband.

The city was the site of a desolate scene impossible to describe. The streets were filled with blood, the houses were open and had been pillaged. Long lines of women in mourning-black were heading toward the plaza, moaning as they went to find the bloodied cadavers of their loved ones.

Vital and her companion followed the doleful procession.

When they arrived at the fateful plaza that had been turned into a horrible hecatomb, each one of those unfortunate women searched among the bloody remains for he whom death had taken from her.

All of a sudden, Vital screamed and collapsed unconscious to the ground.

Among the bodies of the two hundred officers executed the day before, she had recognized that of her husband....

VII

From that day on, Vital turned into an unreal being who slid among the living like a ghost. She never stayed still; sleep never came over her; her lips were silent; and only when the sun set and she saw her own shadow drawn in long silhouettes on the dry grass of the fields, would she interrupt her perpetual silence and exclaim with an infinite sweetness: "Horacio!"

The years came and went; but her strange existence did not change in any manner whatsoever. The inhabitants of the neighboring fields still find her on summer nights, in the moonlight, under the fragrant foliage of the orange trees, wandering, pale but serene, weaving orange blossom crowns that she places on her hair, which is still rich and black—for time, which usually leaves such deep marks, has passed by without touching even with the tip of his wing the smooth, white features of that face, after thirty years of dementia.

Ah! But who knows if that mystery that men refer to with such horror as "madness" is not very often the anticipated vision of eternal happiness!

# 4

# The *Mazorquero*'s Daughter[1]

*A Historic Legend*

## I

Roque Black-Soul was the terror of Buenos Aires. He was a killer par excellence in an association of killers called the Mazorca; devoted body and soul to the dreadful founder of that horrible brotherhood, he counted the hours in the day by the number of crimes he committed, and his hand, perpetually holding a dagger held above his head, never came down except to stab someone. He left blood behind him wherever he went, and all traces of mercy had left him so long ago that his heart did not even have a memory of it; the cries of orphans, wives, and mothers found him as insensitive as the cold blade of steel that he drove deep into the chests of his victims. All semblance of

........

[1] The Mazorca referred to the "Sociedad Popular Restauradora," a secret police force designed to ferret out Rosas's opponents and secure his power in Argentina. The Mazorca took its name from the corn husk that appeared on the emblem of the society. Founded in 1833, the Mazorca was the subject of many tales of terror, resistance songs, and obscene doggerel written about the Rosas regime. Rosas's wife, Doña Encarnación Ezcurra, was reputedly an active organizer of the society and issued directives to agents of terror who then committed atrocities in the name of state security or organized popular rallies in defense of Rosas. The Spanish title of Gorriti's story refers to Roque Black-Soul as a member of the Mazorca. Gorriti employed the popular orthography of the time and frequently took liberties, hence she occasionally uses *mashorquero* instead of *mazorquero*. —Ed.

humanity had disappeared from that man's countenance and speech; he was the true expression of the name that his offenses had earned him, a combination of fierceness and blasphemy that made anyone who had the misfortune of coming near him turn pale with fear.

Within that terrible vocabulary of cruelty and irreverence, however, like a flower growing in slime, there was a blessed word that Roque always uttered.

When that bloodstained man came home at sunrise, fatigued from the crimes he had committed that night, he always said: "Clemencia." And in response to this name, which seemed like sarcasm on the lips of that murderer, a voice so sweet and melodious that it sounded like it came from a choir of angels, would answer tenderly: "Father." And the figure of an angel, a sixteen-year-old with big blue eyes, crowned with a halo of blond curls, would come out to meet the *mazorquero* and embrace him with pained effusion. Clemencia was his daughter.

Roque loved her like a tiger loves its offspring, with a ferocious love. He would have gone to the end of the world for her; he would have spilled his own blood for her; but he would not give up even a single drop of his vengeance, nor sacrifice any of his homicidal tendencies.

Clemencia lived alone in the wicked home of the *mazorquero*. Her mother had died a long time ago, the victim of an unknown ailment.

Clemencia had seen her languish and slowly expire in a drawn-out agony, without being able to bring her back to life with her tender care; nor was she able to get from her mother's heart, not even with pleas and tears, the fateful secret dragging her to her grave. But when her mother died, when she saw her disappear under the black lid of the coffin, and when, frightened by the immense void that had formed around her, she went to throw herself into her father's arms, she saw them stained with blood, and an appalling revelation suddenly came to her. She looked back and recalled scenes that had been a mystery to her then; but now she saw them clearly, distinctly, and quite horrendously. She remembered the curses directed toward Roque the *mazorquero* that affronted her ears so many times, and that, in her love, in her veneration, for her father, she had been unable to believe could actually be intended for him. She who until that day had lived in a world of love and mercy found herself suddenly in a completely different one, filled with crime and horror. The entire truth was revealed to her, and comparing her own pain with the pain that her mother had accepted in silence, she understood why her mother had preferred eternity over life, and the cold pillow of the grave to that of the conjugal bed. But feelings of bitterness did not mix with the sorrow Clemencia felt. The beautiful girl's soul was very much like her name—all sweetness and compassion. Her awful discovery in no way diminished the affection she professed for her father. On the contrary: Clemencia loved him even more, because she loved him with a deep pity. And seeing him walk alone with his crimes on a path flowing with blood, carrying hatred on his back and vengeance in his head, far from envying her mother's eternal rest, Clemencia wanted to live so that she might accompany her wretched father on that road of wickedness like a guardian angel; and if it was not possible for her to take him away from it, at least to offer God a life of suffering and atonement on his behalf.

Clemencia rejected with dread the luxury that surrounded her, for she saw in it the rewards of crime. Forgetting that she was young, forgetting that she was beautiful and that the world is filled with heavenly pleasures for youth and beauty, she hid her svelte figure and her delightful shape under a long, white gown, covered the silky curls of her magnificent hair with a thick veil, quieted her beating heart's desire for love, and devoted herself entirely to the relief of the unfortunate. Overcoming the deep horror in her soul, she looked at the bloodstained lists where her father recorded the names of his victims, and, guided by these gloomy facts, she rushed off to adopt the orphans and the widows that his dagger had left in the world unprotected. To save them, she used the talents she had acquired under her mother's meticulous education: She gave music and drawing lessons, and devoted all of her hours to her work. The poor girl filled her mind with doleful thoughts, and although her heart was always heavy with sorrow, she played joyful polkas to which her students danced happily and merrily. In the frightful solitude of her nights, she who had said her adieus forever to all the joys of life, occupied herself with embroidering sheer bouquets in the veil of a newlywed or in the transparent and coquettish folds of a dance dress, without being disheartened by the painful thoughts awakened in her soul by those accessories of happiness of which she could no longer dream. Once these tasks were completed, the cost of which was filled with so many sad emotions for her, she would rush over to spread comfort and peace in the home of someone who had been sacrificed by her father's ax. She caressed and helped educate the children like an affectionate mother, she watched over sick ones with the fervent solicitude of a sister of charity, and she assisted the dying with passion and mercy.

Completely forgetting herself, Clemencia seemed to live only for the life of others. And yet the world smiled at her from afar, opened its arms to her, and showed her its delights. Quite frequently, in her charitable outings, Clemencia would hear enraptured voices behind her that exclaimed:

"Look at how beautiful she is! Blessed, a thousand times blessed, is he who is worthy of a look from those eyes!"

But those gallant words of love in the middle of the funereal silence of the desolate city offended Clemencia's ears, as if they were profane songs among the graves of a cemetery; hiding her face behind the folds of her veil, she would hurry off, her heart heavy with sadness and disgust.

II

One evening, Clemencia saw a group of men enter her house and head to her father's room; they had a sinister, hair-raising appearance, and were wrapped in long ponchos, in the folds of which could be seen the bright blades of their daggers. Clemencia foresaw something evil in the presence of those men, and after hesitating a brief instant, she hurried to put her ear against the keyhole of a door that led into her father's room.

Roque, standing near a table, held some papers in his hand; he was speaking in a loud voice to his audience.

"Yes, my friends," he said, "this is a war to the death against those Unitarians! A war to the death against those villains! You think that you have accomplished a great deal? Well, you are only fooling yourselves. All you have to do is read the list of our executions for this month and compare it with all the denunciations that we have received even just today. Read and you will see that there is still much work left for the blade of the Mazorca to do; when you compare the number of those who have fallen with the number of those who will fall... yes, who will fall, even if they hide under the mantle of the Virgin Mary herself!"

"Queen of Heaven!" Clemencia murmured, putting her hands together in pain and turning toward the image of the Virgin, her only companion in that solitary abode. "If that blasphemy reached even the feet of your divine throne, do not listen to it, heavenly Mother! Ignore it with indulgence and shine a smile of compassion on that wretched soul who walks in darkness."

After uttering these words, Clemencia turned back to hear her father, who was reading out loud:

"'Tonight, at nine o'clock, a masked man will stop at the foot of the obelisk in the Plaza de la Victoria, and will whistle three times. That man is Manuel de Puirredon,[2] the incorrigible Unitarian conspirator, Lavalle's friend, who has emigrated to Montevideo.[3] The signal is for the daughter of a Federal who has joined with him in secrecy and, turned into his most powerful aide, passes on to him her father's secrets. Informed by that signal of the return of the conspirator, she will surely go to meet him in order to help him with whatever base plan he is bringing for her in Buenos Aires.'

........

[2] Manuel de Pueyrredón (modern spelling) (1802–1865) joined the army of independence against Spain and later took sides with Lavalle in his struggle against Rosas's supporter, Dorrego. He was imprisoned by Rosas in 1835, and, upon his release, emigrated first to Montevideo and then to Brazil. —Ed.

[3] Juan Lavalle (1797–1841) joined the regiments of San Martín and later unleashed the civil wars that divided Argentina by his assassination of Dorrego in 1828. Rosas sought revenge against him, opening a series of battles that were to last until Lavalle's murder in 1841. —Ed.

"Do you hear that, comrades? And our daggers still in our belts?" Roque exclaimed with ferocious anger.

"Death to Manuel de Puirredon!" the murderers yelled, drawing their long daggers.

Clemencia looked through the keyhole to the clock in front of her father and trembled. The hands marked 8:55.

"Five minutes to save a man's life! Five minutes to prevent my father's committing another crime! Oh! God, stretch out this short amount of time and lend my feet wings."

And wrapping herself in her long, white veil, she ran out of her house and down the street toward the plaza, not without turning her head around many times in fear that the murderers would catch up and pass her, foiling her desire to save the unfortunate one who, without knowing it, was that very moment walking to his death.

When she reached the corner of Calle de la Victoria and Calle del Colegio, Clemencia spotted a black shape crossing the plaza diagonally toward the obelisk.

"There he is!" she murmured in a quivering voice and ran to meet him, catching him right when he reached the iron fence.

There were many people strolling around that night in the evening breeze, and they impeded Clemencia from speaking with the stranger directly.

So she turned sideways and walked passed him, touching him lightly on the back and making an imperceptible sign for him to follow her.

The masked man turned around impetuously, went up to Clemencia, and exclaimed, "Emilia! My Emilia!" He grabbed the young woman gently with his arm, and she was unable to stop him, for she was afraid to call attention to them.

Thus forced to remain quiet, Clemencia looked through her veil at the man, whose face she could see just at that moment by the way the rays of the moonlight illuminated him under his mask. He was a young and handsome man the likes of which Clemencia had never seen in all of her sixteen years of life, even in her lyrical dreams. He was tall and svelte. All of his movements revealed that easy, almost careless, elegance gained only through a knowledge of the world and a distinguished birth. His beautiful eyes, at once deep and languid, looked out with an irresistible power of attraction that, combined with the magical harmony of his voice, helped make him one of those beings who cannot be forgotten once one has looked upon them, and who always leave either an indelible mark of happiness—or of grief—in our lives.

The stranger, carried away by the misunderstanding, continued speaking in Clemencia's ear:

"Emilia, here I am, my love, not as a conspirator to entwine you again in the ruin of my unrealistic dreams, but as a passionate husband, to snatch you away from your father's arms and take you into mine, so that we may go far, very far from here, into the desert, to some unknown spot that your love will turn into a delightful Eden for me. Come, my Emilia, let us leave behind this ill-fated country of ours. God has cursed it, and our efforts and sacrifices to save her are in vain. . . .

"Oh!" the exile continued in a hushed voice, holding Clemencia even tighter against his chest. "You see, Emilia: This idea tears my heart to pieces . . . but you are here to calm my pain and fill it with joy. . . .

"And our son? He will be so handsome! How much you must have suffered when you had to separate yourself from him because of the cruel need to hide his existence. . . !"

At that moment they reached an empty part of the plaza. Clemencia looked around her and pulled herself quickly away from the stranger; then she raised her veil so that he would realize his mistake.

"Heavens!" he exclaimed. "It is not Emilia!"

"No, sir; but if your name is Manuel de Puirredon, you must get away from this fateful place where each second is a step toward death for you. . . . Do you not see them?" she continued, terrified, pointing to a group in black at the other end of the plaza. "That is them, the blood-stained daggers of the *Mazorca* waiting to ambush you. . . . Flee from here, in the name of heaven, for your wife, for your son. . . . Go with them, far from this den of beasts, to carry out that beautiful dream of happiness that fills your mind. . . . Go, go," she repeated, directing the exile toward a dark street and hurrying down another herself.

### III

When she got home, Clemencia went and kneeled down at the feet of the Virgin, hiding her face under the veil of the sacred image, crying for a long time, murmuring mysterious words between sobs. These perhaps revealed some sweet and painful secret that she wished to keep for herself, and that she dared only trust to the one who holds the keys to the hearts of all virgins.

From that day on Clemencia's enchanting and melancholy face turned even more pale, and her features held a deeper sadness. Who knows what joyful vision crossed her mind when she heard the passionate words that that man spoke! Who knows what emotions were set in motion in that young and lonely heart!

At times, she would smile sweetly and stare out into space; but then, as if she had been assaulted by a bitter memory, she would shake her head in painful resignation, and whisper under her breath:

"You are the daughter of misfortune, an inheritor of heaven's punishment, a victim who must atone for the sin's of another—remember your vow, and do not forget that this world is not your kingdom."

Plunged again into her implacable sorrow, she would devote herself with even more passion to the mission of piety that she had assigned herself.

"Clemencia," the *mazorquero* said one day to his daughter, "why do I find you sadder and more pensive all the time? Who dares to cause you such sadness? Tell me his name and, upon my life, I swear that you will soon be able to say—poor unfortunate wretch!"

"No one! Father. . . no one!" she answered, her body trembling, and raised her hand instinctively to her heart, as if she feared her father might read some secret written there.

"No. . . you are lying to me. . . . For some time now I have noticed tears even in your voice when you come to embrace me."

"Father . . ." the girl answered, interrupting him, and looking into his bloodstained eyes with her blue and merciful ones, "can you not guess what it is? When, after a night of staying awake, filled with anxiety, I see you finally arrive and I come out to embrace you, I think with deep grief that the children of those unfortunate ones that your band's ax silences daily will no longer be able to enjoy the happiness that God still grants me. Oh, Father! Is that not a good enough reason to be sad and full of tears? In the middle of those bloody scenes, have you never put your hand on your heart and asked yourself what you would do if you were to see a hand holding a dagger come down upon your own daughter and behead her. . . ?"

"Be quiet. . . ! Be quiet, Clemencia. . . !" the bandit yelled. "What would I do? Hell itself knows no rage like that which would drive Roque's arm until I had avenged your death. . . . But you are mad, girl! Do you not know that the savage Unitarians do not have hearts like we do, that they do not know how to love and hate with equal strength, as we do. . . ?"

"Father, you know that that is not true! What do those mothers' heartbreaking screams, the wails of those wives, and the sad cry of those orphans I hear at all hours rising to heaven against us say to you? Do they not say that the fibers broken by your dagger at the bottom of their souls are just as sensitive as ours?"

"Be quiet," he repeated, "be quiet, Clemencia! Your voice is so insinuating and persuasive that you might start to make me believe what you are saying; and what would General Rosas think of his loyal servant then? Can you imagine how much Salomón and Cuitiño would mock their comrade! No, no. . . . Do not go on! I cannot stand listening to you say those things, especially not today, when Manuel Puirredon, that Unitarian bandit who I have sworn myself to behead, roams free among us, as if he were protected by some supernatural power. . . . Oh! But I am only worrying myself in vain. . . what madness! My heart is full of hatred; there is no chance that compassion will find any room in it at all. . . . If you do not believe me, just listen to this story. . . .

"A few months ago, I went to the Church of the Succor to hear Mass."

"Father! You dared enter the temple of God with your hands stained as they are!"

"Stained with blood? Yes, of course. And why not, for they are stained with Unitarian blood, and the Unitarians are the enemies of God.

"I went in, as I was saying, to the Church of the Succor. The Mass was just beginning when a man kneeling next to me turned suddenly toward me and stared at me for a moment, as if to make sure I was who he thought I was. Then he gave me a look of contempt, and left my side with insolent repugnance, going to the opposite side of the church. His look and his deed gave him away as a Unitarian. The wretch had recognized Roque; but he did not know the extent of Roque's vengeance.

"I did not take my eyes off him during the entire Mass; after he left the church, I followed him, until he went into a small, run-down house.

"That night, while that man, having completely forgotten his affront to me, was spending the evening peacefully with his two small children in his arms, next to his wife, who was embroidering the decorations on the wardrobe for a third soon to be born, I led the *Mazorca* to his house. And, while he was still in the arms of his wife and children, I plunged my dagger a thousand times into his chest, splashing blood everywhere, even on the diapers of the baby who had not yet seen the light of day.

"Clemencia! Clemencia! What is wrong with you?"

The murderer reached out to hold up his daughter, who was shaking and swaying unsteadily, trying to keep him away from her with an expression of horror, which she could barely disguise, on her face.

"For some time," he continued, "I thought I felt the feeling that they call remorse, for I could not erase that memory of blood, screams, and tears from my mind; my imagination kept recalling it to me. But, no! It was not remorse, but rather the joy of satisfied revenge. The day that Roque comes to know compassion or remorse, the blade of this weapon will dull.... And look at how brightly it still shines today," the bandit said, brandishing his wide dagger in front of his daughter's eyes.

Then, quickly sliding it back into the folds of his *chiripá*,[4] he went off, doubtlessly to return to his horrendous labors.

Clemencia felt completely crushed under the weight of the appalling words she had just heard. Weak, disheartened, faint, she went and collapsed at the feet of her divine protectress, raising her hands toward her, beseeching her in anguished supplication.

As she prayed, hope and faith slowly returned to her heart. When she stood up again, her countenance once again glowed with the serenity of resignation.

"It is never late for your infinite mercy, God" she said, turning her eyes toward heaven. "The time of repenting has not yet arrived; but it shall come, it shall come."

Immediately she went to the chest that she kept for the unfortunate victims. She took a basket of goods and a small bag of gold with her, and with the aid of the shadows of the night, she headed off to look for the house that her father had just spoken about.

She recognized the house by the marks made by the bandit's axes in breaking down the postern, leaving it wide open. Clemencia was about to cross the threshold into an empty and miserable room when she heard a voice inside and stopped to take in the sight that presented itself to her.

In one corner of the room, on a simple bed with few coverings, a woman was lying; she was young, but pale and thin, and held a newborn in her arms. Further on, a six-year-old boy, and another of four years of age, were sitting under the covers of a small bed suspended like a cradle by four ropes tied around a crossbeam in the ceiling.

The dim light from a candle burning on the floor lent the dwelling a gloomy appearance. This, plus the thought of the dreadful scene that had recently taken place there, broke Clemencia's heart.

........

[4] The *chiripá* are the pants worn by gauchos, made of an embroidered worsted shawl with a corner drawn between the legs over lace pantaloons. —Trans.

"Mother," the youngest of the two boys said in a sad voice. "What did you do with the bread we ate yesterday?"

The mother sighed deeply, a mournful exhalation, while the other boy answered in a serious, resigned tone:

"We ate it, Enrique, we ate it and Mother does not have any money to buy another one because she is sick and cannot work. Do not torment her; let us just go to sleep, like the poor little angel that heaven sent us yesterday."

"Oh! He has my mom's breast and I'm hungry. . . . I'm hungry!" Enrique said, crying.

"My God!" the mother exclaimed between sobs. "If in the wisdom of your designs you deigned that the murderous ax should cut down the strongest tree, I welcome your will and resign myself to it. But have mercy on these tender flowers that are just now starting to open themselves to the rays of your sun. Dear Lord! You who feed the birds of the air and the worms of the earth, and who hears my children crying, hungry, can you not send one of the thousands of angels who live in heaven down to help them. . . ?

"Ah! There it is," she murmured, as she saw Clemencia kneeling down in front of the children's bed, handing them the goods she had brought.

The mother put her hands together and stared with religious fascination at the beautiful young woman, whose white veil, folded back like a halo around her face, seemed to illuminate the darkness that surrounded her, and who, bending over the children like a merciful spirit, looked at them with eyes full of affection and pain. The poor woman thought Clemencia was an angel who had come down in response to her prayers; she sat motionless, afraid that just one move, one gust of wind, would make the divine vision vanish and bring them back to their dreadful reality. When Clemencia approached her bed, the simple woman stretched her hand out anxiously to touch Clemencia's to convince herself that she was indeed not a supernatural apparition.

"Oh! You, who have come to deliver comfort in this home full of suffering," she exclaimed, putting her arms around Clemencia's knees, "who are you, you angelic creature?"

"I am a miserable being, just like you, and I have come looking for fellow suffering companions. I have come to say to you: Christian mother, trust in he who wipes away all tears and silences all cries. He watches over all of us from the heights of heaven and can turn the weakest of creatures into an instrument of his mercy. You have been left alone and without protection? I will be near you and you will be my dear sister. Your children are in need of a protector? I will be one for them. You are in need of just about everything? I have brought gold so that you may buy it."

"Ah! You are a saint!" the widow said, bowing down devotedly, "bless my child and give him a name, for he has not yet been baptized."

And she placed the newborn in Clemencia's arms.

"Call him Manuel," she said in a low voice. As she uttered the name, the virgin's pale face blushed over and her eyes shone with a strange brilliance.

"Manuel," she went on, kissing the baby shyly, "I shall be your solicitous and loving godmother. But your own mother will not be jealous of me, for all your caresses will be for her. All I will need to be happy is the joy of being able to say every day, 'Manuel, I love you!'"

"Oh, my!" the poor mother exclaimed, grabbing Clemencia's hand, covering her own eyes with it, and crying deeply. "You will be everything to him soon enough. My husband calls to me from heaven. The murderer's dagger was unable to break the bond that joined our souls; although I do not wish it, and I cry bitterly for these other souls who will stay behind, suffering on earth, my soul will soon be leaving this world to join my husband again," the poor woman said, pointing to her children in a desperate gesture.

Clemencia listened to her, terrified. The murderer's daughter was thinking, trembling, horrified, about her father's crimes, the image of which had never presented itself as frighteningly and clearly as this. But overcoming the gloomy thoughts that overwhelmed her, she reminded the mother of her duties while she was still in this world, and reminded both of them of the need to resign oneself to heaven's will.

"Mother," the oldest boy said when they were alone again, "which of the Lord's angels was the one who just came to visit us? She has such beautiful hair, in long curls like those of our Lady of Succor!"

"And her eyes, Mother," the younger one said, "her eyes were blue like the sky. And her eyelashes, is it not true that they looked like the rays of that star looking down at us through the window?"

"Yes, my children," the widow said, smiling sadly at her boys, "she is a beautiful angel that God has down here on earth to comfort sad, unfortunate ones."

"Ah! She's an earth angel—that's why she was so unhappy. I saw her crying while she was making our beds."

"What is the angel's name, Mother?"

"Whatever it might be, let us bless it, my children, and pray to God that he dries her tears as she has dried ours," the widow said, making the boys kneel down to say their evening prayers.

V

Clemencia, meanwhile, walked away with slow, unsteady steps. The expression on her face revealed a deep sorrow. She was thinking of the omnipotence of evil and of the impotence of good. Just one blow from a dagger was all it had taken her father to tear open the unfathomable abyss of misery she had just beheld; whereas she, with a whole life of sacrifices and abnegation, what had she accomplished? To relieve hunger and provide clothing; to cure material aches—but for the sorrows of the soul, she had been able to provide nothing but tears. And it was this thought that made Clemencia feel overwhelmed and tremendously disheartened. But as always, when she feared her faith might be wavering, the virgin girl raised her thoughts toward God, and asked him for some large sacrifice that would reveal the secret of how happiness might descend where sadness now reigned.

Then she heard a name repeated many times in fierce tones; this awakened Clemencia abruptly from her sad meditations. She looked around her and realized she was right next to a group of men whose sinister appearance drew her attention. They wore long ponchos and were carefully guarding a door, all of them armed with daggers. Those men were her father's comrades; that building was the headquarters of the intendancy, the site devoted to secret executions, where Unitarians entered in peace never to come out again, and inside the vaults of which the finger of terror wrote Dante's lugubrious inscription.

While Clemencia, shaking and quivering anxiously, tried to hide behind a column to hear what those men were saying, a rider arrived mounted on a black horse; he pulled hard on the reigns of his racing, spirited steed, cursing as he did so and making his long sword belts knock loudly against the butt of the spear that he brandished in his hand. Then he approached the group guarding the door.

"Lieutenant Corbalan,"[5] he shouted in a hoarse, curt voice from atop his horse, "take twenty men and circle down to the Bajo, while I do a sweep in Barracas. With the devil as my witness, I swear that I will cease being who I am if the sun rises tomorrow and the day does not see Manuel Puirredon's head on the end of this spear!"

And digging his spurs into the sides of his horse, he galloped off like a dark whirlwind.

Clemencia, pale and cold with fright, fell to her knees. The man who had just made that horrible oath was her father.

"Corbalan," one of the bandits said, "take me with you. . . . I want to kill men, not stay here and guard women."

"If Black-Soul had given you the woman that is down in the cell of the Three Crosses, it would not have been so hard for you to guard her, would it?" another one of the men said in a frightening tone.

........

[5] Manuel Corvalán (modern spelling) (1774–1847) defended Buenos Aires against the English invasions, and collaborated with San Martín. When Rosas came to power, Corvalán became his adviser and close confidant, loyal to Rosas throughout his days in power.

"Ah! That old tiger! He surprises the beautiful woman waiting for her loved one, he ties her like a lamb to the back of his saddle, he brings her hidden under a poncho to the intendancy, he locks her up in the cell of the Three Crosses, which is the site of over fifty graves. . . . I wonder what he plans to do with her now."

"No more and no less than kill her instead of her husband, or kill her with her husband if he is able to catch him!"

Clemencia had heard enough. She got up, strong and determined, and walked boldly toward the leader of the bandits. Then she raised her veil and looked at him with her father's black eyes, saying in a commanding tone:

"Lieutenant Corbalan! Do you know who I am?"

"The commander's daughter!" the *mazorquero* exclaimed, unmasking himself.

The bandits moved out of the way respectfully, and the young lady, without deigning to say another word to them, walked directly past them and into the shadows of the ominous building.

In the darkness of the gloomy entrance hall before the patio with the cells, Clemencia saw a man standing motionless, leaning on a halberd. He wore a guard's uniform; she thought that he must be a sentry. But when she approached him, she started.

The young woman did not need to see his face, which was covered by the wide sleeve of one of the hoods used by the men in the quarters, to recognize him.

"You poor soul!" Clemencia whispered into his ear, grabbing his arm in fright. "What are you doing here? Did you not hear what the men just said outside?"

"Yes," he answered, cutting her off. "I am the one who those murderers are looking for so fiercely. Their daggers are hanging over my head, but I have come to save my beloved, or to perish with her. Look," he went on, kicking a shapeless bulk lying on the ground next to him, "I have killed a guard, and now, dressed in his uniform, I am waiting here and will drop to my feet the first man that comes through the threshold of that door."

"Manuel Puirredon!" Clemencia said, uncovering her beautiful face and staring into the eyes of the exile with an indescribable look, "do you remember me?"

"It is she. . ." the Unitarian exclaimed, "the angel that saved my life. . .!"

"Do you trust me? Would you leave to me the task of saving the woman you have come to rescue?"

"Ah!" he answered, with an enraptured passion that Clemencia tried to ignore, frightened, "just for saying those words, beautiful creature, you have me at your feet, at your service. Ask me anything . . . to spill my blood. . . for my soul. . . I give you everything."

"Leave this foreboding place, then. Walk through that fateful door, and go wait for your beloved where she was waiting for you not so long ago."

"No! I will do anything. . . except take even one step away from here without her."

"Oh! My Lord! He is determined to get himself killed! . . . Very well, then. In that case, swear to me that you will stay here, with your disguise on, without moving, and not attack anyone, no matter who they might be, who comes through there."

"That is a hard promise to make! . . . But since you wish it, so be it!"

"Thank you! Thank you!" she exclaimed, squeezing the exile's hand, on which he felt a tear fall. "Be happy, Manuel Puirredon. . . . Good-bye!"

The young woman lowered her veil and disappeared into the shadows.

The Unitarian heard the clanking sound of locks and bolts opening in the distance and said:

"That is the door to her cell. . . . Emilia! My Emilia!"

And with his eyes and ears perked up, he waited attentively in the silent night in anguish. And in that manner, two, five, ten minutes went by, each seeming to last a century. Puirredon, in his implacable restlessness, was finally about to break his oath and run after the woman who had imposed it on him.

But then, from a distance, he suddenly saw Clemencia's white veil appear in the darkness of the gloomy corridor. Puirredon saw that she came alone, and, forgetting his promise, forgetting the danger he was in, forgetting everything, he let out a pained moan and ran to meet her. But when he reached her, he felt affectionate arms embrace him around the neck, and fiery lips drown out his shout of pleasure.

"Silence, my beloved!" a sweet, loving voice said in the ear of the exile. "I have been saved by a miracle. The Virgin of Succor has come down to my cell to set me free. Yes. I recognized her in her sky-blue beauty and in the melancholic smile of her divine lips. This is her sacred veil. . . it will protect us. . . . Let us get away from here. . ."

And the enshrouded woman dragged the exile away with her.

When the fugitives reached the door, they saw a rider who made his horse prance into the entrance hall, then jump to the ground, and, drawing his dagger, head in a fierce silence toward the patio with the cells.

As they saw him, Puirredon felt his partner's hand shake in his, and he heard her murmur under her veil in a terrified tone:

"It is Black-Soul!!!"

A little later they both crossed the evil threshold and were able to breathe in the fragrant air of freedom.

Meanwhile, Black-Soul crossed the patio; upon reaching the cell of the Three Crosses, he shoved open the heavy bolts and felt his way into the darkness.

A stray ray of light from the waning moon slid through the narrow window of the vault; it formed a leaden stain on the wet stone floor and made the darkness of the frightening dungeon around it even darker. The bandit's greedy eye, however, spotted the white shape it was looking for in the corner.

He stormed toward her, reached out with his bloodstained hand, and, feeling a woman's throat, plunged his dagger into it, shouting in anger:

"You are an informer, you have given away our secrets. You are an accomplice of the vile Unitarians, and now you will die in place of the conspirator you love. But you should know before you do that not even your bones will be together, for your grave will be at the bottom of this dungeon."

Then he let out a loud, terrifying laugh.

When she felt herself to be mortally wounded, the poor girl reached with her hands for her sliced throat and tried to hold back the blood spurting from the wound.

"Oh, God!" she murmured. "My sacrifice has been consummated! Now that the mission that I set for myself here on earth has been fulfilled, make my blood, oh Lord, cleanse that other blood that cries out to you from this world."

When he heard that voice, Black-Soul felt his heart break and his hairs stand on end. He got up quickly, picked his victim up in his arms, and ran to the light under the window, where he looked at her bloodied face in the moonlight.

"Clemencia!" the murderer shouted in a horrible howl.

"Father! . . . My poor father! . . . Turn your eyes toward heaven and look for her there," the girl stammered in her sweet voice as she exhaled her last breath.

The bandit collapsed to the ground, holding the decapitated body of his daughter in his arms. . . .

But the virgin's blood found grace before the eyes of God and, like a baptism of redemption, it made a divine ray of light shine down on that man, and it reformed him.

# 5

# The Black Glove

*paints a picture*

## I. A TOKEN OF FRIENDSHIP

It was one of those delightful nights in the Argentine countryside. The moon bathed the banks of the Río de la Plata in its silver beams and lit up the plants and trees of the shadowy orchards and the poplar-lined promenades of the thousand beautiful country homes and manors that surround Buenos Aires. Although it was not so very late, everything was quiet and deserted outside the great city, and the only sounds that could be heard were the rippling of the waves of the nearby river, and the whistling of the wind through the leafs of the willow trees.

All of a sudden, a human voice, a woman's heavenly voice, joined these sounds of nature; her voice rising softly and timidly from one of those avenues lined thickly with trees, the woman began to sing with an inexpressibly melodious voice that adorable aria from "Romeo and Juliet":

*Sei pur tu che ancor rivedo?*[1]

........
[1] "Is it you whom I see again?" (Italian) —Trans.

But the song was interrupted by the sounds of an approaching carriage.

An elegant covered carriage stopped at the foot of the front steps of one of the country manors. A hunter dressed in luxurious livery opened the door and offered his hand to a beautiful young lady with a svelte and graceful figure and a quick, imperious look; light as a bird, she jumped off the footboard and raced up the front steps and into the entrance hall of the house.

When he saw her, the concierge in the first vestibule bowed deeply.

"My friend," she said, glancing around with restless eyes, "is your young master sleeping?"

"My master is wounded, madam, and. . ."

"I know, I know; that is why I am here. Take me to his room."

The concierge bowed again and led the young lady through a gallery that opened into an inner garden. He then stopped in front of a door, which he was about to open so as to announce the lady; but she brushed him aside, smiling, and opened the door herself. She ran through an elegant hall and entered a bedroom illuminated by a gas lamp; at the far end, between two mounted gauntlets, there was a bed, and in it lay a young man with a handsome and sympathetic physiognomy. His wide, broad forehead showed the signs of haughty intelligence, while under long eyelashes, his large, black eyes flashed, revealing the clash of strong and opposing passions. His bright hair flowed in thick curls down to his neck, and a black, silky mustache, quite enviable indeed, was wound gracefully above a mouth that could make a woman quiver with fear, or love.

The young lady ran toward him; then, raising her veil over her lovely face with one hand, and handing him her other, she said, "Wenceslao! I have taken too long to come, I know!"

"What is this that I see? Manuelita![2] You, here?"

........

[2] Manuela Rosas (1817–1898), daughter of Juan Manuel de Rosas and Encarnación Ezcurra. A legendary figure in literature written by opponents of the Rosas regime, Manuelita was represented as a gentle figure who extended herself to aid Unitarian supporters oppressed by Rosas's secret police. Lettered men such as José Mármol often depicted Manuelita as a

"Did you think me ungrateful? Oh! The fact is that, although I was dying of impatience and desire to see you, I could not pull myself away for even one moment from my father's looks, or from that awful crowd of suitors and flatterers that is always around me."

"Me, think you ungrateful? Oh, no, Manuelita! I know that you have thought about me; besides, even your slightest regards are so precious to my heart that I believe I could not properly repay them even if I were to sacrifice my whole life and soul for you. . . . But allow me to convince myself that this happiness at seeing you here, at this hour, leaning over my bed, is not a dream."

And removing the black, tulle glove embroidered with arabesques that covered her lovely hand, he impressed upon it a kiss that must have been quite passionate, for Manuelita quickly withdrew her hand and looked down as a scarlet cloud descended upon her face.

"Oh, you flatterer!" she said, trying to calm herself and smile. "There is nothing more natural than for me to be here, at this time, leaning over your bed like this. A wicked gentleman attacked my honor, believing that he could thus discredit my father's administration—as if dishonor, thrown like that in the face of a young woman, could cast a shadow over the bright star of the mighty Rosas. But you stood up to defend your childhood friend, disarming your adversary and forcing him to admit the falsity of the claims he made from Montevideo.[3] In the process, however, you were wounded, and it is my duty not just to come to see you, but to be your nurse. How sweet it would have been to my heart to devote myself entirely to you! But I have been kept far from you by my father's need for me and by the terror of that world that has taken over my life in order to destroy it, as if I were not already sad and vexed enough! Oh! Wenceslao! Why can we not turn the clock back and be with your mother and mine in the cool shade of Luján once again?"

---

lost soul in need of rescue by Unitarians, while women writers opposing the Rosas regime often depicted her as a perverse and sinister figure (cf. Juana Manso de Noronha, *Los misterios del Plata*, 1846). —Ed.

[3] Montevideo was the city to which many opponents of Rosas fled. —Ed.

The daughter of the dictator raised her eyes, perhaps to keep tears from flowing down her cheeks, and rested her lovely head against one of the columns of the bed.

Sitting up, Wenceslao pressed the young lady's hand against his wounded chest and exclaimed, "Manuelita, beautiful flower among brambles! The world in which you live is not worthy of you. Unable to understand you, it seeks to defame you; but if it is at all possible that a loyal, committed, and energetic man might do anything about your misfortune to live in a world that does not understand you, you have but to command me—my life is yours. This heart, which beats under your hand, is completely faithful to you. Confide in it, impart some of your sorrows to it."

Manuelita pressed the young man's hand tenderly and a melancholy smile spread across her face.

"Oh, my friend!" she said. "The much envied fate of Manuela Rosas has condemned her heart to loneliness and isolation, removing all her friends from her one by one. Those who have not emigrated have joined the army of Lavalle, that implacable enemy of my father; and although I know that they still hold a tender memory of my friendship, duty demands that I eject theirs from my heart.[4] You yourself, Wenceslao, the last and dearest of them all, shall only be near me for a short while longer; I saw on my father's writing desk your dispatch as second in command to the regiment led by your father Colonel Ramírez, and the order for the regiment to head North."

"What is this? Leave you behind! Leave Buenos Aires! Oh!" Wenceslao exclaimed in a voice that expressed a mysterious sorrow.

The young lady understood, quickly got up, and covered her face with her veil. She said, "Good-bye, Wenceslao," stretching her hand out over the bed cover to retrieve the glove that he had removed. "It is eleven o'clock and I do not have much time to reach Palermo

........

[4] Juan Lavalle (1797–1841), independence war hero and initially a comrade of Rosas. When, ill-advised, he ordered the execution of Dorrego, civil war erupted and Rosas turned against him. —Ed.

before the house doors are closed. . . . But . . . what did I do with my glove?"

"I have it," Wenceslao said, uncovering his chest to show the glove resting on his heart. "Manuelita, I would like to save it forever in memory of this evening. But how should I keep it? As a memento of a conquest or as a token?"

"As a token of friendship," she answered, raising the tip of her veil with graceful coquetry and sending Wenceslao a kiss from the door.

"She loves me!" he said when the door closed behind Manuelita. "She loves me and I could be her husband and thus realize the happiness and prosperity that I have dreamed of for my country for so long—if only a fatal love had not come to darken, with tempestuous winds, the bright horizon of ambition and glory that had opened up before me. Isabel! Isabel! Why did I have to meet you? Why did your eyes and voice penetrate so deeply into my heart?"

At that moment the voice that had sung in the avenue lined with poplars was heard once again.

"That is her voice! That is she!" Wenceslao exclaimed, sitting up and pushing open the spring of a secret door at the head of his bed.

## II. THE BLACK GLOVE

The door opened and revealed the countryside illuminated by the moonbeams in the distance; through it entered a white, airy, and ethereal figure, like a wili from a German ballad. It was a young woman wrapped in a long, white dressing gown, with a gauze veil over her head. She was fairly tall; her long hair, bright and jet-black, fell in dark waves to the floor; and her slanted, black eyes, with their wide pupils, had that long, penetrating look attributed to those who can tell fortunes.

When he saw her, the memory of Manuelita, and with it all thoughts of glory and ambition, fled from Wenceslao's mind.

"Isabel! My beautiful angel, my kind fairy!" he exclaimed. "You are here! Oh! May my mother forgive her son's ungratefulness. But how I thank God for her absence, which forces you to come to me like a guardian angel, among the shadows and the silence of the night, to cure my wound with your hands, and to flood my heart with pleasure from the magic of your eyes, of your voice, of your smile! . . . But . . . you are pale! . . . Trembling! Do you not have even one caress, even one word of love for he who loves you? Isabel! What sorrow darkens your brow, my love?"

"Nothing has changed with me," she answered, kneeling at the foot of the bed and forcing Wenceslao to lie back down on his pillow. "Nothing has changed—the sun has shone brightly; the birds have sung their lovely melodies to me, since my harp has been silent ever since your suffering began; the beautiful stars of our skies smile upon me as always; you, whom I love passionately, are right here, near me, and I see your love in your eyes; and yet, there has been something in that sun, in those fragrances, in those melodies, in the night, in the stars, and in your eyes, something doleful that weighs down my heart like lead!

"Listen, Wenceslao. When my mother was carrying me in her womb, she heard me cry one night, when she was up thinking about the being to whom she was about to give birth. There is a belief in our country, a superstition, if you will, that asserts that if a child cries inside its mother's womb, and if the mother keeps this event secret, then the child will be born with the gift of divination. My mother kept quiet, believing that she was thus giving me something joyous. Oh, poor Mother! She did not know what a mournful present she was in fact bequeathing upon her daughter's destiny! Weighed down like everything that exists to that eternal order called fatality, I feel misfortune arrive, but am unable to avoid it; I recognize its approach in the air, in the light, in the shadows, but I am ignorant of from whence it comes and of the moment in which it will strike me. When my father fell to the blows of the Mazorca, that organization of savages, I had already seen the entire event in my dreams. Each of the misfortunes of my life has first been revealed to me in my heart. Today, I have been pursued by the most horrendous hallucinations; my spirit has witnessed horrible scenes in which murder exercised its bloody actions; and I have heard the voice of jealousy, that fatal disease of the soul, scream in doleful tones: 'Betrayal! Treachery!' Right now, Wenceslao, when I entered your room, I felt a shadow near me, an enemy spirit that blocked my way; and, like the hand of a rival, it sought to keep me far away from you. My heart suffered so much that, as I approached your bed and found you alone waiting for the presence and care of your Isabel, I actually thanked God for your wounds, as they have delivered you exclusively to my love, and I even wished that your sufferings would last forever so that you would never cease to need me!"

"My love," Wenceslao answered, kissing the young woman's hands fervently, "there are words that are only meant to be heard on one's knees, and such are the ones you have just uttered. What have I done to deserve the love of a being as beautiful and sublime as you? And, possessing this joy that would be the envy of all the angels in heaven, would I repay it with treachery, instead of with eternal adoration? Oh, my Isabel! Banish those senseless fears that are but an affront to you and your love."

Wenceslao spoke sincerely, for, as has been said, his thoughts of ambition had vanished in the presence of Isabel. The young woman smiled with tenderness and shook her head sadly.

At that moment the clock in the hall struck midnight.

"My God!" Isabel said. "It is midnight, and I have not yet looked after your wound."

A terrible image flashed like lightning through Wenceslao's mind, and he quickly brought his hands up to his chest.

But it was too late! Isabel had uncovered him to change the dressing on the wound.

A deep silence reigned in the room. Wenceslao, struck dumb with confusion and terror, looked at Isabel; she, pale as ghost, now held a black glove in her hands, inspecting it with a fierce and steady gaze.

Then, all of a sudden, her large eyes opened inordinately widely; a muffled cry burst from her chest; her arms fell listlessly to her sides; her feet faltered; and, falling on her knees, she slumped to the floor, hiding her face.

Inside the glove, on the band that covered the elastic, Isabel had read the name of Manuela Rosas.

"Isabel! My love, oh, please deign to listen to me for a moment! Do not condemn me without hearing me out!" Wenceslao exclaimed, stretching his arms out to try to lift her up. But she rejected him silently and stayed as she was.

She remained motionless in that position for a long while, silent and indifferent to Wenceslao's pleas.

Then she raised her head, brushed her hand across her forehead, as if recalling a memory, and stood up.

"Oh, my poor father!" she exclaimed, crossing her arms and turning her deep eyes up to the heavens. "This blow to my heart is due punishment for a daughter guilty of betraying her oath and leaving your bloody shadow roaming behind, forgotten, irreverently exchanging your unrequited vengeance for the love of a Federal.

"Ah, Father! Perhaps it was necessary for him to push me from his heart so that the memory of your ill-fated death and the sense of my duty might return to mine. But it is not too late, Father. The oath that I made to you in the dark vaults of your prison cell shall not have been made in vain; I hereby renew my pledge to consecrate the doleful existence that still awaits me to carry out your vengeance and to pursue the triumph of your cause, the testimony of which you sealed with your martyrdom!"

And, turning toward her lover, who had listened to her in great dismay, she said, "Good-bye, Wenceslao! This is the last time that I will ever say your name, that name which my lips once took so much pleasure in ceaselessly repeating as it resonated in my heart like a delightful melody. Good-bye forever! May you love in peace that Manuela Rosas, whose reward for love you wear on your heart; and when you think about Isabel, remember her without any regrets, for your betrayal has led her to the path of duty, as it has led you to the path of honor and happiness."

Wenceslao had remained motionless until this moment, oppressed by the weight of the indisputable proof. But now he raised his pale face with pride and said to the young lady, who had already taken a step toward the door: "Isabel! In the name of your father, listen to me for a moment, for just one, brief moment!"

Isabel turned her white countenance back toward him.

"Oh! Isabel! Do you refuse to listen to me? Deign, then, to tell me yourself, my love, what can I do to convince you that no other image has ever approached the sanctuary that you hold in my heart? Speak! Even if I have to go down to the very pits of hell to rescue your love, there I shall go."

A deep sob raised Isabel's chest; wavering and trembling, she lowered her eyes so that Wenceslao would not see her love for him in them.

But her gaze suddenly fell on the black glove that lay on the floor, and a convulsive shaking ran through her body, and a flash of tremendous anger blazed in her eyes. Then one of those evil thoughts, born of jealousy and capable of transforming angels into demons, flashed before her and grasped at her heart.

"Let him die for my love," she murmured, "as long as he leaves her forever!"

And fixing her bewitching eyes on Wenceslao, she said:

"There is a place from which you could persuade me that what I have seen tonight has been nothing but a dream, one of those nightmares that comes to torment one's heart; but that place is. . . that place is among the ranks of the Unitarian army!"

And she disappeared into the shadows that stretched out beyond the door.

Wenceslao remained motionless for a few moments, crushed by the weight of those terrible words. His eyes closed, his heart stopped beating, and cold beads of perspiration covered his forehead. Then an immense sense of desperation invaded his heart and shook him with terrifying force.

"I have lost her forever!" he exclaimed, striking himself on the top of his head. "She does not love me anymore, for she wishes me to be dishonored. She wants me to abandon the cause that my sword has defended ever since I was a small child, the cause of my illustrious benefactor. . . the cause of my childhood friend! In short, she wants me to become a traitor! Oh! Isabel! . . . Never. . . never. . . . But what am I to do with my empty and silent life, now that it will no longer be illuminated by your love? How am I to bear all those hours, all those days that were made so delightful by your presence? For losing you means more than just losing the heart of a woman; it means losing the very air, the light, the sky. . . . Oh! I would be better off dead!"

And taking a homicidal hand to his own chest, he pulled the bandages off his wound, tearing it open again.

The blood gushed onto the bed; then, little by little, the desperation that had been devastating Wenceslao's soul was slowly lulled to sleep. A bluish haze spread before his eyes; a disorienting rumbling invaded his ears as he ceased to hear external sounds; the cold of death began to take over his limbs; and his heart filled with that sense of peace that must surely await us all on the other side of the grave, and which is always seen painted on the faces of the dead.

### III. A MOTHER

All of a sudden, a soft, sweet voice came to interrupt the silence of his agony.

"Oh, my God!" the voice was heard to utter between sobs. "I have arrived just in time to save him! Wenceslao!"

"Isabel!" murmured the dying young man faintly.

A woman rushed over to the blood-soaked bed. She was tall, with a countenance sweet and beautiful in spite of the extreme paleness that now covered it. Her look revealed a soul that had suffered greatly, and a fire burning inside her chest.

With Wenceslao's head resting on her chest, and her arms around him, she tried to stem the flow of blood gushing out of the wound. She spoke to him in a soft and loving voice, as her tears fell on the youth's face.

"Oh!" she said when she heard his lips utter Isabel's name. "He does not recognize me; he loves another, but it does not matter! God bless the name that brings him back to life! Oh, God, return him to me, even if he only thinks of me after all his other loves! For I know that although he fills my entire soul, I am not the one who should fill his."

Who was that woman, who loved so greatly and was also capable of carrying out a saintly self-sacrifice stronger than jealousy, that powerful demon that builds its hell within the confines of the human heart?

She was a mother.


### IV. THE LETTER

A few days later, that same woman was walking, or rather wandering about aimlessly like a shadow, alone under the tall trees of the gardens of the country manor. Her countenance was even paler than before, and her eyes revealed a gloomy restlessness.

"My God!" she was saying. "What could be the origin of that deep sorrow, of that horrible anger, that has taken over my husband ever since that government spy handed him that letter. I have heard him murmur Wenceslao's name, accompanied by awful curses. Oh! What misfortune still threatens my beloved son? Most Holy Virgin!" she continued, kissing a reliquary containing the image of the Virgin Mary and a strand of Wenceslao's hair. "You who suffered so much in this vale of tears, have mercy on the suffering of a mother, in memory of your own suffering! Protect my son! If there are any dangers still awaiting him in his path, save him, as you have done before! Make him happy, and give me, instead, all his woes in this world. . . .

"But I cannot go on any longer with this terrible uncertainty that is making me suffer so much, that is making each moment seem like an entire century. That letter must be in. . . it must be in his writing desk. . . . I know that he is not there right now. . . that he has gone to the drawing room. . . . What would happen if I went quickly to look at the letter? Yes, I will go! Oh, Ramírez, do forgive me! I am not an imprudent wife scrutinizing her husband's secrets; I am a mother watching over the fate of her son."

She hurried along one of the long avenues lined with trees, under the already darkening evening, opened a low window, and, after looking around carefully, climbed in.

"There is no one around," she murmured, "no one," and entered a room surrounded by bookcases, with weapons mounted on the walls, and a writing desk filled with papers, above which hung a portrait of General Belgrano in an elegant frame.

Among a thousand other ones, the mother's eyes recognized the letter she sought, which contained the information she so feared. She grabbed it with a shaky hand; then, looking at the writing on the envelope as she opened it, said, "My God! It is Wenceslao's handwriting—my son!"

A black glove slid from within the folded letter and fell at the feet of Wenceslao's mother, making her scream suddenly.

"Oh! Why has this object frightened me so much? As if it were the hand of death come to take possession of my heart!"

After looking around her, she began to read:

"Isabel.

"The man to whom you have given the horrible alternative of either being a traitor or living without you, that strong man whose friends have referred to as a lion when he fights, has succumbed miserably in the battle between love and duty. Oh, shame! Honor, duty, friendship, gratefulness—all the noble sentiments of the heart have been silenced by the thought of losing you forever, of renouncing the joy of looking at your face, of burning under the fire of your eyes, of feeling the touch of your hand, of hearing the sound of your voice.

"Your lover, for whom honor is everything in life, will soon bear the mark of desertion on his forehead, a baptism of shame so strong that even death itself will not be able to erase it. The army of Lavalle is currently a two-day journey from here, and soon the sun will see me among its ranks, turning my vilified sword against the cause that once held all my sympathies, against my protector, against my own father.

"In this letter you will find that glove that was at the root of so much pain. Send it to Manuela Rosas, and tell her that her childhood friend, the man in whose heart she had searched for an asylum from slander, is no longer worthy of owning that token of friendship, because he has now become a traitor.

"Isabel! Thus have you wished it! So be it!"

The poor mother was unable to read the last words of the letter. A convulsive trembling shook her limbs, a frozen fear invaded her heart; the letter slipped out of her hands, her legs folded beneath her, and she fell on the floor like an inert weight. When she came to, her mind still befuddled, she heard two voices nearby. The weakness that paralyzed her limbs impeded her from moving; she remained hidden in the long pleats of the carpet.

"Bracho!" Colonel Ramírez was saying to his favorite servant, who was thus called because he had been born in the hot desert of the same name.[5] "Although I have absolute confidence in you, I need you to swear to something."

Bracho responded in military fashion:

"At your service, my colonel! Your loyal soldier is ready to obey you."

The colonel went up to him, took his hand firmly, placed the other one on his own heart, and said to him in a solemn voice:

"Bracho! Swear to me on the days of our many past troubles and glories, and on the immaculate laurels that we earned together through thirty years of service on so many battlefields, that you shall remain absolutely silent about everything that I am about to tell you, and that you will take it with you to the grave."

Bracho's grave, bronze-colored countenance became graver still. His hand responded to the colonel's pressure; placing his other hand on his own heart, he answered in a firm voice:

"I so swear!"

"Bracho," the colonel continued, pointing to a pick and shovel lying on the floor. "Take those tools that I have had brought here, and dig a hole in that corner of the room over there; make it about seven feet long and six feet deep."

With that cold blood of his—at times admirable and at other times frightening, and so characteristic of the native sons of this land—Bracho pulled up one of the corners of the carpet where it was nailed down and began to follow the orders of his master. For a long

........

[5] Bracho is a desert in the province of Tucumán. —Ed.

time the only sounds heard were the colonel's labored breathing and the rhythmic blows of the pick that Bracho wielded.

A horrible premonition invaded the mother's soul, but she held her breath and continued to listen.

Once the hole had been dug, Bracho leaned on the pick and turned back to face his leader.

The colonel went up to the pit's black opening and measured its depth by sight.

"Bracho!" he said in a doleful voice that sent a cold, deadly feeling into the mother's heart. "In a few hours that pit will contain a corpse! Listen," he went on; "today, in this very place, a great crime will be judged and punished, one as of yet unknown among Argentine soldiers, one that has never before stained our military annals—that of treason!

"Go now into the city and look in the barracks where my regiment is stationed for the second in command; tell him that I order him to meet me here immediately, and advise him to keep absolute secrecy about his destination."

Bracho made an involuntary movement expressing painful surprise when he heard his order. He hesitated and looked at his master, as if he wanted to say something; but a severe look from the colonel made him obey silently.

### V. A MOTHER'S LOVE

"A deserter!" the colonel exclaimed once he found himself alone. "A deserter! An Argentine soldier, a Ramírez, is a deserter! Oh, soul of Belgrano!" he continued painfully, addressing the portrait of the national hero. "Majestic soul of Belgrano, do you not tremble with indignation when you hear the name of your friend—once repeated with honor in the accounts of a hundred battles—now allied with infamy? Do you not moan with pain when you see your old companion's scars dishonored? But no, not dishonored, thank God; the crime has not yet been consummated. And that grave, and this dagger, will soon bury it forever along with the guilty individual."

When she heard the metallic sound that the colonel's thick dagger made as it fell on the table, the poor mother, who until then had been trying to convince herself that all of this was a dream, felt her insides tremble madly. Her heart seemed to sense the cold blade destined for her son's heart. Then, letting out a bloodcurdling scream, she suddenly stood up; she was so pale that she looked like a ghost to her husband's eyes. The startled colonel took a few steps back, and exclaimed:

"Margarita! What are you doing here?"

"Ramírez!" she yelled mournfully. "Oh, have mercy! Tell me that I am insane, and that the horrendous words that I have just heard you pronounce are all part of my delirium! Ramírez! Ramírez! In the name of God, tell me that that grave, that dagger, that frightening sentence, are merely the hallucinations of a horrible nightmare that has taken possession of my mind! Tell me that it is not true, that you are not planning to murder our son! Our son!"

"Your son! Our son!" the colonel exclaimed in an explosion of pain and indignation. "You no longer have a son, you most unfortunate woman; he who was once our son is now a traitor, driven by passion to abandon the sacred flag of our country. His moments in this world are already numbered; they belong only to my judgment. Margarita! Go pray for him, and forget your son's name forever."

"Oh!" the mother exclaimed in a loud and frightening tone. "Pray for him, as if he were already dead? Forget my son's name, that beautiful name of the one who has been the apple of my eye for the past twenty years? Who is telling me to do this? Who? . . . Oh, nobody. . . nobody! Oh, God! I must be mad. . . mad!"

The poor wretch paced back and forth in the room as she said this, wringing her hands, then pressing both palms against her temples, as if she were trying to make the madness burst out of her head.

The tremendous voice of affronted honor had drowned out that of paternal love in the colonel's soul; but it was in turn muted by a mother's desperation. Ramírez felt his heart break and his terrible resolution waver. He stretched his arms out to his wife and said sadly:

"Margarita! Poor mother! Come, cry on the chest of your husband, your friend! I also need to shed tears."

But his eyes suddenly met those of Belgrano; and the firm and penetrating gaze of the national hero, shining clearly from the back of the gloomy room, seemed to reprimand him for his weakness.

Shame then covered the colonel's contorted and livid countenance in shades of purple. His fiery eyes burned, and a long scar on his forehead, a memento of past glories, turned pale on his reddened face, making it look as if he were wearing a sinister crown.

"No!" he said loudly to his wife, and stormed over to stand before the portrait of his old leader. "He who has served by your side," he exclaimed, addressing the portrait of Belgrano, "and has stood calmly in the face of death while the shrapnel of battle flew all around him, will not disprove his courage in carrying out his duty, as terrible as it might be. If my heart gets in the way," he continued, striking himself in the chest, "I will break it, but honor will have been saved; the guilty individual will perish!"

"Oh!" the mother screamed, hurling herself at her husband and shaking his arm wildly. "Could it be true? Do my ears not deceive me? Ramírez! Ramírez! Is it true that the horrible thought that my lips cannot even utter has found a home in your soul? Ah!" she continued, falling at the colonel's feet and grabbing him by the knees. "If you need blood, here—take mine! Take that dagger and cut open each one of my veins, one by one; martyr me, tear out my heart, bury me alive in that empty grave, but have mercy on my son! Respect his life, that precious life that is just now beginning to flower. Oh! Ramírez! If you have forgotten that you are a father, remember at least that you are a man; take pity on his youth, on his beauty and his future, on that wonderful horizon of dreams and promises that you wish to steal from him. The crime has not yet occurred; there is still time for him to repent. What right do you have to be even more severe than God, who always allows the guilty time to recognize and repent for their mistakes?"

But the moment of weakness had already passed for the colonel. His white, severe lips smiled bitterly and disdainfully.

"Repent?" he exclaimed. "Can he redeem himself from a crime that is dishonorable, even if it exists only in the form of a thought?

Margarita! You know that it is not possible! You, who as a young wife told your husband, when he found himself awaiting his death unguarded and staying where he was only because he had given his word of honor to do so: 'Ramírez! It is better to stay and die than to break your word and lose your honor! Nothing can cleanse one's honor once it has been stained!'"

"Ah!" she answered, crying. "But I was a wife then; now I am a mother! Oh! A woman once carried you in her womb and fed you with her own blood; in memory of her, have mercy on a mother who begs you on her knees to save the life of her son!"

The sound of a few horses resonated from the patio of the country manor.

The colonel took his wife violently in his arms, and tried to carry her out of the room; but she grabbed one of the legs of the writing desk, and the woman's thin and delicate fingers became as strong as steel springs that the colonel's strength could not unwind.

"No! I will not be carried out of here," she muttered; "I want to save my son from death, and you from a horrendous crime! I want to put my chest between his and the blows of a murderer!"

"Margarita!" he exclaimed in a solemn tone of voice. "Do you want to watch while your son dies? So be it! You will watch him die, for I swear that nothing can save him!"

When she heard these words, the mother's eyes lit up like those of a wounded lioness. Her tears suddenly dried up, and, standing up, her countenance white and terrible as the image of death itself, she shouted out as she went toward her husband: "Ramírez! Is it true that nothing can save my son from the horrible fate that you have in store for him?"

"Nothing!" the colonel answered firmly.

"Nothing!" she repeated in a strange tone of voice. "Nothing, not my pleas, nor my tears, nor the memory of all the happy days that he has given us in his twenty years of life!"

"Nothing!" he repeated dolefully. "I am a judge, I have condemned a criminal, and I myself will execute the sentence."

"Then you will die!" the mother yelled. "You will die, because I want my son to live, even if it is in a world of ruins."

And seizing the dagger that was lying on the table, she plunged it deep into her husband's chest.

At the same time, the door opened, and a painful, terrifying scream resonated in the room.

"Mother! What have you done?!" Wenceslao exclaimed, throwing himself on the colonel's body, which had fallen, dead, without his having even let out a moan.

The mother turned toward him with the impassability of desperation.

"My husband had sworn that he would kill a traitor," she said; "that traitor was my son. I have killed my husband to save my son!"

The next day, at the head of his regiment, the pale and somber Wenceslao, carrying in his heart the grief of being three times a mourner, marched off to join the army of General Oribe.[6]

Duty had placed a terrible oath between him and happiness. Standing before his father's blood-soaked body, in the hands of his dying mother, he had sworn to forget Isabel forever.

### VI. QUEBRACHO HERRADO

The night of November 28 had descended upon that same man's field.[7]

That day, the sun had witnessed the victory of Oribe's troops and the defeat of the Unitarian army; the latter, composed of warriors who were as generous as they were brave, had stayed and fought the battle with inferior forces and on disadvantageous terrain, rather than undertaking a forced retreat and abandoning the large group of people who were fleeing and had attached themselves to them. But luck did not reward these heroes' courage and sublime self-sacrifice; instead, it crowned the heads of their enemies—who, by the end

........

[6] Manuel Oribe (1792–1857), born in Montevideo, served Artigas, and later became president of Uruguay. A supporter of Rosas, he fought against Lavalle and was named head of the Federal troops. —Ed.

[7] November 28, 1840. Oribe defeated Lavalle at the Battle of Quebracho Herrado. Here, Lavalle lost 1,500 of his 4,200 soldiers. —Ed.

of the day, had become the masters of the field—with the laurels of victory.

What followed the battle was a frightful scene; pillaging, murder, and violence satiated their horrible thirsts on that immense group of venerable old men, beautiful virgins, and innocent children.

But now the tumultuous sounds of the weapons, the screams of the soldiers, and the wailing of the victims had ceased. Darkness veiled the lakes of human blood that had been spilled on the earth; the night winds spread the delightful fragrance of the nearby aromatic forest across the funereal field; the sweet light of the stars reflecting off the faces of the dead lent the scene the appearance of a sweet dream—nothing, in short, revealed that there was a battlefield there, except for the deep silence that reigned everywhere, a silence interrupted only by the long, sad song of the *coyuyo;*[8] the insects, hidden among the dark branches of the carob trees, seemed to bewail the fate of the fallen heroes.

## VII. THE PREDICTION

All of a sudden, the distant echo of a sweet, sad voice was heard, quieting the sad melody of the insects. The voice came nearer, singing Juliet's last song:

> *Oh! Fortunato atendimi. . .*
> *Non mi lasciare arcor. . .*[9]

A white figure, airy and ethereal, emerged from the darkness. The lead sentry of the victorious army, who was camped a few hundred feet in front of the field, crossed himself and closed his eyes when he saw her, believing her to be the soul of one of the deceased from the battle.

........

[8] The *coyuyo* is a large cicada found in the Argentine pampas. —Trans.
[9] "Listen to me, oh fortunate one. . . / Do not leave me yet." (Italian) —Trans.

The white shade entered the area of the battlefield. She was, in fact, in spite of the extreme frailty of her figure, a young and beautiful woman.

Her thick, black hair was lavishly spread on her long, white robe, which looked like a wide mourning veil blown back by the night wind. The look in her large, black eyes was vague and strange, as if there were a shadow between her and the objects around her; as she stopped before the bodies of the dead, her lips alternated between murmuring Juliet's song, praying for the deceased, and saying Wenceslao's name.

"Lezica!" she said, leaning over a corpse and softly brushing aside the silky, brown hair that hid the face of a youth whose beauty had not been stolen by death.[10] "Lezica! You poor child, who came into this world surrounded by luxury and wealth—who could have told your mother, when she rocked you in your cradle, wrapped in gold and silk, that you would sleep your last night on the barren ground of a desert?! And when she kissed your beautiful, blue eyes, how far she must have been from imagining that they would end up, at the end, belonging to the vultures!

"Varela!" she exclaimed, contemplating the stiff, motionless face of a man lying nearby in a pool of his own blood.[11] "Noble scion of that family of swans that has enchanted with its songs the banks of the Río de la Plata. Death has placed its black mark on the laurels of your face; but why?! For there, while the jackal drinks your generous blood, while the tiger devours your heart, in which so many sublime inspirations once burned, the murderer's dagger prepared itself in the shadows to forever silence the poet's song and the patriot's shout for freedom with one single blow! Oh! Oh!" And starting her funereal song anew, she walked on.

The terrain that she crossed was sown with hundreds of corpses and watered with streams of blood, which stained the feet and the

........

[10] Juan Antonio Lezica (1812–1874), a second lieutenant at Quebracho Herrado. He was not murdered but was taken prisoner by Oribe; he later immigrated to Montevideo. —Ed.

[11] Rufino Varela (1815–1840), fought with Lavalle against Rosas and, after Quebracho Herrado, accompanied political prisoners to Oribe's camp and was then executed. —Ed.

white robe of that fantastic traveler. One might have said that it looked as if the sword of the angel of death had cleared a path through there, or that the human hand that had cut short the lives of so many men, had done so to carry out a great act of vengeance, or to redeem itself of a grave deed.

In the distance, and at the end of that blood-soaked road, surrounded by corpses, fired rifles, broken swords and spears, lay the body of a warrior whose noble and handsome face still maintained, even in death, a threatening expression. Although everything indicated that he was the one who had wreaked such havoc on the ranks of his enemy, the latter's blade had not dared to come near him; for that svelte body, elegantly dressed, was untouched, except for the place at which the single bullet that caused his death had entered his heart. His hand still held his sword by its handle, and that terrible, red ribbon, along with a portrait of Rosas and the Unitarian death sentence, waved in the night wind.[12]

The strange traveler came nearer, glancing across the bloody and mutilated faces of the dead, calling their names out in a doleful voice:

"Mons! Torres! Bustillos![13]

"Wenceslao! Wenceslao!" she screamed suddenly; she was carried away by a mad, senseless sense of pleasure and fell to her knees, embracing the corpse of the handsome warrior. "Here I am, my love! I have arrived too late, but you are the one who left your gentle bed at

........

[12] Along with the red ribbon and a portrait of Rosas, the phrase, "Death to the savage Unitarians," was a common way to express loyalty to the Federalist cause. —Ed.

[13] Gregorio Manuel Mons (1773–1840) served in the independence wars and later fought against Rosas. At the battle of Quebracho Herrado, he was taken prisoner and executed several days later by order of Oribe. Manuel José Bustillo (1817–1840) was pursued by Rosas for his conspiracy against Maza in 1839. He joined Lavalle's forces and was killed in the battle of Quebracho Herrado. Of the many oppositional figures bearing the surname Torres, it is most likely that Gorriti refers to Prudencio Torres (1799–1843), who served under Lavalle and Paz, though he intermittently served the cause of the Federals as well. In April 1840, at the battle of San Cristóbal, Torres commanded one of Lavalle's divisions against Urquiza's forces. He later served Lavalle in the Battle of Familliá (September 19, 1841). Following this military defeat, he immigrated to Bolivia. —Ed.

the shores of the Río de la Plata to come and lie down on this distant ground, burnt by the sun and soaked with human blood.

"When I heard your voice calling me, the darkness that had earlier blinded my mind suddenly dissipated; I saw you in my soul's eye lying in a nuptial bed, stretching your arms out to me and shouting, 'Isabel! My love, my wife, come!' And I broke the powerful chains that held my feet and walked long distances, guided always by that voice that kept calling to me, 'Isabel! Isabel!' And here I am, dressed in a newly-wed's white sendal to join my arm to yours in an eternal embrace! . . . But. . . oh! My God. . . ! His chest is cold and motionless, his lips white and stiff, his eyes fixed and veiled by a sinister shadow. Ah! It is that ill-fated talisman, that ill-fated black glove! From the very moment that I first saw it, it brought pain to my heart, and its very touch drove me mad."

Then, resting his inanimate head on her knees, she quickly undid the shirt of the dead man to look at his chest.

"Oh!" she screamed, her eyes fixed to a deep, circular wound with black edges. "It is the hand of Manuela Rosas, who has torn open his chest to steal his heart from me! There she is, still coming to claim him, to throw between us—as if to defy our love—the black glove that drove us apart. Retreat!" she screamed, standing up, stretching her arms out over the body. "Get back! Your very presence is fatal to those who love you! Your virgin's white veil is stained with blood! A cloud of tears hovers above your head! Get out of here!" she went on, moving forward as if to block the phantom that her mind presented to her. "Do not touch him! Because the dagger of the *Mazorca* will fall on him. . . . Ah!

"No, it is the ghost of my father, moaning and wandering among the cold remains of his compatriots! Father! Listen! This is not the last blow of the iron hand of fate that will be unleashed upon the defenders of liberty! Do you see those streams of blood running through the field? It will continue to flow like that, for a long time, throughout our beautiful land. But the earth cannot absorb it! Do you see how it rises up to the sky instead, so that it may one day descend, in the shape of God's blessed dew and mercy? Look, over there, in the distance, on the horizon. . . . Do you not see a valiant warrior who stands out among the ranks of the Federal army? The entire world also looks at him in wonder, because he is the hero who will raise the banner of liberty once again over his imprisoned brothers; he will overthrow tyranny from its bloodied throne and restore splendor and glory to our country.

"Go, rest your head once again on the peaceful pillow of death, while my husband holds me in his arms on our new wedding bed."

And silence reigned once again in the field. The pampero[14] mixed the fragrances of the flowers with the foul smell of the blood; the flowers from the carob trees fell on the mangled faces of the dead bodies, and the *coyuyo* began to sing its sad song once again. . . .

. . . . .

It is said that every time that the tyrant of Buenos Aires was about to decree one of his bloody executions, one of those horrible acts of butchery that have desolated the city, a strange-looking woman would appear in the wee hours of the night, covered in a long shroud, with her hair blown about at the whims of the wind, and she would circle the city three times, all the while singing in a doleful voice the somber melody of *"De Profundis."*

whim

[14] The pampero is a cold wind that blows from the Andes across the South American pampas to the Atlantic. —Trans.

# 6

# If You Do Wrong,
# Expect No Good

## I. THE ABDUCTION

It was late in the day in the middle of spring. The sun was setting behind the mountains in splendorous glory, spreading with its last rays mother-of-pearl on the snows of the range across the way, drawing long shadows of fleeting silhouettes from the goats that wandered here and there among the steep rugged rocks, picking at the leaves of the shrubs and the spiny thistles of the thickets.

Everything was peaceful and silent in the lonely, rustic landscape. The woodpigeons, hidden in the boulders, added their sad cooing to the rumbling of the waterfall, which rose up from the valley where the waters of the Rimac River fell like distant thunder.

Suddenly, a sweet, sharp voice let out a joyful shriek.

"*Mamay*," it said in the tongue of the Incas, "see those pretty golden flowers glowing down there among the stones? I am going to get some for you."

And a beautiful five-year-old girl, plump, ruddy, and wearing a cute *anaco*,[1] skipped happily toward the valley down a steep path. At the same time, a young Indian woman came out from behind a large

........

[1] An *anaco* is a loose skirt worn by Indian women of Bolivia, Peru, and Ecuador. —Trans.

boulder and yelled in a distressed tone, "No, Cecilia! No, my daughter! Those stones are near the road. . . . Listen, you can hear the soldiers coming on horseback! If they come this way. . . There they are! One is coming over here. . . . My daughter! . . . My daughter! . . . Oh!"

And, in fact, a regiment was approaching along the waterfall.

When it reached the valley, an officer pulled away from one of the last companies and called an orderly to him. He said a few words to the soldier, pointing to the girl in the distance who was gathering flowers from between the rocks standing by the side of the road.

The soldier galloped down to where she was. When he reached her, he leaned over the side of his horse and seized her in his arms. But when he straightened back up and began to turn around to place the girl on the hind bow of his saddle, he felt two hands of steel grab him around the throat and throw him to the ground.

The Indian woman had run to rescue her daughter; holding the soldier's head down with her knee, she was looking with ferocious eyes for a stone with which to finish him off.

She finally grabbed a small, dense rock; but just when she had raised it above the soldier, someone pulled her off of him by her hair.

The officer who had ordered the abduction dragged her away and threw her mercilessly over a cliff.

The blood-curdling scream of the mother rose up from the precipice as the officer laughed and said:

"What a weak, effeminate fool! To let himself be strangled by a woman! Luckily I arrived in time. . . . But . . . what a funny coincidence! . . . Yes, it was right here, in this same place, or very close to here, in any case, where that young woman . . . Be quiet, girl, be quiet. Oh! She is so beautiful! Look at those black eyes, that silky hair, that little coral mouth. She will make a pretty little present for my beautiful Pepa, that witch who likes to amuse herself by torturing other souls. . . . Be quiet, little girl; you are going to be very happy. You will have candies, cookies, and . . . hard slaps at the discretion of that evil woman.

"Here, take her, Mariano. Gallop until you catch up with the muleteers, then tell mine to take this little mestizo girl with the greatest care; but also tell him that when he arrives in Lima he should not be so dumb as to take her straight to my house. Have him leave her with the guard at the sentry box at the base of the Road of Wonders until I get there. Do you understand?"

Then he returned to his place in the march, while the soldier galloped passed the front of the regiment, taking the girl, who was crying desperately, with him. But her cries were soon lost in the distance, as they blended with the moaning of the wind and the sound of the waters, leaving the valley behind in complete silence.

## II. THE BANDITS

Both night and fog were starting to spread over the Rimac; a wintry silence reigned through its dense thickets. But in the distance, on the road that comes down from Chaclacayo, the bells of a pack of animals could be heard more and more distinctly.

Then, from the dark mass of the bushes, came a long whistle.

Soon afterward, three well-equipped men, completely armed, on horseback, came out of the nearby gully. They dismounted, hid their horses behind the dilapidated walls of a *huaca,*[2] and crouched behind the shrubs by the side of the road, where they waited in ambush.

Not far from there, some ten mules loaded with chests and bags appeared around a bend in the road, guided by four muleteers.

The travelers walked along peacefully, guiding their beasts of burden without any worries, adding the notes of a *yaravi*[3] to the sound of their footsteps.

All of a sudden, a strong hand grabbed the harness of the mule walking in front and made the entire pack stop. The muleteers saw the outline of the three wide barrels belonging to the three muskets, and did not need to see the three large Negroes holding them before scuttling into the bushes and disappearing like shadows.

........

[2] *Huacas,* or *Guacas,* in the Aymara and Quechua languages, are places in the Andean countryside demarcated as sacred, often containing idols and other religious items. —Trans.

[3] The *yaravi* is a sweet and melancholy indigenous song. The word comes from the Quechua verb *arawi,* meaning to compose poetry. —Trans.

The highwaymen then began to go over their spoils.

"Fourteen mules," one said.

"Eighteen chests," another one shouted.

"Three military hatboxes," a third one said.

"A little mestizo girl," the first one said.

"Leave the mestizo girl and the hatboxes behind and bring the rest up the hill with us."

So they spoke, and so they acted.

The thieves, mounted on their magnificent horses, rounded up the pack and headed back into the gully from whence they had come. A few moments later, the poor girl was the only one left, crying, abandoned and alone by the side of the road.


### III. THE PROTECTOR

Several hours later, when the girl's loud cries had diminished to sobs that made her body shake, a rider appeared, galloping down the same rode as the muleteers had come, wrapped in his riding cloak and carrying a large bag on the croup of his horse. He stopped abruptly and jumped to the ground to pick the girl up in his arms.

"Who has abandoned you like this, my poor little girl?" he asked her affectionately.

But the traveler spoke in a language that the girl did not understand. To all his questions, she cried and answered, "Mama!"

"Poor little creature!" he said, deeply moved. "It shall not be in vain that you call out that name, whose meaning is universal! You will be my daughter from now on and will comfort me in my solitude. I do not know your name; but I will give you the same as that of my lost little one, who sleeps under the shadows of *du Père Lachaise!*[4]

The traveler held the girl against her chest, and with her the memory of the dead daughter he was recalling.

........

[4] Père Lachaise is a cemetery in Paris, celebrated for many illustrious figures buried there, among them Victor Hugo. —Ed.

He mounted his horse again, and, protecting the girl under his cloak, added, like a good Frenchman always does, *le petit mot pour rire*.[5]

"I can now say that I have faithfully completed my role as a naturalist. My bags hold my samples from the vegetable and mineral kingdoms. And up here, with me, is the sample from the animal kingdom. And so, back to France I go!"

He hugged the girl again, laughed, dried off a tear, and galloped down the lonely road. . . .

### IV. TWELVE YEARS LATER

"Father," a beautiful young woman said to a lavishly decorated colonel one night after the theater, "do you think I have time to write my brother a letter?"

"There is more than enough time; the steamship does not weigh anchor until tomorrow at noon."

"I will write him tonight, then, to rid myself of any remorse for not having written him sooner. I will be able to sleep in peace afterward," she said, frowning.

The colonel smiled ironically, kissed the girl on her pretty forehead, walked her to her alcove, and retired to his own rooms.

When she entered her room, the charming girl smiled at herself in the mirror, tossed her feather fan on the dresser, took off the garland of roses she had worn on her head, hung it like a votive offering at the foot of the Virgin mounted above her bed, and shook out her long hair. Then she opened up a secretary desk, sat down, and began to write:

'There is such a tremendous emptiness, my dear Guillermo, such a tremendous emptiness in my life since you left! How horrible is that ailment of the soul known as "missing someone"! The doctors are satisfied calling it by a scientific name—"nostalgia!"—they say,

........

[5] Literally, "the small word to laugh," in French. In other words, the punch line. —Trans.

smartly. And if it is a young woman who suffers from this disease, they then add, smiling:

"'Have this girl taken to Chorrillos, have her take baths and lots of fresh air, have her go out on promenades and amuse herself in every way possible, and it will pass."

'Quite right! Since they think that the only things we girls from Lima love is to dance, live luxuriously, and squander everything . . . !

'Oh! Guillermo, what is the right punishment for those who slander us so? But I do know what it would be. I would have their heart suffer the same pain that your absence has caused in mine. That way they would "*feel*" how strongly a girl from Lima knows how to love.

"And you, my brother? Oh! With you it is different! First of all, regardless of what they say, the one who leaves has a thousand distractions that absorb him and lessen his pain. The events onboard the ship, the arrival into unknown ports, the new faces that appear endlessly one after the other. And then, I suppose that brothers never miss their sisters.

'What is, in essence, a brother usually like to a sister? A tyrant who tries to monopolize all her emotions, who treats her like the cruelest of despots, who always thinks less of her, and says she is ugly and stupid, and . . .

'But, oh, my dear Guillermo! Please forgive me! To compare you with those other impious brothers! What an atrocious injustice!

'You have always loved me with the tender care of a father and the exquisite gallantry of a lover. But you know I mistrust my own words, for having lived in Paris for two months, you have forgotten your sister; you have neglected your promise of sending her a detailed account of your life there every fifteen days!

'Oh! Even at the risk of showing disrespect, and even if you cross out the following phrase because of its vulgarity, I shall say it, and angrily at that: What nerve you have! There, I have said it!

'If there is a serious reason, love, for example, that occupies your mind . . . But if it is a tiring assignment from the government, dances, outings, shows, promenades . . . Guillermo, if that is what has kept you from writing me, there is no excuse.'

Soon thereafter, the fastidious sister received this response:

'Well, my beautiful, angry sister, it was a serious reason, it was love that made me, not forget you, not even for a single moment, but rather remain silent before sending you some news that I am certain will fill you with pleasure—news that our father already knows and has kept from you at my request. You have a sister now; she is as good as you, and, like you, is beautiful as an angel, and in fact resembles you in a surprising and striking manner. Just listen to my story.

'I was taking a walk one afternoon under the funereal groves of the Père Lachaise. The day was drawing to a close. The reddish light of the setting sun pierced the dense foliage like strands of fire.

'The gloomy place was deserted and silent, and the last gusts of the afternoon wind moaned like ghosts among the leaves of the cypresses.

'After wandering about for a long time in the city of the dead and visiting the tombs of Abelardo, Ney, Lavedoyère, and Foy, I sat down under the laurel tree that covers the tomb of Carlos Nodier with its shade.[6] Reading his epitaph, I remembered the wild enthusiasm with which, back home under the jasmines in your garden, you read his fantastic "Tale of the Little Bitty Fragments,"[7] and the gullible determination with which you ran through the hills of Amancaes in search of the "beautiful mandragora."

'I recalled one memory after the other of you, to the extent that your image finally appeared before me so vividly in my imagination that I looked around involuntarily, expecting to see you there.

'Imagine my surprise when I actually did see you near me, you yourself, right there, a few steps away from me, dressed in mourning and leaning against the pilaster of a tomb.

........

[6] Charles Nodier (1780–1844), romantic novelist and poet, author of fantastic fiction. His *Contes fantastiques* circulated widely, as did his stories about generous and noble outlaws, heroes similar to those constructed by Gorriti. —Ed.

[7] Gorriti refers to Nodier's best-known story, "La fée aux miettes" (1832), a dialogue between a narrator and his valet about madness and the fusion of dream and waking states. The search for the beautiful mandrágora named by Gorriti is a reference to Nodier's story in which the hero goes in search of an ideal, symbolized by a mandrake that sings. Some consider this tale a breviary for adult education, teaching about the codes of freemasons. —Ed.

'Without thinking, I ran to touch you, to see if the vision was real. But as I drew near I realized that it was only the case of an enormous resemblance, and that I had committed a gross indiscretion.

'But the young woman dressed in mourning did not even take notice of my presence. Her cheek was resting against the marble of the epitaph, her eyes were closed, and her lips were moving slowly. She was praying.

'At that moment, I heard dogs barking loudly in the distance.

'I remembered that it was the time at which the concierge releases his formidable mastiffs to guard the place at night. Quivering with fear at the thought of the danger threatening the beautiful young woman, I seized her in my arms and ran down the cypress-lined path that leads to the exit.

'At the suddenness of my action, the young woman opened her eyes, screamed with fright, and fainted.

'A hired car awaited her at the entrance of the cemetery. I set her inside, sitting next to her myself to hold her up.

'As I looked at her, I contemplated lovingly the marvelous resemblance of her beautiful countenance to yours, my dear Matilde. It was the very image of your face, of your every feature, but without the extravagant vigor that is one of your greatest charms. She, instead, was delicate and slender, and her tawny cheeks had that velvety paleness so admired in France, but which in Lima causes so much alarm in all caring mothers.

'That same paleness made her black eyes shine even brighter when they finally opened, reminding me even more of my sister, whether with her sweet smile, or with her mild seriousness.

'Amelia is the daughter of a wise traveler who devoted his life and fortune to science; he died, leaving her only his illustrious name and his austere virtue.

'A poor orphan, but with a heart rich in poetry and sentiment, Amelia has divided her life between the sublime melodies of her piano and the funereal silence of the cemetery. A strong-tempered soul, everything in life is serious for her; and in her eyes, in her voice, and in her attitude, there is an extremely sweet melancholic expression, always grave and pensive, which is completely lacking in the turbulent daughters of France, and which she undoubtedly acquired from the solemn expression found in the desert, under the veils worn by Arab women, in the distant regions through which she traveled with her father.

'Such is your new sister. Am I not correct in saying, my beautiful and amazed soul mate, that you will be very happy to embrace her when you meet her?'

### V. REMINISCENCES

On a summer day, not long afterward, Guillermo's fastidious sister, dressed with a fair degree of coquetry, like someone who likes to stand out, was on her way to the steamship Panamá aboard a gondola.

No sooner was the small boat brought alongside the steamship than the charming young woman from Lima climbed up the slippery steps, wet with the morning's fog, with a sure step, and threw herself into the arms of her brother. Then she stepped back from the fraternal embrace so as to turn and hug closely against her bosom, in a passionate gesture, a beautiful young woman, tawny and pale, who resembled her with a startling likeness.

The foreigner welcomed her caresses with tender abandon. But why did she seem distracted at times? Why did her eyes stray from the coast full of flowers and gaze into the distance at the blue silhouettes of the mountain range?

"Guillermo!" she said at last after they had disembarked. "I have seen those mountains before. . . . But I do not know where!"

"You must be confusing them with the Alps," Matilde said quickly.

"No. The Alps do not have outlines as crisp as these."

"Then it must be the Pyrenees," the haughty girl replied, determined to show off the geography she had learned at school.

"No, even less so. In any case, I know that my feet have stepped on rustic paths like those that wind through those tremendous slopes."

"You must have dreamt it, my dear Amelia," Guillermo said to her; "you must have dreamt about those mountains in your fervent yearning to come to the Americas."

"To dream about mountains!" the bewildered sister exclaimed with a charming frown that made Amelia smile. "To dream about mountains, having our beautiful Rimac right there, with its cool poplar-lined promenades, its fragrant gardens. . .

"You know, my own garden is quite divine. It is filled with roses, jasmines, cherimoya trees, white frangipani, acacias; and in its shade you will find in full bloom all the flowers found in Europe. I planted them myself. . . .

"Allow me the honor of helping you disembark, Amelia. Give me your hand. I do not want you to turn an ankle on the slippery, old steps of the platform."

But the beautiful stranger was barely listening. Distracted by strange thoughts and worries, she did not notice the speed with which they were moving; the wide fields and the dense groves passed before her eyes like the unreal haze of a dream.

The colonel was waiting for them at the station in Lima. Guillermo delivered his wife into his father's arms.

The colonel loved his children dearly, and Amelia was welcomed with extreme tenderness. But why did she tremble when she felt the gray hairs of his mustache touch her forehead? How strange!

Right away, though, laughing at her own childish fear, she responded to the colonel's affection with a beautiful daughterly kiss and leaned her trusting head against his chest, which was adorned with medals and crosses.

. . . . .

For Amelia, the days sped by swift as the wind and clear as dawn. She was a spirit with exquisitely perceptive senses, and she savored like no one else the delights of the magical life of Lima, where everything is pleasing to the soul and the senses; where everything, from the sky to the ground, is full of fragrance, light, and harmony.

But many times, running with her new sister through the groves of the garden, she had to stop suddenly, gasping for breath in the thin air of our atmosphere—a delightful but lethal air that both vitalizes the most beautiful flowers, but also causes them to wither.

And then a day arrived when Amelia, grown thin and pale, gasped in vain for the breath lacking in her chest, and when the rays of the January sun could no longer warm her greatly deteriorated body.

The doctors gathered gravely around Amelia's bed, and, very deeply worried, agreed:

"This girl is to be taken up to the Sierra; she is to receive complete rest; and she is to drink goat's milk; she is to be distracted; and the rest will depend on God's will!"

The next morning, Amelia, accompanied by her husband and her new father, set off toward Jauja.

They were followed by Matilde and the large contingent of friends who always surrounded her in that loving way that causes such a sense of both happiness and sorrow at farewells.

Everyone kept their silence—the silence with which people accompany those who go up the ominous Road of Wonders hoping to recover their health; a road that so many go up, but that so few come down.

When they reached the hills where the road begins to get difficult to climb, the colonel stopped his daughter's horse and said to her friends:

"Gentlemen, the day is drawing to a close and we have already come quite far. You must turn back now!" And then, pointing to Matilde, he added, as if to lend a more joyful tone to the sad solemnity of the farewell:

"I entrust you with this fair lady. I induce you to use your swords as necessary to defend her from the thieves that roam through this rugged area. Until we meet again!"

When she heard these words, Amelia trembled. A strange scene appeared suddenly in her mind; one of those series of images that, like reflections from heaven, appear suddenly to the spirit, and come and go with the brightness and quickness of a flash of lightning.

When Matilde came away from embracing Amelia, she said to her escorts in between tears:

"Amelia will not return! She is going to die. There is a strange look in Amelia's eyes that I have never seen before."

From that moment on, Amelia began to have an endless succession of hallucinations.

For the briefest of moments, in the furthest reaches of her memory, she would see a fantastic and impossible world. But when she turned to look at it, it would disappear, only to catch her eye again later.

At other times, she had strange intuitions that would make her say to herself, "Around that hill there is a large group of houses between two sets of stables." She would go up the hill, her heart beating wildly, and, upon reaching the summit, she would be struck dumb with surprise, as she saw the group of houses and the stables just as they had been dreamt up by her imagination. At times like these she would try to persuade herself that everything that had happened since she left Lima had been but a drawn-out nightmare; for she was afraid, afraid that she was experiencing the fatal deliriums of madness.

A time arrived when, pale, her heart overwhelmed by a strange sensation of anguish, she thought:

"Over there, around that bend in the road, a deep ravine will open up. It is formed by two tall mountains that rise straight up, blocking out the sky. From its bottom can be heard the roaring waters of a waterfall." Upon going around the bend, right where she had anticipated, the gloomy ravine appeared, at the bottom of which the white waters of the Rimac River roared along from the nearby waterfall.

Amelia, seized with an indescribable fear, looked around anxiously, searching among the stones by the side of the road for some object that might differ from, and thus belie, what her fantasy had imagined.

Suddenly, pale and trembling, she said to herself:

"Over there is a plant with golden flowers. A girl gathers a few of them, and then cries, fighting against . . . against what? . . . Oh, dear Lord! Help me remember what that *something* was that made that little girl cry!" Without knowing it, Amelia had started sobbing bitterly. Her husband and her father went tenderly to help her.

At that moment, a strange figure, a woman wrapped in a black shawl, pale as a specter, came out from behind a large boulder, screaming dolefully:

"Who is crying here? No one has cried here since that day. . . ." And suddenly spotting the colonel, she jumped toward him, grabbed the reins of his horse, and exclaimed: "I have finally found you! Thief of honor, thief of children, you hide in vain. In vain have you put snow on your hair to disguise yourself, for I still recognize you! You decorated highwayman, what have you done with my daughter?"

"It is the crazy shepherdess from Huairos," the muleteers shouted. The colonel, meanwhile, spurred his horse and freed himself from the sudden attack.

But the strange apparition followed them at a distance. As they traveled through the mountains, Amelia saw her behind them, always at the same distance, walking slowly but surely after them.

When they reached the tambo, however, she looked for her but did not see her—the figure had disappeared.

That night Amelia was unable to sleep, as is often the case with those whose chest is sick; so she left her bed and paced, lost in thought, by the light of the fire in the gloomy room of the tambo. Guillermo and the colonel kept her company and asked anxiously what was worrying her.

The poor young woman could not put it into words; but she was filled with fright. She felt, within her, a new being moving, as if it were awakening: a half-forgotten being that identified with her soul and beat with her heart.

And she would put her hand on her chest in anguish, wondering if perhaps it was a ghost remembering its past life.

The reddish flame from the fire threw fantastic shadows on the empty walls that served to augment her excited state.

All of a sudden, a cautious hand slowly opened the door, and a black figure glided into the room.

It was the apparition from the ravine.

The madwoman looked around with her lost eyes, as if she were searching for someone. She walked silently to the fire, rigid and solemn as a statue, and grabbed a log whose end was on fire; then, using it as a torch, she started to look all around the room.

Amelia and the others saw that the woman holding the fire in her hand was still young, but greatly deteriorated. Deep wrinkles furrowed her withered face, and her eyes had that frozen and, in a word, ethereal look of the dead.

When she saw her, Amelia's anxieties disappeared; moved to the very core of her soul, she approached the demented woman and said to her in a sweet voice:

"What are you looking for over there, poor little one? Come and rest, I beg you; it is late already and very cold."

"I am looking for the decorated man," she answered without looking at Amelia, and went on in her relentless search.

But Amelia took her hands gently, and, holding them tenderly, guided her and sat her by the fire.

### VI. THE STORY OF THE MOUNTAIN ROAD

With sad docility, the wretched woman allowed herself to be led. She crossed her hands on her knees and stared for a long time, pensive and silent, at the shifting flames of the fire.

Little by little her listless eyes became animated and shone as if they were illuminated by an internal light, and her lips curved into a youthful smile that made her white teeth glow like pearls in the darkness.

"Esteban!" she shouted all of a sudden. "Who said that Esteban is dead?! It is a lie! There he is, young, tall, and quick as ever, coming down from Casa-Blanca with the sheep. It is him, it is really him; his eyes, his black hair. He is calling me! But, no! Stay back, Esteban. The priest does not want our flocks to graze together, we are still too young to get married. As if one could not love, praise God, and be happy at any age. To be happy! Oh! I will never be happy now that the priest has separated us. Off you go, take your flock up to the heights, and I stay behind in the valley, alone, alone with the sheep; and they jump about happily, but I cannot share in their joy at all. All of this you know perfectly well; but—oh!—what you never knew is that . . . He is leaving me! He does not want to listen to me! Come back Esteban; come back. I will tell you now, now that time and sorrow have hardened my countenance, and my cheeks no longer burn with shame.

"Over there is the hill where I was crying, waiting, that afternoon, that afternoon that we were to meet by the light of the fire, under the willows in our patio. Then, from that dell over there, I heard the voice of a soldier, calling me. I was afraid, and ran; but he was riding a horse, and came after me very quickly. He caught me, jumped off his horse, brought me down, and raped me. . . .

"And from that day on, I was afraid to see you, and I fled from you . . . . And I said to you, 'Esteban, I cannot be your wife now.' But I loved you then more than ever. You, however, must have thought that I was a fickle and loose woman. You left me, crying, and cursed me.

"Then . . . Then one day my father took a long look at me and said to me:

"'You are a vile woman; you have dishonored your family and stained your father's house. Get out!'

"And raising his hand over my head, he cursed me.

"And I wandered aimlessly for a long time, fleeing like a wild beast, from valley to valley, from mountain to mountain, naked, hungry, miserable. But in my sorrow a blessed happiness was growing. God had taken mercy upon me, and in my road of misfortune, had made a flower be born. . . . My daughter!"

She uttered these words in a tone of intimate affection, impossible to reproduce, and heard only in the huts of Indians.

Amelia was crying, Guillermo found himself deeply moved, and the colonel, pale and somber, was lost in deep thought.

"My daughter!" the Indian woman continued. "My daughter! I never tired of repeating it, and in doing so, I forgot your name, Esteban. Do not be angry with me; the same happens with all mothers.

"Then, instead of hiding, I went asking for work and bread in the nearby homes.

"The shepherds of Huairos took pity on me, sheltered me among them, and gave me a cabin.

"I took care of some of the sheep, with my daughter curled up on my back, like a baby bird in its nest. Every day, from morning until night, I looked at her, and each day I was happier.

"But as my daughter grew, my joy began to turn into restlessness. I became reticent and suspicious, and I trembled with fear every time a stranger came near my daughter, because—oh, Esteban!— poor Indian women are not allowed to keep anything in peace, not even their own children.

"They say that our fathers were powerful in another time, and that they reigned in this land that we have to pay so dearly for now, and that the whites came from a foreign land and stole their gold and their power. I do not know if this is true, but now that we are poor, now that we have nothing for them to take from us, they steal our children and make them slaves in their cities.

"That is why I protected my little girl with a fear that grew and grew as she became more and more beautiful each day. I never left her alone at home; and even though the poor little one would get tired, I always took her with me to the fields, guiding the sheep through the areas that are furthest from the roads used by soldiers and travelers.

"In this manner, hiding her from everyone, from the subprefect, from the landowner, from the priest, my daughter reached her fifth birthday.

"Then, one day . . . " and the Indian woman screamed out; she put her hands over her eyes and leaned all the way down to the ground.

Amelia, sitting on her knees, was listening without moving, without uttering a sound, attending to every word the Indian woman said. Every once in a while she would pass her hand across her forehead as if she were trying to remember something. The Indian woman continued:

"One day there was not enough grass in the heights, and I had to go down into the valley.

"Frightened to death, carrying my daughter in my arms, I walked with the sheep, hiding among the large boulders and in the hollows of the hills.

"The hours went by, the area was deserted, the sun was about to set, and I was already on my way back up to my cabin with the sheep, when, all of a sudden, my daughter saw a bunch of *arirumas*[8] by the side of the road. She let go of my hand and ran off, ignoring my screams to come back."

Amelia was standing up now. With her hands held together, her body leaning forward, her eyes fixed on the Indian woman's face, she concentrated and listened as if the voice were coming from far away.

"At that moment," the Indian woman continued, "I heard bugles somewhere in the valley, and then a regiment began to file along the shores of the river.

"As I was running down the rugged hillside, chasing after my daughter, I saw a soldier come galloping up to her and pull her up onto his horse.

"I got there and retrieved my daughter; but just as I had done so, a man jumped on me, and, dragging me by the hair, threw me over the cliff.

"I fell and could not move, but I saw who the man was. It was the officer who six years before had raped me in that same area. Now he was stealing my daughter, my poor little daughter who was calling out to me. . . . Oh . . . ."

The Indian woman suddenly stopped talking. Her eyes had come to rest on Amelia's face. She stared at her, her eyes full of an anguished uncertainty, and then shouted:

"Cecilia!!!"

"*Mamay,*" Amelia murmured, fainting, and fell into the arms of the Indian woman.

Guillermo ran toward her and took her in his arms. But Amelia, coming back to, pushed him back, terrified.

. . . . . . . .

[8] *Arimuras* (Quechua) are yellow flowers of intense fragrance (Clydanthus bolivianus). —Ed

"You poor wretch!" she exclaimed. "You have to get away from me. Do you not understand? I am your sister!"

The colonel, pounding his fists against his temples, ran out of the room, wailing madly.

The next day, the shepherds from the nearby mountains found his corpse, devoured by vultures, at the bottom of a ravine.

### VII. CONCLUSION

One day, in the monastery of Ocopa, not long afterward, two solemn ceremonies took place simultaneously.

Inside the church a new priest was taking his vows.

In the cemetery a coffin was being laid in the ground.

The prelate, at the end of the ceremony, gave the novice his blessing, saying to him:

"May your soul find the Lord's peace, brother Guillermo."

Above the grave a stone was mounted with the following name on it: *Cecilia*.

The novice, his eyes looking down, his feet bare, leaned on his staff, kissed the prelate's hand, and left to carry out missions in distant lands.

The gravestone remained alone. Swallows came and rested peacefully on its marble ledges and stretched their quivering wings out in the sun. But when night fell across the valley, and the stars began to shine in the sky, the priests from the monastery always saw a shadow glide through the path under the poplars, enter the cemetery, and, bent down on its knees, keep a motionless vigil over Cecilia's grave.

# 7

## Gubi Amaya

*The Story of a Highwayman*

### I. A LOOK AT THE MOTHERLAND

It was a fiery afternoon in October. The sky to the east was dark, covered by dense, threatening clouds, shattered repeatedly by flashes of lightning; to the west, some patches were clearer, the cloud cover burned through by the rays of the setting sun. The electricity from the storm made the leaves of the trees vibrate, and their shaking produced a dull rustling, like the sound of the distant ocean. The air was hot and stifling. The cicadas made their shrill and monotonous call from hiding places in the hollows of the tree trunks, and flocks of birds of all shapes and colors, brushing the tops of the trees with their wings, quickly fled the approaching, gloomy, and majestic tempest.

How can I put into words even part of what was taking place in my soul as, all alone, I traversed that forest, which in other times I had traveled with my cheerful family—a family that has since been torn from its native land by a blizzard of extraordinary misfortune, devoured in the midst of its full bloom by death, reduced now to five weak scions, thrown great distances from one another!

Every thought that could torment the mind and torture the heart weighed upon me. I walked with my head bent, absorbed in the most sorrowful reflections. When I raised my head and saw the trees clearing before me, I realized I had reached the end of the forest and the beginning of the prairie where, surrounded by hills that formed an amphitheater, our old home once stood.

I stopped, suddenly shocked at having arrived. My heart beat wildly in my chest, and I was terribly afraid of being alone at that ultimate moment, as if the doors of eternity were about to open before me.

My eyes gazed deeply, and took in with inexpressible pleasure, with inexpressible sorrow, the enchanting view, which I had never ceased to behold in my memory, and which now appeared before me in reality.

In that small universe that seemed as if it were from another time, only I had changed—everything was exactly like the day, like the very moment, that I had left it. The hills that bordered the prairie on the northern side were as green and full of flowers as always, with the same trees and the same pleasant slopes as when I used to skip merrily through them completely trusting in our future. To the south, the river's waters still flowed unchangingly, with the same song, over its bed of sand and colorful little pebbles. In front of me, rising on a solitary stone hillock, were the ruins of the Jesuit castle; its tower, still intact, was a black outline against the tempestuous horizon in the light of the last rays of the setting sun. Further below, finally, on the gentle slope of a hillside, the beautiful house that my father had built, and in which I spent my childhood, appeared before my eyes; it was white and radiant, just as it always had when, coming back from the bath, I would stop to look at it distractedly, with what were then fortunate eyes.

Each tree, each leaf, each turn in the road awakened an entire world of painful memories in my soul. From this carob tree now flowering above me, I had once grabbed a nest filled with small birds; then, after spending the whole night crying and thinking about the grief of the poor mother, I had gotten up at dawn to return them to her.

The road to Ortega cuts through the seemingly endless prairie. We used to go there quite frequently. And on that green esplanade, we would gallop, turn around quickly, and, with our horses, circle my mother's coach; she would scream from inside, frightened at our stunts, warning us in vain to be careful, and begging my sisters and I to get in and suffer the unbearable monotony of her carriage with her. Poor mother! She could not foresee then the real dangers that threatened her children from afar; she did not yet see the black cloud of pain and tears gathering above our smiling faces. How merciful you are, oh God, to hide our futures from us! For my mother was therefore able to enjoy long days of peaceful happiness, with flowers hiding the abyss that has since devoured us.

The storm, meanwhile, had begun with a violent rain, and it covered the hills and the plain with its gloomy veil.

But neither the large drops of rain whipping against my face, nor the powerful voice of the cyclone, nor the terrible crashes of the thunder could tear my soul from its painful contemplation. Standing there, without moving, with one hand over my beating heart and the other leaning against the old tree trunk, I had been transported in spirit to the past; its scenes appeared before my saddened mind as if they were reflected by a magic mirror. I saw my father again among his many children in the beautiful gallery from where, gathered around him, hiding in the folds of his cape, we would look with both curiosity and fear at the torrents of water and the columns of lightning with which the storms ripped apart the trees in the forest. I heard again the screams of happiness with which we greeted the gusts of wind that swept away the clouds, making way for the first rays of sunlight that would break through and shine brightly on the drops of water suspended in the green leaves like the diamonds of a diadem. I saw how each one of us would run and jump, hurrying out to the garden and the fields, to see how many flowers had bloomed, and if the little birds needed our help to repair their nests, destroyed by the water, and how many foxes had been killed by the lightning.

Oh! Where were all those bright youths that once lived in that Eden? Tadeo! Pedro! Celestina! Severa! Julián! Antonina! Teresa! What has become of you?

In response to each of these names, a gloomy echo answered from the bottom of my heart: Look to the grave for your answer.

Of all those beings full of life, whose hearts beat with youth and hope before the doors of an immense and smiling future, only I had returned, devastated, to cry and lament like the prophet over the ruins of the past. And now, a stranger in the paternal house that I contemplated, I had not inherited from my parents even a single rock on which to lay my head. Everything had been exchanged for the bitter bread of foreign lands.

A harsh voice and a solid hand grabbing my shoulder brought me back to the present. A fifty-year-old man, tall and strong, with bright, dark skin, gray hair, black eyes, and thick, overgrown eyebrows was standing next to me.

"Sir," he said, fooled by my dress, "do you enjoy getting wet, or do you wish to insult me?"

"Me, sir!" I replied, frightened by that gesture of abrupt familiarity, and feeling my woman's heart beating loudly under the outfit with pistols with which I had heroically adorned my belt.

"Yes," he answered, "since being only two blocks from my house, you choose to take shelter under a tree, as if you were in the deserts of Arabia."

His words and accent revealed to me that he was a Spaniard. He was the new owner of the land.

That simple and benevolent invitation, so common to the frank and generous character of the sons of Spain, caused me pain. "My house," he had said, pointing to the home in which I had slept in my crib as a baby. I found myself once again deprived of my inheritance and felt as if the walls of the house were rejecting me, saying: Get out of here, stranger, we do not know you!

When I went into the house, sweet and welcoming voices drove away my sad thoughts. The women of the family came out to meet me; they greeted me, welcoming me with friendly simplicity and alleviating my weariness with such tender solicitude and such frank cordiality that, for a moment, I wondered if the past had been only a dream and if that family was not my own.

Oh! Only the exile, the ill, the orphan, and the traveler can appreciate how noble, generous, and affectionate are the souls of my beautiful female compatriots. Powerful men find them haughty and untamable, like the forbidden garden in the sacred book, because they save the treasures of their hearts to help the destitute.

Daughters of the Río de la Plata, guardian angels of that Eden marked with gravestones and abandoned for so long to horrible killings, there is nothing that compares to your divine charity, to your sublime abnegation. In comforting those who suffer, you put aside your own misfortunes; devastated mothers and wives, you stifle the cries of your own mourning to lend sweet words of hope to a prisoner; and though exiled and without a home, you visit the battlefields to grab the dying back from the claws of vultures and bandage their wounds with the veils of your chaste bosom. May God bless you, and keep you in his thoughts for the redemption of our unfortunate motherland.[1]

## II

My hosts, once they had looked after everything I might need, left me alone in the room in which visitors stayed. Everything there was as it had been before. Hanging on the walls were some paintings that belonged to my sister, among which I saw a masterpiece that had been drawn by my own pencil. It was of a guardian angel with which I, not knowing the least bit about drawing, tried to equal my sister's dexterous brush.

Looking at that image, I admired the power of will, which had guided my ignorant hand and given the figure of the protecting numen of our gloomy road the ethereal curves of a mysterious and sad beauty and an ineffable expression of tender melancholy with which it seemed to smile down on the poor traveler.

Oh! What a difference between those times and the present! What a difference between the girl with blond hair and flushed cheeks who, talking wildly, had drawn that picture—and the pale, tired, and sick traveler who now looked at it in silence!

........

[1] Author's note: written in 1850.

While my eyes and my thoughts wandered from one object to another, from one memory to the next, the storm passed and now howled in the distant rustic mountains to the west.

I went to the window that opened out to the countryside and watched as night fell and the moon rose over the Colorado Mountains.

Everything outside the house was peaceful and quiet; the only sounds were the distant mooing of the cows and the dripping of the water as it fell drop by drop from the tiles of the roof. A moist breeze that brought with it many smells gently rocked the large trees that grew near the window, murmuring sweetly; their shifting shadows seemed to play with the moonlight in the darkness of the room.

The servants interrupted the charming scene when they entered with their lamps.

When I was alone again, I left the welcoming room, closing the door carefully behind me. I glided along the gallery, went down the front steps, and headed quickly up the path lined by carob trees that leads to the spring and the ruins.

As I walked, it was as if there were two people within me, one the daughter of those rustic woods, the other the traveler of distant countries who had come to visit them; and I was telling myself the story of all those places, which I knew so well, everything from the cave of the tiger to the home of the deer, from the gigantic tree to the minute blades of grama grass. Over there, I said to myself—as if to convince myself that I was not dreaming—over there are the prickly pear trees where those snakes hide their offspring, the snakes that make a whistling sound as they perfidiously imitate a bird's song in order to bite the hand of anyone who reaches unaware into the hollow of a tree trunk to grab the bird. Over there are foxes' dens; further along is the jackals' lair. I once had to climb to the top of that pear tree to get away from a huge bull that I had foolishly called with a red handkerchief; it forced me to stay in the tree for half the day as it pawed at the ground and growled angrily. . . . And that piercing cry coming from the depths of the forest? Oh, yes! It is the song of the *pacui,* a nocturnal bird so reticent that no one has ever seen it; it is known only by its song and by the fantastic legend associated with it.

The story is that there were once two shepherds from the forest, Pascual and María, who loved each other very much. They were always together and always lovingly took their herds to graze in the flowered prairies or in the dense forests. There was no one in the entire region as happy as they.

But Pascual was very jealous, and he doubted even the shade of the oak trees.

One day, when he was going to meet his lover, who was resting beside a fountain, he thought he heard the sounds of someone leaving as he approached.

It might have been a deer that had come down to quench its thirst. But Pascual became somber and taciturn. He looked at his beloved with a long, strange, and piercing gaze, as if he wanted to see all the way to the bottom of her soul. What did he see in her eyes? A lover's eyes are very telling!

Later, Pascual took María to a distant forest, where he showed her a flower that was as big as he and wonderfully beautiful, at the top of a very tall tree. Its broad petals captured the colors of the rainbow, and the sunlight made the drops of water from the morning dew shine like stars in its broad calyx.

María loved flowers. Shrieking in admiration, she rushed to the tree and began to scale it. When she got to the top, she reached greedily with her hand to grab the desired treasure. But the beautiful flower, as it came loose from the chord that held it, came undone in the girl's fingers and turned into a thousand small flowers that had been bound together by an artful hand.

María thought that her lover had wanted to play an innocent joke on her, or test her agility, so she looked down at Pascual with a smile. But her smile froze on her lips and her shocked eyes looked with fear at the tree she had climbed; from the very high place where she was, she saw that all the branches that had assisted her climb up had disappeared, and the trunk was now smooth and terrifying. She called

Pascual, but the only answer she received was an echo, repeating Pascual's name with a satanic sneer.

The wretched girl cried all night long, uttering her lover's name between sobs. But when the first rays of dawn shone their light upon the forests, the tree was deserted. María had disappeared. Ever since, when night extends its sad cover over those lands, the sorrowful voice of the young woman calling out her lover's name is heard.

"Holy Mary, Mother of God! He is going to cross the bridge!" I heard someone exclaim at the very moment I was about to set my foot on the beam that was used to cross the spring. I looked down and saw an old Negro woman filling a pitcher with water; she left it by the side of the water, and climbed to where I was. She approached me with that benevolent solicitude, almost maternal, that old women of her race have toward the young. Putting her hand on my shoulder, she looked around her suspiciously, and said to me:

"If it is your intention to go to the ruins, sir, do not do so, in the name of God!"

"But why?"

"What! Do you not know?"

"I do not!"

"Do you not know that he," she said, and made a cross over her mouth, "that he roams through the ruins of the castle every night?"

"And who is he?"

The Negro woman came closer to me, her countenance expressing even more dread, and said in a terrified tone, "He is a . . . a necromancer. Oh! Sir, if you value your life at all, do not go there."

And crossing herself, quite scared, the Negro woman lifted the pitcher of water and walked away into the night.

III

The poor Negro woman's fears made me smile. Her story of the necromancer was clearly one of those thousands of frightening tales that people of the region tell about the castle. When I lived there with my family, before the devastating winds of the civil wars left it in ruins, I heard old women tell similar stories under the trees of the neighboring cabins, when there was a full moon.

The castle was a Jesuit construction, one of those fortresses that, disguised under the humble name of *Reducciones*,[2] the Order of Loyola had built toward the end of its reign. After their expulsion, the castle and its riches, as well as the broad expanse of land associated with it, were confiscated. And while their owners disappeared as if they had been swept away by the four winds, the poachers carried off to Spain the gold that the Jesuits had accumulated in their bastions of power in the Americas.

There was an old man, however, who had lived through those events, and he always shook his head and smiled slyly when he heard about the confiscation. He had been a servant of the Jesuits when he was a child and still lived, clinging to the walls of the castle like an old ivy. He had put together a strange story, which was a combination of the delirium of old age and some vestiges of the reality he remembered, and he would sometimes tell it to children and servants in the kitchen.

"The Jesuits of that congregation," he would say, "were warned a few hours before their expulsion. So they held a secret council, secret as all the actions in the life of those mysterious creatures. When they came out of the council, they closed all the doors of the second enclosure, which was the area that contained just the rooms where they lived. Later, when the doors were opened again and the servants entered to serve dinner, they found the patio flooded with wine, and the cellar that had contained large barrels of it, completely empty.

"No one ever knew what became of those barrels. But," the old man would add, with his mysterious smile, "no one, except the 'Fathers,' knew where the underground tunnels of the castle were located, either."

........

[2] A *reducción* refers to a village or colony of Indians in South America converted and governed by the Jesuits. The Jesuits were in Latin America from 1578 until their expulsion, by papal edict, in 1767. In Argentina, the Jesuits established their missions in the northern triangle formed by Misiones, Córdoba, and Humahuaca. —Trans.

When he reached this point, he would give free reign to his powers of imagination and would start to ramble irrationally, saying:

"Thus, while the new owners of the castle sleep peacefully behind their locked doors, the 'Fathers,' the legitimate owners—because everything the 'Motherland' sold had been stolen—the Fathers, the legitimate owners, as I was saying, arrive two by two, as they once did. They cross the cemetery so silently that even the ends of their long soutanes do not touch the daisies and the passion flowers that grow there. Then they symbolically knock three times on the large door, and in response to this signal, the Reverend General of the Order, who has been sleeping for the last two centuries under his epitaph, slowly raises the block of marble that covers him—or rather makes it rotate on some hinge from the other world—and, with a solemn gesture, goes to open the door of the church to the living. Then, led by him, they go down one by one to the sepulcher, where they stay until the sun rises. But the next evening, before the light disappears over the horizon, they always return, always two by two. And the dead man, after closing the door, returns to his tomb."

Every time the old man told this story, crouching in the kitchen with his hands shaking over the fire, a greedy excitement would take over the servants. And the next morning, they would go and stomp loudly on the floors and walls of every corner of the castle, searching for the door that led to the underground tunnels—in other words, to the desired barrels, and the gold they held.

My father put an end to these searches, forbidding them severely.

He loved the castle not only for its history and tradition, but also for the picturesque location it occupied, atop a stone hillock, looking down at the most delightful view my eyes have ever beheld. Without ever changing anything in it, he cared for it meticulously; when he bought the beautiful building from the state, he planned to retire there after the long War of Independence and rest. But God did not wish it to be so. The castle was now in ruins, the lands belonged to a stranger, and the old veteran never saw even a single day of rest dawn for him until the one on which he fell to rest for all eternity in his grave under a foreign sky.

With these thoughts racing through my mind, I climbed the steep stone slope to the top without realizing it and suddenly found myself at the door of the cemetery.

Beings rested there whom I had loved and cried over. The silver moon lighted their tombs, lending them a peaceful white quality, as if they were their summer beds.

Here lies Urbana, the girl whose father left her to me in his death throes; I, a girl like her, took her in my arms, from where she quickly departed for heaven. There is Manuel, my sister's beautiful boy, who died of grief because his wet nurse abandoned him. Over there is the grave of Enrica, the beautiful and merciless coquette. God, one day, turned the tables on her, and she found directed toward her the same torment that she had taken pleasure in torturing others with throughout her life. For there came a time when the love she had parodied, and with which she had deceived everyone, awoke in her heart for real, and then she ceased being a coquette; she became timid and doubted the power of her own beauty. She was actually right to do so, because she loved someone who had loved her only when he had been toyed with, dejected among the throng of his rivals, but who rejected her disdainfully the moment she became worthy of being loved.

He was a good man, merciful and generous. But for some strange inconsistency, he enjoyed pitilessly slicing to pieces the heart of the one who loved him; he would search for its most sensitive fibers and cut into it with the infernal dexterity of a torturer. And the poor heart, untiring in its fatal love, would yearn more and more for the being rejecting it. After each new deception, after each new wound, it would retreat, moaning; but then it would forget everything and kiss with a smile the hand that was hurting it, thus returning once again to its path of pain.

I was a girl back then. When, aided by the negligent trust that young age inspires, I was able to see into the darkness in which that soul had sunk, and I examined with the timid wonder of childhood the tempests that devastated it, those terrible and for me incomprehensible scenes, those trances of love in which a heart that someone wants to kill insists on living, I would look around restlessly and ask myself what could be causing such a frightening devastation for a young woman who was beautiful, rich, and loved and spoiled by everyone.

Later, when years and sorrow had darkened my skies and the happy songs of childhood had turned into sobs, the image of that woman returned to my mind. I saw her as I had seen her so many times before, pale, trembling, and quivering, her black hair loose on her shoulders. With the bitter smile her lips formed, she seemed to be saying to me, "Look at me here, so peaceful now! The pillow on which I rest knows no insomnia or nightmares. But you, who now know the secret of my pain, tell me, is it not true that it is horrible to say: I am young, I am beautiful, my soul is full of poetry, I am capable of giving and receiving torrents of love and happiness; and yet, desperation lives in my bosom, and I feel it devouring my heart?"

At other times, when I came to visit these tombs, I cried a lot; I wanted my cries to wake up Urbana, Manuel, and Enrica. But now I envied their immobility and their eternal silence; even if I had had the power of bringing them back to life, I would have said to them, "Stay. Rest in peace!"

I left the cemetery and, walking through the church, whose dome had collapsed, I entered the immense mass of ruins.

IV

A heavy silence reigned all around me, a silence interrupted only by the distant shrilling of the cicadas and the rustling of the night wind through the destroyed galleries and the overgrown grass of the cemetery. The moon, high above, shone its pale and uncertain light on the desolate scene like the gaze of a dying man and cast upon it such a fantastic spell that it caused my imagination to run wild. I started to doubt whether I myself was not a shadow that had left its grave for a short while, and had come, drawn by the dense darkness, to visit the place of its birth. But my heart's fast beating brought me back to the present and made me feel that I was still very much entirely in this vale of tears, where each hour is accompanied by a new sorrow, and each object we contemplate is accompanied by the memory of a lost happiness.

I approached the tower, which rose white and majestic above the ruins of the fallen buildings. And sitting in its shadow, like the old girlfriend who remained behind in the midst of the ruins, disconsolate, I cried with barrenness for my parents' destroyed and lonely home.

I do not know how long I stayed there like that, without moving, with my mind absorbed in thinking about the past.

The sound of a horse's footsteps shook me abruptly out of my deep and heavy contemplation.

A strong, healthy-looking rider had stopped before me.

The man was completely wrapped in a large poncho; its broad and fabulous folds fell to his feet, on which he wore boots with enormous spurs.

The man's features were hidden by an immense gray beard that came down to his chest. An excessively small hat left his abundant and wavy hair completely uncovered. His left hand distractedly held onto the reigns of his spirited horse, while his right rested on the handle of a long dagger.

If I had seen such a somber figure so close to me, without moving or speaking, at that time of night and in the middle of the ruins at any other moment, I would have been terribly afraid. But the strong emotions that then stirred in my soul made me immune to all fear.

I stared straight at him and was going to ask him what he was doing in that place at such a late hour, when he beat me to the question with a strong and deep voice that burst from that tremendous mass of facial hair.

"I am a traveler," I answered, "and am visiting these ruins."

"And has no one informed you that at night these ruins belong to me? Has no one spoken to you, sir, of Miguel the Horse Master?"

When I heard this name, I brought my hand quickly to my mouth to hold back the scream that was about to burst from my chest. Miguel the Horse Master! I had before me, without having recognized him, and without his realizing it, my childhood friend —a man who had devoted his life and soul to my siblings and me with an immense and tireless affection unequaled in the human race. The memory of that loyal servant had never left our hearts, and in our conversations in exile, the name of Miguel had often been mentioned. We remembered him as an exemplary being whose mysterious and tutelary loyalty we bitterly missed.

Tears of happiness and sorrow prevented me from speaking; but he attributed my silence to a bout of fear and immediately attempted to reassure me by stretching out his hand and offering me a cigar, a sign of comradeship between men like him.

"My little friend," he said to me in a sad voice, "do not be afraid. There is more to Miguel than his reputation would lead you to believe. I like to have this area to myself at night so that I can 'conjure up ghosts,' as they say down there," he added contemptuously, showing his white teeth in the darkness. "It is true!" he continued. "Ghosts who are dear to my heart come to visit me among these destroyed walls, and smile at me sadly, reminding me of days that are far, very far behind us. And since you are already here, stay. It is so strange! Miguel, who for fifteen years has denied his heart and prevented tears from rising to his eyes, and whose lips have not uttered a single moan of complaint, feels a huge need to unburden himself tonight."

He dismounted and came to sit beside me on the slab of a fallen column.

He remained silent for a long time, his elbow leaning on his knee, his hand lost in his thick beard.

I did not say anything either. I looked from the imposing figure of the friend beside me to the solemn view that nature presented to us. The night breeze brought to my ears the hushed murmuring of the river, like a distant echo of times past, of a time when the same Miguel who sat next to me without recognizing me would come at night to see the children, and after having hugged us and given us the flowers, honey, and birds he had brought, would say to us, so that we might let him go:

"If I do not go now, my horse could drown. Can you not hear how the river is not as loud anymore? It is because of the flooding. If I do not get back before the moon sets, I will not be able to find the ford of the river."

The same objects surround us now as did back then. We were surrounded by the same hills; we saw the same mountains outlined against the horizon; above us, the night stars shone with the same brightness; the same warm and perfumed breeze brushed against our faces, bringing the distant rustling of the forests to our ears. The scene was the same, but there were only two actors now, and when they came to represent the denouement of the lugubrious drama, the strong man and the smiling child who arrived were now stooped over, the one under the weight of years, the other under the clutches of her sorrows.

V

Miguel, like all the people of the area, began his narration with a question.

"Sir," he asked me, "if you were separated from every interaction with fellow human beings by a life of crime, if you were rejected and cursed by everyone, and then you found a man who tore you away from the miserable state in which you found yourself, and brought you back to life with his high regard for you, and comforted you with his friendship, sheltering you under his own roof, even trusting you to protect his children; and if once you had become accustomed to that peaceful existence of honor and happiness, that friend, that family, that home were suddenly taken from you, leaving you alone and isolated like before, what would you do?"

"I would cry for a long time, and would always miss that friend and my lost fortune. But I would resign myself to God's will, for it is he who determines our happiness as well as how long it lasts."

"You have spoken like a woman, sir," Miguel said, looking at me with contempt. "To resign oneself, having here," he said, touching his chest, "having here a heart that demands vengeance, and two strong arms that can execute it! Child, resignation is only a virtue for cowards. God says: 'I shall help he who helps himself.' Remember this, for it could be of use to you in the future.

"For my part, I did not resign myself. My friend was dead, his children exiled, and I was being pursued; but my courage did not waver. I found his enemy, I was able to get near him, and a few hours later, a huge multitude gathered around a corpse, contemplating in awe the deep hole that the bullet from my rifle had left in his chest."

"You murdered him!"

"I killed him loyally, sir. Miguel has not murdered anyone, thanks to that man who is resting over there in his grave, and who converted into the honest and upright Miguel the man who had once been the . . . the wicked Gubi Amaya."

"Gubi Amaya!" I exclaimed, frighteningly recalling bits and pieces of the formidable legend. It seemed to me that the figure of Miguel grew and took on horrendous proportions before my very eyes.

"Yes," he replied, in a sad and solemn tone, "I was once that bandit who is so frightfully remembered. This man you have before you, who has tenderly rocked the crib of children and kept vigil over their sweet dreams, was once the terror of the region and the nightmare of the law. Do you see that cemetery?" he continued, stretching his hand out toward the place of eternal rest. "My dagger has sent many to their graves there.

"But before I tell you the second part of Gubi Amaya's life, let me tell you the first."

### VI. THE STORY OF A HIGHWAYMAN

Miguel looked sullenly at the vast horizon, as if he searched there for some painful memory from his past. Then, startling me with a terrible and bitter smile, he moved closer, and continued:

"You, sir, you who make the laws, those of you who have decided upon the punishment that condemns a criminal to death, have not, before sanctioning it, thought about the causes that might lead a man to such an awful extreme. When the prosecutor tells you the story of a criminal, presents him in chains before you in your courts, from where you send him on to the scaffold, you are content to say: 'He was born evil.'

"Oh! Luckily for humanity, and for the glory of God who created it, this is not true. Good and evil exist within us; we have them both since childhood, like two equally unknown roads. We do not choose: Destiny chooses for us, and brings about circumstances, joyful or ill-fated, that throw us down one or the other path. Let me give you an example.

"Do you see over there, on the side of the range across the way, that mountain that is cut vertically from its top and the immense cliff that glows white in the moonlight like the dome of some fantastic city? At its base, in the middle of a delightful gully, in the shade of an orchard, there once stood a lone cabin, which knew only peace and virtue, in which an old woman and a youth once lived.

"The old woman dedicated her entire life to loving God and her son.

"The youth loved only his mother, until the day she left him and returned to heaven.

"The youth found himself alone; this was his first sorrow in life. But the sorrows of youth are like clouds in the afternoon: A hopeful sun glows on them, and lends them a magical, golden spell that makes them love the very sorrow.

"Still crying ceaselessly over the loss of his mother, the youth yearned with the longing of an impassioned soul for a being to love. One day he came across a man facing death; he threw himself before the danger that threatened this man, and saved his life.

"He thus made his first friend.

"But then, feeling an empty sanctuary inside his heart, he looked about him for the idol, for an ideal beloved, that could occupy it. He looked, and his eyes found those of a woman.

"Natalia!" Miguel exclaimed in a voice full of passion. "Natalia!" he continued, in a somber tone. "Natalia!" he repeated, in a long sob torn from his heart. "Oh! Why did you appear before my eyes so beautiful and pure, only later to fall from the lofty pedestal upon which my love had placed you into the mire of common women? Why did you allow me to dream of a perfection that does not exist on earth?" Miguel dropped his head into his hands and fell into deep thought.

"Oh! Oh!" I said, trying to get his attention and lighten the gloomy mood of his story, not knowing why I was afraid. "Oh! Were you the one who lived in that cabin and who loved Natalia?"

"Yes," he answered, "that obedient and loving son, that lover who idolized in material beauty a beauty that comes only from the soul, was me. Oh!" he said, looking into my face, still fooled by my disguise: "You are still too much of a boy to understand the vehemence of the first love of a strong, fervent, and pure soul.

"Natalia belonged to an illustrious family. Her father was a powerful man, whose pride would have found the mere idea of a plebeian daring to rest his eyes on his daughter criminal; and yet I loved her; and although everything seemed to drive us apart, the love burning in my heart was immense, and I had to communicate it to her. And she loved me. . . .

"Did she love me? Oh! With a doubt that has consumed my soul like the fires of hell, I have asked that same senseless question of all the forces of creation. Did she love me?

"Yes! I must believe it, for this knowledge is the only ray of light that shines amidst the gloomy memories of my soul. Yes, she loved me, then. If not, why did she come down from her golden palace to meet me in the depths of the forests, defying the frightening solitary night? What else did those long and profound looks say, when she gazed upon my face, upon my lips, into my eyes, her head resting on my bosom, her chest on my knees? What else were those chaste but fervent caresses, the memory of which makes my heart quiver, even now, under the ice of all these years?

"Yes, she loved me. And drunk with that love, I forgot everything: the world, the memory of my mother, and . . . even God. She was my universe, my heaven, my God. How bright my days, illuminated by my memories of her! How beautiful my nights, which brought her to my arms!"

As he said these things, Miguel's voice sounded young and harmonious. He looked up proudly, and all traces of the many years that had since passed disappeared from his face, which glowed now as if it still reflected the light from those days of love he was recounting.

And I, leaning before him, looked on admiringly at the man who had such deep sentiments, but who was also endowed with such heroic serenity. I would have liked to have been a stranger, to have been able to examine with the cold gaze of a philosopher the terrifying depths of that soul's many abysses.

Suddenly Miguel's countenance darkened; a somber brightness shone in his eyes, his lips contracted in a sarcastic laugh, and, mocking himself, he started repeating his own words with a bitter sneer:

"She was my universe, my heaven, my God! Oh! Oh! Oh!"

His dismal and sinister laugh echoed in the ruins. He went on:

"One night, my heart was racing, exalted by some strange restlessness, and it called out to her more longingly than ever. But Natalia did not come. The moon rose above the top of the trees and halfway up the sky, and found me alone still.

"'She is dead!'" I said to myself. "'What else other than death would keep her from me? Has she not come looking for me even when she was delirious with fever, or when she has had to walk through whirlwinds caused by cyclones, or through the thunderbolts of tempests? Natalia is dead!'

"And shaking with an overwhelming terror, I headed straight for the opulent house where she lived.

"When I arrived, I saw there were lights inside the palace, and I thought that each one of those lights was a lugubrious candle burning around her coffin.

"Blinded by this strange hallucination, I ran through the prairie like a madman, climbed swiftly up and over the tall fences, and with my forehead awash in a cold sweat, with my hair standing on end, staring wildly in front of me, I reached the foot of one of the windows from which bright light poured out into the darkness of the country. I lifted myself up by the golden bars and looked inside with my anxious eyes.

"Oh! Oh! Oh!" and his laughter was sarcastic, sharp, and cold, like a double-edged sword. "Oh! Oh! Oh! The woman who had come to meet me, defying cyclones and the booming thunderbolts of storms; the woman who had spent nights lying against my bosom, intoxicating me with her caresses; the one I believed had died, was right there, inside, beautiful, young, smiling, wearing a wreath of roses, in the middle of a bright circle. Next to her was a man to whom she was giving her hand, swearing to love him forever. And before them a priest was blessing her oath."

Miguel interrupted his story, gave me a long look, and said with a dark smile:

"Are you not going to ask me who that man was? He was the one who called himself my friend, the one whose life I had saved."

When I heard the story of that horrible betrayal, painful memories rushed into my soul, burning and heartrending.

I, too, had awoken one day to the light of a terrible reality. Hands that I had once warmed in my bosom turned cold by death had broken my heart. At that moment I felt its wounds reopen and begin to bleed again.

Miguel noticed the emotion on my countenance.

"Poor child!" he said. "He is crying! Is it out of pity for that betrayed heart, or out of fear for the punishment awaiting the guilty ones. Do not worry, for their crime went unpunished. Oh! Never trust your vengeance to your fury, for it might fail you. Just when the steel bar had bent and snapped in my trembling hands, just when, touching the blade of my dagger gently, I was about to return a wound for a wound, a death for a death, a wave of blood flooded my chest, drowned my throat in an angry scream, blinded my eyes, and knocked me senseless.

"When I awoke, the awful vision had disappeared. It was already daylight; the pinkish shades of dawn colored the sky, and the stems of the flowers by the cornices of the wall swayed in a cool and fragrant breeze. The palace was silent; in the distance, on the royal road, a bright party was moving quickly away, shouting joyful exclamations in the morning breeze.

"I got up angrily. Pale, shaking, with my hands in tight fists, I ran after the happy convoy.

"What did I want? I do not know. All I know is that I was mad, and that I ran, yelling the whole time in a hoarse voice stifled by a maddened fury: 'Natalia! Natalia!'

"I quickly reached the carriage, and, pushing my way through the large retinue accompanying it, lunged toward the door and tried to open it. But Natalia's husband stepped between me and the carriage; he drew a pistol from his belt and fired at my chest.

"His shot was on mark; I fell unconscious in the middle of the road.

"I did not feel anything other than a burning wave that washed over my entire body and stopped the beating of my heart.

"I do not know how long I lay there, stretched out on the ground, lying in my own blood, teetering between life and death. In the double agony that darkened my eyes and my mind, I could see birds of prey gliding above my head, in steep circles; and although my hearing was impaired, I could still make out the sinister screeching with which they celebrated my agony and awaited my demise.

"Night came and the cooler temperature gave me new spirit. On my lips, dry from fever, a few dewdrops formed, and I swallowed them immediately, as I was parched with thirst.

"I raised myself with much difficulty from the pool of blood in which I lay and dragged myself on my knees, with one hand on the ground and the other on my wound, to the foot of a tree by the side of the road, where I fell again, without the strength to go on.

"When I got there, my memory, which had momentarily left me, suddenly returned to strike me with a horrible host of recollections. I wanted to retreat into the depths of my heart, but found only a pile of ruins there. Love, faith, hope—it was all destroyed!—and the bitter waves of a sea of pain crashed in the darkness of my soul. Carried away by an impotent fury, I broke down and cried; my tears were drops of fire that burned my cheeks, and my wailing a horrible bellow to which the tigers roared back from the depths of the forest. And tearing at the wound on my chest with my fingernails, I sent my blood straight to the sky, cursing horrendously. Fallen into that strange fit, I spent hours that seemed as long as a reprobate's eternity in hell.

"All of a sudden, an unbelievably loud and frightening sound exploded deep inside the earth, filling the entire circumference from east to west, and quieting all the voices of creation. The earth shook and trembled horribly; the trees pounded the ground with their long branches; the air became filled with noxious vapors; an abyss opened up, and from its bowels torrents of boiling water and whirlwinds of fire escaped; and the mountain, splitting from the top of its summit to the very bottom of its base, collapsed like a wall, covering everything with its tremendous mass.

"The birds of the sky, frightened from their nests, flew about uncertainly; and the fierce beasts, running from the falling and crumbling boulders in their caves, fled down the hillside in tremendous confusion.

"And of all those multitudes of beings raising their voices to the heavens asking for mercy, only one stood up, calmly and serene: the one who just a short while before had lain there, overwhelmed by anger and pain. And with an irreverent smile on his lips, he directed his steps toward the area that had witnessed his past fortune. . . . But when he reached the gully where he had lived his entire life, he saw only a vast mound of boulders. The cabin and the palace, its prairies and its gardens—all had disappeared.

"When I beheld that sight, an infernal joy shook my heart. The earthquake, that upheaval of nature, had erased all traces of the past on the earth—and now I wanted crime to erase it from my soul.

"With my arms crossed on my blood-soaked chest, I embraced the vast ruin with my gaze and let out a dark burst of laughter, which was repeated, as if by the voices of all eternity, by the echoes in the huge precipice.

"Sitting on the mountain of rubble like Lucifer after his fall, I called on 'evil' and began to dream of it.

"While I sat there motionless, lost in my horrendous thoughts, I saw a group of savage-looking men on horseback, dressed strangely, and even more strangely armed, invade the place and rush upon the ruins like a flock of birds of prey, trying angrily to lift the large piles of stone to which the cataclysm had reduced everything.

"I was so lost in my thoughts that it took me a long time to comprehend their intention. But when I finally understood, when I saw that they wanted to dig up the palace—on whose collapsed towers and arches I had begun to walk with such rancorous pleasure—in order to pillage it, I went toward the man who seemed like the leader of the band, and drew my dagger defiantly.

"He was a man of superior height, dark-skinned, and of herculean limbs and features. When he saw my threatening stance, he looked at me with an ironic smile. But it did not take long, once we began to fight in the middle of the circle formed by his sinister companions, for him to learn that the youth whom he mocked was possessed by an infernal strength. His sarcastic laughter turned into a roaring fury and was then hushed altogether by his rasping last breaths of life. My dagger had pierced his chest, and he lay at my feet.

"When they saw their leader dead in front of them, the bandits bowed before me, filled with fearful admiration.

"'Who was that man?' I asked.

"'Our captain.'

"'What was his name?'

"'Gubi Amaya, the Terror of Tucumán. He brought us to attack the ranches of the neighboring region.'

"Gubi Amaya! When I heard the name of that bandit, so infamous back then, a diabolic thought immediately crossed my mind.

"'Good has abandoned me,' I said to myself, 'and here is evil, come my way. Let me join its cult, and devote myself to it. Let me embody it; from now on, I shall be as one with it.

"I turned to the disheartened group.

"'Do you want to see your leader replaced?' I asked.

"'Yes,' they exclaimed together, 'as long as it be by you.'

"'Well then,' I yelled, stretching my hand with the bloody dagger out toward them, 'in the name of the destructive power that has just laid waste to the earth, I promise to increase the fame of Gubi

Amaya, and to leave the most atrocious acts behind in this name. Furthermore, to seal this oath, I require a solemn baptism to formally lay claim to the name.'

"The bandits let out a howl of joy, which was repeated by a formidable echo from the mountain. With the corpse of their leader at their feet, they took some of the blood gushing from his wound, spread it on my forehead, and baptized me in the name of violence, theft, and murder.

"For the next two years, I lived a life of horror and destruction. I never forgave, and those who had the misfortune of coming across my path did not live to tell about it. Zealous in my vengeance, I alone did the fighting, unless the entire band was attacked. And when I attacked, my arm sufficed; my comrades knew that in these encounters they had to satisfy themselves with merely being witnesses. Many perished at my hands for breaking this order.

"Thus, there may have been much savagery in the war I declared against humanity, but there was never any cowardice. . . .

"One time, however . . . !"

The bandit's voice became shaky, and a shadow of remorse darkened his brow.

"One time . . . ! It was a spring day, one of those days in which the soul opens its doors to happiness, or to sorrow, with surprising greed. I was alone. Lying down at my horse's feet, under a group of willow trees along a solitary path, I was thinking of my past life. The warm breeze from the prairies brought the memory of its destroyed happiness in perfumed waves to my heart. A beloved and hated image, the image of happiness, idled about me, now mixing with the soft gusts of wind, the warbling of the birds, and the rustling of the leaves, now smiling in each of the flowers swaying in the gentle breeze. While my body lay there motionless, my soul was tormented by a tumult of emotions. In the air, on the earth, in the branches, and in the foliage, there were mysterious murmurings, chirpings, sighs; the sweet vitality that flowed through everything in nature throbbed in my veins and a deep compassion invaded my heart for the first time in a long,

long time. I thought about my childhood, about my mother, about God; I was horrified by my present life, I hated all the days I had lost, devoted to the cult of evil; and the soul that had wallowed in crime suddenly felt a thirst for love.

"All of a sudden, I heard a sweet and harmonious voice singing a tender lament in the distance. A few moments later, at the end of the path, a young woman appeared. Dressed in white and covered with a veil that the wind curled around her like a blue haze, she walked slowly, her arms at her side, looking up at the sky. She seemed lost in some sweet thought, her entire being exuding tenderness, abandon, and passion.

"When I saw her, my heart began to race as it had done in past times, when happiness resided in it.

"'Divine goodness,' I exclaimed, 'have you sent this woman to me as an angel of redemption?'

"And getting up impetuously, I ran toward her.

"My presence seemed to frighten her, but she did not grow too disconcerted.

"'You are a bandit and I know what you want,' she said to me, taking a diamond ring from her finger. 'Here is my engagement ring. Take it, and tomorrow, at this same time, in this same place, I will give you a large reward for it. Do not worry about my not keeping my word; tonight I am going to marry a wealthy man who has laid tremendous fortunes at my feet; and even though I loved another, I prefer being rich. Right now, as a matter of fact, I was sending off the last of the memories from that love to the wind.'

"Betrayal! This ideal being had a soul of mire! The sentiment that shone in her blue eyes, which was heard in her melodious voice, was not love—it was greed!

"I fell once again from the high region where I had hovered, and caressed a deceiving chimera.

"'You vile creature!' I exclaimed, as the woman suddenly embodied for me the memory of the perfidious girl who had deceived me, and the tender emotions in which my soul had been swimming turned into an enraged fury. 'You vile creature! So your heart loves gold, does it? So you walk about with a smile on your lips and your eyes turned to the heavens dreaming your evil dreams and coldly preparing a betrayal, condemning to eternal pain the soul that loves you? So you want gold? Have it then, and with it the prize of your betrayal!'

"And I plunged my dagger deep into the woman's bosom, and opened up her chest, and tore out her heart, and threw it, still beating, to a vulture waiting nearby for the spoils. Then I filled the bloody hole left behind with all the gold I had with me...."

The man's voice, which at the beginning of the narration of the terrible episode had wavered and trembled, gained speed and fury as it went along, rushing like a torrent toward the end, shaking horrendously.

"Three times deceived by good," he continued, once his exaltation had calmed down, "I swore not to believe in it again, and I plunged myself once more, this time deeper than ever, into my life of crime. I lay waste to the region, burned houses to the ground, and made the roads impassable.

"The men of the law actively pursued me. But I always mocked them, and aided by the astonishing quickness of our horses, stolen from the best breeders of the neighboring provinces, I would disappear just when they thought they had me in their hands, and immediately appear far away, accompanied by my terrible band, bringing death and destruction wherever I went.

"As I carried on in this manner, it did not take long for superstitions to be added to the fear that my name already inspired. I was thought to be a supernatural being sent by hell; inside the cabins they spoke of Gubi Amaya in low voices full of terror.

"One day I was waiting in ambush on a road in the Forests of the Swamp. It was November ninth," he added, raising his head with a solemn gesture and gazing up to the sky vaguely as he seemed to become lost in the memories of that distant day.

"The sun was nearly setting, my band was waiting for me three leagues away, and I was getting ready to retire for the day when I heard the sound of branches cracking and the steps of someone approaching. Soon afterward, I saw a man appear, mounted on a magnificent horse that I longed to have at once. I determined that I would take it from him right there and then.

"I jumped in the middle of the road and shouted loudly: 'Stop!'

"When he heard my cry, the man, who had been riding along distractedly, looked up, and our eyes met.

"'You are Gubi Amaya,' he exclaimed, 'I have finally found you, villain.'

"And he came at me, not with the anger of an attacking aggressor, but with the energetic serenity of a judge passing judgment.

"There was something in the countenance and in the voice of that man, though he was still quite young, something so imposing and majestic, that—how strange!—I, the cold-blooded highwayman, who had done away with all fear and had always acted boldly, froze with fright for the first time in my life, and fled into the forest as fast as my horse would go.

"He followed close behind me; but he was less accustomed than I to galloping through the dense forest and was thus at a great disadvantage, despite the agility and quickness of his steed.

"We reached a small clearing in the middle of the trees, where my pursuer gave a strong kick to his horse, certain that he could catch me there.

"I anticipated his move. Pulling suddenly back on my horses' reigns, I made a quarter turn to the right, and bolted again for the covering of the trees. But at that point my enemy reached suddenly into a coat pocket, took out a fistful of gold doubloons, and threw them at my head with surprising strength, shouting in his loud and terrifying voice: 'You vile creature! So you want gold? Have it then!'

"Those words, combined with the awful blow of the coins, which cut into my forehead, made me fall listless to the ground—for those were the same words that I had uttered when I carried out the only cowardly action of all the crimes that marked my life—words that reached my ear as prophetic and solemn, as if they had been uttered by the mystical trumpets of Judgment Day.

"Through the syncope that clouded my senses and hindered my

faculties, I felt the tremendous hand that had knocked me down now turned into an instrument of restitution. It touched my bruised body gently and charitably and stopped the flow of blood gushing from the wound on my head with the dexterity of a doctor and the solicitude of a brother.

"My drowsiness then became so heavy that I did not feel anything besides a rough and continual movement shaking my body, and the pain this motion caused my head wound.

"When I came to again, I was lying on a bed in a dimly lit room; a man was reading by its light, his head resting on his hand. Although his back was to me, I still recognized him: It was the man who had knocked me off my horse.

"I sighed involuntarily, and the man turned around. Seeing I was awake, he stood up, grabbed a cup that was next to him, came up to me, and had me take a refreshing drink. He checked my pulse; after fixing the pillows and the position of my head, he went back to keeping his vigil and reading.

"What else can I say? The man continued taking care of me in this manner for the seven days it took for my wound to heal. On the eighth, after helping me get dressed, he had me sit up in a chair, sat himself next to me, and gave me a grave and sad look.

"'Do you feel,' he asked, 'that you have enough strength to hear me out and answer me?'

"I did not feel like I did, in fact, for the man exercised a strange power over me, and I had feared this moment ever since I had fallen into his hands. My pride, however, rebelled against this mysterious influence. Wishing to overcome it, I turned my eyes away from the severe gaze with which he looked at me.

"'It is useless,' I answered, 'to waste time with words. There is nothing for you to know about me. My actions speak for themselves; they are written everywhere. If you do not believe me, ask the burned-down houses, the devastated fields, and the countless crosses found by the sides of the roads of the region. I have killed, I have stolen, I have destroyed; and now I am at your mercy. So, what will you do now? It is simple enough: Send me to the scaffold!'

"'Yes,' he replied, 'you have killed, stolen, destroyed, and left waste and devastation everywhere you have gone, like a man-eating tiger. But I know, you poor wretch, that in the depths of your soul there is a voice that you have tried to drown out, a voice that speaks louder than your thirst for blood and your greed for gold. Do you deny that you hear it all the time, in the silence of the night, and in the middle of the pillaging and the moaning of your victims?'

"'Yes,' I interrupted vehemently. 'There is a voice that cries out ceaselessly in my soul, a voice that blends with the murmuring of the night wind, and the clamoring of the pillaging, and the moaning of my victims. The voice of a deep and bloody wound, opened by a human hand. And do you know what it says to me? "Vengeance! Vengeance!" That is what it says!'

"'So you wish to be my judge and question me? Very well, then. Listen to my story, and tell me if you would not have done the same if you were in my place!' And although just a moment before I had refused to answer him, I was overcome by the man's irresistible superiority, and proceeded to reveal to him the entire drama of my life.

"He heard me out gravely and silently, and immediately responded with the following:

"'Almost at the same time as you, I began to open my eyes to life and my heart to hope. You dreamt of finding your happiness in love, I in science. I loved it passionately, and even as a child, I devoted every moment of my life to it. I was the son of a wealthy merchant, and my father's fortune opened the doors of the universities to me, where I drank thirstily from the cup of human wisdom. The sky and the earth revealed the treasures of their mysteries to me, and I began to delight in that existence of perpetual ecstasy that arises from a life of wisdom. Who knows what heights I might have achieved in those bright regions where my soul soared among celestial objects . . . !

"'One day, however, I had to tear my mind from that beatific vision and return to the mire of everyday life.

"'My father, brought down by a partner's fraudulent bankruptcy, saw his huge fortune disappear in one day, and died of grief. His large family became the victim of creditors; they were thrown into the street, and their goods were sold in public auction.

"'With this fateful turn of events, my golden dreams vanished; the severe voice of duty ordered me to renounce them and to run to the aid of my dear ones.

"'I asked for and was granted a term in which to redeem my father's honor and my family's well-being. I abandoned the investigations of the geologist and the telescope of the astronomer to take up the hoe of the farmer. I secluded myself in a deserted area, plowed the earth, fertilized the fields, received huge winter pastures, bred a large number of cattle, and in two years I paid off all the debts hanging over my father's memory and reestablished my family's splendor.

"'The Wars of Independence arrived and offered me a new chance to do good. United with the phalanx of the free I saved our old oppressors from their vengeance a thousand times; and just as many times, after serving as their shield, I suffered as a victim of their perfidy.

"'Then one day—this was during the revolution, when Liniers was marching south with his troops[3]—a man covered in dust and pale with fear and fatigue suddenly entered my house and fell at my feet.

"'"Save me!" he exclaimed. "The viceroy and all his men were captured in the middle of their march, and he is in the hands of the rebels, who are certain not to forgive him his life. I am the treasurer of the expedition. I was able to escape in the darkness, but they are following close behind me, and very soon they will be here to take me back. I have an immense fortune deposited in Potosí. This document proves it. Take it, I give you all I have if you save me from the scaffold that awaits me."

"'I did not even have time to reject the paper in which the man offered me his fortune, when the house was surrounded by a military unit, and the leader asked me to turn the prisoner over to him. In his

........

[3] Santiago Liniers y Bremond (1753–1810), penultimate viceroy representing Spain in the Río de la Plata, organized royalist troops to suppress the independence movement. When most of his soldiers deserted, he was pursued and trapped by Colonel Antonio Balcarce and was subsequently executed. —Ed.

place I gave a letter of guarantee to the Governmental Junta of Buenos Aires.

"'That same night, giving the man a passport and a safe guide, I had him flee to Perú.

"'Go in peace with your usurped fortune," I said to him as I sent him on his way, "but remember that the man who saved your life today is the son of the man whose life you took with your wicked bankruptcy."

"'For that man was my father's murderer. The fortune he offered me in exchange for his despicable life was the fortune he had stolen from him.

"'So, here we have, one in front of the other, your life and mine: antipodal roads, the one streaked with monuments, the other with ruins. Look at how much you have destroyed and how much I have rebuilt! My father's honor, the wealth and happiness of my dear ones, even the joy and safety of the family of the man who sent my father to his grave.

"'God has rewarded me for my deeds, and has given me a wife of whom I am worthy. She shall give me children, and I will be completely happy.

"'As far as you are concerned, I implore you in the name of the only good thing that has survived in your soul—loyalty—to tell me if it is possible for repentance to enter your soul. If not, I will let you go free today, because you are my guest. But tomorrow I will go after you even to the furthest corners of the world to turn you in to the law.'

"With God as my witness, I swear that it was not fear, but rather repentance, that this man's words inspired in my heart, and made me fall at his feet, hitting my chest and exclaiming:

"'I have sinned! Forgive me! Have mercy!'

"It would be impossible to describe the expression of angelic joy that shone on the man's noble countenance then. He lifted me up with kindness, embraced me, called me his brother, and offered me his friendship.

"'Oh!' I said then, like Cain. 'You have forgiven me in the name of God; but what about the others? They will look at me with horror!'

"'No one shall know who you are,' he answered; 'your identity will remain a secret between God and I. Gubi Amaya has died; you are now Miguel. I have thought of everything; if you do not believe me, just look. . . .'

"He opened the door and showed me where we were.

"It was Gualiama, a cattle station, and he and I were the only ones there."

When I heard these last words, I realized in awe that this terrible story—that I had treacherously heard, thanks to the disguise of my clothing—was a secret being told to a stranger, a secret that my father had kept and taken with him to the grave.

I thought then that I would hear the voice of my father rise from the ruins and accuse me of impiety.

"Forgive me!" I cried.

"Who are you?" he said.

"Do you not recognize me by now, Miguel?"

"No!" he answered, strangely moved by the sound of my voice, and looking at me with an anxious gaze.

"Have you forgotten the blondest of the children that you loved so much?"

"My little Emma!" he exclaimed with a deep cry. And embracing me, he lifted me with his robust arms up to his face to take a good look at mine.

"My little Emma!" he repeated, putting me back down on the ground.

And resting his face on my head, he cried bitterly.

Then he grabbed my shoulders and stretched me out at arm's length to look at me.

"Yes," he said, "you are my girl, alright! But why has your blond hair turned black? Why has your smiling countenance grown sad?"

As he said this, he suddenly started, and looked around him.

"And the others?" he said, more with the expression in his eyes than with his voice. "Where are your brothers and sisters?"

I bent my head down and did not answer.

He must have understood, for he moved away from me and went

to lean against an old column, where he covered his head with the long folds of his poncho.

He was crying!

Every once in a while doleful sobs reached me through the silence of the night. Oh! He did not know that of those children whom he loved so much, the happiest were the ones who were already "resting in peace"!

Miguel's horse seemed to grow restless at its owner's long absence and called out for him with a loud neighing.

When he heard his friend's voice, Miguel raised his head slowly, and came toward me.

"My companion grows impatient," he said, "and wants to return to the other shore."

"He is not quite like the *Lobuno*,"[4] he added with a sigh, "but he is good and strong, and he runs faster than most. Look at him, if you do not believe me!"

He showed me from a distance his magnificent and well-harnessed reddish-brown steed, with its long mane and very fine legs. The moonlight reflected off the large silver medals on its bit and breast band.

"I miss the other one, though, my poor, old *Lobuno!* But he was less resilient than I. When he saw that instead of wading through the ford of the river to come to *Sala*, I wanted to take him at night to fight the Federals, and that the joyful voices of the children were replaced by rifle shots and the harsh screams of the fiends we were fighting, he would go no further, and died of grief.

"This one also comes every night, but there is no one to pet him, and the only cries he hears are those of the owl on top of the tower."

Then he looked up at the sky.

"It is getting late," he said, as he used to say before, a long time ago. "Orion's Belt and the Southern Cross are about to set. You have not forgotten that that means it is time for bed, have you?

........

[4] *Lobuno* is a nickname used in Argentina to refer to a horse that has long hair and somewhat resembles a wolf. It literally means "wolfish" in Spanish. —Trans.

"Let us go home."

How sweet were those words to my heart! It had been so long since I had heard anyone say them! It had been so long since I had had a home, and since my father's home had been reduced to a pile of ashes!

All of a sudden, the fantastic silhouettes of two riders appeared atop a mound of debris, black against the deep blue of the sky.

The ethereal wanderers looked around anxiously. Then, believing themselves to be alone, they jumped to the ground and went for Miguel's horse, which neighed in distress, trying to shake itself free of the ties of its hobbling straps.

Miguel saw the riders, wrapped his poncho around his right arm, brandished his dagger in his left, and charged toward them—all in a single instant. Miguel, in fact, was completely eclipsed. He was replaced by Gubi Amaya, appearing in all his somber magnificence.

When the thieves, who had at first prepared to hold their ground, saw the herculean figure—his angry eyes shining in the dark like burning embers—they retreated, terrified. They jumped on their horses with unexpected agility, and rode off, yelling:

"It is the necromancer! The necromancer!"

Miguel tore the hobbling straps off of his horse and jumped on his fast *Sebruno,* racing after them with lightning quickness. The three riders disappeared in the shadows like a mysterious whirlwind, leaving me where I was, paralyzed by surprise and terror.

When I came out of my stupor, the moon was starting to grow pale in the first light of dawn. I found myself alone, sitting on the slab of the column where Miguel had told me his dark story; the dew from the night moistened my hair, and around me there was not even the slightest trace of the strange scenes that had passed before my eyes. I would have thought them the ravings of a delirious mind if Miguel's large figure had not come to stamp on them a seal of reality with its imposing emphasis.

## VII

I found myself once again alone in the middle of the ruins; my fantastic protagonist had disappeared with the night. But I could still hear his words in my ears; they seemed like a deep wake connecting back to the somber torrents of the past. I felt a strange split in my soul and in my body, as if I had lived two separate realities that night. I stretched out several locks of hair to see if they had turned gray.

But as I left behind the area of debris where I had passed the night and came down from the high plain, the pleasant scene that opened before my eyes—while it did not erase the memory of Miguel and his terrible story—brought to my mind a new set of impressions.

The blooming *turcales* and the line of tall trees that marks the course of the creek were turning gold under the first joyful rays of the sun. The pungent fragrances of spring perfumed the air with their voluptuous scents. Bands of mountain hens sang to each other in the clearing under the foliage, and outside the immense corrals that extend behind the house, hundreds of cows mooed for their calves, locked inside the yards of the dairy. In the distance, the farm hands ran after the cattle in the forest while singing mournful laments in their magnificent voices, improvising with fervent inspiration. The slight trill with which they make the notes vibrate is one of the charming aspects of those plaintive melodies.

When I returned to the house, I found new guests had arrived. An old military man, who had been expected since the day before, had arrived in the middle of the night accompanied by his daughter. He was a colonel, an old comrade of San Martín, one of the few brave men who survived the immortal campaign that liberated Chile and Perú.[5]

His daughter was an angel of beauty. Her name was Azucena Rosalba. Fair-skinned, blond, and slender, there was something in her

........

[5] José de San Martín (1778–1850), commander-in-chief of the revolutionary army of the Andes in the wars for independence from Spain; considered Argentina's national hero. —Ed.

light blue eyes, as in her entire person—something ethereal and supernatural—that invaded my heart when I saw her, like a sad foreboding. Oh! I was not wrong. Azucena was under the attack of that inexorable illness that tends especially to consume the young and the beautiful; that illness that rolls along slowly like lava from a volcano, but inevitably catches and devours its victim.

Born along the Río de la Plata, Azucena had breathed its fragrant breezes in vain hoping for relief from her suffering. So the doctors had ordered her to go north for the change in air. Her father, who had heard speak of the wonderful climate of M——, had brought her here, driven by the hope to which his soul clung. What the poor father would not have given to transfer to his daughter the gales of life that his broad and strong chest breathed with ease!

As far as she was concerned, however, she was cheerful and happy, and thought only of having fun. The moment she saw me, she ran up to me with a sly smile on her lips; and when my hosts introduced me, with my male name, she threw her arms around my neck, gave me a kiss, and said, "God bless you, Emma . . . nuel." From that moment on we were inseparable. I carried her on my shoulders as we strolled under the jujube trees; I milked with my own hand the glass of milk I took to her bed; and at the table she would only eat what I cut for her. But oh! My care, and that of her father, were to crash impotently at the feet of that terrible angel with black wings whose name is Phthisis!

During the day Rosalba felt fine, and the warm southern wind that reigns on our plains when the sun is above the horizon vitalized her chest. But when night fell and the air from the mountains descended into the prairies and the dew began to condense on the fields of grama grass, the poor girl would start to feel the deadly shortness of breath that tormented her. She would run around, her face in anguish and her temples throbbing, in search of the air that she lacked in her lungs, which were being destroyed by the relentless disease.

The colonel would spend the night walking with her through the gallery, as this was the only way she could breathe more freely. With her head resting on her father's chest, Rosalba would sleep long hours, abandoning the weight of her body with that trust that we love so much in children.

I always accompanied the colonel in his vigils with the girl. Sitting on a stool at the end of the gallery, I heard him tell his daughter the adventures of his long life, legendary epics that in the veteran's noble language seemed like strokes of fire against the dark background of the night. The tall, lean, imposing old man carried the white, ethereal, fragile girl in his arms, and her long blond hair became mixed with his white hair, intertwining like fresh ivy around an old trunk. Speaking of distant men and long-forgotten events as he walked to and fro, his voice sent my mind down a strange road—and I thought I was watching the ghost of the past lifting the shadow of the future in its arms.

Then, one day on which Rosalba was suffering more than ever, I suggested to the colonel that he take her to the hot springs in Rosario.

My idea would have seemed absurd to anyone who did not know about the marvelous properties of those famous springs in our country. They are a panacea for everything from leprosy to fever, apoplexy, dropsy, gout, and pulmonary diseases.

Only the backwardness in which we live due to the long civil wars can explain the little attention that has been given to building more roads and lodgings in and around that important place, a true sanctuary for health.

Numerous caravans from throughout the republic go there to try out the effectiveness of the springs. There the leper, the cataleptic, the paralytic, witness their horrible misfortunes disappear; and invalids who have been abandoned by science, and those on the verge of death, are brought on stretchers from long distances and recover their life and health in the miraculous waters.

They gush forth in a boiling stream from the hollows of the large boulders at the foot of the Hill of the Silver Fountain. They then descend quickly into a riverbed containing deep pits designed for the baths, and trace a path, winding along, emanating vapors that decrease in density as the water cools under the dense shadows of the forest, until it joins the Orcones River.

The colonel welcomed my suggestion with an exclamation of joy, and Rosalba jumped into my arms, despite the fact that I was wearing a man's shirt.

"Maybe there . . . !" she exclaimed, with a glowing gaze that expressed faith and hope.

We quickly prepared to depart.

The colonel saddled the horses while Rosalba's servant and I put all the belongings that she considered necessary for her comfort into a carriage: rugs, cushions, perfumes—in a word, luggage worthy of an oriental princess. That same day, late in the afternoon, we said farewell to our generous hosts. We left along with two girls who lived in the house, two lively and rowdy girls who ran ahead of us, filling the forest with their happy laughter and dragging in their childish racket the pale invalid, who looked like a romantic illusion between those two robust little women.

It was six o'clock. The sun had set, and the moon was starting to shine its silver rays over the blooming grama grass of the countryside. We forded the river and were heading along the shore on a pebbled path. This meant torture for the impatient girls, as it forced them to hold their horses back at an unbearably slow pace.

Our guide, an artful old man, a true son of nature, dark-skinned, with the eye of a vulture, went ahead on his cinnamon-colored colt. He wore huge spurs that clanked loudly against the side strips hanging from the saddle, startling the cattle that we passed on either side. An old resident of the region, he knew the history of every place we passed by heart, and told it in his picturesque language better than the most talented chronicler, often naming his own horse as witness to the truth of his assertions.

"Sir, let's hurry passed this area. It's a very hard and heavy place, for it used to belong to two brothers who have already passed on, two brothers who loved each other very much, but were caudillos of enemy parties: one was Unitarian, the other Federal. You should've seen those two, sir! When they got together and no one was around, they'd hug and cry sure enough. . . . One would cry, that is, for the other was too much of a man and swallowed his tears. But if they met when they were at the head of their bands, God save us then! They'd go at it until the earth itself would begin to bleed. Right over there there's still a pile of bones, their owners suffering in purgatory. The other night, as a matter of fact, a ghost rose up from that area and left me shaking in my boots. My cinnamon colt himself can vouch for the fact that he broke into a full gallop and ran for half a mile, making me lose his hobbling straps and three locks off the breast band of the harness."

"Be careful, my friend, Contreras," Rosalba answered him, laughing, "that if that half mile gallop did not knock you off your horse, that tall tale just might."

"Fine! Fine! So the child doesn't believe in ghosts! I should leave her in Esteco for a night during the last quarter of the moon, and then she'd see apparitions so horrible rising from the rubble over there that it would make her heart stop."

"Esteco! And where, pray tell, is that?" Rosalba asked, looking over and winking at me.

"Right over there, child, at the head of that hill, on the other side of the river, as a matter of fact. Haven't you heard speak of the city whose inhabitants were so arrogant that they only wore gold and silver, and so cruel that they used to burn their slaves alive? Well, that's where it was, right over there. And if they were still alive, we would hear the sound of their dances from where we're standing right now, for it is said that their dances lasted for months on end, for the people there had no need to work, since they had mines of gold ingots that they could cut into with a chisel right on their own hill. But you know how it is, sir. Sometimes God gives his consent, but not forever. One night, the earth swallowed them up, just like that.

"None of them ever came out again. But their gold cups and vases and their diamond necklaces sure did, carried by floods to the bottom of the ravines. Many times I have found rings with green stones and plates that shine like the sun, as a matter of fact. But I never took one. Instead, I've thrown them far off so that those evil objects don't tempt another Christian. It's true, sir! Here's my cinnamon colt, who was present at the time, and he wouldn't let me tell you a lie, now, would he?"

And Contreras would put grave emphasis on his appeal to his horse, certain that the poor cinnamon colt would not contradict him.

Meanwhile the night was progressing. The wind had died down, and only once in a while would a warm breeze reach us, full of the intoxicating fragrance of the heliotrope, among the thickets of rock-roses along the riverbed.

I rode next to Rosalba, who for some time now had traveled in a deep silence. I could hear her sigh often, and gasp anxiously in the night's warm air. She seemed oppressed, short of breath, and restless, and would turn around to look at her father every time he stopped to light his lighter for those of our companions who smoked. All of a sudden, breaking abruptly away from my hand, which had been resting on the neck of her horse, Rosalba raised the bridle and kicked her horse forward, making it jump over the tall weeds, and galloped off in a desperate run.

I followed close behind her, despite the great disadvantage I had due to the superior speed of her horse.

After galloping for an hour through the dark paths of a wood, Rosalba finally came to a stop at the end of a shady gully filled with wild fragrances. She was extremely pale, and yet a smile rested on her countenance.

"You must confess, Emmanuel," she said to me, with a burst of laughter that sounded like a bird singing in the clear air of the night, "you must confess that this time, at least, I scared you. I am sorry! You did not know that when I feel short of breath, the best remedy for me is to run. Yes. I run from my fierce enemy and leave it far behind," she said, and turned around with a mocking expression on her face, as if she were in fact defying the fury of an adversary.

"What a beautiful place!" she went on, looking about her. "What peace and solitude! How cool it is here! Can you feel the soft breeze and the air that expands in your lungs? How well one can breathe here! Look at the ruins of that ranch. How happy the people who lived under that thatched roof must have been, in the shadow of those carob trees that in spring must have scattered its flowers on them like snow . . . !

"But, what is wrong, Emmanuel? You seem preoccupied, as if you were dreaming. . . . I do not know! But I am certain that your soul is far from here."

Yes, my soul was far away, very far; for it was roaming through the past, where it recognized that gully, those trees, that ranch. I had been there once, on a night with a full moon like this one.

One day, my brother and I, tired of being at home, had solemnly resolved to retire from the world and make a pilgrimage to Jerusalem, to go on from there to the desert, and, like Saint Jerome and Saint Paula, become hermits. Although Saint Paula was only eight years old and Saint Gerome six, it took them less than an hour to get their project under way. Two gentle women had come to bring honey and bread to our mother; we took their horses and rode with devoted spiritual absorption, heading in a full gallop into the forest.

Everything was going wonderfully well while the sun's joyful rays penetrated the dense foliage. But the afternoon started to fall, and we began to realize that Jerusalem was further away than we had imagined, and our pious plans turned into fear, and our ascetic sobriety into a hunger that would have seemed immense had it not been overshadowed by an overwhelming thirst. We cried and frightened each other with our screams. It was growing dark, and we went further and further into the thick forest.

During one of those moments in which we were going along in silence, terrified, we heard a dog bark in the distance. We began to cheer up, and screamed out, asking for help; but soon thereafter, a tremendous roar made the entire forest shake and left us dead silent with horror. There was no mistaking it: That had been the sound of a tiger—only from its tremendous jowls could such a roar have come. But our horses continued on calmly, as if they had not heard anything.

We began to cry out again, and again the roar was heard, even more terrifying this time. But then we finally heard a voice shouting in the distance:

"Antolín! Antolín! Come here, my son! Good God! I send you out to retrieve those poor creatures, and you go and frighten them to death! Over here, children, do not be afraid, come here."

We reached a clearing in the forest and saw at the end of the gully the thatched roof of a ranch. Next to a hearth burning on the front patio, we saw a woman dressed in white, waving to us with the end of her blue rebozo.

Then an urchin came to meet us. He was between fourteen and sixteen years of age and looked like a real-life bandit—he had a watchful eye, a shameless gaze, and an impudent smile.

He jumped up, agile as a cat, on the rump of my brother's horse, grabbed the bridle, and led us to the house. There, overwhelmed with fatigue, we fell into the woman's arms as she approached to help us dismount.

Our host noticed that my lips and mouth were completely dry and parched and went into the house. She came out a moment later with two wide cups made from ostrich eggshells full of carob mead. Then she had us lie down next to the fire on two wooden benches and immediately saddled a horse, which was grazing nearby, and sent her son off quickly in case we were in need of assistance. He headed down the same road we had come to tell them at home about our edifying crusade, and to have them come retrieve the exhausted pilgrims.

My mother said farewell to the woman, giving her many presents; and every time she spoke of her it was with deep gratitude.

Four years later, in 1831, the Southern Front rose up en masse against the constitutional government. The rebels, engaged in the fiercest pillaging ever seen, brought theft, murder, and fires everywhere they went. My father, under the martial law for which the legislative body had voted, was given forces to go against them. One day, after a bloody skirmish, he was presented with one of the caudillos of the rebellion; he had been taken prisoner after desperately resisting at the end. He was a famous murderer who had stood out in the insurrection for the refined cruelty of his actions. His battle name was

"The Butcher"—a name that made his already dark life story seem even darker. Under martial law, the crimes of which he was guilty condemned him without trial. Despite the severity with which he had fulfilled his duty, my father had previously found ways to save many of the misguided men against whom he fought; but although he was especially impressed by his extreme youth, he could do nothing for this one, no matter how much he wanted to. He was forced to abandon him to the ominous destiny that soon awaited him; my father retired, disgusted by the fatal mistake that induces us to lay the foundations of the social edifice with the blood of capital punishment.

All of a sudden, a woman, pale white and trembling, ran into the tent, screaming, "My son! Antolín!" Seeing my father, she was about to throw herself into his arms, when the blast of the rifles was heard and she fell at his feet.

This tragic event moved my father deeply and left a painful mark in his generous soul forever.

My mind was absorbed in the memory of what had happened back then, and for a few minutes I forgot about Azucena. When I turned back to look at her, I found she was staring straight at me, saying, "If your head is not in Lima, it is clearly on something that is making you sad."

We met up again with our companions, and by six in the morning we had reached the baths of Hot Springs.

There were several families there when we arrived. Gathered in a circle of tents, they entertained themselves in peaceful activities, such as bathing, hunting, taking long excursions in search of beehives, eating delicious *picanas*[6] together on long tablecloths under the fragrant foliage of the forest, dancing, singing, playing games of forfeits, and telling all sorts of stories—from serious dramas to witty and spicy anecdotes.

........

[6] *Picanas* is the meat from the haunch or rump of the cow. —Trans.

They gave us the most cordial of welcomes. The ladies hurried to prepare the *mates*[7] with the spurts of boiling water gushing from the boulders. They offered them to us, excusing themselves for not being more dexterous in their preparation, assuring us that we would drink better ones when the "master of ceremonies" returned. The latter, it turned out, was in charge of this task and many others. Everyone called her "The Soul of Society" because of her liveliness and inexhaustible happiness. She had gone to Rosario to get some provisions, and they awaited her return with much impatience.

She finally arrived, riding a bay colt devilishly fast, pushing branches from the trees out of her way with her hands, and at times grabbing them, holding on to them for a moment, and then releasing them with a crazed laughter. She had on the croup of her horse a large, full sack, which she dropped to the ground before she reached the camp. Sliding down from the saddle by herself, she ran to meet the colony that came out en masse to welcome her with shouts of joy. She hugged everyone, men and women; she told each one of them the news they had asked her to find out; she brought them up to date on everything—told them about the priest, about the neighbors in town, about the parties, about the stagecoaches that had arrived on the royal road. Then, turning to the young women, she added, gesturing silently: "An Italian is coming, *bello e mesto come un trovatore;*[8] but he is mute, my daughters, mute as a post. I caught up to him at the turn of the river, and even though I did absolutely everything I could to get him to speak, the only thing I could get out of him is that he is coming from Tucumán and traveling wherever his horse takes him."

I looked at the woman and could not believe my eyes. It was María Montenegro, a friend and contemporary of my mother's; and yet, she was still as young and beautiful as when she was twenty years old. Still, María had not had a happy life; great misfortunes had fallen upon her, and the future had appeared ominous. But she was a coura-

........

[7] The *mate* is an infusion of tea-like leaves consumed in South America. It is also the name of the gourd or calabash in which the infusion is served. —Trans.

[8] Beautiful and melancholy as a troubadour (Italian). —Trans.

geous soul who knew how to smile in the face of sorrow; she had let it slide right off her countenance, and it had not left any traces on her smooth features.

How strongly I wanted to embrace her and tell her who I was; but I had to remain incognito—only Azucena and her father could know my secret!

Another surprise awaited me yet—Miguel was also there. He had caught the thieves, captured them, and taken them to Rosario, where he turned them in to the mayor. There he had met a few ladies from the bath colony; they had begged him to accompany them back, and he had now been at the springs for several days. This very much pleased the young ladies, for he looked after them in their daily excursions, and at night served as the holder of the tokens in the evening games of forfeits. That day he had gone out in search of bee-hives. When he came back in the afternoon, loaded with honey and flowers as he used to do so long ago, I had the enormous pleasure of being able to run up and meet him, as I used to do when I was a little girl. Jumping up, I put my arms around his neck and stole from him the sweet plunder he was bringing.

A little later the taciturn Italian reached our camp. He said hello with serious courtesy and asked permission to spend the night there with us. The men quickly offered him their tents; and the ladies, in love with the air of sadness on his handsome countenance, welcomed him with extreme friendliness.

No matter how hard they tried, however, they could not get him to accompany us on the expedition to Red Hill that we were planning for the next morning. We therefore set out at dawn, leaving our guest alone in the camp.

The outing was truly a delight. We roamed all day through the narrow canyons of the mountain range that the common people claim is full of ghosts and apparitions. The area does indeed have a rugged look to it, imposing and sinister like the nomadic tribes that live there. Trees of gigantic girth and height, with strangely shaped and colored leaves, rise here and there, and their top branches are perpetually shaken by the wild and impetuous winds, rocking the old vines that wind between them. At night, therefore, they can look like ghosts dancing and howling in the darkness. Tall grasses, many of them poisonous even to the touch, grow with an amazing richness of vegetation on the reddish sand, covering the ground in the area and presenting incredible electrical phenomena in the summer nights. The tempests never leave those mountains. Lightning bolts flash ceaselessly around their summits, and the crash of the thunder is answered from the depth of the valleys by the roars of tigers and the rattles of snakes. Eagles and hawks make their nests on those rocks, and they can often be seen rising and screeching, hovering in the air in magical circles, a lizard or snake clutched in their claws.

There is nothing as pleasant to behold, however, as the view of those canyons and mountains from afar, even if, when seen up close, they do fill the soul with an invincible sentiment of terror. But from a distance, one sees how they rise like a blue wall, making a straight silhouette against the horizon, the base adorned by a green strand of forest; and further below, the plentiful Pasaje River stretches its silver ribbon, adding its shifting reflections to the rich tones with which dawn colors this amazing view.

When we returned to our camp after our extended excursion to Red Hill, night had long since fallen. The full moon, rising behind the mountains we had visited during the day, shone on the tops of the trees, and its rays slid obliquely through the foliage, crossing like strings of light in the darkness of the forest. One might have thought them silver nets thrown by the spirits to capture drifting auras.

With the bridle of my horse in my hand, I stood motionless and contemplated, thoroughly enthralled, the magical contrast of the scene composed of two opposing principles: that of light and that of darkness. I was staring so fixedly, in fact, that little by little I began experiencing unusual optical phenomena. At times I would see the translucent wings and the swaying clothes of a nymph shifting in the thickets; at others I would see the metallic scales of a dragon and its shining eyes glowing like burning embers. At once I would see the horrible head of a demon coming out of the twisting tree trunks; then I would see, in the distance, the bright face of a smiling angel.

To my amazement, the last vision I saw did not disappear. A celestial being approached me, and as its ethereal shape became more and more perceptible, the melancholic smile on its lips became sweeter and sweeter. When it reached my side, it put its hand on my shoulder, and, pointing to the forest, said in a very soft voice:

"*Nel mezzo del cammino di nostra vita.*"[9]

It was Azucena. She had left her riding skirt behind and now wore a white muslin gown. Its undulating folds waved about her in the night breeze, lending her a fantastic and supernatural appearance, which awoke in my heart that lugubrious foreboding that I had already felt when I first saw the beautiful girl.

But she did not notice my melancholy. Instead, she continued speaking, with a gracefully comical gesture of grief:

"Woe to us, who live in the century of weak nerves and hysterics! Oh! Oh! Oh! The ladies, frightened as always, have asked for a bonfire to be lit, and . . . look at how our *selva selvaggia*[10] is not even *oscura*[11] any more."

And, sure enough, the forest was suddenly illuminated by the light of the large bonfires that the servants kept lit all night to keep the tigers at bay.

Azucena remembered our country soirée, and we both hurried back to our tents.

It was time already. The small society of the baths was gathered under the predetermined walnut tree. No one was missing, not even the taciturn and mysterious Italian who had arrived the night before. Sitting on the root of a large tree, his head resting on the trunk, he was looking up at the stars with a contemplative attitude and seemed completely removed from everything happening around him.

After we had sung, danced, and discussed politics, storytelling time finally arrived.

........

[9] In the middle of the road of our life (Italian). This is the first line of Dante's *Divine Comedy.* —Trans.

[10] Wild wilderness (Italian). Also from the *Divine Comedy.* —Trans.

[11] Dark (Italian). The pun depends on a sustained reference to Dante's *Divine Comedy.* —Trans.

Miguel, according to the established custom, gave his hat to Azucena's servant to collect the tokens of forfeit from everyone.

The unknown Italian, once he was told what was expected of him, took a ring from his finger and put it in the hat.

Ms. Montenegro, walking by me, whispered in my ear:

"The Italian leaves tomorrow. We must get him to contribute his share of storytelling tonight."

Then she went up to Miguel, who had turned around to draw a token impartially, and, handing him the hat, said to him softly:

"For God's sake, my old Miguel, make sure you find the thick ring that is in there somewhere."

Miguel winked, one of those typical gestures of the region; then, after stirring the tokens in the hat noisily, lifted his hand. The Italian's ring was on his index finger, shining.

Everyone turned, therefore, to look at the stranger. The ladies brought their chairs closer to hear better; and Azucena, leaving the pillows that her servant had brought for her, came to sit next to me on Miguel's poncho.

The foreigner realized that all excuses were hopeless; thus, smiling melancholically, he bowed to the company with that gallant and exquisite courtesy that distinguishes Italian noblemen.

Then he seemed to fall back into himself. He looked up at the sky, shaking his head sadly. And as if he had forgotten that he had an audience encircling him, like a somnambulist evoking memories from the past under a magnetic spell, with a voice that sounded at times like the moaning of the wind, and at others hoarse and threatening like crashing thunder, he began to speak.

## A DRAMA IN THE ADRIATIC

### I

"Venice, the beautiful bride of the Adriatic," he said. "Venice, that magical queen as powerful in other times as she is now defeated and in chains, forgot for the time being that she was a slave, and, covering her chains with fragrant garlands, abandoned herself to the wild joys of Carnival. Her palaces, magnificently illuminated, opened their golden doors to the numerous guests who invaded them, going noisily up the many marble steps. Thousands of gondolas wound through her mysterious canals, filled with masked men and women going to the dances, to rendezvous with lovers, to carry out vendettas, or to hold concerts in the lagoons. And from the entirety of that vast concert of palaces, cafes, taverns, terraces, balconies, streets, plazas, and canals, a single and tremendous shout rose up, made up of all the sounds that the human chest can let out: shouts of joy, exclamations of surprise, interjections of fear, howls of anger, sighs and words of love, twice as lovely for being expressed in the sweet and poetic language of Tasso. Here the deafening, discordant clamor of a *cencerrada;*[12] there, the delightful melody of a serenade; further along, a hundred happy Punchinellos crowd together in a gondola exquisitely decorated with bunting, going along, singing and laughing under the somber arches of the Bridge of Sighs. Their songs and laughter sounded satanically ironic under the lugubrious domes that have seen so many pale faces go by, and whose echoes have repeated so many cries of anguish. But now, all this was forgotten. The terrible Tribunal of Ten,[13] its mysterious judgments and its many victims, passed by like the glory days of Venice, and this Nereid, who is always happy to admire herself, looking so beautiful in the clear mirror of her canals, had forgotten her past splendor and her present humiliation, and smiled at her tyrants, opening her arms and her golden palaces to them, singing and dancing with them—but instead of her own rich

·······

[12] A *cencerrada* is a noisy serenade of bells, horns, etc., on a widower's second wedding night. —Trans.

[13] The Tribunal of Ten refers to a legislative council that exercised a secretive and oppressive tyranny over the Venetian Republic. In the eighteenth century, Enlightenment thinkers viewed the Venetian Tribunal of Ten as a horrid anachronism at a time when more democratic aspirations were vaunted. In *The Social Contract*, for example, Jean-Jacques Rousseau went so far as to condemn the Tribunal of Ten as a "tribunal of blood." —Ed.

national dances, it is the loud and barbaric songs of the north to which she danced."

As he spoke thus, the Italian's voice trembled, and his almond-shaped, black eyes shone with indignation.

"But not all the sons of Venice," he continued, "looked on with indifference at the Austrian chains that held the claws of the Lion of St. Mark imprisoned.

"There were still a few strong cubs left who roamed in the darkness, roaring bloody threats under their breath.

"And if the day of vengeance had not yet arrived, if the chalice of indignation had not yet spilled over, there were still, in each of the palaces on Rialto, as in each of the humble houses on the Lido, in each of the wealthy gondolas of the aristocrats, as in each of the poor boats of the fishermen, hearts pounding with hatred at the mere mention of the name Austria. And Venice, like all of Italy, was undermined by numerous secret associations all occupied with the same objective: the independence of the motherland."

## II

"The Punchinellos who had so pleasurably just passed under the bridge that held so many terrible memories, had been traveling along the canals, picking up many masked men as they went along, all wearing the same costume. The gondola finally stopped under the balconies of an old, decayed palace.

"The happy costumed group let out a loud, long, and drawn-out hurrah, repeated by the echoes of the somber building. At this signal, a hand raised the latticed window of a balcony, and a young man with a pale face and a long, black mustache leaned out over the canal. When he saw him, the leader of the Punchinellos stood up, raised his hand, and made some kind of strange sign. Then the group let out another hurrah, like before, and the gondola disappeared into the darkness.

"Another gondola was following close behind them; inside, the masked men sang the parts of *Hernani* and repeated the chorus:

'*Allegri beviamo!*'[14]

"The young man closed the balcony and called out to someone. An old man came before him.

"'Giovanni,' he said to him, 'our Orient will be holding a solemn meeting tonight, and all of its members will be present. Carry out your duties as a concierge and prepare everything accordingly. At midnight, twenty gondolas will arrive, one by one, at the secret door, and the underground chamber will be occupied by five hundred Punchinellos. Under their masks, you will find our brothers' determined and vigorous countenances.

"The old man and the young man each grabbed a lamp. The old man walked through a long gallery covered with portraits, stopped before the last of these, and touched a spring hidden in the frame. The portrait spun on hidden hinges, revealing a wide staircase leading down into darkness. The old man headed down the lugubrious spiraling steps with the lamp in his hand.

"The young man, meanwhile, walked by a long line of rooms covered with magnificent reliefs and frescoes, and stopped in front of a dark and silent chamber.

"'Blanca!' he said in a low voice. 'Are you sleeping, dear sister?'

"'I am awake, like you,' a sweet, sad voice answered.

"'You are up all alone and in the dark!' the young man said, with an affectionate reprimand, and went into the room.

"The light from his lamp illuminated a simply adorned boudoir and the beautiful figure of a young woman who seemed lost in painful thoughts, her arms crossed on her chest.

"The sheer folds of the long white tunic covering her body would have given the young woman a fantastic air, were it not for the thick waves of black hair that revealed her to be a youthful and living treasure. If there are names that coincide especially well with the individ-

........

[14] "Let's eat and be merry!"(Italian) The opening choral piece of *Ernani*, in which rebels and bandits amuse themselves before the dramatic crisis emerges. *Ernani*, an opera in four acts by Giuseppe Verdi (1844) and modeled after Victor Hugo's drama (1830) of the same name, finds its way into Gorriti's texts as a frequent citation. Ironically, the opera is sustained by masked identities and concealments, appropriate to the plot of "Gubi Amaya." —Ed.

ual qualities of the people to whom they belong, that of Blanca, given to that young woman, was one of them, for her skin was diaphanous and bluish, and seemed to darken her translucent crepe dress. There was, furthermore, an extreme paleness, added to that whiteness, and a somber restlessness in her beautiful blue eyes, which were not hidden by the affectionate smile with which she approached her brother."

## III

"'You were up alone, and in the dark,' he continued, holding her hands in his and gazing into her eyes with a searching look. 'Blanca, dear sister, what has been going on in your heart for some time now? Your youthful joy has suddenly been replaced by a deep and sorrowful restlessness. I have found you here many times, on your knees, with your face in your hands, crying bitterly and so overwhelmed by this unknown grief that you did not even take notice of my presence and my caresses, nor of my tears and my supplications; you were instead as unresponsive as the marble upon which you laid your head. Now you no longer cry, but your eyes have grown somber, and you often run alarmed and trembling into my arms, as if some invisible enemy threatened you. What gloomy secret are you hiding from your brother's heart, from your childhood friend? Have I not loved you enough for you to trust me? Did I ever hesitate to fulfill any of your desires?'

"The young woman's face became even more pale, and her eyes expressed a tremendous sorrow.

"'Dear Octavio!' she exclaimed, hugging her brother. 'My good and generous protector! Yes . . . you have been everything to me. To a brother's love you have added the tutelary solicitude of a father, as well as the care and tender abnegation of a mother. When you were still a child, at that young age when one usually lives only for oneself, you came to sit at the foot of my crib, which death had forsaken, and kept vigil over your little orphan sister. Still young, handsome, and at the age when most youth pursue their illusions, the only flowers of life, you risk your very life and stay behind, disguised and hidden, and devote to your sister the years which, without her, you would be spending in a foreign country enjoying the pleasures and glory to which your illustrious name and brilliant talents entitle you.'

"'Well then, my dear Blanca,' he interrupted her; 'if you still carry in your soul the memory of those days so satisfying to me, when there was nothing you did not have at my side—in the name of those days I ask you to pour your sorrow into your brother's heart, so that you might unburden yourself of some of your tears and stop suffering by yourself and in silence any longer.'

"Blanca gazed straight at her brother with an ineffable expression of tenderness, but then quickly turned her eyes and looked downward. A violent internal battle made the crêpe covering her bosom quiver. She hesitated, shook, and rested her head against her brother's chest; then her knees bent as if she were about to fall at his feet; making a supreme effort, however, she raised her pale but smiling face up to look at him.

"'Yes, my friend,' she said to him, 'I am suffering. But your tender solicitude exaggerates my sorrow and mistakes its nature. Is there not in everything around us many reasons to make us grieve and cry?'

"'Oh! It is true. . . .' Octavio answered in a bitter voice. 'I was such a fool to ask you for the cause of your sorrow! You see our motherland enslaved and its best sons exiled or in chains. You have seen our own father die at the scaffold, and, without a doubt, our friend from childhood, the brave Mario who loved you so much, has disappeared under the murderous "weights." You see your brother, the last scion of a race of heroes, pursued, errant, forced to hide shamefully in the shadow of the monuments raised by the glory of his ancestors. And you yourself, the heiress of immense treasures, have to live out the miserable life of an ordinary worker, and pay with the sweat of your own brow for the right to live under a dark name, in your parents' ruined palace. But take comfort, my sister. Our affront and your sorrow will soon be over. The hour of liberty for Italy is at hand. Even as

I speak, thousands of fearless hearts, thousands of strong arms, are busy filing down our chains. Very soon, everywhere in our country, from the Alps to Mount Etna, a tremendous shout of triumph will be heard. And then, surrounded once again by the grandeurs that were taken from you in your childhood, you will see open before your eyes a horizon of happiness as yet unknown in your life.'"

IV

"As he spoke thus, Octavio's countenance was radiant; the fire of faith glowed on his countenance.

"Blanca stifled a moan, and reached out to grab her brother's hand.

"'May God protect your efforts,' she said to him, 'and bless the holy work to which you are devoted. As far as I am concerned, the only possible happiness for me is that which can come from you; when I see you happy again, I will be so as well.'

"A drawn-out shout, the hurrah of the Punchinellos, was heard in the distance. When he heard it, Octavio hugged his sister with sudden enthusiasm.

"'Yes, my dear friend. God protects our glorious cause and will soon smile again upon this land of his. Do you hear that distant sound? It is the voice of Italy calling out to its scattered sons; it is a prophetic shout foreshadowing our victory. Good-bye, my dear Blanca. . . . You who are an angel, pray and wait. . . . Good-bye!'

"'Octavio . . . !' Blanca shouted in a weak voice, stretching her arms out after her brother. 'He cannot hear me. . . . He has disappeared and with him all hope of anyone delivering me from my crime. Oh!' she continued, covering her face with her hands in an outburst of delirium. 'There is that accusatory shout erupting within me, from deep in my soul, repeating those tremendous words: "Cain! Cain! What have you done to your brother?!"'

"'You have sold him out!' a voice answered, making Blanca tremble. 'You have sold him out miserably; you are a sister committing a crime worst than the first fratricide! You have turned him over to the hands of his enemies. But why, unworthy daughter of Italy, why have you exchanged your motherland, like the whores of Zion, for the love of the tyrants who have enslaved her?'

"'Mario!' she exclaimed, and ran toward a man who was looking at her with a severe gaze, his arms crossed and his head held high.

"'Yes,' he answered, rejecting her with contempt; 'it is I, Mario, who was buried in the *pozzos*[15] by the Austrian you love to quiet the only voice that can denounce him before the holy association to which he has introduced himself by assuming and thus debasing an Italian name. . . . Mario, who was buried in those dungeons to which living beings are sent to find a bed made from the bones of their predecessors. . . . Mario, who, tearing off his shroud, and raising the stone off his grave, has arrived in time to save his brothers from the scaffold that the spy is preparing for them, and to tell you, who were just capable of listening to your brother's noble words without dying of shame and remorse, that you are the accomplice of a traitor. You have sacrificed your name, your motherland, your family, and my love for a man who has sold you out as you have sold us out. That wretch who joined our Orient under the name of Marelli, that Austrian who you love under the name of Estevan Landoberg, is the son of Radetzki. He is the favorite of the queen of Hungary, one of the pawns that the proud Austrian woman uses to tear from the hearts of our women the secrets of their fathers and husbands.'

"Blanca moved her hand over her heart as if she had received a deadly blow.

"'Oh, infamy . . . ! Oh, shame . . . !' she exclaimed.

"'Yes . . . !' Mario answered with a fierce smile. 'Shame and infamy that will be washed with blood . . . with the blood of the traitor who has made of you an instrument with which to scale into the sanctuary in which we have been preparing the liberty of our motherland.'

"Blanca stumbled back, pale as a corpse. Then she stepped under the frame of the door and shouted with a determined voice:

. . . . . . . .

---

[15] Cells or pits (Italian). —Trans.

"'No! No, you will not kill him! That man's life belongs to me. . . . His death might suffice for your vengeance, but not for mine. I want him to live so that he will always remember his perfidy and my love . . . because Marelli, Landoberg, or Radetzki . . . whatever his name might be, I love him!'

"And closing the massive door behind her, she disappeared like a shadow among the lugubrious galleries.

"'Curse you!' Mario screamed with a howl, rushing to the door and trying desperately to open it."


V


"Beneath the foundations of the solitary palace, in a circular underground chamber illuminated by a large bronze lamp suspended from the top of the dome, Octavio sat on a purple seat of honor, presiding over an imposing assembly, wearing on his chest the blue band overlaid with gold of the grand master of the Masons.[16] Gathered around him were young patricians representing the most illustrious names of Venice, old warriors who had grown gray from going to all the battles of Europe in search of Italy's liberty, messengers from other associations, and exiles, finally—all of whom, wishing to breathe the air of the motherland, came to look for it in the bowels of the earth.

"'Yes, my noble brothers,' Octavio was saying in a vitalized and inspired tone, 'let us trust the liberty of our country to the single effort of our arms. Or faith and the justice of our cause will lead us to victory. Any foreign intervention is shameful. . . . Let us reject it, then. And you, honorable emissaries, go and tell your brothers in Naples and your brothers in Milan that this is the last time that we

........

[16] The Masons were of great importance in the cultural imagination of Argentines, having recruited prominent patriots and statesmen (San Martín, Belgrano, Rivadavia, and Sarmiento among them) since the first lodge was established in Buenos Aires in the eighteenth century. —Ed.

will meet like this to deliberate, that we are saying good-bye to the darkness of these caverns, which have been a haven of our exiled existence for such a long time, and that our next assembly shall be in the Piazza of St. Mark's, weapons in hand, under the light of our beautiful sun. Long live Italy!'

"'Hurrah!!!' the five hundred men responded in unison with wild enthusiasm.

"Then, all of a sudden, a woman dressed in white, pale and disheveled, rushed into the underground chamber and looked around full of fear.

"'Estevan of Landoberg . . . !' she exclaimed. 'Run away, your life is in danger!'

"At the sound of those words, a man stood up; he drew a pistol from his belt and fired. At that same instant, all of the entrances leading into the underground hall opened, and the chamber was filled with Austrian soldiers.

"'In the name of the emperor,' shouted the man who had given the signal, going toward Octavio, 'I order you to surrender. You are unarmed. All resistance is futile.'

"'Fellow Italians!' Octavio exclaimed, with majestic determination. 'Do you wish to perish slowly in dark Austrian dungeons, or do you wish to die now, gloriously, with the sweet taste of vengeance?'

"'Die now!' the men answered unanimously with a tremendous shout that thundered in the underground chamber.

"'Die now!' Octavio repeated, pressing a hidden spring on the back of his seat of honor.

"A horrible crackling was heard, and the ground broke open in the center. The chamber sank and disappeared, dragging everything with it, leaving only a deep and silent black abyss behind, at the edges of which the waves of the Adriatic broke with a lugubrious murmuring.

"Of everything that had just existed and moved there a moment before, the only thing left was the large lamp hanging from the ceiling of the dome, shining a light over the fatal scene like a funereal torch."

## VI

"At that moment, a man, his clothes disheveled, stepped panting onto the last steps of the staircase leading into the palace. When he saw the horrible catastrophe, he stopped, pale as a ghost, and stared for a long time into the abyss with an indescribable look.

"'God has wanted it so!' he exclaimed. 'Everything that I loved in this world lies here annihilated. Italy! I am now entirely yours. Before this immense tomb where all my hopes and all the links that kept me tied to life have fallen, I swear to liberate you or die. . . .'

"And yet," the unknown man went on in a hushed voice, "this man has not fulfilled his oath. Italy has once again fallen under the chains of slavery, but he still lives, for death has forsaken him everywhere he has gone looking for it. Bullets destined for his head have fallen weakly at his feet, the steel of his enemies has missed his chest, and the battlefields have returned him back to his sorrow."

The foreigner remained alone, his face hidden in his hands, lost in his thoughts. He disappeared the next morning; we never saw him again. Who was that man? No one ever found out. Silently he joined us, and silently too he left, like an image that enters the mind in a dream, and quickly leaves again.

# 8

# A Year in California

*For Ernesto Quesada*[1]

## I. THE WATCH CHAIN

One day, very late in the afternoon, tired, sick, and freezing cold, I was pushing my horse to reach the underground sanctuary of *Uchusuma;* it was in the middle of a long and difficult journey eighteen leagues in length, the most dangerous stretch of road between Bolivia and Tacna.

I had already left Mauri and the steep mountains surrounding it behind and was galloping across the dry plains, regularly swept by cold north winds and covered with bogs. These plains are bordered by a group of rocky outcroppings, made by an old cataclysm, at the center of which is the entrance to the cave, the only shelter for the traveler in those frozen barren lands.

All of a sudden, through the gusts of wind that were making it so difficult to see, I spotted a bright object shining among the small pebbles on the road.

........

[1] Ernesto Quesada (1858–1934), son of Vicente Quesada, a patron of Gorriti and close family friend. The younger Quesada, a child at the time Gorriti dedicated this text to him, became a diplomat, historian, and cultural journalist of distinction. —Ed.

I turned back around, got off my horse, and went to see what it was. I found an elegant and eccentric piece of jewelry and picked it up. It was a watch chain made of twelve gold stones of different shapes and colors. They were linked together by matted rings of the same metal, some of which had pieces of slate and horn encrusted in them.

I had concluded that the jewel had recently been lost by someone, and that I would look into it further down the road, when I saw a man in the distance coming toward me. He was riding along, leaning far over the neck of his horse, moving the long grass aside as if he were looking for something on the ground.

He spotted me and galloped in my direction, displaying visible signs of distress, which I quickly allayed by going to meet him and showing him the jewel I had found.

It would be impossible to describe the expression of joy that shone on his face when he laid his eyes upon it. More than taking, he snatched the object from my hands, and he held it against his heart, hooking it onto the watch and the buttonhole of his vest with a yearning that wavered between veneration and greed.

Then he turned toward me, as if he were emerging from an ecstatic rapture. He greeted me, thanked me, and begged me to forgive his reaction.

"You certainly had good reason for it, sir," I answered ironically. "To lose twelve ingots of gold is no small matter."

"Oh!" he answered with a hurt tone. "It is not the intrinsic value of the item that makes it so valuable to me. It is the fact, rather, that each of these stones holds memories of suffering and ineffable abnegation."

I very much believed him. For although the darkness made it impossible for me to see his face, his harmonious voice was that of someone young, who spoke frankly and without any premeditation.

We continued down the road together and finally reached the grouping of boulders that I had been looking at on the horizon, like a druidic dolmen, for the previous half hour.

We unsaddled our horses, and, numb with cold, took refuge in the cave. Inside, we were looked after by an old Indian, dry and black like a burnt tree, the only survivor of a family devastated by typhus.

The hapless old Indian got up from the stone where he laid, alone and curled up like a mummy, to look after the care of the lodgings with the diligent attitude of his race. He gave water to the horses, fed them barley, and covered them with their blankets. Then he immediately went to gather dry shrubs to start a fire, which gave us light and hot water.

I was then able to take a look at my accidental companion.

He was a youth with an open and pleasant physiognomy. His hat had kept the original coloring of his face around the top of his forehead like a halo; below, it had clearly been tanned by the sun during long travels or hard work in the elements.

The time of day, the place, the fortuitous circumstance of our meeting, and especially the difference in our ages—he a young man, me a mature woman—led to us trusting each other immediately. We made coffee together, applying both our knowledge to the task, laughing at our Brillat-Savarin technique.[2] But when we were about to pour it, we realized we did not have any sugar.

My companion sadly set his cup down on the rock that served as our table and looked at me with envy as I drank my coffee Turkish-style.

Then I remembered that I had a *bonbonnière*[3] in my pocket, full of those tiny capsules of sugar that the nuns of the Holy Conception give to their favorite guests.

"Come on, you spoiled child," I said to him, emptying the contents of the *bonbonnière* into his cup, "there is your sweetened coffee. Go ahead, drink it, but from now on, you better get used to bitter tastes on your palate, and in your life."

........

[2] Anthelme Brillat-Savarin (1755–1826), French lawyer, economist, and gastronomist, famous for his witty treatise on the art of dining, *La Physiologie du goût* (1825) [*The Physiology of Taste*]. —Ed.

[3] A *bonbonnière* (French) is a fancy box for holding sweets. —Trans.

A slight smile appeared on the young man's lips that made mine disappear, and I was reminded of the words he had spoken in response to my observation at recovering the watch chain.

Encouraged by the friendly familiarity that already existed between us, I asked him to tell me the story of the jewel. He told me the following:

## II. A MOTHER'S LAP

"I was born under the full force of a hostile destiny. My father died in Uchumayo, near Arequipa, defending the entrance to the city of Salta against the invaders; I arrived in the world amidst tears of widowhood, and the abandonment of orphanhood. . . .

"No, that is not right! For I first saw the light of day from a mother's caring arms. And when a child has a mother, he has all the treasures of the world. He is the king of his home and possesses a marvelous kingdom: his mother's heart.

"The first years of my life went by pleasantly, like the dawn of a spring. Our small house on the shores of the Chili River, clean and cool under the shadows of fig and pear trees, always had a festive spirit, and my mother's eyes shone with such fervent tenderness that I mistook all this for happiness. Thus, after spending the day playing or reading next to my mother, surrounded by flowers while she sat at her loom making lace garments, night would fall, and I would fall asleep in her arms listening to the peaceful murmuring of the river, and it seemed impossible to conceive of a life happier than ours.

"But as I grew up and reason began to shine its cold and severe light upon my spirit, those beautiful mirages began to dissipate, and the sad and naked truth began to appear before my eyes. I saw my mother overwhelmed with work so that she could provide me with joy and comfort. My soft bed, my delightful meals, and the education I received at the finest school in Arequipa were paid for by her very long hours and difficult privations.

"This revelation produced a great change in my moral being. I ceased being a rowdy boy and became thoughtful, and the lazy indolence of my young age underwent a transformation as I became fever-ishly active. All of this surprised my teachers, who had been unhappy until then with the little attention I had paid my studies.

"When I would go home, however, and cross the threshold into our small house, I would once again become the same selfish child, allowing myself to be spoiled at the price of my mother's hard work. To me, she looked so happy and diligent when I was around, that it seemed natural that she should sacrifice herself on my behalf.

"But an incident occurred that made my transformation complete.

"One night, I was sleeping next to my mother while she sewed by candlelight, my head resting on her lap, when a loud voice abruptly woke me.

"I opened my eyes and saw a round-faced, stout woman with a masculine look standing with her hand on her hip, speaking the most irreverent phrases to my mother.

"'Let me tell you, Doña María,' she shouted, waving her finger threateningly, 'let me tell you that I will no longer put up with these delays of four and six days that you have been accumulating time and again in the payment of your rent. Five pesos is so little, you could find it anywhere, even under a stone, and I will not wait until you decide you are ready to give them to me. Especially when there are other solicitors who are ready to offer me eight shiny new ones, and in advance.'

"'Oh! Señora Gervacia,' my mother answered, her voice trembling, her eyes full of tears, 'I hope you will not commit the cruelty of throwing me out of my house. Please remember that in the ten years I have lived here, I have always brought you your money on the first of the month. But oh! You know how much the value of work has declined for some time now, especially that of sewing and needle-work. Just look at these soldiers' uniforms: They have so much inter-lining, so many pieces and backstitches. And yet, they only pay one real for each one. I have done ninety-nine of them. This one here is the last one; I am just putting the finishing touches on it now. Tomor-row I will receive twelve and a half pesos: five for you, and the rest for my son's school, and to buy him shoes.'

"'Shoes! And why, if you are so poor, do you not let him get used to going barefoot? And why, if you cannot pay your rent, do you spend so much for his schooling? I say put a spade in his hand and hire him out to the nearest farm.'

"'Oh! Señora Gervacia! How clear it is that you do not have any children!'

"'Children! God save me from such a plague. I leave all of that to you. That is why I am nice and plump, and you are so thin and withered. That boy is eating you alive. You spend everything you have on him.'

"'My poor son,' my mother exclaimed, smiling bitterly and caressing my head, 'what do I give him other than a life of misery? Oh! How different our fortune would be, if only my dear Solis were still alive!'

"'He would be, if he had not gone like a fool to serve for the interests of others. Why did he not do as my husband, who, as soon as he saw the politics start to stir up, changed hats and learned how to negotiate with both sides like you would not believe?! Bah! A man, burdened with a child and, besides, one who is also married without the appropriate license, without the widows' and orphans' fund, I mean—just look at how many reasons you have right there not to risk your life!'

"'I am not going to judge what your husband did. But as far as mine is concerned, it was his duty to fight for the motherland, which was invaded by a foreign army.'

"'The motherland! Hah, hah, hah! Do you still believe that lie? Does anyone do anything that is not for his own good? Go on! I did not think you were such a simpleton!'

"When I heard these insolent remarks, I wanted to jump and go at that woman, but my mother held me down firmly.

"'That is just fine, Señora Gervacia,' my mother replied, with as much sweetness in her voice as there was impertinence and harshness in the other's. 'Tomorrow at eight in the morning, I will take this work to the contractor, and at nine you will receive your money, which I promise to pay punctually from now on.'

"'I will count on that. But let me warn you that I will not put up with any more of these delays. You have until tomorrow at nine, and no later. Do you understand?' the woman said, and left.

"Unable to release my anger by throwing the witch out myself, I broke down in tears, which my mother dried as she tried to comfort me. But she too cried furtively.

"The next day I quit school and went to work in the house of an Italian Jew who dealt in jewels and hardware items.

"Samuel Tradi was a man who spoke in a very sweet tone of voice and said affectionate things; but he was miserly and greedy, a son of his race. Living in a country where the sweet virtues of women make domestic life a true paradise, he lived alone. His heart, devoid of any fondness for anyone whatsoever, lay instead with the cash register and the stock of his store.

"Once he was convinced of my aptitude to handle his books and write commercial correspondence, he gave me a hug, called me *carissimo*,[4] and offered me a job working fifteen hours a day at the desk and behind the counter, for room and board and a monthly salary of ten pesos.

"His miserly proposal riled me. But thinking that this salary, small as it was, would help my mother, I accepted at once, without complaining or making any demands.

"To seal the agreement, the Jew quickly advanced me a month's salary. I took this to my mother triumphantly, and told her that it was half my monthly pay—a merciful lie designed to make her better accept my decision.

"She was very much opposed to my leaving school. However, in light of our circumstances, she finally gave in, but she did so only after shedding bitter tears. This was especially so the first night, when she closed the door and found herself alone in the house where she had lived with me ever since I was born. Nor was that night that I spent away from her for the first time any less painful for me. I felt each hour

........

[4] "Dearest" (Italian). —Trans.

go by, and as much as I tried to add a sense of serenity to my resolution, I was brokenhearted, and my eyes were filled with tears.

"The following morning, when the first light of dawn revealed the desk where a part of my work awaited me, and, further off, hanging from a nail, the keys to the store I was to take charge of, I understood the seriousness of my duties. From that moment on, I ceased being a boy and became a man.

"When I went to see her, my mother noticed this change at once. Her reaction, at first, was to smile proudly; but then I heard her sigh and murmur under her breath.

"'Oh! Poverty! Poverty! You snatch children from their mothers when they are laughing and smiling. And at an age when they should be playing games, you condemn them to sow the seeds of Adam's sorrows!'

"She and I, however, became accustomed, little by little, to our separation. It was compensated, in any case, by the special pleasure we both derived from Sundays, which we always spent together, from six in the morning until nine at night.

"Those days were a true celebration for my poor mother. Possibly depriving herself of what she needed during the week, she would await me with all kinds of gifts, and our meals on those days were always feasts. We enjoyed them holding hands under the shade of the fig trees. These, rustled about by the wind, would drop their delicious fruits on our table, and we would eat them, laughing and making sweet plans for the future—a future that my mother's lively imagination, as she was still young and a daughter of Misti, painted with pleasant scenes that were always set in the beautiful countryside of Arequipa.

"Wishing to give our dreams an air of reality, we would go and spend the remainder of those delightful days out in the country, pointing out the places where we would build our house, and the surrounding gardens and orchards.

"Thus the years went by. Samuel Tradi became happier with me every day that passed. Practice made me so good at working behind the counter that the establishment prospered in extraordinary fashion. However, no matter how many compliments and caresses he rained down upon me, the Jew made quite sure never to raise my miserable salary by even the slightest amount.

"Then, one day, he announced he was leaving Arequipa and moving to Valparaíso, drawn by an opportunity to expand his business. He offered to take me with him, but added right away that the conditions under which I would work for him in Chile would be the same as those in Arequipa.

"It was hard for me to move so far from my mother, and even harder as I knew the pain our separation would cause her. But it was also necessary for me to continue the career I had begun, and in which I had made so much progress. I had already established a reputation with Samuel that it would take a long time to acquire anywhere else, during which time my mother would miss my salary—which, small as it was, went a long way for her.

"This last reason, combined with the others, convinced me to follow the Jew in his new pursuit.

"My mother accepted this new blow with angelic resignation, and hid her tears to make the move less bitter for me. She smiled, and although she was heartbroken by my upcoming departure, she spoke of how happy my return would be, and the joy we would feel when we saw each other again and were finally together forever.

"As far as I was concerned, her apparent calm, combined with the novelty of the upcoming trip, distracted me from my grief; I was almost happy when the day of our separation arrived.

"We were to leave after sunset to cross the hot desert that separates Arequipa from Islay by night.

"To shorten our farewells, Samuel came with me to say good-bye to my mother; to my great surprise, however, we did not find her at home. It took everything I had to follow the Jew, who tore me from the threshold where I wanted to wait for her, and behind which I was leaving my entire universe and felicity.

"Only then did I begin to sense how painful it was going to be to live apart from my mother. Had it been possible for me to undo the commitment I had contracted with the Jew, I would certainly have stayed behind.

"We departed.

"It had grown dark, and the moon shone a sad light on the white domes of the city, adding a fantastic element to the oriental aspect it had at night, and helping to augment my grief. I could not resign myself to leaving without seeing my mother; I prayed silently, stifling my sobs, while Samuel explained to me the details of the commercial operations he planned to carry out in Chile, as well as the outline of my new duties as his dependent in the new market. Absorbed in his business speculations, he headed away from the white city that had been his home, from the majestic Misti and the enchanted countryside, without looking at or thinking of them even once.

"This is how his forefathers must have left Canaan as they followed the scent of the fruits of Egypt.

"I saw someone sitting immobile at a turn in the road, on the slope of a hill. It was my mother. She had not wanted me to experience the pain of saying farewell in our own home and had gone there, where she had been waiting for me, crying.

"When I approached, she stood up, dried her tears, and embraced me, trying to make her voice sound firm so she could say her last words of advice to me. Then she gave me her blessing, stepped aside, and immediately knelt down and began to pray. She followed my departure with her eyes until we reached the windy, narrow streets of Yanahuara and lost sight of one another.

"I was baffled, in my sorrow, about the laconic farewell she had given Samuel, and why she had abstained from asking him to look after her son. My poor mother! Time was to teach me how well she knew that making any such request of that coldhearted soul would have been in vain.

"A month later, we were established in Valparaíso, and Samuel Tradi's store already enjoyed a great reputation. The son of Israel possessed by direct lineage the science of how to run a lucrative business. Without letting up on his valuable speculations in jewelry in the least bit, he also began dealing in foodstuffs. He bought a ship and started trading along the coast with a new associate who captained the vessel: A compatriot of his, David Isacar was a renowned

Jew who looked like a true bandit, with dark skin and fierce, treacherous eyes.

"David and Samuel's relationship went back a long time. It had been interrupted elsewhere and was renewed one day in a chance encounter on the shores of Valparaíso.

"These two men, so different on the outside, shared, however, a point in common that in both constituted the core of their being: greed. This sentiment should have split them apart, like all evil passions do; but in their case it was combined with some other unknown drive which served to unite them in a tight bond, making their two lives seem as one.

"Around this time, news of treasures discovered in California began to spread throughout the world like an electric current, driving a universal pilgrimage to that marvelous land. Chile became deserted and its granaries emptied, as everyone rushed to the gold-bearing shores, dreaming of striking it rich.

"The miner, the farmer, the merchant, the speculator, the gambler—all saw their imaginary castles there and rushed off to find them. The Pacific was filled with ships sailing from all points of the globe, carrying contingents of men to tear from the earth the precious metal hiding beneath it.

"It almost need not be said that Samuel Tradi was one of the first to undertake this pursuit.

"Sure enough, after holding long conferences with David Isacar, he recruited the latter's ship, filled it with wheat, flour, and jerked beef, packed up the most valuable things from his jewelry business, and sold everything else from his store. He organized, at once, a corps of child workers, all more or less about my age, taken from the needy classes. Then he shipped all of them aboard and employed them, from then on, in the duties aboard the vessel."

## III

"He came to see me, smiling, touched my cheek tenderly, and said, 'My dear Andresino, of course you will come with me. I cannot leave you behind, can I, especially now that we are about to make millions in that golden country?'

"'And what about my mother?' I thought.

"But the novelty of the unknown seduced me with its shifting horizons, and I decided to follow the Jew to California just as I had followed him to Chile, without setting any conditions.

"I wrote my mother, providing as much rationale as possible to make her accept the immense expanse of space that would separate us. A few hours later, we were leaving the bay of Valparaíso and heading out to sea.

"Sitting on the stern of our brig, the *Luiggi,* surrounded by Samuel's child workers, I watched the port and its green hills spotted with houses and pleasant gardens grow smaller and smaller as we left it all behind us.

"When the last hill had vanished and the blue sky had merged with the blue ocean, the poor children began to cry.

"By the rags they were wearing, it was clear that almost all of them were orphans; but they were leaving behind their native ground and its gentle breezes, and they already missed it.

"Since we had to pick up the rest of our cargo in the port of Callao, we stopped there, and were thus able to see the beautiful city of Lima, an oasis surrounded by wild lands. Gas and steam had not yet arrived in full force to obscure the beauty of Mount Carrizal, or the fragrant evenings of the city, and it could still be referred to as the place of Amat the lover and his beautiful Perricholi.[5]

"There, too, as in Chile, gold fever had gotten into everyone's head. Thousands of men uprooted their homes and families and left daily in all sorts of conditions, in ships that weighed anchor at all hours from the port of Callao, destined for California.

........

[5] Manuel de Amat y Junyent (1704–1782), a Spaniard, governor of Chile (1755–1761) and later Viceroy of Peru (1761–1776). He was the lover of Micaela Villegas, known as Perricholi (1739–1819), a young *criolla* actress in Peru. According to Ricardo Palma, the name origi- nates in the derogatory combination of *perra* (dog) and *chola* (Indian), used to reproach Vil- legas's scandalous romance with Amat. —Ed.

"We took on two passengers while we were there. We were already hoisting up to get on our way when a young man showed up and asked to come aboard with his sister. He paid her passage and hired himself out as a sailor after demonstrating his skills as a seaman to Daniel, who was in charge of the ship.

"Alejandro S. was a navy officer who had splintered off from his squadron for political reasons. Poor, without anyone to whom he could leave the girl, his only family relation, he took her with him in search of a fortune that his homeland had denied him. Spirited and stoic in his misfortune, he resigned himself to his new position as if he had never done anything other than pull cables and mend sails.

"As far as his sister went, I have never seen a creature as precious as her. A truly feminine kind of girl from Lima, everything about her was graceful and beautiful, from her long hair to her graceful feet. Her name—Estela—was written in her amazing black eyes, whose gaze, at once chaste and voluptuous, was of a splendor that made me, a boy, dream of heaven, but which must have aroused violent and terrible passions in virile souls.

"From the moment we first saw each other, an affectionate sympathy drew us together, and an unknown sentiment began to beat in my heart—that of fraternal love, a tender balm that expanded my soul, which had previously been constricted by the cold contact with selfishness and avarice around me.

"Breathing the sky-blue air of childhood, we loved each other like two migrating turtledoves, like two angels lost in space.

"Always together in our strolls on deck, in our readings, in our prayers, it seemed impossible to us to live life any other way. Our conversations knew no end. She spoke to me of her dead mother, I of mine so far away. With the grim memories of my childhood, consumed by study and work, she combined the pleasant memories of her own, spent playing joyfully by the blooming jasmines along the Rimac River. In our two lives, mixed together in past and present, what one knew came to supplement what the other had ignored. I had more book knowledge than Estela, she more knowledge of life than I. I showed her the latitude at which we sailed, guiding her eyes along the lines of the map; she taught me to see the sordid instincts of Samuel and David in their tone of voice and the expressions on their faces.

"Alejandro S. gladly welcomed this attachment, which replaced him in the care of his sister, and allowed him to devote himself to the duties of his post without worrying about her.

"I, as a matter of fact, declared myself to be Estela's servant knight from the first day we met. I gave her my cabin, served her meals on my table, and went against the despicable niggardliness of the Jews, surrounding her with all the comforts that could be procured aboard the ship. I placed soft cushions on deck, and we sat out there and spent long, sweet evenings following with our eyes the outline of the stars and the phosphorescent waves of the ocean. . . .

"But you must forgive me! I am abusing your attention with these childish details. It is just that it is so pleasing to me to let my mind dwell upon these memories, which have left such a bright mark upon my life!

"A problem with the rudder forced us to head to Panamá and stop there for a few days to repair it.

"We found the streets, houses, and hotels invaded by a world of Yankee emigrants of all sorts and religions. Soldiers, freebooters, frontier hunters, Methodists, Quakers, Mormons, Spiritualists—all on their way to California—turning the city into a true pandemonium, carrying out all manner of eccentricities.

"One gathered a pile of stones, climbed atop, and preached his political or religious doctrine; but then a thousand others arrived, fell upon him, pulled him down from his pedestal, and used those same rocks to stone him, leaving him half-dead. Over here, we see two ruffians in a fistfight. Over there, a couple of swordsmen stab each other as they thrust their weapons at the same time, and both fall dead to the ground, dropping their weapons at their side, at which point the witnesses continue their battle, sending another two or three off to the other world; they finally go off to finish the business, drinking and toasting each other, as well as the dead ones.

"These scenes, and the looks of their protagonists, astonished me. But I later had occasion to learn that the normal Yankee existence is made up of all manner of incredible peripeteia, as the Yankee is a giant in all respects, from his highest virtues to his strangest extravagances.

"Among all these men there was one who stood out, less because of his stature than because of his race and physiognomy. He had copper-colored skin, a full head of straight black hair, sharp, spread-out white teeth, and the eyes of a vulture, which fixed their gaze on Estela with anxious greed.

"Through some mysterious form of intuition, seeing this man produced a feeling of hatred in me, as if I recognized him as an enemy. Even Estela, who, as a girl from Lima, was fairly accustomed at having to hold herself with regal serenity under the furtive glances and looks that her beauty attracts, was seized with fear under that black, tenacious, and persistent gaze that seemed to follow her every step, until we were finally back aboard the ship.

"But even after we had set sail and Estela's white veil waved in the afternoon breeze toward land, we saw the man near the port, leaning against the trunk of a coconut tree, immobile, his gaze fixed upon our ship.

"We moved away from the shore, and very soon the coast of Panamá disappeared into the fog in the horizon. But the impression of terror that the emigrant had left on Estela's mind did not vanish quite so easily.

"She was overcome by a mysterious restlessness, a childish fear that would not allow her to venture out if were it not in the company of her brother.

"When I tried to coax her to meet for our usual nightly stroll, she stopped me with a terrified expression on her face.

"'What are you afraid of?' I asked her. 'Am I not at your side?'

"'Oh, Andrés!' she answered. 'You are a boy and would not be able to defend me.'

"'Defend you from what? Are you not completely safe here?'

"'I do not know! But I do know that I am too afraid to spend a single moment up there after nightfall. I shudder to think that we spent so many long evenings on deck before, two weak children alone, in the dark . . . Andrés . . . ! What an awful gaze that copper-colored man had! Do you remember it? It has etched itself upon my brain. When I sleep, I see it in my dreams. When I am awake, I see it shifting behind my every thought, and it causes me distress at all hours.'

"The anxiety and terror that tormented Estela spread a shadow of sadness over our fraternal intimacy and neutralized its enchantment.

"During the day, when the sun shone its golden rays on everything around, she was the first to laugh at her irrational fears, and promised me she would leave them behind. But as soon as the day drew toward late afternoon and evening and the shadows of our sails stretched out in long silhouettes over the dark, blue sea, Estela's pleasurable mood would vanish. The poor girl, sad and thoughtful, would lock herself in her cabin, or spend the night wrapped in a long cape, sitting beside her brother, who kept watch over the rudder.

"Alejandro became aware of his companion's somber mood and tried to discover its cause. But Estela obstinately kept it hidden from him and made use of her influence to impose the same silence upon me.

"The journey, which had until then been a series of delightful days, became tedious and unbearable. And even at the cost of not being close to Estela anymore, I yearned for the end of the voyage, at which point we were to separate, in the hope that a change of surroundings, and the sight of new things and places, would dissipate the strange fear that afflicted her.

"Finally, one morning in May, at dawn, we looked out toward the horizon and saw a forest of masts with the flags of all the nations of the world hoisted upon them.

"It was the San Francisco Bay. We had reached California, the land of so many golden dreams.

"When we dropped anchor among the multitude of ships, we noticed that the majority of them were deserted and abandoned. Like the fantastic ships of Eastern tales, they rocked back and forth on the water, colorfully decorated with bunting, but silent and completely alone.

"We had the answer to this mysterious enigma very soon aboard our own vessel. An hour after our arrival, the entire crew had deserted, rushing to join the phalanxes of adventurers that already populated the gold-bearing riverbeds of Sacramento.

"The Jews found their crew reduced to just the children from Chile. Isolated and without the means to escape, they stayed where they were, although it is true that Samuel, fearing they might follow the example of the sailors, bestowed the most paternal of caresses upon them and did not lose sight of them, leaving them locked up in the hold of the ship while we went ashore to look for lodgings.

"It was no small task to dock at one of the piers, as they were all surrounded by ships full of people struggling to jump ashore.

"Finally, after a long wait, we were able to set foot on that much yearned-for shore.

"We found the beach full of luggage abandoned by its owners, who must have had no means to transport it and been unable to find a place to store it. Chests, boxes, bags made of good Moroccan leather were spread about here and there, blocking our way, without anyone having tried to pillage them. With no rust on their locks, they had not even been touched by the elements. Thus, the thirst for gold, at its most elemental level, had overcome the greed for all other goods.

"The city looked as strange up close as it had from the port. An enormous number of tents of all kinds of canvases and colors—from the dark hide of the Arab camel to the red brocade of China—had been set up and extended in parallel lines right next to the houses made of wood, forming endless streets filled with crowds of rowdy and excited individuals all mixed together. They seemed to speak in all the languages of the world, everything from the harmonious tongue of Cervantes to the unpleasant cackling of the Macanese,[6]

........

[6] The Macanese—the inhabitants of Macao (a Portuguese city and territory on the south coast of China), especially those of mixed Chinese and Portuguese descent—speak a Portuguese creole language. —Trans.

from the purest Gallicism of the Touraine region to the wild grunts of the Apaches.

"But even within this cosmopolitan emporium of nationalities, the Yankee element always dominated. All the inns were Yankee, as were the theaters; and the only institutions that gave a shadow of a guarantee over the life and property of individuals in the middle of that formidable clash of opposing personalities and interests were Yankee. Everything, in a word, foretold that this race of titans—which is destined either to soar up to the sky or to sink under the weight of its own size—would very soon plant its star-spangled banner there.

"We began to make our way through the assorted mass of people heading in every direction. Lieutenant Alejandro entrusted me with the care of his sister while he walked ahead, carrying their light luggage on his shoulder, followed by Samuel. The two of us brought up the rear, holding hands and chatting happily.

"Estela, enchanted to be on land again, breathed with delight the perfumed breeze that blew in from the surrounding meadows.

"Dressed in white muslin, with a small straw hat resting atop her long curls, she looked fresh and beautiful as the spring morning; she laughed, her fears forgotten, with the trusting abandon of childhood, adding exclamations to her joyful laughter.

"'My God! What a beautiful country! Look at those hills covered with such tall pine trees! Look at the feet of that *gringa;* she is wearing sandals that look just like two little ships . . . ! And that man mounted on an ox! And look at that flock of white birds flying across the sky; you can hear their song down here. And what are those men doing in there, the ones you can see through that hotel window? They are playing dice! Each one has a pile of yellow stones in front of him. . . . Oh! It's gold! . . . California gold! What angry expressions on their faces! Oh, I am sure that the game is going to lead to a fight. All the men look like they are carrying guns. . . . Oh . . . !'

"Estela's voice trailed off, and she suddenly let out a scream of terror.

"One of the gamblers had raised his head and fixed his eyes upon her.

"It was the copper-colored man we had left behind in Panamá, staring at her as he leaned against the trunk of a coconut tree.

"Pale, upset, and shaking, Estela ran off and went straight to her brother's side.

"'And now, Andrés,' she said to me, 'do you still laugh at my fears? You saw him yourself. That man possesses some kind of infernal power! How is it that we find him here, after we left him behind in Panamá?'

"'That is very simple to explain. Remember that when we left the isthmus we saw the *Oregon* make a stop there on its way to California.'

"But even though my reasoning helped dissipate some of Estela's superstitious ideas, it was unable to do anything about the fear that had overcome her again at the sight of the immigrant.

"I myself began to feel a deep anxiety about the state in which I saw her. I would have given half my life to be two years older so I could go and find that man and settle the score with him for the fear he inspired in Estela.

"At the entrance to a small square, between a sawyer's cabin and the store of a distiller, we finally found a spot large enough to set up our tents. Samuel, meanwhile, negotiated the selling of our cargo and made the necessary preparations for our trip to the placers of Sacramento.

"The moment of our separation had arrived. Alejandro took his sister with him and went to look for Madame Gerard, a modiste from Lima who had recently moved to San Francisco and with whom Estela was to stay while he went off to the mines.

"I followed them as far as the Peruvian consulate, where they stopped, and sad, sad as the day I separated from my mother, I left them to board the ship, bringing the order to Isacar to disembark.

"The day was drawing to a close. Lights were starting to come on, and the city took on a fantastic look, with its improvised wooden palaces, its oriental shops, and the enormous number of people that filled its streets.

"Crossing a plaza, I saw a group of men with a mysterious air about them gathered in a circle, talking. They were dressed as if they came from Sonora, with large serapes, and they spoke a strange tongue, full of rough and savage sounds, like the rustlings of a forest.

"As I went past the group, I saw that, in spite of the cloaks that covered them, the men's faces were in fact painted with the red and black hues used by the Navajos. The men were disguised Indians.

"At the center of the circle, a taller man spoke with vehemence, holding the attention of all the painted men. They crowded around him, captivated by his words, listening to him with displays of enthusiasm and submission.

"His hat and his serape partially covered his face, but I did not need to see him entirely to recognize the ominous character whom Estela feared so much—the copper-colored man. But there was more. I recognized a surprising racial affinity between his features and those of his companions. Their eyes, which flashed in the shadow of the black arabesque facial paint, had the same bold and sinister glow as those that had taken a hold of and darkened Estela's mood; and their teeth were as spread out and sharp, glowing white in their set mouths as they listened to him attentively. Finally, he spoke to them in their own barbaric language, with the speed and fluidity of one's mother tongue.

"Yesterday, he had crossed from the Atlantic to the Pacific with a phalanx of adventurers; today he had been gambling piles of gold with elegantly dressed card players around a green felt-top table; and now, finally, he was leading this conference, mysteriously wrapped in a disguise, with the sons of a reprobate tribe. Who was this man, in reality?

"I walked off, filled with a vague sense of anxiety. The strange fear that this man had inspired in Estela began to present itself to me as the foreshadowing, or, more accurately, the intuition, of some imminent danger. What danger? I could not say. To look at a woman, especially if she is attractive, to follow her, even—there is nothing more natural than that. But recalling the gaze that frightened Estela in the plaza in Panamá, and which had just terrified her again through the window of the hotel, I found it to hold, in addition to impetuous desires, a fixed determination, unyielding, threatening in its dark relentlessness.

"Instead of going aboard, I went back to look for Estela in the Peruvian consulate. But she was no longer there; her brother had already taken her to Madame Gerard's house. The French modiste had a storefront somewhere; I searched for it extensively, but was unable to find it in the city's labyrinth of streets and alleys.

"At last, telling myself that I was no longer Estela's companion, but rather Samuel Tradi's dependent, I forced myself to overcome my anxious yearning to watch out for her, and, burying my heart under a stone, I continued on my way to deliver the message to the ship. It was only then that I realized how fond my heart had grown of my past friend, whose path had crossed mine by sheer chance. Also, never before then had the submission of one's own will to a foreign one—which turns man into a passive being and annuls the power of his own will—seemed so odious to me.

"I found Isacar aboard the ship, on deck, in the company of three men whose expressions and physiognomy resembled his so much that one would have thought them to be related, or, at least, to be old comrades of his. They were speaking excitedly, apparently discussing some project of theirs.

"Distracted by the excitement of their discussion and the topic that so absorbed and preoccupied them, they did not at first notice my arrival, and Isacar was startled when he finally saw me. But the astute Calabrian composed himself quickly. He took up, or rather, pretended to take up, the previous conversation, posing some question about nautical navigation, and soon thereafter said good-bye to his ugly companions.

"Two days later our cargo had been sold and everything was ready for our trip inland.

"Isacar was to stay behind, in charge of the ship, the strong brig, taking shipments to and from ports to the south, and Samuel would head with us to the placers of Sacramento.

"Fearing the high fares, the Jew determined that we should travel by land and bought a carriage in which he, I, the children, and the equipment needed for the extraction and washing of the gold were all to travel.

"But just when everything was set for our departure, a new line of river steamships was formed. It tried to compete with the previously existing one by reducing its fares to a minimal amount, while the old one gave out tickets nearly for free to drive the other one out of business.

"This development led Samuel to change his mind; he decided to travel by steamship. But he was very careful not to purchase tickets on the line that was trying to woo passengers like him, fearing some manner of retaliation for the eccentric generosity. So he determined, after methodically considering the situation, to board a vessel named the *New World,* a beautiful steamship, luxuriously decorated, that belonged to the original company.

"Meanwhile, I was unable to learn anything further about Estela's whereabouts. I found myself consumed with anxiety. Would I depart without seeing her? Would I be separated from them without confiding to her brother the sinister misgivings that worried me so?

"The days passed, however, and the day of our departure approached. The evening before our departure arrived without my being able to learn anything further about them.

"That night, I slept and dreamt restlessly and had many nightmares. Then, all of a sudden, I was awoken by a strange sound, mixed with curses, yelling, and moans. I rushed outside our tent; when I saw the scene before my eyes, I screamed out in terror:

"'Estela!'

"Gigantic flames were rising from a sea of fire, whirling high above the city. Driven by a strong wind from the east, the fire enveloped everything in whirlwinds of smoke and spread with startling quickness toward the port. Large groups of people rushing through the smoke, and the sparks shooting from the fire completed the infernal image.

"'Estela!' I yelled, and ran toward the flames.

"The elegant buildings that had so captivated my attention when we arrived were collapsing around me, and the multitudes rushing along the streets, fleeing from the fire, were being buried by the burning debris.

"With my heart beating madly, my eyes blinded by the flames, my ears listening attentively, my breathing choked by the smoke, I ran, making my way through the loud multitudes, running aimlessly, not knowing in which direction to head, falling, getting back up again, but always running, screaming out for Estela with shouts that were stifled by the hot breath of the fire.

"At one point, when I was being carried by the momentum of the mass of people, running with it without my feet even touching the ground, I spotted a tall man heading in the opposite direction and carrying someone wrapped in a sheet. His imposing figure stood out among the crowd as he walked against the flow of people at a steady pace.

"The human wave that dragged me along brought me closer to him, and I recognized him. It was the copper-colored man with the sharp teeth.

"A scream of anger erupted from my chest. Making a supreme effort, I was able to reach out and grab the body he carried in his arms. But the multitude forced me along and dragged me far away from him. Flowing into the center of a plaza, it left me lying on the ground, my heart filled with fury and my soul with desperation. I had no doubt about it: The person he was carrying was Estela. That mysterious man was stealing her away!

"All of a sudden I realized I was holding something in my trembling hands. It was a strip of the sheet I had reached out and grabbed when I was trying to save Estela.

"Among the folds that my twitching nerves had made of it, I found a lock of blond hair. This discovery partially allayed my fears. It had not been Estela, then, wrapped up in that sheet.

"But what had become of my dear friend in the middle of the catastrophe that took place that night?

"Dawn found me wandering down the streets, my hair singed, my clothes torn, calling out among the multitudes for Estela and her brother in vain.

"I eventually had to abandon my search and go back to meet up with Samuel again, for the time to depart had arrived.

"But how could I leave with such a horrible sense of uncertainty? It was impossible!

"I communicated as much to Samuel. When he answered me, he added a scolding tone to his mellifluous voice.

"'You ungrateful wretch!' he exclaimed. 'You want to abandon your old friend, who looked after you right alongside your mother when you were a child, for someone you met just yesterday! Of course I will go and tell your mother all about it, but first I will curse you before her!'

"These words awoke a sentiment that was latent in my soul: remorse. Swayed by the sweet emotions of a new love, I had, in actuality, begun to forget my mother's love; the Jew's severe reprimand sounded to me like a voice speaking from my own conscience.

## IV

"'Let us go! Let us go!' I answered, and hurried after him.

"As I mentioned earlier, the *New World* was a beautiful steamship, containing not just all the necessary commodities, but all manner of superfluous luxury as well. Its poop deck had an elegant gallery decorated like a large hall, with rich hanging curtains. It was filled with many passengers, coming and going, all laughing and speaking at once, making the most animated of scenes, while the steamship glided smoothly upstream along the picturesque shores of the Sacramento River.

"Leaning against the railing of the deck, surrounded by blooming flowers, I looked sadly back at the city, which stood out in the distance like a mirage against the blue backdrop of the ocean. 'Estela! Estela!' I murmured under my breath.

"Someone's hand touched my shoulder from behind. I turned around and shouted with joy. It was she. We hugged each other like people do when they see each other after surviving a catastrophe.

"When I calmed down enough to speak, I asked her:

"'How did you get here? I looked for you for so long in vain.'

"'My brother has been hired aboard this ship,' she answered. 'As far as the reason that I had to leave Madame Gerard's house. . . . Oh! Andrés! . . . That copper-colored man is always there, wherever I turn! That threatening specter follows me everywhere I go! Oh! You cannot imagine what happened last night!

"'Emilia Gerard and I were sleeping in a small room; it was divided by a canvas partition from Madame Gerard's room, and by a thin wood wall from the house next to us, in which the fire started.

"'I woke up, choking because the air was densely saturated by the strong smell of tar. Almost at the same time, a reddish glow filled the room with light, and smoke poured into the room through the cracks between the wood panels of the thin wall.

"'I was about to wake Emilia up when a sudden blow, like a heavy hammer cracking wood, broke a hole through the wall. Then, against a backdrop of flames, I saw the outline of a colossal figure stick his head through the opening. Its teeth, sharp as a dog's, glowed white in the reflection of the light from the flames. It was the copper-colored man!

"'I barely had enough time to slide under the bed. Then I heard his heavy footsteps as he entered the room. I was absolutely terrified and did not even dare to breathe.

"'Emilia, meanwhile, continued to sleep.

"'The cupreous man felt through my bed, but, finding it empty, headed over to where Emilia was sleeping. He picked her up in his arms and walked back through the hole in the wood wall that was already burning, and disappeared.

"'When she felt herself getting picked up, Emilia screamed out; this woke her mother. But when Madame Gerard came in, she found the room empty and engulfed in flames; her daughter had disappeared, and I, hidden under the bed, had fainted.

"'The screams of the poor mother woke me from the deep fainting spell in which I lay. It was time to move. The flames were about to consume everything.

"'At that point, my brother and the consul from Perú arrived with Emilia, whom they had found all alone in the middle of the crowd.

"'When she found herself taken away from her bed in the middle of the night, the poor girl had lost consciousness. Her own fright, however, had prompted her to come back to, at which point she had started to scream, asking for help. But when Emilia's abductor heard who she was calling for, he abruptly set her down. Then he looked at her with a gaze that made her quiver, and left, disappearing into the crowd.

"'Madame Gerard's establishment has been destroyed by the fire. Luckily, her son recently returned from the mines having made a million, and they are planning to return to France. I would have died of grief if I had led them to their ruin. For I am convinced that that man started the fire. So tell me now, Andrés, if I should leave my brother's side for even a single moment? Keeping my fears, as well as the story of how that man has haunted me, from my brother in order to avoid his becoming involved in a fight, I convinced him to take me with him. Andrés, my dear friend, say you will stay with us!'

"'You know that my heart desires nothing else,' I answered. 'But duty calls me far from you. Samuel trusts me to help him carry out his plans.'

"'That miser is going to sell you out eventually. Is he capable of keeping his word to anyone? He would cut off the wings of his own guardian angel to sell its white feathers. Oh! You are going to abandon us for that infidel!'

"This, and more, my heart said to me as well. But Samuel had invoked a name that held an enchanted place in my memory; and the small house on the shores of the Chili, and its solitary inhabitant, seemed to call out to me, throwing my ungrateful forgetfulness back in my face.

"Estela understood what was going on in my soul and did not insist any further.

"Leaning against the railing of the deck, side by side under the starry sky, with the swaying current under our feet, we rejoiced to find ourselves together again when we least expected it, drifting on a fairy palace up a magnificent river surrounded by prairies covered with flowers; we became the joyful children of yesterday once again. Our separation, the fire, and even the memory of that mysterious man whose obsession with Estela tormented her so, disappeared from our minds, and were replaced by the pleasant images that happiness bestows upon its chosen ones.

"The gallery was illuminated by colorful lamps, giving the vessel an animated and picturesque look.

"Estela and I walked along, holding hands, exploring the ship and the heterogeneous groups traveling aboard it. Over here, a circle of Yankee smokers sat comfortably on chairs, reclining on soft cushions with their feet up on a table, puffing spirals of fragrant smoke from their Havana cigars into the air. Over there, sitting on the pillows of a divan, a group of women was holding a meeting, discussing fashion and soirées in low voices. And over there, amid a circle of curious onlookers, a hard-fought game of chess was being played. Further along, the ominous sound of the dice box, shaken by feverish hands, indicated that someone was playing the ultimate game, the terrible *monte*.[7]

"We stopped to observe this last group, made up of the captain of the steamship, two Canadians, and a Mexican. The game was fiercely contested, and the stakes for which they played were very high. Before too long, luck began to tilt repeatedly toward the side of the captain and one of the Canadians, and most of the gold on the table slid into their hands.

"At one point, the Mexican player stood up, apparently overcome by a wild emotion; asking permission to get a breath of fresh air, he walked off toward the deck. Meanwhile, tea was brought, and the players took a short break.

"Shortly thereafter, the Mexican returned. He had calmed down. He stood with his hands behind his back, looking straight down at the dice lying on top of the felt table.

"'Captain,' he said, turning to the man he was addressing, 'may I ask a favor of you?'

........

[7] *Monte*, also called *monte criollo*, a popular card game in rural and urban areas. At one time, it was forbidden to play the game for money because of the violence it incited. —Ed.

"'Certainly. Name it.'

"'Allow me to kiss these dice, which have taken so much gold from me.'

"'You are perfectly welcome to do so.'

"Then, with his hands still behind his back, the Mexican leaned all the way down until he touched the dice with his lips, and kissed them with a humorous graveness.

"Everyone, even the other Canadian who had lost, laughed at this eccentricity. But the Mexican, imperturbably serious, went to sit by the other loser.

"'Well, sir,' he said, enunciating each of his words very slowly, 'you know, I do not mind losing. It is losing with fixed dice that I mind.'

"'Fixed dice!' the captain yelled, dropping his cup, outraged. 'Who dares to accuse me? The dice are mine, and I declare that they are good and honest.'

"'Very well!' the Mexican said, with a mocking tone of voice. 'If such is your conviction, all we need to do is cut them open and inspect them.'

"'Bring me a knife!' the captain exclaimed. 'But you had better understand, you vile slanderer, that after cutting the dice, the second function of the knife will be to cut your tongue out.'

"Someone brought a knife; the captain grabbed it. Then, with one swift blow, he cut one of the die in two pieces, showing its interior, which was made completely of ivory and free of any guilt.

"The captain delivered a blow to the other die; but after cutting it, the knife fell from his hand. The die was filled with quicksilver.

"'What infamy!' the captain yelled, white with anger. 'I do not understand how anybody was able to switch my dice! I always keep them locked up, and this is the only key.' He showed a key that he carried in the case of his pocket watch.

"But Estela, whose eyes were as sharp as they were beautiful, had seen that the Mexican, instead of kissing the dice, had gobbled one of them into his mouth and left another in its place.

"The captain returned the sums he had lost and, in a fit of chivalrous indignation, threw the money with which he had begun the game overboard.

"He was a Yankee in every splendid meaning of the word: extreme in all his actions, especially those associated with honor.

"Traveling with him was his daughter, a very beautiful girl. From the first moment she set eyes on her, she became tenderly fond of Estela, who became no less attached to the graceful little Yankee girl.

"Their mutual affection was impeded by a single difficulty: Neither of them knew the other's tongue. But their eyes, Estela's black and the Yankee's blue, spoke the same language of smiles, and they understood each other perfectly.

"At that point, the ladies who had been sitting on the divan tired of their discussion, and broke off for the piano. One of them ran her fingers over the keys in dexterous arpeggios, playing the prelude to the waltz "La Festa" from the fourth act of *Hernani*.[8]

"When they heard this tune, so meaningful to American ears, the two girls looked at each other and smiled. They were both thinking the exact same thing.

"With one of those quick movements so normal for her, Estela grabbed the blue felt *calañés*[9] that the Yankee girl wore atop her blond hair, took off its long white veil, fastened it on the other's hair, and pulled the comical little hat down on her own head. Then she linked arms with her friend, and, lending her actions a theatrical air of courtly gallantry, she marched forward with her partner to the center of the circle.

"Their arrival there produced much excitement. The ladies moved

........

[8] *Ernani* (1844), an opera in four acts, by Giuseppe Verdi, was modeled on the 1830 drama by Victor Hugo, which centers on a revolt staged in Aragon against the Spanish king. The citation of this opera is significant here insofar as the ill-fated Elvira, heroine of Verdi's opera, is found in a situation similar to that of Gorriti's character, Estela, a woman desired by many men who compete for her love and attention. After many secrets, threats, and revelations, Elvira's moment of happiness is interrupted by the call of fate. —Ed.

9 A *calañés* is a stiff, low-crowned hat with rolled up brim, formerly worn by Andalusian peasants and still used by Spanish gypsies and flamenco dancers. —Trans.

out of the way and retired to the area around the columns of the gallery, from where they sang the distant song of the chorus.

The pianist, enchanted at an opportunity that allowed her to shine in her accompaniment, began playing the main part of the song.

"'*Cessari i suoni...*'

Estela sang in an admirable contralto voice.

'*...He come gli astri, Elvira mia,*
*Sorrider sembrano al felice imené...*'

she continued, filling the hall with excitement.

"'*Cosí brillar vedeali...*'

answered the young Yankee in her sweet soprano voice.

"It would be impossible to describe the magical effect their singing produced as it rose in the middle of the night and mixed with the murmuring of the current and the rustling of the nearby forest, contrasting with the silence in which everyone listened to them. After the first emotions had passed, numerous "bravos" burst forth from throughout the gallery, while the accompanist played the ritornello.

"'*...Sí, sí, per sempre tuo...*'

Estela sang at the end. And joining their two voices, they sang the duo:

"'*Fino al sospiro estremo*'

concluding with the terrible curse:

"'*Maledizione di Dio!*

"And adding the corresponding bodily posture to her voice, Estela stretched out her hand toward the emptiness and sang:

"'*Non vedi, Elvira, un infernal sogghigno?*'"[10]

"But all of a sudden we saw her turn pale, scream, and fall senseless to the floor.

........

[10] Gorriti draws upon act IV of *Ernani* in which Elvira and Ernani, about to celebrate their union and rejoice in the brightness of their love, are violently interrupted by Silva, who has come to demand that Elvira be his as promised. Abandoning hope, Ernani takes his life. The appearance of the copper-colored man who threatens Estela is anticipated by this dramatic moment of Verdi's opera, announcing the imminent appearance of the man who will destroy the couple's love. —Ed.

"While the passengers of the *New World,* enthralled by Verdi's melodies, had been listening to the young dilettantes, a steamship belonging to the new line had pushed its engines forward and passed so close alongside of ours, that one of its passengers was able to jump aboard.

"It was the copper-colored man. He had appeared suddenly in front of Estela, like the ominous masked villain in the song.

"'It is Falkland the Freebooter,' an old sailor said when he saw him.

"'What? That is Hawk-Eye the Killer,' a panther hunter said.

"'If it were not impossible,' a young man from Sonora commented, 'I would say that the man we have before us is the chief of the Navajo bands, the terrible Tabahoe, the Man Who Has Scalped a Thousand Heads. . . . The one who almost, almost, made mine into number one thousand and one.' And he showed those around him a deep scar across his forehead.

"But the man recognized as so many different individuals disappeared just as he had come.

"While we looked after Estela, the steamship made stops in San Pablo and Venice, where new passengers came aboard.

"When she recovered her consciousness, after a long fainting spell, Estela gave me a long, anguished look, which I understood at once. She feared that I had told her brother everything. I took hold of her hand and pressed it gently to allay her worries; she thanked me for my silence. But from then on she became sad and thoughtful, and neither her brother's care nor the tender friendship of the captain's daughter was able to tear her from the dark fear that had once again taken hold of her.

"We finally reached Sacramento, a lovely city that was starting to grow and expand in the midst of a picturesque prairie full of flowers stretching out like a tapestry at the foot of tall mountains. It was the waters descending from these that not only kept the plains green, but also brought hidden treasures under their surface.

"Leaving my friends was very difficult. Estela threw herself into my arms and cried.

"'Andrés,' she said. 'I have the strangest feeling that some awful misfortune is about to happen to me. Please, pray for me.'

"Then she hugged me again and went off sobbing."

While my young companion had been recounting his memories to me, new guests had arrived to the underground sanctuary. Two miners from Corocoro and an Italian baritone had entered, carrying their night sacks and their horses' saddle padding. They set up a kind of divan with their equipment and stretched themselves out comfortably by the fire. They too listened to the story with much interest as they smoked cigars.

The narrator, however, was absorbed in the visions of his past and did not even notice the new members in his audience.

"A few days later," he continued, "we found ourselves along the shores of the American River, a part of a strange town, sullen, taciturn, ragged, that stretched out along the slate canyons of the river's shores, where the inhabitants dug ardently around the clock.

"The town was divided into two camps, made up of two different nationalities, the two equally hostile toward each other.

"One was a camp of Chileans; the other was a Yankee camp.

"Bloody fights had already taken place before we arrived, the deadly consequences of which were revealed by the large number of crosses on raised mounds by the sides of the roads.

"A given position or placer, the possession of a tool, looking at a woman a certain way—any of these, and much less, was enough of a reason for a tremendous fight to break out, in which the North Americans would attack the Chileans or vice versa. The bodies of the opposing sides would be left with bloody wounds from the guns of the former and from the daggers of the latter.

"The Chileans were in the habit of cutting off the ears of their prisoners. The Yankees, returning one good measure with another, would slash their prisoners across the forehead.

"Despite the many dangers, however, thousands of men could be seen bent over the blood-covered land, their eyes blinded by greed, silent, mistrustful, somber, searching through the wet sand they moved around with their pick for the gold spark that would elicit a shout of joy, in turn quickly stifled by fear. Indeed! For woe to him who allowed anyone even to suspect that he had found something, for his death was then assured. Yes, for the place was swarming with hundreds of disguised bandits who would jump upon him, and even his corpse would disappear.

"When you reached the area of the placers, it was necessary to choose between the camps. If someone set up independently, wishing to remain neutral, he was lost, for both sides would destroy him. They would attribute to him the anonymous misdeeds committed in the area; in no time at all, he would be caught and lynched.

"In light of these considerations, and not wanting, for reasons of his own, his young workers to be among their own kind, Samuel set down on Black Hill, where the North Americans had their placers and their camp.

"The next morning, before putting them to work, Samuel gathered all the children around him.

"'My little friends,' he said to them, 'it has now become necessary for me to modify the previous conditions of your situation, conditions dictated by dreams, which have in turn been greatly modified by reality. The salary stipulated in our agreement will be given to you on Sundays, which I declare to be your own day, in exchange for the salary from the rest of your week, which will go to me.'

"'What do you mean? We are free; we want to work on our own.'

"'Free? Oh! My children, and who is going to pay me for the voyage that brought each of you here, which cost me a fortune? Free! No one is free in this world. We all depend on each other, to greater or lesser degrees. Besides, you will have everything you need here. You will be well fed, you will live in comfort, and you will be protected from all the evil people in the area. Furthermore, and above all else, you will be loved.'

"The poor boys bowed their heads dejectedly.

"'As far as you are concerned, my dear Andresino, for you, it is different,' he said to me. 'I look on you as my own son. And is it not natural for a son to work for his father without any hesitation or self-interest?'

"'What about my mother?' I said, deeply disturbed by the Jew's tone.

"'Your mother! Do you not know how many resources the excellent lady has available to her? In the first place, she has her love for her work. Then she has the liveliness and strength of her spirit. Finally, and above all else, she has her moderation. What does she need anything else for?'

"'What? Is my mother going to go without the salary I have been earning for her?'

"'Dedicate your Sunday's work to her. Your religion, which is not as severe as mine, does not proscribe it as the day of the Lord.'

"I realized how useless it was to argue any further with the miserly speculator, so I decided to rely on no one but myself to resolve my mother's fortune.

"Under Samuel's guidance, the new workers had magnificent results that day. The waters of a small creek had been redirected to form numerous rivulets that flowed through the fissures of the canyons of Black Hill. Rich deposits were discovered there under the quartz creek bed, extending and increasing as they went along, all the way to the shores of the river.

"After a month, Samuel had collected large sums. He sent these regularly to Isacar; they were destined to expand his business speculations. At the end of each week, he took a shipment to Sacramento and returned happier and happier each time at the news he received from his partner.

"Despite the good luck that my companions were having in the lower part of the canyon, I refused to associate myself with their labors from the very first day and always stuck to my resolution, preferring to carry my work out on my own. I followed the course of the creek up to where the canyon narrowed abruptly and the current came down much faster; the waters there were white as they raced between the two black slate walls that sped up its flow.

"I found thick stones of gold in the crevices of the waterfall that had formed there. Although they looked strange to me, they made me believe that there might be one of those marvelous 'pockets of ore' nearby—that dream that everyone prospecting for gold in the region shared.

"My work was extraordinarily prosperous. In less than three months, the waterfall in the upper part of the canyon had given me much more gold than I would have needed to make my own fortune. But from what my hands extracted, the only part that belonged to me was what I found on Sundays. And, as if an enemy power were involved, the product of my work, regardless of how plentiful it was on all the others, always seemed scarce and poor on Sundays.

"I always religiously saved it, however, depriving myself of even the most basic necessities. By the end of the month, I would exchange it for a thick gold stone and send it to the Peruvian consulate in San Francisco, so that they would sent it on to my mother.

"Meanwhile, the time of year when the snow melts arrived. Floods covered the fields, breaking off all means of communication and making most forms of transit nearly impossible.

"It was not long before scarcity began to make itself felt; hunger soon followed. The price of food and supplies went up incredibly. Bread and meat were available only to those who could pay their weight in gold; even then, there were disputes, often with guns or daggers in hand.

"The general penury was, for us, a true calamity. Samuel broke the central article of his second treaty. Driven by greed, he sold the provisions he had stored for our sustenance and starved us to death. It should be noted, however, that he seasoned our scant food with picturesque eloquence.

"'Come, my dear little ones,' he would say with the sweetest of voices, 'come try this delicious rice that I have prepared especially for you with my own two hands. Have you ever seen anything so appealing and tasty? Can you smell the delicious aroma coming from it? It is from a small bundle of thyme that I gathered on that hillside over there and steamed along with the rice in the covered pot. And just try that buttery part there: That is butter from Switzerland (it was actually drippings from whale oil candles that a servant had sold him for next to nothing) that I bought yesterday from the innkeeper at the

Large Pines. Eat, eat, my dear children . . . special dishes like this one are made for eating it all down.'

"And he would add action to his words, setting an example for us by eating with a pleasure that would have made a dead man hungry.

"But after fifteen days of this monastic diet, Samuel and I found ourselves alone on Black Hill. The boys had deserted, one after the other, and gone over to the camp of their compatriots.

"The Jew was enraged; he cursed their desertion passionately.

"'Those ungrateful wretches!' he would yell. 'Oh, those no-good creatures! To choose the company of those soulless criminals over the tenderness of my loving care! Oh! You pick them up out of nowhere, you educate them, you get used to them, and then, when things are at their best, they abandon you and leave you brokenhearted!'

"Still, after working the canyons for four months, those children had given him enormous quantities of gold, raising the value of his fortunes to a very high level.

"Samuel followed my example and went to work where the creek was narrower.

"I gave my position up to him and went further up to a place where the fast waters of the creek came down and made a hole through the slate and quartz creek bed near the shore.

"A little further down and to the side, this layer of slate was cracked in large pieces as the water went through a large number of crevices, disappearing from sight in a low murmuring and reappearing a few meters away, flowing among the colorful pebbles back to the creek.

"I set my pick aside and sat down on one of the slabs of slate. I sank my hand into one of the small pools of water and brought it back out—it was full of gold. I reached into all the other pools; each time I pulled my hand out, it was full of gold, gold, and more gold!

"That day was magnificent. It was a Saturday.

"A Saturday. In other words, the day before the one devoted to my mother.

"The result of my labors that day left Samuel dumbfounded. He exclaimed: 'Another week like this, and we will be able to buy back Canaan, the lost homeland!'

"He thought about his homeland; I, about my mother.

"That night I was unable to sleep. The laughing vision of a tangible happiness spun all around me, stretching its arms out to me and pointing toward the light of a new day that would make it come true.

"Near dawn, in the middle of the heavy sleep that followed my insomnia, I believed I heard a strange noise, something akin to gushing torrents, but I thought it was the blood throbbing in my brain.

"The first light of morning found me at the shores of the creek, my arms by my side, completely disillusioned.

"The golden crevices whence I had withdrawn so much treasure the day before had disappeared, along with the slabs of stone that had formed them. The noise I had heard in my sleep had been an avalanche; it had come down from the mountains, dragging everything along with it as far as the rough waters of the American River.

"The radiant dream from the night before had vanished right when I was about to reach out and make it come true. The hour I had so yearned for—to see Estela and be at my mother's side again—receded and was lost on a distant horizon.

"I sat down in the shade where the creek turned, my body and soul completely shattered, my eyes staring at the black, dried-out creek bed, my mind unable to think. The outer edges of the creek bed, now that the force of the avalanche had passed, were starting to air out and take on a bluish color.

"I do not know how long I sat there, lost in an abyss of dark thoughts. The sun, piercing through the branches of the pine tree that shaded the rock on which I sat, shone a light into the darkness of the bend in the creek.

"All of a sudden, a thought flashed through my mind, quick and bright as lightning.

"I jumped up, grabbed my pick, and hit the outer edge of the dried-out creek bed as hard as I could. The top layer of slate broke into many pieces, revealing a wide hole, the bottom of which shone so brightly that it left me completely astonished.

"The brilliant reflection was produced by the enormous quantities of gold that had been deposited there—accumulated, without a doubt, for centuries on end by the flow of some underground stream.

"I, a weak and inexperienced child, had found the fabulous pocket of ore for which the professional miners had been searching in vain. There it was, right before me. As I stood there, immobile, contemplating the precious material that glowed in the sunlight beneath the black slate of the creek bed, my soul was overcome by a rich man's joys and fears. It was not gold that my eyes beheld in that marvelous treasure I had at my feet, but rather my mother's and Estela's happiness, the joy of being free and able to see them again and of bringing everyone together into a single family, together forever.

"But how was I to extract that treasure? How to hide its existence from the thousands of adventurers who wandered around the placers pretending to be working, while only trying to be in a better position to pillage and steal when the opportunity presented itself?

"I had to make a decision, and, above all, to do so quickly.

"With my head held high, looking around me attentively, I followed the course of the creek and walked back down to the camp.

"It was silent, nearly deserted. The workers spent their Sundays in the nearby taverns, or in the forests, hunting birds and rabbits. Even Samuel, pleased with the rich finding of the day before, had given himself a day off and was playing dominoes in a fellow countryman's restaurant.

"I ran to the room in which Samuel and I slept in a store that sold straw mats. I moved aside the buffalo skin that served as my bed and dug a hole in the ground deep enough to hide my treasure. Then I put the buffalo skin back in its place, covering the hole I had made to hide the mound of earth I had just dug out, I put a pile of clothes on it.

"I rolled up a canvas shirt with very strong pockets, covered myself with a Mexican serape, and headed back up to the bend in the creek.

"Seven times did I fill the wide and deep pockets of my shirt and the front pocket of the serape with gold, and just as many did I make it disappear into the hole hidden under the buffalo skin.

"But the pocket of ore was enormous. It seemed to extend under the entire creek bed, along the whole width of the bend. From its depth at the margins, one could only guess at what it might hold at the center of the creek bed.

"It was simply marvelous. The astonishing reality far outshone the Jew's hopes and dreams: Not in a week, but rather in the twelve hours of the Monday that was soon approaching would Canaan be his.

"The sun had set, meanwhile, and the distant sounds indicated that the workers were beginning to return to the camp.

"I ran back to our room, deposited the contents of my last trip inside the hole—now filled with enormous quantities of gold—moved the earth I had dug out to a place far from the tent, and returned everything to its usual place. Completely worn out, but with my soul soaring through infinite space, I lay down on my bed and closed my eyes, less to sleep than to lose myself in my thoughts. But these were interrupted by Samuel, who came into the tent in a happy mood, holding some pastries in one hand and a bottle of champagne in the other.

"'My dear Andresino,' he said in an affectionate tone. 'The Swiss man told me about the bad luck that your labors suffered last night and how the avalanche destroyed the area where you had been working. But it does not matter. You are intelligent, you will look for another place, and you will find it. The important part has already been earned. After all, did you not make your friend a true fortune yesterday? I sent 14 pounds of gold to Isacar to be included with the shipment to the Hobber Company. It is on its way to San Francisco at this very moment.

"'Meanwhile, my son, have a little of this delicious pastry I brought you and chase it down with a glass of champagne. It tastes especially good after a hard day's work.'

"I realized I had not eaten all day long. In the midst of the tumultuous emotions of the day, I had completely forgotten about my usually demanding boy's appetite.

"I ate the pastry without really wanting it, but when it came time for the champagne, I raised my glass up high and toasted with Samuel:

"'To my mother's health! To Estela's! And to all the happiness that our wealth will bring us!'

"Samuel seemed to hear some allusion in my toast that made him anxious, and he quickly added, in response:

"'Once you have found that wealth, of course!'

"I laughed at his comment, thinking about the incredible surprise I was saving for the Jew, and drank my glass of champagne quickly, full of excitement.

"The bubbles of the champagne eased, little by little, the fervent rushing of the thoughts in my mind. I finally fell asleep; but it was a heavy, sluggish sleep, full of nightmares and misgivings.

"Bands of highwaymen, their daggers in hand, scaled the walls of my brain as they sought to attack me. Some gazed at me with the sinister eyes of Isacar the Jew; others laughed satanically, displaying the sharp, glowing teeth of the copper-colored man. With greed painted on their countenances, they tore open my chest, looking through my insides for my hidden treasure.

"A hand grabbed me by the shoulder and shook me, dissipating the agonizing nightmares.

"It was Samuel, yelling at me: 'Andrés! Andrés! . . . The avalanche has shaken loose again up in the mountains, but this time it is coming down in torrents, and it is heading straight for our camp. Can you not see? . . . Everything is flooded! The Yankees have fled. Let us go, we have to get out of here . . . ! Look at the water rising, it is going to reach us if we stay here. . . . Let us go! . . . What are you waiting for? Let us go!'

"And he ran off to the top of Black Hill, which was filled with people.

"But I had no intention of running away. If I was going to lose the treasure that had already led me to dream of so much happiness, I did not want to go on living. Immobile as a sentinel, I stood between the place where the treasure was buried and the flood that was going to take it away from me and looked at the advancing waves as they roared down the side of the hill. A little further down, and I would be covered under its black whirlwinds.

"The light of dawn, as the sun was rising behind the black tops of the fir trees, added to the desolation of the scene, presenting it in all its horror.

"The picturesque canyon at the foot of Black Hill, as well as the American camp at its foot, had disappeared, along with the trees and the tents that had been set up in their shade. It was all covered by the creek now, which had become a raging torrent, its rushing waters tearing along with a frightening roar.

"By sheer chance, the first waves of the flood threw some large tree trunks and boulders not far from our tent, forming a kind of dam that redirected the course of the flooded creek toward the neighboring gully, saving our tent from the general devastation.

"After the main thrust of the flood had passed, I was able to climb up to the bend in the creek where I had found my treasure, but I found its bed of slate completely dry. The impetuous avalanche had dug it out, and the creek had opened up a new bed, under which it now flowed as if it were a natural bridge. Somebody else might have collapsed at that point, destroyed at the sight of the incalculable loss. But I was not moved by it at all. I was still a child, and my dreams had not turned into greed. It only weighed upon me that Samuel would not be able to collect now the enormous wealth that, without his knowing it, would have come into his hands.

"Four days later, the Yankee camp had moved higher up the hill, and the bottom of the canyon, which had been completely covered with the waters of the avalanche, was full of workers. Every time they stuck their hands into the muddy puddles, they brought them back out full of thick gold stones.

"These were the contents of the immense pocket of ore deposited through the centuries under the creek bed.

"No one had as much right to those riches discovered and lost in so few hours as I did. However, following my isolationist system of working, I took my search to the neighboring canyon.

"The water had left a broad quagmire there, and its surface was beginning to turn green with a new layer of grama grass, indicating that no one had gone prospecting there yet.

"Suffice it to say that with the first shovelful of mud, I dug out a multitude of small chunks of gold, some embedded in larger pieces of quartz, others loose, as if they had been melted in a crucible.

"When I returned to the tent toward nightfall, I could barely walk up the short, steep incline of the canyon. Such was the weight I carried.

"How much joy would fill Samuel's gold-loving soul when he saw the tremendous product of the day's work, all of which belonged to him!

"But, to my great surprise, he did not respond to the signal we had between us that announced a large find. I walked faster, went into the tent, and found him stretched out on the ground, his face ghost-white, his eyes staring off into space, and his body twisted in a horrible convulsion. At his side was an opened and crumpled-up letter.

"I lifted him up, and, with great difficulty, managed to get him to his bed. His body was as stiff as a corpse's.

"I got him to drink a few drops of water; then I ran to get a French doctor who happened to be passing through the area.

"As soon as he saw him, the doctor declared that the patient was suffering from cholera.

"'But,' he added, examining the patient's jaws, which were closed in a tight contraction, 'this particular incident was brought about by a sudden burst of emotion of pain or anger.... And ... yes, right over here we have precisely the letter that will explain to us what the subject felt before succumbing to the attack that has put him in his current state. A condition, I may add, that you, who are no doubt his son, or his dependent, need not fool yourself about—this is a dead man we are dealing with here. But with this drink that you can give him in two separate portions, he will recover his ability to speak.'

"And turning to poor Samuel, who was apparently unconscious, the doctor said to him: 'Is it not true, sir, that you can hear me, and find yourself in control of your senses?'

"Samuel answered by letting out a heavy sigh.

"'Very well, then!' the doctor continued, with the typical self-assurance of one of his profession. 'You will be able to speak again after you drink my medicine. But my advice is to make good use of it.'

"And he sauntered out, after leaving his terrible prescription.

"As the doctor had said, drinking the medicine gave Samuel the use of his speech again. He turned his dulled eyes toward me and exclaimed:

"'The God of my forefathers has forsaken me, for I have forsaken his ways and have followed the ways of the wicked!'

"Samuel's countenance looked more and more pale and sickly, and the mark of death was drawn deeply across the outline of his features.

"'Yes,' he continued, with a lifeless voice, 'I have exchange the God of Abraham for the golden calf, and have sacrificed to it my youth, my life, and all the affections of my soul. . . . Right now, even as my strength leaves me and pain has taken over my body, the idea of losing my treasures is my greatest sorrow. . . . But . . . what am I saying? . . . Oh!!! Isacar, you vile scoundrel! . . . Give me back my gold . . . my gold . . . my gold . . . !'

"A horrible convulsion shook his entire body and silenced a scream in his throat.

"'In the name of God,' I exclaimed, frightened by his desperate agitation, 'Samuel, my friend, calm down! You want more gold? I will give you all the gold you want. You cannot even imagine how much there is! I found it by the handfuls in the quagmire of the neighboring canyon today. . . . Look!'

"And I showed him my bucket, nearly full of the gold I had found that day.

"When he saw it, the Jew's eyes, already wild and glassy, glowed with a dark and fierce fire.

"'Good God of Jacob!' he exclaimed, stretching out his trembling hand and sinking it into the splendorous metal. 'Will you not give me just a short amount of time out of all your eternity to enjoy this marvel with my eyes and with my hands? After that, you can send my soul wherever you wish it to go. . . .'

"A horrible convulsion drowned out Samuel's voice. He thrashed about in violent spasms for a few moments and then came to a complete rest.

"I believed him to be asleep.

"Then I remembered the opened and crumpled letter on the ground, next to where Samuel was lying half-dead on his bed. I looked for it and found it at my feet. The handwriting belonged to Isacar. Thanks to my knowledge of the Calabrian dialect, I was able to read the following, from which I shall leave out the countless atrocious insults and affronts, so common in the popular Italian diction, which it contained:

"'For too long have you abused our ignorance in the matter of numbers. You have been a disloyal depositor of our gold pieces. We earned them at the risk of our own lives and at the price of our own blood, only to have you steal them, you miserable coward. Your only value was knowing how to hide our money from us. So well, in fact, did you hide it, that you made it look like an illusion to we who had earned it in the first place. But all things must come to an end, and your time embezzling from us ends today. We hereby close our accounts with you; but not your way, the way you did it up in the Abruzzi Mountains, but rather cleanly and neatly, in one fell swoop.

"'You should know, first of all, that I, for leading you into this trap, have taken possession of all your gold, which I received in ten shipments. Bepo, Estefano, Bambino, and Testa di Fuoco, who arrived here as if they had fallen from heaven, have taken a harpoon aboard the *Luiggi,* our good, old sail brig; they will sail up and down the Pacific and plunge the weapon so many times into its unsuspecting passengers, that their coffers will be filled in no time at all.

"'As far as this servant of yours is concerned, he is going to Italy. He will buy himself a palace in Naples the Beautiful and spend the rest of his life in the delightful shade of a garden, under blooming orange trees.'

"'A thief! A member of a band of highwaymen and pirates!' I exclaimed, turning my eyes toward Samuel. But he was lying immobile, his face suddenly thinner, his skin a pale, bluish tone.

"I reached down and touched him. He was dead.

"Even though the revelation I had just reached made me look at him with horror, he was already a corpse. And death gives everyone a certain prestige, a halo of virtue, lending crime a veil with which to attenuate its deformity.

"Alive, Samuel would have been a repugnant villain before my eyes; I would have distanced myself from him at once. But dead, I forgot that he had been a vile shelterer of thieves; that he had been an unscrupulous miser; that he had behaved despicably toward me, cheating me out of the worth of my work to the detriment of my mother. All of this I forgot, and I remembered instead his affectionate words and his charming voice. I felt attached to him by the invisible but strong ties of habit, which take such deep roots in the souls of children. I cried tears of true sorrow for him and spent the entire night keeping vigil beside his corpse.

"The next morning, when I went outside to look for someone to help me bury the dead man, I found there was no one anywhere near our tent. The fear of contagion had emptied the surrounding area completely.

"No one wanted to assist me at all, and it was with much difficulty that I carried out the task on my own.

"But, as the saying goes, every cloud has its silver lining. Thus it was that people's fear had favorable results for me, as it allowed me to dig a grave under the tent itself, take out my treasure, and leave—all without anyone's suspecting the least thing.

"For the purpose, I used the carriage in which we had brought our work tools from Sacramento. It was a kind of box, mounted on two tall wheels, especially designed to cross the muddy plains.

"I bought from a German man the horse on which he had just arrived; it was a strong beast in good shape. I placed my gold between the bottom of the carriage and a wooden plank of the same size, and covered it with my clothes and some provisions. Then, after mounting a cross atop Samuel's resting place, despite his being a Jew, I set off on my own.

"Soon afterward, on a hot afternoon in June, covered in rags but sitting atop a treasure, I reached the crowded streets of Sacramento with my carriage. My appearance made impertinent people laugh at me, and girls pointed at me. How many of them, if they had only known my secret, however, would have bowed before me!

"Being a transit point for the mines, and containing rich seams in its surrounding areas, the city of Sacramento was occupied by thousands of prospectors; they filled all the hotels and houses and even set up their tents under the trees of the outlying neighborhoods.

Having said this, I almost need not add that a ragged boy like myself was forced to resign himself to this latter manner of spending the night. This was even truer given that I could not trust anyone with the knowledge of the existence of my treasure, and that it was impossible for me to leave the carriage that contained it unattended.

"So I rode straight through, crossing the city without even thinking about asking for lodgings anywhere. I stopped only to buy a few supplies and some items of food. At the store, the merchant was reading a newspaper to two neighbors and exclaiming loudly about some tragic event recounted therein.

"'To lose such a beautiful ship!' he exclaimed. 'It was clearly the best that the old line had.'

"'And to think that so much misfortune came simply from the carelessness of a fire stoker,' one of the neighbors commented.

"'From carelessness? You should say from intentional arson, rather, and you will have hit it on the head. Listen to what it says in this paragraph here:

"'"After all the investigations, it has been impossible to find the stoker who started this horrible incident, which cost the lives of more than twenty people. His disappearance has led officials to suspect his actions were intentional and criminal in nature."'

"When I heard the merchant read this section, my heart trembled, and a horrible thought crossed my mind.

"'In the name of God,' I said to the merchant, 'could you please allay a terrible anxiety for me. That tragic incident you were just reading about, is it referring to the ship the *New World?*'

"The merchant (a Yankee) looked me up and down, from my head to my foot, as if to say, 'Who is this unknown boy talking to me, and such a poor one at that?' Then he gave me the goods I had purchased, put away his money, and showed me the door.

"I had to leave, although my soul was burdened by a gloomy foreboding.

"Once I had left the last streets of the city behind me, however, and found myself in the beautiful countryside covered with flowers and the shade of the different trees, the clouds darkening my spirit began to dissipate. There was nothing in the article from the newspaper, nor in what the merchant had said, that should lead me to think that the victim of the disaster was the *New World*, the ship of Estela and her brother.

"I followed this line of thinking and gradually grew more tranquil; the peacefulness of the beautiful country around me occupied my soul, and hope once again flooded into it.

"Night, meanwhile, had fallen across the land. Stars bloomed in the sky, and the fragrant breezes filled the prairie with perfumed air.

"Half an hour outside the city and a short distance from the river, a caravan had stopped under a growth of sycamore trees. It was a colony of Germans heading to the canyons near Sacramento.

"I approached them and asked if I could spend the night in their company.

"They very kindly took me in and made room for me next to the fire, necessary at those latitudes due to the cold nighttime temperatures.

"Once my place was set up, the Germans engaged in a serious conversation and left me to my own thoughts. These were rose-colored indeed, as I saw my future filled with pleasant images, the distances of time and space shortened, and I brought to the present the happiness my heart was forging for the times to come.

"The light of the bonfire, reflecting off the moving branches of the sycamore trees, provided marvelous decorations for my illusions.

"Then, at one point, when the bluish flame, agitated by the breeze, shone a clearer and brighter light on the surrounding area, I saw a white shape come out of the underbrush near the river. It began to walk, wavering hesitatingly, toward the area illuminated by the fire.

"When I saw her, I shook my head and rubbed my eyes, thinking that I must be dreaming. But convinced, at last, that I was indeed awake, I screamed out and ran toward the apparition.

"It was Estela! Not the ruddy, smiling, and elegant Estela I knew, however, but rather a sad, somber, and frightened Estela, with her clothes all disheveled.

"At first she did not recognize me and tried to run away. But when she heard my voice, she jumped into my arms. She tried to talk, but her strength failed her and she fainted.

"The women of the colony were filled with pity at the sight of her; they took her into their tent and assisted her every way they could.

"The women and I were busy trying to revive her, when we suddenly heard a loud noise outside in the middle of the camp. A group of armed men on horseback had invaded; without dismounting, they whirled silently among our things, looking through everything as if searching for something or someone.

"One of them, leaning over the side of his horse, lifted the flap of the tent in which the women surrounded Estela, hiding her from view as she lay on the ground.

"The light of a lamp inside the tent shone on the face of the mysterious visitor, making his phosphoric eyes and his spread-out and sharp teeth glow in its reflection.

"It was the copper-colored man.

"He was wrapped in the black-and-white striped shawl of the Apaches; his head was uncovered, and his long, straight hair flowed back under a red bandanna.

"He looked so fierce that the women all screamed when they saw him.

"He, for his part, looked all around the tent with his vulture's gaze. Then he straightened himself up, kicked his horse, let out a hoarse and guttural yell, and rode off, followed by his band, like a dark whirlwind in the night.

"At the sound of that last yell, Estela, who had been lying without moving, shuddered, as if her body was shaken by an electrical discharge. She moved her stiff lips in a supreme effort and pronounced her brother's name, and then moaned. Her weak cry led me to a painful revelation, as the story that the merchant had read earlier that afternoon returned to my mind, followed now by its gloomy conclusion.

"Estela finally came to from her long fainting spell. She got up abruptly, as if she had been awakened by some terror, and looked all around her with completely disheartened eyes. 'Andrés!' she exclaimed, seeing me at her side. 'Did you hear that yell? It is a sign. It is . . . it is the copper-colored man. . . . He started the fire on the steamship and killed my brother and snatched me away from him as he lay dying. . . . I have just miraculously escaped from him; but he is after me, and he will catch me. . . .'

"She tried to run away, tearing herself from our arms, but I stopped her.

"'You have nothing to fear,' I said to her, 'you are with me.'

"Estela looked around her, sadly, and said in a voice full of sorrow:

"'I am all alone in the world!'

"'What about me?' I exclaimed. 'Do I not love you, and am I not also your brother?'

"'Oh! Andrés! Life is just beginning for you; you belong to your mother, who is waiting for you back home. If you want to see her again, you must leave me behind. The infernal being who is following me has killed everyone who has come near me: He killed Alejandro; he killed the captain's daughter; and he will kill you, too, if you do not run away from me.'

"'No, on the contrary. I am here, at your side, and will stay here forever. But tell me what happened? How did all these awful things happen? Why are you out here, all alone, in the middle of the night?'

"'Oh!' she answered. 'It is a horrible story! All good has suddenly sunk deep into the abyss of evil; happiness has shipwrecked just as it was about to reach the port of good fortune! . . . And it is all my fault!'

"'What are you saying?'

"'Just listen. Not that long ago my letter recounted to you how happy Alejandro, Lucy, and I were aboard the steamship. That is how it was. Life spent between two people I loved so much, traveling up and down the river on a perpetual voyage through prairies blooming with flowers, was like an enchanted dream for me. Alejandro and Lucy were in love. I was an additional link between them; their union was not far off. Only you were missing to make our happiness complete. But you were nearby, and it delighted us to hope and think that one day soon you would come and join us.

"'That is how the year went by. I devoted myself to my music, to pleasant conversations, and to other joyful activities, and it was the happiest year of my life.

"'The captain, once his daughter married my brother, planned to form a new company and establish a line of steamships to travel between San Francisco and the southern ports of the Pacific. He would be in charge of one of the ships; Alejandro, another; and Lucy and I would move to Lima. What a plan! Homeland, friendship, family . . . !

"'But, alas! It was all an enchanting mirage, seen briefly, only to vanish like fog in a strong wind.

"'The day before yesterday, as the day was drawing to a close, the engines of the *New World* were running and its passengers and the large amounts of gold it carried were all aboard as it prepared to weigh anchor from the pier of Sacramento.

"'I had left a letter behind for you. In it, I recounted to you our wonderful, new plan, reserving a special place in it for you. Happy with the pleasant news I was sending you, my mind racing with sweet thoughts, I was lying down on the deck in the same spot in which I had found you when you were leaving for Sacramento nearly a year before.

"'Now, as then, the gallery was full of people coming and going, talking excitedly. But this time I was lost in my own thoughts, and I heard the loud murmuring of the passengers without paying any attention to it.

"'From where I was, because of the layout of the ship, I could see the furnace of the steamship burning at maximum intensity.

"'My eyes wandered about distractedly and were drawn to the reverberation of the fire, where they finally settled to look at the bright furnace glowing in the night like a fire in hell. The scene was complete: Two men, whose features were covered under a thick layer of coal, were stoking the fire, and their faces, glowing red in the light of the flames, had a terrifying appearance.

"'One of them, in particular, was of colossal size; his hair was standing on end from the heat of the fire, and under it he had the face of a devil.

"'Just imagine, if you can, my fright at the sight of the man when he turned around and I saw two vulture's eyes glowing in the shadows, looking right at me, and under thick lips, grimacing threateningly, two rows of sharp, wide-spread teeth. In a word, it was the figure that happiness had only just begun to erase from my mind: that of the copper-colored man!

"'My immediate terror at first glued my feet to the floor; when I overcame this paralysis, I ran off and went to hide with Lucy and Alejandro. They saw how pale I was and became alarmed at once.

"'I was going to speak. I was going to tell my brother everything; but, like always, I did not, for I was afraid that it would lead to a fight between him and that terrible man—an awful fear that led to the entire disaster.

"'So I did not speak. Instead, terrified, I went and locked myself in my cabin.

"'My spirit felt so fatigued that I eventually fell asleep, but I was immediately overcome by a horrible nightmare. A sea of fire raged and whirled above my head, while loud, wild screams, mixed with all sorts of cries and curses, filled my ears. The air was hot and suffocating, and a mysterious weight pressed down against my chest.

"'All of a sudden, I was awakened by a loud noise.

"'The cabin door fell and gave way to a man who broke through a wall of flames, carrying the inert body of an unconscious woman under one arm. Grabbing me with the other, he tore me from the voracious fire that was quickly consuming the ship.

"It was Alejandro, saving the lives of his fiancée and his sister.

"But just as he reached the gangway and was ready to jump into the water with us, I, leaning against his shoulder, saw a terrible, black, colossal figure rise up and whirl two lead balls attached to two cords in the air, which he then swung down on the heads of my brother and his fiancée, dropping them both dead to the floor. . . .

"'The cold water brought me back to my senses. I opened my eyes and saw the glowing vulture-eyes, the frightening smile, and the sharp teeth of the copper-colored man right beside me.

"He was holding me in his arms and swimming for the shore, and he sent out a signal in that direction by letting out a hoarse and sinister yell.

"'My fear gave me strength. I made an abrupt movement, slipped out of his arms, and let myself sink to the bottom of the river.

"'When my feet touched the slippery sand at the bottom,' Estela continued, 'I let myself drift down current with the tide until I was out of breath, at which point I came back up to the surface.

"'I found myself in the middle of the river, surrounded by a deep darkness. I heard cries of anguish and moans of agony everywhere around me. My memory abandoned me. How had I gotten there? What had happened? I could not remember. I knew only that I was fleeing from an evil spirit and that I had just escaped his hands. How? I could not remember that either. Furthermore, overcome with terror, I barely dared to stick my head above the surface of the water more than to breathe a bit of air; then I would swim underwater, against the current, with the strength my fear gave me. Oh! Who could have foreseen that when I played with my friends in the delightful cove of Chorrillos on other, happier days, and learned the art of swimming from Ceferino, that it would one day save my life and honor?

"'I finally reached the shore at a place that was steep and covered with brambles whose sharp branches sank into the water.

"'Exhausted, extremely weak, short of breath, I pushed them anxiously aside with my hands. But I suddenly let go of them and fell back, terrified.

"'Tangled in the branches was someone's long hair, keeping afloat the body of a woman's corpse. . . .

"'The next thing I knew, I was coming to from a fainting spell, the length of which I could not gauge. I found myself on a deserted beach, thrown ashore by the river, among some tall thickets. My limbs were numb, and I could not move. A funereal silence reigned there, interrupted only by the murmuring of the waves and the chirping of the nocturnal birds.

"'I tried to get up and managed to drag myself as far as the densest part of the weeds. The darkness, my pain and fear, all conspired to form terrifying visions around me.

"'Then, all of a sudden, distant but distinct, and very frightening, the savage shout of the copper-colored man reached my ears. Soon afterward, a group of mounted men rode by very close to me; the steely hoofs of their horses sparked against the pebbles on the ground.

"'Fear once again gave me the strength I would not otherwise have had. I ran off in the opposite direction and arrived near here, where I hid in the middle of some dense thickets. Finally, the cold night drew me out, and I went toward the light of the fire. What I do not know is what miracle of Providence has brought you back to me!'

"The next day, we all left together: the Germans to their new destination, and we toward the port of San Francisco.

"We rode slowly through the most beautiful of prairies, sitting side by side, with a treasure at our feet, and above our heads was the splendor of a summer sky streaked with mother-of-pearl clouds and dotted with flocks of birds that filled the air with their various songs.

"But Estela was no longer even a shadow of her old self. Her grief had taken on a sinister character, and she remained silent, without shedding any tears.

"I would invite her at times to come down from the carriage and walk along next to it. She would give in to my request with sad acquiescence, and we would walk, literally, on a bed of flowers. But she, whose soul had once loved nature so, passed these magnificent landscapes with the coldest indifference.

"Finally, one morning, with the first light of dawn, the city of San Francisco and its bay full of ships appeared before our eyes. Soon afterward, we were traveling through its streets, heading toward the port where we hoped to find a ship leaving soon for the port of Callao, as Estela longed to leave far behind her the land that had been so fatal to her life and fortune. I myself, moved by some strange restlessness, wished fervently to return to my homeland.

"As if in reply to our wishes, a large sign attached to a column of the porch of a consignment house announced the departure, on that same afternoon, of the brig *Pietranera*, headed for the port of Callao. The sign added that excellent accommodations for cargo and passengers were still available.

"For the first time since the horrible catastrophe in Sacramento, Estela's countenance showed a slight sign of happiness at the sight of this notice.

"Pleased by the good omen, I took just the minimum time needed to change our gold for exchange bills and buy Estela the clothes, ribbons, and other trifles that make up the obligatory luggage of a young lady. Then I purchased the tickets in the same consignment house, and that afternoon we boarded the ship.

"They were rigging up the vessel when we came aboard. It was a recently painted ship, and one could see that they had also equipped it with a new set of sails and had changed the main masts and yards.

"As I walked up the platform, as I went down to the cabins, I sensed something strangely familiar about the vessel. Later, when I introduced myself to the captain, who was standing on the prow with his first mate and the head steward, I thought I had already seen those same dark and roguish countenances on some other occasion, gathered together in the same way.

"I strolled about on deck, worried by a memory that seemed to retreat just as it reached the edges of my powers of recollection, and

then come back, only to retreat again. Finally, Estela, who had left me
to take possession of her cabin, returned and whispered in my ear:
'*The Luiggi!*'

"The revelation flashed in my mind.

"We were aboard Samuel's ship, in the hands of the bandits who
had stolen it from him, and whose strategy for getting rich was to
throw passengers overboard and steal their gold. And they would no
doubt do so with us before too long.

"As much as it grieved me to alarm Estela, I had to tell her about
the desperate situation we were in.

"But, to my great surprise, her countenance, at first flustered with
grief, suddenly became calm and was incredibly transformed into a
picture of tranquility.

"'Sir,' she said to the captain, smiling with childish innocence, 'I
was just consulting with my brother to see if it might be possible for
me to ask a favor of you.

"'When we brought our luggage aboard, a wave hit it and everything got wet. Would you allow me to stretch our things out on the
deck for them to dry?'

"I listened, terrified. The chest that held Estela's clothes also contained our exchange drafts, and my bag contained a large number of
thick gold stones that I had set aside for my mother.

"My fear only increased when, after receiving the captain's permission, Estela turned to a sailor who was nearby and asked him to
retrieve our luggage from her cabin.

"Once the bag and the chest had been brought on deck, Estela
searched her pockets and took out the keys of one and the other with
much ado. Then, right in front of the captain and his companions,
whom she encouraged to stay nearby, she opened and completely
emptied the contents of the bag and the chest and proceeded to
stretch all our clothes out. These were, in fact, completely wet. Estela
had poured all the water she had found in her cabin on them.

"And the gold and the bills had disappeared!

"I was entranced.

"Estela, without ever giving herself away, moaned in grief at the sight of each of her wet garments. She smoothed out with her fingers the silk laces ruined by the water, and asked me, in the most anguished of voices, if I would ever again, in our whole life, be able to buy what that awful wave had ruined.

"This ruse of hers saved us.

"Estela, with the restless curiosity inherent in women, which makes them notice and register everything they see, had found a kind of hiding place in a corner of her old cabin. Formed coincidentally by the way two boards fit together, it was so well concealed that only eyes as sharp as hers could have spotted it. Terrified, like me, at the memory of Isacar's letter, she had hidden the gold and the bills there and had come up with that plan and proceeded to completely pull the wool over their eyes.

"But despite the security we enjoyed once the bandits were fooled, the presence of Estela among them filled me with anxiety. Sleep fled from my eyes, and I spent every night at the door of her cabin, standing, immobile, my ears perked up, my gaze staring into the darkness, and my hand clutching the handle of a dagger.

"One day, at last, we looked out and saw, through the first fogs of autumn, the Peruvian flag hoisted atop a tall tower.

"An hour later we arrived in the port of Callao.

"When she saw the port, whence she had left with her brother, a tear rolled down Estela's cheek. But she quickly dried it and recovered her sad serenity.

"As soon as we were moored, the customs officials came aboard for their inspection.

"A thought crossed my mind at this point, and I was troubled, as I faced a difficult decision. On board were the three bandits who had stolen the ship and planned to use it as a stage for future thefts and murders. Should I denounce them and turn them in to the hands of the law? Or should I remain silent and make myself responsible for the blood they would later spill?

"I looked at Estela; she understood my doubt.

"'Let us leave to God the punishment of those who do wrong; let us not stain our lips with a denunciation.'

"We did take advantage of the presence of the customs inspectors, however, to retrieve our fortune.

"A fury raged in their eyes when the bandits saw a bag of gold and a wallet full of exchange bills in my hands, and they looked at Estela with a burning gaze.

"The railroad, built during our absence, took us to Lima.

"When we set foot on the tiles of the station, Estela grabbed me by the hand and led me outside.

"'Where are you taking me?' I asked her.

"'To my house,' she answered.

"We set off and walked for a long time.

"At one point, we passed a church, and Estela said, 'Santa Ana! This is where I had my first communion.' She went in, kneeled, and prayed.

"As we left the church, I noticed she was trying to hide her teary eyes from me.

"A block further, I saw a large stone with a hole through it— caused, no doubt, by the flow of water over the years.

"'The Perforated Stone!' Estela exclaimed. 'On Sundays, when I was a little girl, we would dance and sing funny little songs and use these places as the lyrics of our harmonious tunes. Who could have known then that my last steps in the world would be taken near this same place!'

"'Your last steps in the world! What do you mean?'

"'Just wait!' my companion said, and led me into the entry room of the Convent of the Carmelite Order. She knocked on the postern, and a door opened.

"'Estela!' exclaimed an old nun who had been walking through the cloister at the time and had run to open the door.

"'Yes, Mother Abbess, it is I, Estela. I who spent the first days of my life inside these walls, and return now to spend the rest of them here. I ask you for the novice's veil.'

"Estela turned toward me, gave me a hug, and disappeared behind the door—all before I had time to recover from the shock of the sudden separation. A bolt of lightning striking me on the head, a dagger's blow dealt straight into my heart, would not have caused me as much pain. I threw myself against the door in the hope of knocking it down. I cried, I screamed, I called out for Estela, moaning desperately, and spent the entire night on the ground in front of that door; but it remained closed and silent as the grave.

"I finally tore myself away; a few hours later I was aboard a steamship heading south. I went ashore at Islay, purchased a horse right away, and rode all the way to Arequipa without resting more than an hour on the entire trip from Lima.

"'Mother!' I murmured as I ran across the sandy shore between the port and the city. 'My dear mother! All your dreams of happiness are about to come true. Your son is back, and he brings a treasure to lay at your feet.'

"I crossed the desert," the young man continued, more and more emotion in his voice as he went on, "I passed the barren ravines and reached the ones covered with the fragrant grasses of our beautiful countryside, and I climbed the incline of the first height. When I reached this summit, Misti,[11] dark and imposing, rose up before me in its entirety, from its dark base to its snowcapped peak.

"The sight of the sacred mountain, a view that would make anyone from Arequipa tremble with happiness, made me, for some unknown reason, tremble with a strange fear. I looked at it with yearning, asking it for an explanation, for my saddened soul seemed to see sinister omens in its shadows.

"It was nearly night by the time my horse, panting and out of breath, stopped, neighing, on the second height. Darkness had begun to spread across the wide landscape. But the moonlight, however vaguely, revealed all its details; and there, in the distance, was a long line of white roofs and towers.

........

[11] Misti is in Peru, near Arequipa, and is considered to be a false volcano because there is no known history of eruptions. —Ed.

"It was Arequipa!

"I crossed the valley of Congata and the narrow streets of Tiabaya fast as a flash, frightening everyone I passed; they all jumped out of my way as if I were a specter on horseback. My horse was ready to collapse, but I pushed it on, screaming and spurring it along, and managed to keep galloping on.

"Then, all of a sudden, at a turn in the road, the white city appeared before my eyes again, but this time very, very close. I could see its lights and hear its sounds.

"I spur my horse on, and it hurries along in a desperate gallop; I enter the outlying neighborhoods; I cross the bridge; I go up the side of the river, and I am there . . . !

"The small house was right in front of me, dark and silent, under the black shadows of the surrounding fig trees.

"The door was closed.

"'She must be sleeping,' I said to myself. Then I jumped off my horse and knocked on the door with the same series of knocks I had used in other times to let my mother know I was home. But the door remained closed; only an echo answered me from inside—a clean, empty sound.

"'Mother! Mother!' I yelled, putting my face right up against the silent door.

"A woman came out of a neighboring house when she heard my cries, and came to where I was.

"'We took her yesterday to the cemetery,' she told me. 'Her grief and her work finally got the better of her. Here is the key to the house, which she asked me to hold until her son returned.'

"Seeing that I did not move or say anything and that I was lying inert in front of the door, the woman took pity on me and tried to take me to her house. Unable to get me to follow her, however, she finally left me alone.

"I do not know how long I remained there, lying on the ground, my head resting on the doorstep. The freezing night wind finally made me shake out of the deep desolation in which I lay. I got up, my limbs numb. My entire body ached, as if I had sustained a long illness. I looked for the key, was unable to find it, then realized I had had it in my hand the whole time.

"I opened the door and went into the house where I had spent my childhood in such happiness under the wing of that angel who had just returned to heaven after having cried and waited for me in vain.

"I turned on a light and looked around, devastated.

"Everything in the lonely house was the same as it had been; my mother's presence could be felt everywhere. Here was her loom, there was her taboret and her needlework. Over there was my bed, all made up and ready to welcome me. It was right next to hers, which was disheveled, revealing in its disorder that a death had occurred there. At the head of the bed, below the crucifix, I found this item of jewelry resting on a holy palm leaf. It was all the gold I had sent her from California. My poor mother had woven her tender abnegation in the design of this graceful item, saving all the gold for me.

"I sat down next to her empty bed, rested my head in my hands, and sank into an abyss of sorrow.

"I was no longer the boy who had cried four days before over the loss of his companion at the door of the convent, calling out to her desperately, crying and sobbing. The blow I had just received was so severe that it knew no limits; but my tears, the soul's supreme balm, had frozen in my heart.

"The next morning found me in the same position, my lips silent, my eyes dry; but my hair, although still silky and rich with the vitality of childhood, was now streaked with gray."

And the young man passed his hand through his black hair, revealing several white strands here and there.

"That night, in the middle of the delirium of my sorrow," he continued, after a somber moment of silence, "I came up with a plan, which, a month later, I had completed. The project was to carry out my mother's dreams, her wishes for the future, which she had thought up at different times, and which had been engraved upon my mind by the passion of her voice.

"I bought all the land of the places in the countryside that she liked, where she always went on her walks. Then I built the country house, with the surrounding gardens, that her vivid imagination had dreamed up, and filled it with all the beautiful objects that used to please her eye. I purchased, with gold, the lands neighboring our small house at the shores of the Chili River and turned them into a vast garden, enclosing the house in its fragrant grove, like a sanctuary for an idol.

"In the enclosure of the garden, in the middle of a growth of rose bushes close to the old fig trees, I had a tomb built.

"In it rests my mother's remains, which I stole one night from the frozen earth of the cemetery.

"Thus, living next to her grave, surrounding myself with all that remains of her, I have constructed the illusion that she is still alive.

"And that is why I was so deeply afflicted by the loss of this item of jewelry along the road."

Deeply moved, I reached out and held my companion's hand in mine.

In the meantime, the sun had risen, and the Indian came in to tell us that our horses were saddled and ready for us to depart.

We all came out of the underground sanctuary and left together, continuing on the same rough and rocky road that descends quickly from the heights of Tacora to the plains of Pachia.

When we reached the Portada, the young man from Arequipa said farewell to us and turned toward a sugar mill in a dell to the right of the road.

The two miners from Corocoro, the baritone, and I, meanwhile, continued down the road in silence. The story from the night before had affected us all.

"What are you thinking about, madam?" one of the miners asked me as he handed me a glass of beer. "The copper-colored man?"

"Yes, indeed! I can see his vulture's eyes and his sharp teeth in my mind. What an infernal creature! I wonder if he is still engaged in a life of crime, or if he has already gotten the punishment he deserves?"

"Who knows?" the miner said.

"I do!" the baritone answered, silencing us at once.

After the surprise caused by his answer had passed, the baritone was reprimanded by a chorus of exclamations.

"What? You mean you knew what happened and did not say anything?"

"Why did you let the storyteller go without telling him the conclusion of the tale?"

"Without letting him know what became of that evil man who ruined his life?"

"I was very careful not to commit such an indiscretion. What I have to say would have made the young man, already so dejected about his own story, feel even worse. Thus, even though I recognized early on in the description of the one he called the copper-colored man, the horrible protean creature that I will now tell you about, I remained silent to prevent him from feeling any new, painful emotions.

"In 1853, I was in San Francisco as part of the singing company that Catalina Hayes took to California. It was Carnival night; we were performing *I Masnadieri* [12] in the main theater of the city.

"I was standing in a dark corner, off in a wing of the theater, waiting to come on stage, looking out at the immense crowd that filled the hall, which, at that moment, was applauding excitedly for Catalina.

"I was studying in detail the heterogeneous makeup of faces, attitudes, and expressions that made up the audience, with its power, so frightening and terrifying to the artist. Just then, however, my attention was drawn to a scene taking place in the hall.

"Ever since the curtain had been raised, a strange man sitting in the middle of the orchestra section had drawn my attention. Resting on a pair of shoulders and a broad chest that indicated it belonged to someone of colossal height, a head stood out, held high with savage arrogance. With the astonishing development and growth of its sinister

........

[12] *I Masnadieri* (*The Robbers*, 1847), opera in four acts by Giuseppe Verdi, taken from Schiller's drama, *Die Rauber* (1781). Curiously, Gorriti has her characters observe an opera about a band of thieves while the copper-skinned man lurks in the theater. —Ed.

protuberances, this head would have frightened even Doctor Gall.[13] An enormous mass of long hair, some straight and some curly, crowned the head, casting a shadow over the dark, blood-colored face, wherein a pair of deep, black eyes glowed with a fierce fury. To complete this horrible agglomeration, a pair of lips, naturally contracted into a grimace, revealed two rows of wide-spread, sharp white teeth.

"I was so affected at the sight of this man that I did not find it strange that it would produce the same effect on several other individuals in different parts of the hall; these were approaching him imperceptibly, changing seats with others, until they formed a circle around him. I was able to observe all these actions in detail from my hiding place off stage.

"To the right, a little further away from the circle that had formed around the cupreous man, an older man, seemingly a naval officer, was also staring straight at him. But this man's gaze was filled with a painful rancor, discernible in all his movements.

"My entrance on stage came right before the end of the act. I was so distracted when I sang, however, that my timing was completely thrown off. No matter how hard I tried to focus on the orchestra, I could not tear my eyes and my thoughts from the drama taking place in front of me, which had become even more tense. I finally understood that the individuals in the circle were police officers in disguise.

"To the side, silent and threatening, like a warship ready to attack, the old man was watching, his hand in the pocket of his long coat.

"The curtain had not yet fallen when the cupreous man moved, as if to leave his seat. A dozen police agents jumped to apprehend him.

"'Nobody touch that man!' the old naval officer suddenly yelled. 'He is mine!'

"Jumping up, fast as lightning, he grabbed the man by his long hair and shot him in the head with his revolver.

"The next day, a corpse was hanging from the gallows in front of

........

[13] Francis Joseph Gall (1758–1828), Austrian anatomist and founder of phrenology. —Ed.

the jailhouse, although the sentence of death by hanging had been preempted by the old naval officer's act of revenge.

"Large groups of people came and went before the horrible spectacle, constantly telling terrifying stories about the dead man.

"'It is Falkland!' one exclaimed. 'Yes, I am sure of it. That is the arsonist freebooter from Central America, who seemed to enjoy burning entire families to their death after locking them up in their houses.'

"'It is Hawk-Eye! The hunter who we had to chase out of the prairies for plotting with the natives. Yes, it is he. His eyes used to make deer stop in their tracks.'

"'It is Tobahoa! Finally, you have fallen, you evil Navajo Indian, you who stole more girls from our villages than the number of days in your perverse life. You wretched headhunter! Too bad yours is already destroyed! If it were not, I would buy it to comfort the poor man from Sonora with the long scar across his forehead, who lost his beautiful girlfriend because of it.'

"'It is too bad, I agree,' a man dressed in black said, pushing his way through the crowd, followed by two assistants. 'I get permission to dissect this man's cranium, only to find it fractured! But the jaws are still intact, luckily, and I can see that the teeth are a true rarity.'

"Soon afterward, the public study of natural history, directed by Doctor Smith, had a new jewel: a pair of human jaws with widespread white teeth that were sharp as nails.

"Soon thereafter, the newspapers in San Francisco announced the suicide of Mr. Scott, the captain of the *New World*, a steamship belonging to an old shipping company in Sacramento, burnt by a fire stoker to steal the coffers of the ship.

"The chronicles attributed the desperate actions of the captain to the grief in which he lived ever since the death of his daughter, who perished in the catastrophe."

A joyous group of young ladies who lived in Pachia and had arrived on horseback from Tacna suddenly came out from a grove of pepper trees in the valley. They came onto the road and we trotted along with them, dissipating with their joyous laughter the grave mood produced by the baritone's story.

. . . . .

August came and went, spreading mourning and desolation every-where. The cities were hit hard by the winter waves, and their poor inhabitants were drowned or forced to flee. Arica, Iquique, and Pis-agua no longer existed, and Arequipa, the white city of a thousand domes, had collapsed. Its sons and daughters wandered away from the debris like ghosts, afflicted by cold and hunger, and finally came to us looking for food and new lodgings.

All of us who at one time or another had been guests of that beau-tiful city ran to the station every time a steamship arrived from the south, with the hope of seeing a friendly face among the saddened emigrants. Moving scenes filled with hugs and tears were repeated to no end.

One day, among the passengers getting off the train, I saw a man whose features looked familiar to me, but I could not remember his name. He was hidden by a large crowd, and I lost sight of him.

A few days later, I was in the Church of the Carmelites, attending a solemn Mass for a holiday.

The altar was covered with candles and flowers, the incense was burning, and the organ filled the church with its majestic chords.

Sitting in a dark corner behind the iron grating, I suddenly real-ized I was not alone. Near me, at the end of a bench, sat a young man, lost in deep thought, his head resting in his hands.

I would not have recognized his face, which was mostly covered by a large, thick, black beard, anywhere else. But the place, and the emo-tions revealed in his features, brought back to me the memory of the traveler in the sanctuary of *Uchusuma,* and his story.

When I said the name Estela in a low voice, the young man turned his head, recognized me, and squeezed my hand.

"In the name of God," I said to him, "tell me at once what fortune, in the midst of this horrible cataclysm, has befallen your sacred little house at the shores of the Chili?"

"The angel who once lived there still protects it under its wing," the young man from Arequipa answered fervently.

"The enormous domes of the palaces have collapsed," he continued, "but my mother's humble roof remains intact and today houses many unfortunate victims."

"And have you never thought, in the end, of taking her a wife?"

"No!" he replied. "There must have been the seed of a different kind of passion in my fraternal love for Estela, which always places her image between my heart and any new love, filling it with sacred fear."

"Have you been able to see her?"

"I have not had such luck. She is in retreat, and her reclusion will last longer than my time here, as I have come only long enough to buy clothes and supplies for my unfortunate brothers back home.

"I may not be able to see her, however, but I shall at least hear her voice."

At that moment the ringing bells and the clouds of incense announced that the veil of the tabernacle was about to be raised. Everyone got down on their knees, and from the quiet of the silent prayers, a wonderful voice suddenly appeared, intense and sweet, singing a hymn to the Eternal Lord.

I turned to look at the young man, but did not need to ask him; the expression on his countenance told me he was listening to Estela.

I left him kneeling on the floor; he was lost in an ecstatic rapture, in which his sweet and painful odyssey, begun in the Pacific and continued in the parries surrounding Sacramento, must have played a beautiful part.